These men will do their duty—
but marriage and love wasn't
in their plans…

New
Arrivals

ONE SECRET
CHILD

MAGGIE COX
MARGARET WAY
LINDA GOODNIGHT

New Arrivals

COLLECTION

March 2015

April 2015

May 2015

June 2015

New Arrivals

ONE SECRET CHILD

MAGGIE COX
MARGARET WAY
LINDA GOODNIGHT

MILLS & BOON

Published in Great Britain 2015
by Mills & Boon, an imprint of Harlequin (UK) Limited,
Eton House, 18-24 Paradise Road, Richmond, Surrey, TW9 1SR

NEW ARRIVALS: ONE SECRET CHILD
© 2015 Harlequin Books S.A.

Mistress, Mother...Wife? © 2011 Maggie Cox
Wealthy Australian, Secret Son © 2011 Margaret Way
Her Prince's Secret Son © 2009 Linda Goodnight

ISBN: 978-0-263-25374-0

010-0515

Harlequin (UK) Limited's policy is to use papers that are natural, renewable and recyclable products and made from wood grown in sustainable forests.The logging and manufacturing processes conform to the legalenvironmental regulations of the country of origin.

Printed and bound in Spain
by CPI, Barcelona

MISTRESS, MOTHER...WIFE?

MAGGIE COX

The day **Maggie Cox** saw the film version of *Wuthering Heights*, with a beautiful Merle Oberon and a very handsome Laurence Olivier, was the day she became hooked on romance. From that day onwards she spent a lot of time dreaming up her own romances, secretly hoping that one day she might become published and get paid for doing what she loved most!

Now that her dream is being realised, she wakes up every morning and counts her blessings. She is married to a gorgeous man and is the mother of two wonderful sons. Her two other great passions in life—besides her family and reading/writing—are music and films.

CHAPTER ONE

IT WAS a pastime she liked to employ when things got a little slower towards the end of the evening. She'd scan the remaining customers who were lingering over their drinks at tables or at the bar and conjure up a tale about them. Making up stories was meat and drink to Anna... it was the thing that had kept her sane and protected when she was a child. Her little made-up worlds had all been so much safer and fulfilling than reality, and there were many, many times she'd sought refuge there.

Now, as though tugged by a powerful magnet, yet again she considered the handsome, square-jawed individual staring into space in the furthermost corner of the room. He'd occupied the stylish burgundy armchair for at least two hours now, had neither removed his coat nor glanced interestedly at the other well-heeled patrons even once. It was as though they were completely off his radar. All he seemed to be focused on was the inner screen of his own troubled mind.

There was definitely an intense, preoccupied air about him that intrigued Anna. After all, what dreamer with a yen for making up stories *wouldn't* be intrigued or provoked by such fascinating material? Making sure she was discreet, she studied him hard. She hadn't personally looked into his eyes yet, but already she guessed they would have the power to hynotise whoever was caught in their gaze. A small shiver ran down her spine.

Having checked the room to see if she was needed anywhere, she let her gaze return to the mystery man. He had straight mid-blond hair, with hints of silver in it, and appeared to be growing out a cut that had probably been both stylish and expensive. Everything about him exuded wealth and good taste, a well as the sense of power and entitlement that often accompanied those attributes. Although his eye-catching broad shoulders appeared weighed down by his concerns, he also wore a fierce need for privacy that was like an invisible electronic gate, warning all comers that they encroached upon his space at their peril. Had an important deal gone sour? Had someone deceived him or seriously let him down in some way? *He didn't look like a man who suffered fools gladly.*

Anna sighed, then studied him again. No…she'd got it all wrong. The black coat he was wearing suddenly sang out to her. He'd lost someone close. Yes, that was it. He was grieving. That was why his expression was so haunted and morose. As she studied his formidable chiselled profile, with the deep shadow of a cleft centred in that square-cut chin, it seemed almost impertinent to speculate about him further if she'd guessed the truth. *Poor man...* He must be feeling totally wretched.

The third Scotch on the rocks he'd ordered was drained right down to the bottom of the glass, Anna noticed. Would he be ordering another one? Bitter personal experience had taught her that alcohol never solved anything. *All it had done for her father was make his black moods even blacker.*

The hotel bar closed at eleven-thirty and it was already a quarter past, she saw. Collecting a tray, she circumnavigated the tables with her usual light step, her heart thudding like a brick dropped into a millpond as she overrode her natural inclination to stay well clear. In front of the man, she schooled her lips into a pleasant smile.

'I'm sorry to disturb you, sir, but will you be requiring another drink? Only, the bar will be closing soon.'

Glittering blue-grey eyes that contained all the warmth of a perilous icy sea swivelled to survey her. For a startled second Anna told herself it served her right if she received a frosty reception, when his body language clearly signalled that he wanted to be left alone. But just then a corner of the austere masculine mouth lifted in the mocking semblance of a smile.

'What do you think? Do I look like I'm in need of another drink, beautiful?'

There was the faintest Mediterranean edge to his otherwise British accent. But in any case he was wrong. *She wasn't beautiful.* If it weren't for the rippling waist-length auburn hair that she freed from her workday style every night when her shift ended, Anna would consider herself quite ordinary. Yet the unexpected compliment— mocking or otherwise—was as though he'd lit a brightly burning candle inside her.

'I wouldn't presume to think I knew what you needed, sir.'

'Call me Dan,' he said, giving her the commonly abbreviated form of his name which he went by in London, not wanting to hear Dante, the name his mother had gifted him with, tonight of all nights.

The invitation almost caused her to stumble. She dipped her head beneath the glare of his riveting gaze because it was almost too powerful to look into for long.

'We're not supposed to address the customers personally,' she answered.

'And do you always follow the rules to the letter?'

'I do if I want to keep my job.'

'This establishment would be extremely foolish if they were to get rid of a girl like you.'

'You don't even know me.'

'Maybe I'd like to.' His smile was slow and deliberate. 'Get to know you better, I mean.'

That roguish grin was like a guided missile that hit all her sensitive spots at once. Inside, the implosion almost rocked Anna off her feet.

'I don't think you do,' she remarked, serious-voiced.

'You're probably just looking for a handy diversion, if the truth be known.'

'Really? A diversion from what, exactly?' A dark blond eyebrow with tiny glints of copper in it lifted in amusement.

'From whatever unhappy thoughts that have been bothering you.'

The smile vanished. His expression became as guarded as though a wall made of three-foot-deep granite had thundered down in front of it.

'How do you know I'm disturbed by unhappy thoughts? What are you...a mind-reader?'

'No.' Anna's teeth nibbled anxiously at her lip. 'I just observe people and—and sense things about them.'

'What a dangerous occupation. And you're compelled to do this why? You don't have any of your own material to contemplate? You must be a rare human being indeed if that's the case...to have managed to negotiate your way through life without any problems at all.'

'I haven't...gone through life without any problems, I mean. How would I have learned anything or be able to empathise with other people if I'd been problem-free? I'd also be quite superficial...which I'm not.'

'And here I was, thinking you were just a simple, uncomplicated barmaid, when in fact you're clearly quite the little philosopher.'

Anna didn't take the comment as an insult. How could she? As well as the pain glittering in his winter-coloured eyes, locked inside his scathing tone was the suggestion of the blackest kind of despair.

A heartfelt desire to help ease it in some way swept passionately through her.

'I'm not looking for trouble... You just seemed so alone and sad, sitting there, that I thought that if you wanted to talk...well, I'd be a good listener. Sometimes it's easier to tell your troubles to a stranger than someone you know. But anyway, if you think that's impertinent of me, and another drink would help more, then I'll gladly get you one.'

The man who'd told her to call him Dan raised a shoulder, then dropped it again dismissively.

'I'm not the unburdening kind, and if you were hoping I might be then I have to tell you that you're wasting your time. What's your name?'

'Anna.'

'That's it...just Anna?'

'Anna Bailey.'

A cold sweat broke out across her skin, where previously his disturbing glance had kindled the kind of heat that made dry tinder burst into flames. Was he going to report her or something? She hadn't meant to insult him. Her only desire had been to help if she could. Was he an important enough customer for a complaint from him to help her lose her job? *She prayed not.*

The comfortable family-run hotel in a quiet corner of Covent Garden had become her home for the past three years, and she loved everything about it—including her work. She didn't even mind if she sometimes had to work long hours. Her employers were so kind—generous to a fault, in fact—and her recent pay-rise had helped make life a whole lot more comfortable than when she'd worked at jobs she'd hated and for too little money. Lord knew she didn't want to go back to struggling again.

'Look, Mr, er...'

'I told you to call me Dan.'

'I can't do that.'

'Why?' he snapped, his expression irritated.

'Because it wouldn't be professional. I'm an employee here and you're a guest.'

'Yet you offered me a shoulder to cry on. Is that on offer to all your guests, Anna?'

She flushed. 'Of course not. I just wanted to—'

'So the only thing that prevents you calling me by my first name is that you're a stickler for the rules and you work here, while I'm a paying customer?'

'I'd better go.'

'No—stay. Is there any other reason you can't be more informal? Like the fact that you've got a husband or boyfriend waiting for you at home, perhaps?'

Anna stared helplessly.

'No.' She cleared her throat, then glanced round to see if anyone was observing them.

Brian—her young, dark-haired colleague—was wiping down the half-moon-shaped bar and chatting to a customer at the same time, whilst a smartly dressed middle-aged couple sat tenderly holding hands as they lingered over their after-theatre drinks. They'd regaled Anna earlier with tales of the play they'd been to, and their infectious enjoyment was contagious. Twenty-five years married and they were still like young lovers around each other.

Sighing, she turned back to find him broodingly examining her. The sudden jolt of her heartbeat mimicked another heavy brick splashing into a pond as his glance interestedly and deliberately appraised her figure. His gaze lingered boldly on the curve of her hips and the swell of her breasts, trailing sensuous fire in its wake. There was nothing provocative about the purple silk blouse with its pretty Chinese collar and the straight grey skirt that denoted her uniform, but when he studied her like that—as if he were imagining her naked and willing in his bed—Anna felt as if there was nowhere to hide.

A trembling excitement soared through her blood at his near-insolent examination. An excitement that was like a gargantuan powerful wave dangerously poised to sweep her into uncharted waters she'd never dared visit before.

'In that case...I've had a change of heart,' Dante drawled, smiling. 'Maybe sharing my troubles with a sweet girl like you is just what I need tonight, Anna. What time do you finish?'

'Around midnight, by the time Brian and I have cashed up.' How was it possible for her voice to sound so level when inside a roaring furnace was all but consuming her?

'And how do you normally get home? Do you get a cab?'

'I live in, actually.'

Just like a popped balloon, her last defence deflated and it was no longer possible for her to pretend that the handsome, hard-jawed stranger hadn't affected her deeply. The truth was that he held a dangerous fascination for her. She was hypnotised by the simmering aura of sensuality implicit in his rough velvet voice and in the twin lakes of his troubled haunting eyes. As a result, her bones seemed to be held together by running water instead of strong connective tissue. Unable to think straight, Anna knew her returning glance was nervous as she gathered the round wooden tray up close to her chest as though it were a shield.

'Have you made up your mind about the drink? Only I've got to get back to the bar to work.'

'Another drink can wait.'

Unbuttoning his coat for the first time that evening, Dante handed her his empty glass with another long, slow, meaningful glance. His lean fingers brushed hers. *Did she imagine that they lingered there against her skin much longer than necessary?* His touch was like being grazed by lightning—deliberate or not.

'I'm staying here too tonight, Anna. And I think that we should have a drink together when your shift ends... don't you?'

A definite refusal was on the tip of her tongue, but inside the dogged belief clung that perhaps she really *could* help him by being a good listener. Her lips pursed tight to prevent it. But when she turned away it was as if some kind of aftershock from their encounter had seized her, because her limbs were shaking almost violently as she crossed the room to rejoin Brian...

There was no understanding such alternating and violent sweeps of emotion, thought Dante. He had just flown into London from his mother's funeral—the funeral of the one person in the world he had truly loved, who had always been there for him no matter what, who had been like a beacon of light he turned to when he ached to remember that beauty, grace and selfless kindness existed in the world.

Now that she was gone he was heartbroken...truly heartbroken. But another woman also occupied his thoughts right now. His body had somehow acquired a compelling desire to know the touch of a red-haired young witch with sherry-brown eyes that glinted beguilingly like firelight—a girl he had only just met whom he had all but mocked disparagingly when she'd shyly offered him a listening ear. Was it so rare that he met up with a genuinely nice girl that he had to punish her when he did?

His mother would turn in her newly dug grave! Bitterness and despair rising in his gorge, Dante ripped off his wristwatch to discard it onto the nearby polished side-table. His coat followed suit, but he let it fall carelessly onto the bed instead. Several hundred dollars' worth of the finest cashmere—but what did it signify? His wealth had neither made him a better man nor a more generous one.

His personal assessment was brutally frank. All the businesses and property he had accumulated through mergers and acquisitions had demonstrated to him was how driven and ruthless he'd become. Yes, driven and ruthless—because of an underlying fear of losing it all. An impoverished childhood and a father who had deserted him had seen to that. He'd been so poor in the small mountain village in Italy where he'd grown up that his mother had been forced to earn their bread by dancing and singing for men in seedy bars in the nearby town, and Dante had long ago set his hungry intention for any career he might settle upon to make him wildly and disgustingly rich so that he might rescue them both.

His wealth would act as an insulating buffer between him and the rest of the world, he'd told himself. Then no one would have the chance to hurt him or his mother again, and neither would she have to humiliate herself by parading her beauty in front of men for money. Dante had carried that insulation with him into his marriage and into any other romantic relationship he'd briefly flirted with, forever seeking to protect his emotions. He'd become cold…not to mention a little heartless.

'No wonder they call you the ice man of the business world,' his American ex-wife, Marisa, had taunted him.

'You're so dedicated to the title that you even bring it home with you!'

At first his mother had been fiercely proud of his rocketing success. He'd bought her the house of her dreams in Lake Como, and made sure she always had plenty of money to buy whatever she wanted. But lately whenever he'd visited her she'd started to profess concern. With one failed marriage and a string of unhappy relationships behind him, it had only seemed to Renata that her son had lost all sense of priority.

It should be the people in his life who were important, she'd told him—not his business or the grand houses he bought—and if he continued in this soulless way then she would sell the richly decorated house on its exclusive plot by the lake and purchase a hut in the hills instead! After all, she'd been raised as a shepherd's daughter, and she wasn't ashamed to go back to where she'd begun even if *he* was. *Someone* had to show him what values were.

Dante grimaced at the hurtful memory of her distressed face and quavering voice when she'd said this to him in the hospital…

To diffuse his despair he deliberately brought his mind back to the titian-haired Anna Bailey. His reaction was purely male and instinctive, and his body tightened instantly. It was as though someone had stoked a fire beneath his blood and set it ceaselessly simmering. Reaching for his discarded watch, he impatiently scanned the time, all but boring a hole in the door with his naked, hungry glance as he waited for her to arrive—not once allowing himself to think that she *wouldn't...*

As if needing to enquire about something, her brooding new friend had leaned across the bar on his way out and whispered softly to Anna, *'Let's have that drink together in my room. I'm staying in the suite on the top floor. It would mean a lot to me...especially tonight. Please don't disappoint me.'*

His lips had been a hair's breadth away from her ear and his warm breath had all but set her alight. The seductive sensation had been the mesmerising equivalent of an intoxicating cocktail she was powerless to refuse. She knew it would make her dizzy and light-headed, but it still held a potent allure she couldn't ignore.

Anna had watched Dan's tall broad-shouldered physique as he left the bar with her heart thumping. Now, in the privacy of her room, she blew out a trembling breath, dropping down onto the padded stool in front of the dressing table because she hardly trusted her legs to keep her upright.

The enigmatic stranger was staying in the only suite in the building. It was the most luxurious and gorgeous accommodation she had ever seen. With its beautiful Turkish kelims hanging on the walls, artisan-created bespoke furniture and under-floor heating, no expense had been spared in its creation and it cost a small fortune to stay there for even *one* night.

Biting her lip, Anna peered into the dressing table mirror to gauge if her expression was as terrified as she felt. Was she really contemplating visiting a male guest in his room? Talking to that lovely couple who'd been to the theatre earlier, she had felt such a pang of envy at their closeness. It wasn't very often she succumbed to feelings of loneliness, but somehow tonight she *had*. What had he meant when he'd whispered, *It would mean a lot to me...especially tonight?* Was he feeling lonely too? Had the funeral she guessed he'd attended been for someone really close to him? His *wife* perhaps?

A heavy sigh, part compassion, part longing, left her. If anyone saw her go to his room then she really *could* lose her job. Was the loneliness that had infiltrated her blood tonight making her a little desperate? Not to mention reckless? Sighing again, Anna went into the bathroom to splash her face with cold water.

Back in the main room, she glanced unseeingly at the television that sat there. Somehow a late-night movie or talk show didn't hold any draw for her. Neither did curling up in bed alone with her thoughts appeal. She'd sensed an inexplicable overwhelming connection to the man who had whispered in her ear downstairs and it was somehow impossible to ignore it. Tomorrow he might be gone, she reasoned feverishly.

She would be wondering what might have been—and the feeling would gnaw away at her if she didn't act.

With fingers that shook, she freed her hair from the neatly coiled bun she'd got so adept at fashioning for work, then pulled a careless brush through the river of auburn silk that flowed down her back. Pinching her cheeks to make them pinker, she quickly changed into a dark green top and light blue jeans. He only wants to *talk*, she reassured herself as she walked out into the corridor. But her pulse beat with fright because he might have been looking for something more…something that in her heart of hearts she secretly longed for.

Flicking an anxious glance towards the small elevator that would soundlessly deliver her to the topmost floor, Anna sucked in a breath as she walked towards it.

The memory of Dan and his haunting mist-coloured eyes came back to her, cutting a swathe through her sudden doubt. Just because he was rich it didn't mean that he didn't suffer like everyone else…didn't mean that he didn't need help sometimes. And from her very first glimpse of him Anna had known he was tortured by something…

The polite welcome he'd intended got locked inside his throat when Dante opened the door to the vision that confronted him. She wore her bright auburn hair loose, and it resembled a burnished autumn sunset cascading down over her shoulders. His stomach muscles clamped tight and the saliva in his mouth dried to a sun-baked desert.

Finding his voice, he murmured, 'Come in.'

Stepping inside, Anna smiled. It was shy and brief, but it still gave him a jolt that had his heart thrumming with undeniable excitement.

'What can I get you to drink?' Moving across the gold and red Chinese rug that covered the main area of the polished wooden floor, Dante paused in front of the dark mahogany glass-fronted cabinet that contained several bottles of spirits behind it and rested his gaze on Anna.

'Nothing, thanks. Alcohol and me don't mix, I'm afraid. Just one sip is enough to make me dizzy.'

'A soft drink, then?'

'Please...just see to yourself. I'm fine, really.'

Dropping his hands restlessly to his hips, he let a rueful grin hijack his lips.

'I think I've probably had quite enough for one night.'

'You've decided not to drown your sorrows after all?'

'Not now that you've consented to visit me, Anna.'

She crossed her arms over her dark green top, and Dante couldn't think of a colour that would complement her pale satin skin more. Without warning, the fresh, searing pain of his recent loss swept over him. It returned with renewed force and he wanted to reach out, anchor himself to life again, remind himself that even though his mother had gone beauty and grace were still his to appreciate if only he'd take the trouble to see it. If he brushed up close to such admirable qualities in Anna would it relieve him of the bitter, despairing thoughts that pounded on him so disturbingly? Thoughts that confirmed his growing belief that he must be no good?

Yes, his nature was clearly unlovable and unworthy of regard—hadn't his own father abandoned him?—so perhaps he deserved abandonment by the people close to him? Especially when he'd been so ruthlessly focused on making himself rich that he scarcely saw the needs of anyone else.

'It upsets me when you look like that,' Anna confessed softly.

'Like what?'

'As if you don't like yourself very much.'

'Is there no hiding from that all-seeing gaze of yours?' Dante retorted uncomfortably.

'I just want to help you if I can.'

'Do you? Do you really?'

'Of course I do. Why do you think I came? Would you like to talk about it?'

'No, sweetheart. Talking is *not* what I need right now,' he answered, gravel-voiced.

And for a man who had prided himself on achieving anything he put his mind to in life it was ironically too difficult a task to keep the raw need that surged through his body like a tidal wave completely out of his tone.

CHAPTER TWO

IN SLOW motion he reached for Anna's hand. His eyes—those intense, burning, ethereal eyes—held her willing prisoner, right then becoming her whole world.

'What do you want?' she whispered, hardly able to hear over the pounding of her heart. 'What do you need?'

'You, Anna...right now I want and need *you*.'

After that, words became unnecessary. His fingers were slipping through her hair, anchoring her head so that she was placed perfectly for his kiss when he delivered it...when the touch of his lips ignited a heartfelt need that had slumbered achingly inside her for years and promised to more than satisfy it.

She'd always thought that maybe her impassioned secret desires were doomed to remain unrequited. On the rare occasion when she'd allowed herself to overcome her mistrust and be caressed by a man, the experience had never remotely lived up to her hopes. All it had done was leave her feeling vulnerable, scared that she would end up alone and unloved until the end of her days. But now, as his warm velvet tongue so hungrily and devastatingly swept her mouth's interior, the flavours she tasted rocked her.

Along with passion, fervour and consuming need, Anna was alive to the anger, despair and pain that she tasted too. But she didn't let such stark emotions scare her...not when they mirrored feelings of her own that she'd often been too afraid to bring into the light. Because of that she innately understood the tumult that flowed heatedly through his blood—good *and* bad— even if she didn't know the details.

Crushed to his warm hard chest in its dark roll-necked sweater, she felt musky male heat and sexy woody cologne captivate her senses as he ravished her in the starved, insatiable way she'd always dreamt of being loved by a man. Holding on to his hard-muscled biceps to keep from falling, Anna feverishly and willingly paid him back in kind... And in her head echoed the advice from her mother that she'd never forgotten: *Only give yourself to someone you love...*

On the bed in a room where in their haste to be together they hadn't even paused to turn on a light they raided each other's clothes with trembling hands—desperate for skin on skin contact and more drugging open-mouthed kisses that promised to last all night long. And if he'd temporarily lost his mind in taking this young red-haired beauty to bed then Dante heartily welcomed the state. She was the first really good thing that had happened to him in ages, and he wasn't about to question his good fortune.

The intoxicating feminine scent of her body had already taken up residence in his blood, and it thrummed with wanting her. The arresting sight of that rippling blanket of fiery hair on the silk cream pillow behind her head made a stirring, ravishing picture that he would not soon forget. Now, as his hands eagerly caressed the smooth, slender contours of Anna's body, the breathless gasps she emitted made him blind to any other sensation but their wild and heady mutual desire. He was all but desperate to plunge inside her, to forget everything except the unrestrained thundering joy of the chemistry that had exploded between them from almost the first glance, to relegate the darkness that had recently threatened to suffocate him, to the shadows.

Sensing her stiffen a little as he explored her heat with his fingers, Dante rose up to cup and stroke her face. A duty that should have been at the forefront of his dazzled mind suddenly stabbed at his conscience.

'I'm sorry, Anna...I should protect you. Is that what you are concerned about?'

'It's okay,' she sighed, dark eyes shy. 'I'm protected already. I'm on the pill.'

For an indeterminate amount of time Dante got lost in her wide fire-lit stare, and then he came to and kissed her. The caress seemed to gentle her. Then, his blood flowing with increasing desire and demand, slowly, carefully, he drove himself deep inside her. The heat that exploded around him was incredible.

Anna's sherry-brown eyes smouldered and brightened at the same time, but Dante had not missed the momentary flash of apprehension in her beautiful glance either. Too aroused and aching to wonder about it for long, he felt his body naturally assume the age-old rhythm that would take him to the destination and release he longed for…a destination that could and *would* free him for a while from the merciless torment that had deluged him when his mother had breathed her last laboured breath in his arms. Instead of grief and misery, ecstasy and bliss would be his. And for a blessed short time, at least, all the hurt would be swept away…

His strength of purpose all but overwhelmed Anna as she watched him move over her, his arrow-straight hips slamming into hers as his loving became ever more intense, ever more voracious. By instinct and by desire she wound her long legs round his back, until he was so deep inside her that she felt as if her body no longer existed just as one. Instead, she and he had become a single entity, with two hearts beating wildly in tandem and mind, body and spirit in stunning accord. She had given herself to him without doubt that it was the right thing…*destined*, even.

Would it scare him to know that she thought that? A girl he had just met, to whom he probably wouldn't even give the time of day normally?

In the soft darkness that seemed to be growing ever

lighter as Anna's eyes grew more accustomed to it his smooth muscles rippled like warm steel beneath her trembling, caressing fingers. His breath was harshly ragged as he alternately devoured her lips and then, with that same hot, tormenting mouth, moved lower to caress her breasts. He suckled the rigid aching tips in turn, and Anna couldn't withhold the heated moan that broke free. It was as though her very womb rejoiced when he touched and caressed her.

When he rose up again to capture her lips in another hotly exploring and intimate kiss, something inside her started irrevocably to unravel, to spiral dizzyingly out of control. At first, because she was nervous of being so vulnerable and exposed in front of him, Anna tensed, trying to stem the sensation. But at that same moment she stared up at him, to find the corners of his oh-so-sensuous lips lifting in what might have well been a quietly knowing smile, and she completely gave up trying to control what was happening.

Instead, she allowed the fierce, elemental power of the tide that swept through her to take her where it willed. She was scarcely able to steal a breath as the heart-racing journey commandingly held sway. *It was like freefalling over a hundred-foot waterfall.* Feeling stunned, she didn't know if her mind or her heart raced more. Tears surged helplessly and she bit her lip to quiet the sounds that inevitably arose inside her throat.

Anna knew then that she was changed for ever by what had just occurred. Even her mother, with all her tenderly given advice, could not have prepared her for the powerful emotions that flooded her at surrendering herself to this man. Her gaze met his in genuine wonder. Moving even deeper inside her, his hard glistening body pinned her to the bed, keeping her there for long pulsating seconds. The blue-grey eyes that were so reminiscent of a restless stormy sea now scorched her as he silently surveyed her. The raw feeling and emotion he unwittingly revealed ripped achingly through Anna's heart.

Even though they were engaged in the most intimate act of all, he still seemed so isolated and alone. Like a lighthouse, with nothing but the sea surrounding it. She longed to be able to swim to him and reach him. But then, with an echoing shout that sounded as though it had been dragged up from the depths of his soul, a shudder went through him, and he stilled. Scalding heat invaded her.

'Anna...' he rasped, clasping her face between his hands and shaking his head as though she was an enigma he'd never resolve.

When he laid his head between her breasts, Anna rubbed away her tears and then enfolded him in her arms, stroking the impossibly soft fair hair almost as though he were a hurt child in need of love and care.

'It will be all right,' she soothed softly. 'Whatever's happened to make you so sad, it will pass given time. I truly believe that. One day soon you'll start to enjoy life again.'

'If you know that, then you have access to the kind

of faith that's a million light years away from where I am right now. And if my life runs true to form, it'll probably *stay* a million light years away.'

His warm breath skimmed her tender exposed skin like a lover blowing a kiss, while at the same time the shadow of beard covering his hard jaw lightly abraded her. But it was the utter desolation she heard in his gruffly velvet voice that disturbed Anna.

'You mustn't give up,' she urged, sliding her hands either side of his sculpted high cheekbones to make him look up at her.

Although he was surprised by her words, he couldn't disguise his anguish. 'Don't waste your reassurances on me, Anna. I'm okay. I'll survive... I always do.'

'You don't think life can be better than just surviving?'

'For you, angel, I hope it can be. You deserve it—you really do.'

'Sad things, bad things have happened to me too,' she offered shyly. 'Apart from childhood stuff. After a couple of years of doing jobs I hated I found one I really liked and excelled at. But I lost that post when some ruthless hotel magnate bought out my previous employers and installed his own staff. I didn't let myself be sad about it for long, though. I had no choice but to pick myself up and face the unknown. Luckily fate brought me here, to the Mirabelle. Sometimes help arrives when you most need it, you know?'

'Perhaps it does if your conduct has warranted it.'

'I wish you could tell me what's happened to make you feel so low. I thought—I thought perhaps because you were wearing black you might have just lost someone?'

Breathing silently for a while Dante didn't speak. Then he sighed. 'I already told you I'm not the unburdening kind. But I don't feel low right now, *cara*... How could I, lying here in your arms, hearing your heart beat beneath my cheek, having just enjoyed the pleasures and consolation of your beautiful body?'

Hot colour poured into Anna's cheeks. 'If I've brought you some comfort then I'm happy. But I think it's time I went. I really should get back to my room and get some sleep...I've got to make an early start in the morning.'

'So working in the bar isn't your only job?'

'No. I do a bit of everything. I'm learning the trade, so it's great. It's a small family-run hotel and we all muck in. In the mornings I'm a chambermaid.' She dimpled shyly.

'Stay.' Winding his fingers possessively round a spiralling length of her vivid burnished hair, Dante raised it tenderly to his lips. 'I want you to stay until morning. Would you do that for me, Anna? I can't promise you more than this one night, but I promise that I'll hold you close until the dawn comes up... If that's enough...if you're willing to accept just that...will you stay?'

Five years later

Anna flew into the large hotel kitchen, hurriedly unbuttoning her raincoat as she scanned the busy room for

Luigi, the head chef. Defying the stereotype that proclaimed all good chefs should be on the large side, he was tall and thin, with a pointy chin and an abundance of curly black hair with threads of silver tied back in a ponytail. She found him straight away, the back of his chef's whites towards her as he weighed ingredients at one of the scrubbed steel counters, whistling an aria from a well-known opera.

'Did the produce arrive?' she asked breathlessly. 'I spoke to the manager at the deli and he told me it had already left in the van. Is it here?'

Turning round to acknowledge her, the first thing Luigi did was to look her up and down, then wag his finger. 'Have you eaten breakfast this morning? My guess is that you haven't, and yet you run around at a hundred miles an hour as if you can exist on fresh air alone!'

'As it happens I had a croissant at the deli while I was waiting to talk to the manager.'

Crossing her arms over her damp rain-spattered coat, Anna challenged him to disbelieve her. It was sweet that he took such an interest in her welfare and what she ate, but she was no longer the naive twenty-four-year-old she'd been when she first came to the hotel. She was thirty-two, in charge of her own destiny, and the assistant manager to boot!

'A croissant, eh? And how do you expect to survive on such a poor substitute for food as that until lunch-time? A croissant is nothing but air too!'

'It wasn't just air. It had apricot and custard in it, and it was extremely filling and very nice.' Sighing patiently, Anna let her rose-tinted lips naturally form a smile. 'Now, will you please answer my question about the produce delivery? Anita's expecting an important delegation for lunch today, and everything has to be just perfect.'

Luigi threw up his hands dramatically. 'And you believe it *won't* be? You should know by now that Luigi delivers nothing *but* perfection!'

'You're right. I do know that.'

'And, yes, the delivery has arrived—and the black olives are excellent as usual.'

'What a relief. So everything is fine, then? I mean, there aren't any problems?'

With her gaze swinging round towards Cheryl, who was the sous chef, and the three young kitchen assistants scurrying busily about the kitchen, Anna included them all in her question. She hadn't been made assistant manager without developing an ability to notice everything— from the mundane to the much more important—and she was very keen for all to be well.

Anita and Grant, the hotel's owners, had always prided themselves on running a tight ship, but an extremely friendly one too. They cared about their staff. That was why Anna had stayed on. And when she'd fallen pregnant they hadn't said she had to leave. Instead, the couple had been unstinting in their support of her, seeing her potential and insisting she occupy the charming two-bedroom apartment in the basement of the hotel as part of her remuneration for working there. They had also helped her find a reliable and decent local nursery for her baby, and encouraged her to take an online management course with a view to promoting her and helping her to earn a better salary. Consequently, Anna was fiercely loyal as well as immensely grateful to the couple.

'Everything's fine in the kitchen, Anna.' Cheryl nodded, but then the slim, pretty blonde bit down anxiously on her lip and continued, 'Except we couldn't help wondering why Anita and Grant had a delegation from one of the most well-known hotel chains in the country coming here for lunch. Can you tell us anything about it?'

Anna's insides cartwheeled at the question. This afternoon the couple who owned the hotel had scheduled a meeting with her to discuss something important, and all last night and early this morning, as she'd got her daughter Tia ready for kindergarten, she'd been fretting about what the subject might be. The charming little hotel in its smart Georgian building was situated in a very desirable corner of Covent Garden, but Anna wasn't oblivious to the fact that the country was plunged deep into a recession and reservations and consequently takings were definitely down.

Were they going to be bought out by a more commercial hotel giant, and as a consequence would she lose a job she loved again? And not just her job this time, but her home too? *It hardly bore thinking about.*

But now, seeing the obvious anxiety on not just Cheryl's but on the other staff members' faces too, she knew she had a duty to reassure them.

'To be absolutely honest with you I know nothing about it. My advice to you all would be to just concentrate on your work and not waste time on speculation. It won't help. If there's anything concerning us that we need to know, you can be sure we'll all get to hear about it soon. Now, I must get on. I've got to relieve Jason on Reception. He's standing in for Amy, who's phoned in sick.'

Time dragged interminably slowly as the hotel chain's delegation of three enjoyed the superb three-course lunch Luigi and his staff had prepared. Afterwards the two men and their female colleague were closeted in a meeting with Anita, Grant and their son Jason, the manager, for two and a half hours. Anna had never been a clock-watcher, but that afternoon she was.

It was a quarter to five by the time the phone rang on Reception to invite her into Jason's office for the promised meeting with him and his parents. In the meantime, Linda, the girl who did the late shift on the desk, had turned up, and now sat beside Anna powdering her nose.

Standing outside the manager's office, Anna smoothed her hands nervously down over her smart navy skirt, captured a stray auburn tendril that had come adrift from her ponytail, tucked it back into her *faux* ivory clip and then rapped briefly on the door. Greeted by three identically reassuring smiles, she nonetheless sensed immediately that all was not well.

'Dear Anna. Come and sit down, my love.'

The tiny brunette with the stylish elfin haircut, and the smooth, unlined face that belied the fact she was only a year away from the big sixty, welcomed her warmly, as usual.

'Firstly, you'll be pleased to know that the lunch Luigi prepared for our visitors today went extremely well. They were very impressed.'

'The man can certainly cook,' chipped in Grant, Anita's handsome silver-haired husband. 'You could almost forgive him for having an ego the size of an elephant!'

Anna immediately deduced he was nervous, and she perched on the edge of her seat, wishing her mouth wasn't suddenly so sickeningly dry, and that her stomach hadn't sunk as heavily as a giant boulder thrown into the sea. Searching for reassurance, her dark eyes met Jason's. The tall, slim young man whose features were a male version of his elfin mother's tried for a smile, but instead it came off as a resigned grimace. That was the moment when the alarm bells clanged deafeningly loud for Anna.

'So...' Her hands linking together nervously in her lap, she leaned forward even farther in her chair. 'What was the delegation from that commercial hotel chain doing here? Are we in trouble, or something?'

Anita started to speak, but Grant quickly took over.

'Yes, love.' He sighed, pulling a handkerchief out of his suit trousers to lightly mop his brow. 'Serious financial trouble, I'm afraid. Like many other small businesses, the recession's dealt us a heavy blow, and I'm sure you're aware that we've been losing money hand over fist. You've noticed how the reservations have fallen? It's really only the regulars that have stayed loyal to us. If we're to hold our own against some of the more popular hotels we need to reinvest and refurbish, but with the coffers practically empty, and banks refusing loans left right and centre, it's not likely to happen. Consequently, we've had no choice but to try and get some other form of help.'

'Does that mean that you're going to sell the hotel?' There was such a rush of blood to her head that Anna scarcely registered her boss's answer. All she could think of right then was Tia... How was she going feed and clothe her child if she lost her job? More urgently, where were they going to *live*?

'We were offered a buyout, but we haven't accepted the offer yet. We told the delegation that the hotel had been in the family for three generations and we needed some time to think things over.' Anita's usually sunny smile was painfully subdued. 'We have to get back to them by the end of the week. If we do agree to the buyout then unfortunately it means that none of us stay.

They'll want to refurbish and give the place their own look, run it with their own staff. I'm desperately sorry, Anna, but that's our position.'

She was struck silent by the news she'd just heard, but her mind was racing at a hundred miles an hour. Then, because she was also devoted to and protective of the interests of the family that had been so good to her and Tia, Anna forced a reassuring smile to her numbed lips.

'It's a difficult situation you're in,' she quietly acknowledged, 'and it's hardly your fault that there's a recession. The staff—including myself—will all eventually find other jobs, but what will you guys do? The hotel's been in your family for so long, and you love it...I know you do.'

'It's kind of you to be so concerned, love.' The big shoulders that strained Grant's suit jacket lifted in a shrug. 'I'm not saying it'll be easy, but we'll be fine. We've got each other, and that's what matters most in the end, isn't it...? The people you love, I mean.'

Not usually given to expressing his feelings in public, he squeezed Anita's hand. 'And we'll do whatever we can to help you find another flat, Anna. We certainly won't be walking out this door until we know you and Tia are safely settled somewhere. As for jobs... Well, with all the experience and qualifications you've gained these past few years, some grateful hotel will eagerly snap you up. You're a lovely girl and a complete asset... they'll quickly learn that.'

'So you'll let us all know by the end of the week what you've decided?'

'Perhaps sooner... Anita, Jason and I plan to spend the evening mulling things over. As soon as we've decided we'll let you and the rest of the staff know the decision we've reached.'

Getting to his feet, Grant sent Anna a friendly broad smile. 'It's five o'clock, and it's time you were running along to get that little angel of yours from aftercare at kindergarten, isn't it?'

Glancing down at the slim silver-linked watch on her wrist, Anna shot up from her seat. She hated to be late collecting Tia, and as always ached to see her child and learn about her day. Tonight, when she was in effect in limbo about their future, she would make an extra fuss of her, and hold her even tighter before putting her to bed.

CHAPTER THREE

STUDYING the sunlit view of the Thames from his Westminster apartment window, Dante suddenly moved impatiently away, jettisoning his mobile onto the bed. He'd just flown back from a business trip to New York, was feeling fuzzy-headed and tired, and yet the conversation he'd just had with a business friend of his had definitely acted like a triple dose of strong black coffee injected straight into his bloodstream.

The Mirabelle Hotel... It was a name he'd never forgotten. Even after five years. The family who owned it were apparently in dire straits financially, and had been forced to consider a buyout from the commercial hotel chain that his friend Eddie was on the board of. The place was situated in a prime location in central London, and as far as Eddie was concerned it should have been a done deal. But he'd just heard that the owners had quite unbelievably rejected the offer. They had some old-fashioned notion that the business had to stay in the family, come what may.

Eddie had verbalised his astonishment at the number

of people who let their hearts rule their head in business. 'Will they ever learn? How about it, Dante?' he'd asked. 'Fancy giving it a shot? I don't doubt the place is a potential goldmine.'

He had ended the call after agreeing to meet with his friend for a drink later, but Eddie's parting remark had set Dante's mind racing. *That incredible night he'd stayed at that particular hotel had changed his life.* A veritable angel had motivated him to want to do some good in the world instead of just simply taking what he believed his hard work entitled him to. Not only had his aims become less ruthless and driven, but he had discovered a much more exciting avenue, and a way of doing business that far exceeded what he had achieved before in terms of personal satisfaction. It would definitely have had his mother cheering him from the sidelines if she'd lived to see the changes he'd made.

Although he was on the board of several blue chip companies, and still in mergers and acquisitions, Dante had sold off most of his businesses and now specialised in helping family-run concerns make their businesses more viable. He'd also reverted to his mother's surname, instead of the British one he'd adopted when he'd first started out in business here. Once again he was *Dante Romano*, and he had to admit it felt good to be much more authentic. Friends like Eddie still called him Dan, but that was okay. It was a fair enough shortening of Dante.

The Mirabelle Hotel...

Dante flopped down onto the king-sized bed with its opulent aubergine counterpane and picked up his phone. What had happened to the titian-haired beauty he'd spent the night with? Anna Bailey. The memory of her slid into his mind like the diaphanous caress of sensuous silk. *Closing his eyes, he could almost taste her.* He could even recall her perfume...something musky, with hints of orange and patchouli in it. It had been in her long flowing hair, and there had been traces on her milk-and-honey skin too.

His reflection deepening, Dante arrestingly recalled the sumptuously erotic, quivering pink mouth that he'd ached to plunder from almost the first moment he'd encountered it. The experience had been an utter revelation...as though it couldn't have been more right or perfect. For an endless-seeming moment he'd been dizzy with longing for her—his lovely lady of the night, who'd reached out to rescue him when all he could see ahead was blinding darkness.

His eyelids snapped open. Of all the businesses he could hear about that were in trouble...why the Mirabelle? One thing was certain—he couldn't let such an uncanny opportunity pass him by without at least checking it out...

She'd had another sleepless night. Duvet and pillow flung in frustration on the floor during the night. Her bed had become a taunting enemy instead of the safe, comforting haven she craved. And when she'd finally got up, Anna had uncharacteristically snapped at Tia as well.

As soon as she'd seen the child's luminous blue-grey eyes sparkle with tears across from her at the breakfast table, she'd immediately wanted to kick herself. Drawing the little girl urgently onto her lap, she'd kissed and hugged her and told her about a hundred times how sorry she was. Mummy didn't mean to shout. She was just a little bit stressed, she'd explained.

'What does *distressed* mean?' Tia had questioned, absently, playing with a long curling tendril of Anna's unbound auburn hair.

Perhaps her daughter had unwittingly stumbled upon the truth of what she was feeling? She *was* distressed.

'I'll explain when you come home from school, darling,' she'd hedged, praying the child would forget to ask. It wasn't something a four-year-old should be remotely acquainted with, to Anna's mind. Childhood should be joyful and carefree...*even if her own had been a million miles away from such an idyll.*

The Cathcarts had told Anna that they'd turned down the offer of a buyout from the big hotel chain. So when she'd entered the office the following morning to discover that her employers were considering a fresh offer—this one from an independent source who had been told about them by one of the delegation from the hotel chain—her insides had mimicked the nail-biting ascent and descent of a frantic rollercoaster ride for the second time. Once more the possibility of losing her job and home loomed worryingly large.

'Your parents said that an interested investor wants to help them improve profitability and modernise. Can you explain exactly what this means?' Anna had asked concernedly as she left the owners' office to walk with Jason to his.

'Don't look so worried, Anna. It's good news. Major investment is just what the Mirabelle needs. What we're hoping is that this guy will be interested enough to invest a large chunk of his own money in the business to help turn it around. He'll be the majority shareholder, but he won't own it outright. I've been checking out his record and it's quite impressive, to put it mildly. His interests are truly international, but his main concern is helping family-run businesses become more profitable. If we accept an offer from him to invest, it means that we stay running the hotel under his guidance and expertise. We'll have the chance to really take things to another level...even in the recession.'

Jason opened the door for Anna to precede him as they took their coffee into his cramped, cluttered office. Pushing some papers aside on a desk that scarcely had a corner free of paper debris, he left his mug of coffee on a stained cork coaster. An air of bubbling excitement underlaid his usually level tone.

'When he goes into a business with a view to help-ing it perform better,' he continued, 'he takes a good hard look at how it's being run and then advises on the changes that will make it more efficient and profitable. He particularly specialises in helping to resolve any conflicts that might be preventing people from working successfully together.'

Anna's brow creased. 'There aren't any conflicts amongst us, though, are there? Unless you mean Luigi's tendency to lord it over the others in the kitchen... They do get a bit fed up with him from time to time, but aren't all head chefs a bit like that? Egotistic and dramatic, I mean.'

'Generally I think that we all get on great. But that doesn't mean there isn't room for improvement.' As he paced the floor, it appeared as if Jason's enthusiasm was hard to contain. 'Unaired resentments can fester... we all know that. And this guy is a real people person. We thoroughly checked him out before inviting him over for a meeting. Apparently one of the first things he does is to interview everyone to discover how they feel about their job. He passionately believes that their attitude contributes to how well they work, and he has a unique reputation for getting staff and management to work more successfully together. The best thing of all is that the family get to stay doing what they love. We don't have to just sell up and go. Who knows? If the hotel starts to make a real profit, we might eventually be able to buy it back completely. The staff will remain too of course. It means you won't have to search for another job, Anna, isn't that great? Having someone like this Dante Romano guy invest his money in the hotel and take a look at how we can improve things could be the best opportunity we've had in ages!'

'And what's the pay-off for this man? I mean...what's in it for him besides making a profit? I doubt that he's going to do all this out of the goodness of his heart.'

She couldn't help it, but Anna wasn't entirely convinced. It all sounded too good to be true. Perhaps her nature wasn't as trusting as it could be, but then bruising experience had taught her to be alert to the glossily wrapped Christmas present that contained nothing but an empty shoebox.

The earnest dark-haired young man before her in the charcoal-grey suit that was showing signs of fraying at the edges of its cuffs abruptly stopped pacing.

'Of course there's a pay-off for him, Anna. He's a businessman! But his interest in helping us sounds perfectly genuine. I know you're only being protective of Mum and Dad but they're experienced hoteliers, don't forget. They won't agree to anything that remotely smacks of a scam or a rip-off. Yes, this guy might become the main shareholder—but he won't be running the business...*we* will. Plus, his policy is to take a longer-term view of situations, so he won't be in a hurry to just look at what he can get out of the business and then head for the hills.'

'You sound as though you believe this is the answer to all your family's prayers, Jason.'

It did indeed seem the ideal solution in terms of enabling them all to stay put, but Anna would rather hunt for another job and flat elsewhere if it meant that Grant and Anita wouldn't be out of pocket and the couple would have the means to start a good life again somewhere else. What if it really *was* in their best interests for them to sell the Mirabelle to a big commercial hotel giant?

'Nothing's been decided yet, Anna.' Compounding her guilt at being sceptical, Jason sounded subdued. 'But Romano is coming for lunch, and after he's eaten we'll have a proper meeting to thrash things out. Hopefully we'll be able to report back on what's been decided later on that afternoon. Would you mind going to talk to Luigi, to make sure he's got everything he needs to impress our visitor with his menu?'

'Of course.'

Carrying what remained of her half-drunk coffee to the door, Anna flashed him a smile to make up for her less than enthusiastic response earlier, but her stomach still churned at the prospect of the unknown changes that lay ahead for them all. She paused to glance back at the Cathcarts' preoccupied son, guessing that he probably saw the chance of working with this Romano chap as something that would enhance his reputation and ability—assets that were sometimes overshadowed by his much more confident and experienced father.

'I just want you to know that I'll do everything I can to help you and your parents, Jason. I love this hotel too, and I know it's been a very worrying time for all of you.'

'Thanks, Anna...I've always known I can count on you.'

The memories crashed in on Dante the instant he walked through the glass-panelled entrance into the cosily old-fashioned lobby, with its chintz armchairs and worn brown chesterfields.

After that incredible night with Anna he'd left the hotel in the early hours of the morning to jump in a cab and catch a flight to New York. His mother's death had plunged him into a tunnel of despair for a frighteningly long time. It had taken a good year or more for him to be able to function anywhere near normal again because, disturbingly, his work and everything he'd achieved had become utterly meaningless. Life had only started to improve when the warm memory of Anna's tenderness and his mother's unfailing belief that he was a much better man than the world suspected broke through the walls of his grief and his self-imposed isolation and helped him start to entertain the possibility of a very different, much more fulfilling future.

That was when Dante had decided to change his driven, selfish approach to something far more wholesome...

The Cathcarts were a delightful couple, with admirably solid values when it came to business and family. But Dante, although charmed by their unstinting hospitality and the superlative lunch, sensed that some of those solid values were a bit too entrenched in the past and needed to be brought up to date.

At lunch, his cool gaze assessed as much as it could as they talked, including the worn velvet hangings at the stately Georgian dining room windows, the tarnished silver cutlery and the slightly old-fashioned uniforms of the waiting staff. Afterwards he was invited to the Cathcarts' office to discuss the nuts and bolts of an investment.

As the fragrant, elegant Anita Cathcart poured him some coffee—at Dante's nod adding cream and sugar— he sat back in the comfortable leather chair, loosened his silk tie a little and relaxed. The hotel *was* in an absolutely prime location and could—as Eddie had foreseen—potentially be a goldmine. Because of lack of funds and the large debt they had accrued with the bank, it was clear the Cathcarts weren't able to make the best of their incredible asset, and that was where Dante came in.

'We'll get started soon, Mr Romano. We're just waiting for our assistant manager to join us. She's more like family than an employee, and we'd like her to be in on what we decide. She'll be along any minute now.'

Jason, the Cathcarts' slightly built son and manager, smiled diffidently at Dante as he sat down opposite him at the meeting table. He was clutching a pen and a spiral notebook and his hand shook a little. *What was the story with him?* Dante wondered. Was the manager's role too big an ask for him, or was it just that he struggled to assert himself under his parents' guardianship of the hotel?

'Was she informed about the meeting?'

'Yes...of course. It's just that she—'

'Then she should be here on time, like everyone else.'

His chastising glance encompassed them all, but Dante nonetheless tempered it with a trace of a smile. He heard the door behind him open and turned expectantly. A woman with hair the same hue as a bright russet apple stepped inside, bringing with her the faint but stirring scent of oranges and patchouli...

His thoughts careened to an abrupt halt...like a driver applying the emergency brake before hitting a wall. He stared in shock. *Anna...dear God, she still worked here?*

'I'm so sorry I'm late,' she breathed, porcelain skin flushing. 'I was—'

The startled leap in her sherry-brown eyes told Dante she recognised him. His heart—which had all but stalled—pumped a little harder as he realised he'd been genuinely afraid she might have forgotten him. *What a blow that would have been to his pride, when out of all the women he'd seen over the years she was the one that haunted him...*

'Mr Romano,' Grant Cathcart was saying, 'I'd like to introduce you to our stalwart assistant manager...Anna Bailey.'

Rising automatically to his feet, Dante extended his hand, praying hard that his voice wouldn't desert him. Anna's palm was fragile and slightly chilled as it slid into his. Their gazes locked as though magnetized, and though he sensed her tremble, inside he believed that he trembled *more*.

'Miss Bailey…I'm very pleased to meet you,' he heard himself announce.

'The feeling is mutual, Mr—Mr Romano,' she replied politely.

Her warm velvet voice bathed his senses in liquid honey. Arresting memories of their unforgettable night together came pouring back in a disturbing heated rush. Realising that his hand still covered hers, Dante reluctantly withdrew it.

'Why don't you come and sit down, Anna love?' Anita invited. 'There's plenty of coffee in the pot if you'd like some.'

'I'm fine, thanks,' Anna murmured distractedly.

As Dante watched her, she moved like a sleepwalker to a seat at the opposite side of the table, next to Jason, and he didn't miss the spark of warmth in the other man's dark eyes as he silently acknowledged her. *Was something going on there?* A hot flash of jealousy hit Dante a glancing blow as he resumed his seat.

'Well, if everybody's ready, we'll make a start, shall we?' With a respectful glance in their visitor's direction, Grant Cathcart organised his notes and prepared to address the meeting.

* * *

Dante Romano. No wonder she'd never been able to find him! What had instigated the name-change? she wondered. Underneath, was he still as ruthless and cutthroat as it had said in the newspaper reports she'd read when she'd been searching for him? But what did it matter when it had already been decided by the Cathcarts that he was going to be their saviour?

As well as investing a substantial amount of money in the Mirabelle, Dante Romano was taking the hotel, its owners and its staff firmly under his wing. Being satisfied that Anita and Grant were completely happy with the arrangement was one thing. *Only time would tell if Anna would be equally happy.* There was a very big—in fact a *huge* hurdle she had to cross before then.

Shaking her head, she emitted a small groan as she added chopped up red and green peppers to the stir-fry she was busy cooking for herself and Tia.

She'd half believed she was hallucinating when she'd walked into the office to find Dan, or *Dante* as he called himself now, sitting there. And she'd had such a jolt when his incredible winter-coloured eyes had bored into hers. In those electrifying few seconds the world could have ended, and she hadn't been able to drag her hypnotised gaze away.

Five years ago she'd never even asked him his full name. When he'd asked her to stay with him for the night but not to expect anything more she'd agreed— and she'd promised herself she wouldn't speculate on where he would go or what he would do when he left her, even if it ultimately meant he was going from her arms to someone else's.

Consoling herself that she'd helped comfort him in his hour of need, and that no matter how emotionally painful it was it would have to be enough, Anna had never intended to try and track him down afterwards. But when she'd found herself pregnant with his child she'd reasoned that she owed it to him to let him know. However, discovering that the suite's occupant Dan Masterson was a veritable 'shark' in the world of international business, who didn't care who he brought down in his empire-building quest, had definitely given her pause. He might have been tender with Anna that night they'd spent together, and he might have been troubled, but could she knowingly risk inflicting such a driven ruthless man on her child?

She'd decided *no*, she couldn't. Besides, she'd definitely received the impression from her one-night lover that he wasn't interested in a relationship, so why would he be interested in the fact that he'd left his one-time-only lover pregnant? she'd reasoned.

Leading up to that night five years ago she'd been working so hard, what with all the different jobs she did at the hotel—sometimes even working double shifts back to back—and because she'd been extremely tired, she'd absent-mindedly forgotten to take one of her daily contraceptive pills. It had only dawned on Anna to check when early-morning nausea had become a worrying recurrence.

Some months after Tia had been born she'd revised her decision not to get in touch with Dan and decided to try once more to locate him. *It had been as though he had vanished.* The only information about him she'd been able to glean was stuff from the past. There had been nothing to indicate what he was doing nearly eighteen months after they'd met.

From the living room came the delighted chuckle of her small daughter as she knocked down the building blocks she'd had as a toddler that she'd been happily shaping into a wobbling tower for the past ten minutes or so. A wave of sadness and terror deluged her mother all at once. What would Dan—or Dante, as she should call him now—think when he found out that their passionate night together all those years ago had made him a father? How poignant that he hadn't had the privilege of knowing his own delightful daughter. Anna had no doubt that it would have enhanced his life in a myriad different ways. But what could she have done when it had seemed as though he didn't exist any more?

With genuine regret she squeezed her eyes shut, then quickly opened them again. Her terror came from the fact that she knew he was a very rich and influential man indeed—rich enough to invest in a major share of the hotel that was the means of her employment and her place to live. How would it reflect on Anna if Dante's was the controlling share? What if he decided she wasn't up to her job—or, worse still, that he wanted to try and take Tia away from her? A man as wealthy as him must have access to all kinds of power…particularly *legal* power.

Abruptly switching off the burner beneath the wooden-handled wok, Anna wrapped her arms protectively round her middle as she crossed the tiled kitchen floor to examine the collage of baby and toddler photographs of Tia that were framed on the wall there. Behind her, the suddenly ringing telephone made her jump.

'Hello?'

'Anna? It's me—Dante. I'm still in the hotel. You rushed off rather quickly after the meeting and I think we need to talk. I believe you have a flat downstairs—can I come down and see you?'

CHAPTER FOUR

ANNA was struck dumb by Dante's request. What should she do? If she agreed for him to come down to the flat, how to prepare him for her news when Tia was there, large as life, playing happily in the living room? There was no time to prepare for anything!

'I'd love to talk to you—I really would—but—'

'But?'

She could imagine him sardonically curling his lip. He knew she was hedging. God, why couldn't she be a better actress?

'I'm making dinner at the moment. Why don't we arrange to meet up tomorrow? You're coming in to start working with Grant and Anita, aren't you?'

'I think I'd rather come and talk to you right now, Anna. I'll be with you in about five minutes.'

He put down the phone. Anna was left staring at the receiver in her hand as if it was a grenade she'd just pulled the pin from.

'Tia, we're going to have a visitor in a minute. We'll have dinner after he's gone, okay?'

She sped round the compact living room, sweeping up strewn toys into her arms like a whirlwind, then throwing them onto the end of the faded gold couch as if she was aiming to knock down coconuts at a carnival stall. When Dante arrived she would hide her emotions as best she could, she promised herself, yanking her oversized emerald sweater further down over her hips. Yes, she would hide behind her assistant manager's mask—be unflustered and professional, as if she could totally handle whatever he cared to throw at her. No matter that she hadn't been able to so much as *look* at another man since he'd left, because her heart had been irrevocably stolen by him.

She didn't have a hope of concealing her feelings behind a managerial mask under the circumstances. How could she?

'Who's coming to see us, Mummy?' Feeling a tug on her trouser-leg, Anna's gaze fell distractedly into her daughter's. The child's big blue-grey eyes—eyes, she realised with another frisson of shock, that were *identical* to her father's—were avid with curiosity. 'Is it Auntie Anita?'

'No, darling. It's not Auntie Anita.' Chewing anxiously down on her lip, Anna forced herself to smile. 'It's a man called Dante Romano and—and he's an old friend of mine.'

'If he's your friend, why haven't I seen him before?' Tia's husky little voice was plaintive.

'Because—'

The knock on the hallway door just outside completely silenced whatever it was that Anna had been about to say. Rolling up her sweater sleeves, she reached for Tia's hand and led her as calmly as she was able over to the couch, where she sat her down. Crouching in front of her, she tenderly stroked back some golden corkscrew curls from her forehead.

'Don't be nervous, will you? He's—he's a very nice man, and I'm sure he'll be very pleased to meet you.'

As she hurried out into the hallway a surge of irrepressibly strong emotion made tears flood into her eyes. Not now! she moaned silently, wiping them away with the back of her hand. *Why don't you wait to hear what he has to say before you start crying?*

'Hi.' His handsome smile was devastatingly confident, and Anna could scarcely contain the anger that suddenly rose up inside her, let alone analyse it.

'Hello,' she murmured in reply, praying he wouldn't see the evidence of her tears. 'Come in.'

Had he called at a bad time? Dante speculated. Her beautiful brown eyes appeared slightly moist. He guessed she would rather have put off his visit until tomorrow, but the fact of the matter was he couldn't wait until then to see her and talk to her again. Ever since Anna had walked into that office he'd ached to get her alone, find out what she'd been doing all these years... maybe even ask if she'd ever thought about him since that extraordinary night they'd spent together.

Folding her arms, she stood squarely in front of him,

leaving him with the distinct notion he wasn't going to be invited in any farther. Fighting down the sense of rejection that bubbled up inside him, he swept his glance hungrily over her pale oval face. The dazzling fire-lit brown eyes were wary, he noticed, and the softly shaped mouth that was barely glazed with some raspberry-coloured lipgloss was serious and unsmiling.

'You said you wanted to talk…what about?'

It wasn't a very promising start. Apprehension flooded into the pit of Dante's stomach.

'What a greeting. You make it sound like you're expecting an interrogation.' He shrugged, momentarily thrown off balance by her cool reception.

'It's just that I'm busy.'

'Cooking, you said?' He quirked a slightly mocking eyebrow and sniffed the air.

'Look…how do you expect me to greet you after all this time? The truth is you're the last person I ever expected to see again! For you to show up now, because you're the new investor in the Mirabelle, is obviously a shock…a shock that I was totally unprepared for.' Pursing her lips, she was clearly distressed. 'I don't know how to put this any other way, Mr Romano, and please don't think me presumptuous, but I think that whatever else happens round here our relationship should remain strictly professional for as long as we have to work together.'

'Why? Afraid you might be tempted to instigate a repeat performance of the last time we got together?'

Stung by her aloof air, and the distance she seemed so eager to put between them, Dante said the first thing that entered his head. Trouble was, he'd be *lying* if he said the thought of them being intimate *hadn't* crossed his mind. It was practically all he'd been dwelling on since setting eyes on her.

Blushing hard, Anna gazed down at the floor. When she glanced up at him again her dark eyes were spilling over with fury.

'What a hateful, arrogant thing to say! Bad enough that you only thought me good enough for a one-night stand, but to come here now and assume that I—that I would even—' She gulped in a deep breath to calm herself. 'Some of us have moved on.'

Dante nodded, sensing a muscle flex hard in the side of his cheek. 'And you *have* moved on, haven't you, Anna? Assistant Manager, no less.'

'If you're suggesting I got the position by any other means than by damned hard work then you can just turn around and leave right now. I certainly don't intend to meekly stand here while you mock and insult me!'

His lips twitched into a smile. He couldn't help it. Did she have any idea how sexy she was when she was angry? With that fiery-red hair spilling over her shoulders and those dark eyes flashing...it would test the libidinous mettle of any red-blooded heterosexual male. To Dante it felt as if a lighted match had been dropped into his blood, and it had ignited as though it were petrol.

'I didn't come here to insult you, Anna. I merely wanted to see you again in private...that's all.'

'I heard you shouting, Mummy.'

A little girl with the prettiest corkscrew blond curls Dante had ever seen suddenly emerged from a room along the hall. Deep shock scissored through him. She'd addressed Anna as 'Mummy'.

Definitely flustered, Anna ran her fingers over the child's softly wayward hair, captured a small hand in hers and squeezed it.

'Tia...this is the man I told you about. Mr Romano.'

'Why are you calling him Mr Romano when you told me his name was Dante?'

The girl was engagingly forthright. Dante smiled, and the child dimpled shyly up at him.

'Hello, Tia.' Staring into her riveting misty-coloured eyes, he frowned, not knowing why she suddenly seemed so familiar. Quickly he returned his attention to Anna. 'You got married and had a child?' he said numbly. 'Was that the "moving on" you referred to?'

'I'm not married.'

'But you're still with her father?'

Her cheeks pinking with embarrassment, she sighed. 'No...I'm not.'

'Obviously things didn't work out between you?' Dante's racing heartbeat started to stabilise. So she was alone again? It must have been tough, raising her child on her own. He wondered if the father kept in touch and assumed the proper responsibility for his daughter's welfare. Having had a father who had shamelessly deserted him and his mother when it didn't suit him to be responsible, Dante deplored the mere idea that the man might have turned his back on Anna and the child.

'Perhaps—perhaps you'd better come in after all.' Saying no more, Anna turned back towards the room along the hallway, Tia's hand gripped firmly in hers.

Barely knowing what to make of this, Dante followed. The living room was charming. The walls were painted in an off-white cream-coloured tone, helping to create a very attractive sense of spaciousness and light. It was the perfect solution in a basement apartment where the long rectangular windows were built too high up to let in much daylight.

'Please,' she said nervously, gesturing towards a plump gold-coloured couch with toys strewn at one end, 'sit down. Can I get you something to drink?'

She'd gone from hostile to the perfect hostess in a couple of seconds flat. It immediately made Dante suspicious. He dropped down onto the couch.

'No, thanks.' Freeing his tie a little from his shirt collar, he gave Tia a smile then leant forward, his hands linked loosely across his thighs. 'What's going on, Anna? And don't tell me nothing... I'm too good a reader of people to buy that.'

She was alternately twisting her hands together and fiddling with the ends of her bright auburn hair. The tension already building in Dante's iron-hard stomach muscles increased an uncomfortable notch.

'Tia? Would you go into your bedroom for a minute and look for that colouring book we were searching for earlier? You know the one—with the farm animals on the front? Have a really good look and bring some crayons too.'

'Is Dante going to help me colour in my book, Mummy?' The little girl's voice was hopeful.

'Sure.' He grinned at her. 'Why not?'

When Tia had left them to run along the hallway to her bedroom, Anna's dark eyes immediately cleaved apprehensively to Dante's. 'That night—the night we were together...' She cleared her throat a little and his avid gaze didn't waver from hers for a second. 'I got pregnant. I didn't lie when I told you I was on the pill, but because I'd been working so hard I missed taking one... Anyway...Tia's yours. What I'm saying—what I'm trying to tell you—is that you're her father.'

He'd heard of white-outs, but not being enamoured of snow or freezing weather had never experienced one. He imagined the blinding sensation of disorientation that currently gripped him was a little like that condition. Time ticked on in its own relentless way, but for a long moment he couldn't distinguish anything much. Feelings, thoughts—they just didn't exist. He quite simply felt numb. Then, when emotions started to pour through him like a riptide, he pushed to his feet, staring hard at the slender redhead who stood stock-still, her brown eyes a myriad palette of shifting colours Dante couldn't decipher right then.

'What are you up to?' he demanded. 'Has someone put you up to this to try and swindle money from me? Answer me, damn it!' He drove his shaking fingers through his hair in a bid to still them. 'Tell me what you just said again, Anna—so I can be sure I didn't misunderstand you.'

'Nobody put me up to anything, and nor do I want your money. I'm telling you the truth, Dante. That night we spent together resulted in me becoming pregnant.'

'And the baby you were carrying is Tia?'

'Yes.'

'Then if that's the truth, why in God's name didn't you find me to let me know?'

'We agreed.' She swallowed hard. Her flawless smooth skin was alabaster-pale, Dante registered without sympathy. 'We agreed that we wouldn't hold each other to anything...that it was just for the one night and in the morning we'd both move on. You were—you were so troubled that night. I knew you were hurting. I didn't know what had happened, because you didn't tell me, but I guessed you might have just lost someone close. You weren't looking for anything deep...like a relationship. I knew that. You didn't even tell me your last name. You simply wanted—*needed* to be close to someone and for some reason—' She momentarily dipped her head. 'For some reason you chose me.'

Barely trusting himself to speak, because his chest

felt so tight and he was afraid he might just explode, Dante grimly shook his head.

'You could have easily found out my last name by checking in the reservations book. From there you could have found a contact address. Why didn't you?'

She hesitated, as if she was about to say something, but changed her mind. 'I—I told you. I didn't because we'd made an agreement. I was respecting your wishes… that's all.'

'Respecting my wishes? Are you crazy? This wasn't just some simple mistake you could brush aside, woman! Can't you see what you've done? You've denied me my own child. For over four years my daughter has lived without her father. Did she never ask about me?'

'Yes…she—she did.'

'Then what did you tell her?'

Her expression anguished, Anna was clearly struggling to give him a reply.

'When Tia asked me why her daddy wasn't around I—I just told her that you'd been ill and had to go away to get better. What else could I tell her when I had no idea where you were or even if you'd care?'

Lifting a shaky hand to his forehead Dante grimaced painfully. 'And whose fault is that, when you couldn't even be bothered to find me?'

Her skin turned even paler. 'I understand why you'd want to blame me, but at the time the decision not to see each other again was ostensibly *yours*, if you remember?'

'And while I've been relegated to the back of your mind as some past inconvenient mistake...has there been anyone else on the scene?' Dante demanded, his temper flashing like an electrical storm out of a previously calm summer sky. 'Another man who's played father to Tia?'

'No, there hasn't. I've been raising her on my own, and at the same time trying to build a career so that I can support us both. I don't have time for relationships with other men!'

This last statement had clearly made her angry. The tightness in Dante's chest eased a little, but not much. He was still furious with her. Frankly, the idea that his child might have witnessed a parade of different men filing through her mother's life filled him with horror and distress. Children needed stability, support, *love*... The thought brought him up short. He had accepted without dispute the fact that Tia was his daughter—accepted the word of a woman he had only known for one too short and incredible night. Yet the moment he had gazed into Tia's eyes—eyes that were the same unusual light shade as his—Dante had somehow known that she belonged to him.

'Well, now you *will* make time for a relationship, Anna. Your comfortable little idyll of having things just the way you want them is about to change dramatically. You've dropped the bombshell that I am father to a daughter, and now you will have to accept the consequences.'

'What consequences?' The colour seemed to drain out of her face.

'What do you think?' Dante snarled, his hands curling into fists down by his sides. 'What do you think will happen now that I know I fathered a child that night? Did you think I would calmly walk away, saying, *"Oh, well"*? From this moment on I fully intend to be a father to our daughter, and that means I want a legalised relationship with you—her mother. Purely for the child's sake, you understand, and not because it fills me with joy to be with you again, Anna! Not after the terrible deceit you have played on me. So, no... I won't be calmly walking away so that you can happily continue the way you were. It's not just the hotel that will undergo a great change now that I am here.'

'I won't prevent you from playing an important part in Tia's life now that you know the truth...if that's what you want,' Anna replied quietly, though her expression mirrored a silent plea, 'but we don't need to be in a relationship for that. Five years ago you made it very clear that you weren't interested in taking things any further. I accepted that. I've made a good life for myself working at the hotel. The owners have been more than kind to me and Tia, and I'm extremely grateful to them for all they've done. As far as I can see there's no need for that arrangement to change.'

Rubbing his fingers into his temples, Dante breathed out an impatient sigh. He didn't like referring to the past, but in this case he would have to.

'Five years ago I was bordering on burn-out from working too hard and too long…then my mother died. She was Italian. The name I use now is my proper full name—the name my mother gave me. I only mention it because the night we met I'd just flown back from her funeral in Italy. I was living in New York at the time, but I couldn't get a direct flight back there so made a stopover in London for the night. Having just been bereaved, I was hardly in a fit state to contemplate a relationship with anyone. But, like you with Tia, my mother raised me on my own as a single parent, and I saw first-hand how hard life was for her. It made her old before her time, and I worried about her constantly. I'll be damned if I'll visit that hurtful existence on my own child. That being the way things stand, you have no choice but to enter into a relationship with me—a relationship that can have only one destination… Our marriage.'

Sympathetically examining the compellingly handsome face with those searing stormy eyes—the face that she had fantasised over and dreamed longingly about for five long, lonely years—Anna willed her emotions not to get the better of her. She was gratified to hear at last an explanation as to why Dante had appeared so haunted and troubled that night, and for the second time in their association her heart went out to him. But while she understood the fears that their own situation must be raising inside him, because he too had been brought up without a father, she balked at the idea of tying herself to him merely for convenience. Dante Romano might be the father of her beloved daughter, but he was still an unknown quantity to Anna. It would be nothing less than reckless to marry him—even though privately she still held a torch for him and always would.

'I'm really sorry that you lost your mother, Dante. I could see at the time how devastated you were. But I won't be told I'm going to have to marry you just because you're Tia's father. That would be crazy. We don't even know each other. And for your information I don't want to marry anyone. I'm happy just as I am, doing my job and taking care of Tia. I won't stop you from being in her life—I'd be glad of it, if that's what you honestly want. But, like I said before, you and I don't have to be in a relationship for that.'

'Like hell we don't!' He scowled at her.

'And there's one more thing.' Feeling nervous, and knowing she was on shaky ground already, Anna rubbed a chilled palm down over her sweater. 'I'd be grateful if you didn't say anything to Grant and Anita about us knowing each other…at least not yet. It's such an awkward situation, and I *will* tell them, but I need some time to think about how best to broach the subject. Please do this one favour for me, and I promise I'll tell them soon.'

'I'll let you off the hook for a couple of days,' Dante agreed reluctantly. 'But then you *will* be telling them, Anna—about us *and* Tia. You can be absolutely sure about that.'

'I found my colouring book and my crayons!' Rushing back into the room like a tiny blond cyclone, Tia blew out a happy breath and headed straight for Dante.

For a moment he stood stock-still, his lean, smartly suited figure apparently all at sea. Anna realised that, like her, he was desperately trying to get his emotions under control. *Put yourself in his shoes*, she told herself. How would you feel if you were suddenly confronted with the astonishing fact that you'd fathered a child? A child you hadn't even known existed up until now?

'Will you help me colour in my book, please?'

The tall broad-shouldered man whose dark blond hair was slightly mussed from his agitated fingers had let Tia pierce his heart with her big soulful eyes, Anna saw. Her teeth clamped down on her lip, but it didn't stop them from trembling.

'I promised I would, didn't I?' she heard Dante agree huskily, and then he slipped his hand into his daughter's and allowed her to lead him back to the couch. Before he sat down, he shucked off the dark blue exquisitely lined jacket of his business suit, throwing it carelessly onto the cushions.

His arresting light eyes met Anna's. 'I'd like that drink you offered earlier after all,' he commented. 'Coffee would be good. I take it with milk and two sugars, thanks.'

CHAPTER FIVE

BY THE time Dante was ready to leave that evening—
having accepted Anna's invitation to join them for dinner—Tia was completely besotted with the man.

Although Anna's senses had been minutely attuned to
the fact that the man she had so recklessly given herself
to that magical night five years ago was now sitting opposite her at her dining table there had been no struggle
to make awkward conversation. Not when her daughter
had chatted enough for them both. So engaged had she
been with Dante's company that for the first time ever
she'd protested loudly about going to bed. She had only
agreed to go if Dante would read her a bedtime story—
which he duly had.

When he'd emerged from her bedroom half an hour
later his air had been subdued and preoccupied. It had
been obvious that he was trying hard to come to terms
with a situation he probably couldn't have envisaged
in a thousand years. After all, Anna had told him she
was on the pill, so what need had there been for him to
worry?

Assuming he would want to discuss things further, she'd risked giving him a smile, but he had shown no inclination to linger…the opposite, in fact. How was she supposed to confess that she wasn't as heartless as he'd assumed, and that she *had* planned to let him know about her pregnancy, but when she'd discovered his ruthless reputation in the business world she'd been scared that when the baby was born he might try and take him or her away from her? Then, when she'd tried again later, it had been as though 'Dan Masterson' had simply vanished off the radar.

'We've got a long day of discussion and planning about the hotel tomorrow,' he said to her now. 'There'll be plenty of time after work in the evening for us to discuss our personal situation in more depth.' There was a fierce glint in his eyes that said *do not doubt that*. 'For now I'll say goodnight, *innamorata*, and I will see you in the morning. Sleep well. You're going to need to be doubly alert for all we have to face tomorrow,' he added, a dark blond eyebrow lifting a little mockingly even though his voice and manner was still distant and aloof.

Innamorata—didn't that mean *sweetheart* in Italian? Anna shivered hard. Having asserted that she wasn't interested in a relationship, she wondered if Dante would still adhere to his insistence that they marry? A tug of uncertainty mingled with the faintest of faint hopes in the pit of her stomach. *What if he concluded that his association with Tia was the only one that really counted?*

A lonely feeling crept over her. And when she was still lying awake in the early hours of the morning because she couldn't get Dante out of her mind, Anna seriously worried how on earth she was going to get through her working day without at some point falling asleep on the job.

Reflecting on the new partner's all-business tone when he'd left, as well as his warning that she needed to be 'doubly alert', she imagined that would go down like the proverbial ton of bricks. It certainly wouldn't reveal her at her best. And as for the news he had just so shockingly learned…would Dante be so angry with her for not revealing his daughter's existence to him that he would try to punish her in some way? For instance, would her job and her home be under threat now that he was in the driving seat?

Thumping her pillow in pure frustration, Anna released a pained groan. Then, with her eyes determinedly shut, she sent up a swift plea to the universe for the incessant worry going through her mind to grind to a halt so that she might at least get a couple of hours' rest before having to rise for work…

'You're late, Miss Bailey.'

The clipped pronouncement came not from the owners of the hotel, nor Jason their son, but from Dante. He was seated at the head of the meeting table in Grant and Anita's office, wearing another mouthwateringly tailored dark suit that he'd teamed with an elegant black shirt—the only splash of colour came from his vivid cobalt silk tie and his disturbing light eyes...eyes that now pierced Anna like the dazzling beams of sunlight reflecting on water as she stood in the doorway, wrestling with her embarrassment at being reprimanded.

So the gloves were off, were they? Clearly he'd reflected on her news of yesterday and he *did* mean to punish her. Making it clear he was the one in charge, he'd probably make her rue the day she'd kept Tia a secret from him and then had the temerity to say she wouldn't marry him.

'I'm sorry. I'm afraid I had a bit of a sleepless night. When I did manage to drop off I ended up sleeping through the alarm.'

'Tia's not coming down with something, is she?' Anita's perfectly arched brows lifted concernedly.

Straight away, Anna saw Dante's smooth lightly-tanned forehead tighten too.

'No, she's fine. I just couldn't sleep, that's all.'

Frown disappearing, he scanned a document in front of him on the table, then lifted his gaze to examine her coolly. 'That kind of lame excuse for being late is unacceptable, Miss Bailey. I'd advise you to get a louder alarm clock if you want to keep your position here.'

Even her employers' mouths dropped opened at that. As the avuncular Grant shifted uncomfortably in his seat, Anita directed a sympathetic smile at Anna and mouthed *don't worry.*

'Dante?'

The older woman moved her attention immediately back to the outrageously handsome man at the head of the table. Although her voice was soft it didn't lack authority.

'Sleeping through the alarm happens to the best of us from time to time—and we've always called our staff by their first names...especially Anna. As we indicated to you before, she's not just an employee. She's a friend too.'

'And that's precisely what goes wrong in family businesses,' Dante returned, sharp as a blade. 'Whilst I'm all for informality, to a degree, it's still important to monitor it so it doesn't get out of control, or your staff will start taking advantage of your goodwill.'

'How dare you?' With her heart beating a tattoo that wouldn't shame a military marching band, Anna glared at the owners' new partner and took affront at the superior tone in his voice. 'I would never dream of taking advantage of my employers' goodwill. I owe them everything...they've given me a job, a home—'

Pulling out a chair next to Jason and dropping down into it, she firmly closed her lips to stop any further angry words from recklessly pouring out. What was between Dante and her was personal, she thought furiously. She wouldn't drag her personal resentments into work meetings and neither should he!

So she hadn't been able to sleep last night? Dante reflected with satisfaction, ignoring her outburst. His glance swept helplessly over her delicate, now flushed features. Well, neither had he. Learning only a few short hours ago that he was the father of the most engaging and beautiful child he'd ever seen had never been going to help him get the best night's rest known to man. Neither was the fact that Anna had seemed far from keen on the idea of marrying him. *As in the past, rejection was like a scythe, slicing open his heart.* But Dante had already decided she could refuse him all she liked—because in the end he was determined to have his way. As far as his daughter was concerned he would use any means possible to ensure she had the upbringing and the future she deserved. But right now he needed to deal with what was in front of him—his promise and commitment to the Mirabelle, to turn the business around and have it flourishing again. Already his mind was buzzing with ideas for changes and improvements. And he would begin as he usually began when he went into a business to update it and improve its profitability—he would interview the staff...

'Can I pour you some coffee?' Reaching for the newly filled cafetière, Dante glanced expectantly at Anna as she sat down on the other side of his desk.

'No, thank you.' Her sherry-brown gaze briefly acknowledged him then quickly moved away again.

Irritation and disappointment threatened his effort to

be as good-humoured and fair as possible. Was she still brooding about him ticking her off earlier? As much as his pride wanted to cajole her into viewing him more favourably, right now this interview needed to get underway as well as remain professional, and Dante knew a battle of wills wouldn't help. Their personal issues would have to wait until later tonight.

'Fine... Good. We'll make a start, then, shall we?'

'As you wish.'

'For goodness' sake, you don't have to sit there like you're about to climb the steps up to the guillotine! All I'm doing is interviewing you about your job.' Tunnelling his fingers through his hair, Dante knew his breath was slightly ragged as he fought to regain control of his temper. What was it about this woman that always inflamed him? Whether it was lustful desire or a burst of bad temper she always seemed to inspire some kind of volatile reaction.

'Am I going to keep my job, or are you planning to replace me with someone else in your clean sweep?'

'What?' His dark blond brows drew together in puzzlement. Anna was slumped back in her chair, and the fear in her eyes was suddenly clear as daylight to Dante.

'I mean, in your drive to improve things, is my job under threat?'

A flash of memory of that night they'd met came back to Dante, and he recalled her telling him that she'd lost her previous job to a 'ruthless takeover'.

'I'm only interviewing you to find out what your responsibilities and duties are, and if you enjoy your work. I have no plans to replace or fire anyone right now, so your job is quite safe.'

'Oh…' Her sigh was relieved. Her restless hand lifted to play with the tiny heart-shaped crystal on the end of a slim gold chain she wore round her neck. *Had an admirer bought her that?*

His equilibrium coming under disagreeable fire yet again, Dante leaned forward to level his gaze. 'Now that we've got that out of the way, perhaps you could give me a rundown of your duties?'

'I will… Only…'

'What?'

'I'm worried that because you're clearly angry with me about Tia you might deliberately find something wrong about the way I do my job so—so that you can get back at me in some way.'

'What?' Stunned, Dante widened his blue-grey eyes. 'Do you really think I'd resort to the kind of tactics that would jeopardise my daughter's well-being? Think about it. If I tried to punish you in some way, would it not have repercussions for her too? I'd hardly allow that.'

'You see? That's where our sticking point is. I don't know you well enough to know *what* you might be capable of.' Her slender shoulders lifted in a shrug. 'All I know is that it's been a confusing and worrying time, what with the threat of Anita and Grant possibly having to sell up and leave, and then—and then out of the blue you show up, and I learn that you're the man who's looking to invest in the hotel and will become the new senior partner. More importantly, I then have to break the news to you that Tia is your daughter. I had no idea how you'd react. We only spent a night together. You might feel utterly compromised and furious. Or you might...' Her voice faltered a little. 'You might want to try and take her away from me. Can you wonder why I couldn't sleep last night?'

Dante pushed to his feet, because the restlessness and annoyance that deluged him wouldn't allow him to remain sitting.

'Why would I want to try and take her away from you? Don't you think—to use an English expression— that would be rather like shooting myself in the foot? I can see that she adores you, and you her. From what I've seen you've done an admirable job of raising her by yourself. But I'm sticking by my original conviction that she needs her father in her life too. She needs two parents...which is why I said we should marry.'

'Why would you want to tie yourself to a woman you knew for just one night?' Anna's voice was slightly husky as she asked this, and a tiny perplexed crease puckered her brow.

'Because that one night resulted in a child...a child I didn't even know about until yesterday!' He drove his hands into his trouser pockets as he moved away from the desk, briefly presenting her with his back.

Was the impression he'd left her with so poor that she hadn't considered even for a moment trying to contact him? It didn't make Dante feel very good *or* wanted. It just made him mad. Briefly thinking of his father and his ex, he wondered what *rare* quality he had that made it so easy for people to walk away from him. And to make them think he wouldn't be concerned about his own flesh and blood.

'Dante?'

Garnering his composure, he turned back to face the striking redhead on the other side of the desk.

'What is it?'

'I didn't tell you before because I didn't quite know how to put it, but I *did* initially try to contact you when I found out I was pregnant. I did find out your name, and I even looked you up on the internet.'

'And?' Dante interjected impatiently, his heart thudding.

'Your reputation was quite—quite intimidating. To be perfectly honest, it worried me. I didn't even know if you'd remember me, let alone believe me when I told you I was pregnant. Anyway...' Glancing away, Anna heaved a sigh. 'I decided perhaps it was best after all if I didn't contact you. But some months after Tia was born the conviction that you had a right to know about her took hold of me again. For days I followed every lead I could to try and track you down, but it was as though you'd disappeared. Of course now I realise that it was because you'd changed your name. I went back to believing that maybe it had never been on the cards that we should meet again. In any case, for all I knew you could have married and had children with someone else. And besides…that night we were together you did tell me it was a one-time-only thing and that I had to accept that…remember?'

Dante remembered. He sombrely reflected on how he'd regretted that over the years. There had been many lonely nights when he would have been thrilled to have Anna in his arms again. But, to be brutal, at the time all he could have offered her was sex. Not even companionship had been an option. Not after his mother's death. He'd been in too dark a place to take anyone there with him. But it still hit him hard that because of his ruthless reputation Anna had been frightened of trying to make contact. And later, when she'd wanted to try and find him again, he had changed his name back to Dante Romano. He could no longer blame her for anything. Everything that had happened was *his* fault.

'We cannot turn back the clock. That is beyond even *my* power, ruthless reputation or no.' His lips twisted ruefully. 'What has happened in the past has happened, and all we can do now is face what's in front of us today. Besides…our personal issues probably shouldn't be discussed in work time. We'll talk tonight, as previously agreed. Right now I have an interview to conduct.'

He sat down again, automatically switching his brain to work mode. He'd turned that ability into a fine art over the years whenever emotions had threatened to swamp him. The woman sitting opposite him was silent.

'Anna?'

For a moment she seemed troubled. But then the corners of her pretty mouth curved into a smile.

'You mean you're not going to call me Miss Bailey any more?' she teased.

The look on her face was somewhere between angel and imp, and Dante all but groaned—because it was as though someone had shot a flame-tipped arrow straight into his loins. A charged memory of her whispering softly into his ear and moving over his body, erotically sliding her mouth over his as her long hair, carrying its scent of oranges and patchouli, drifted against him surfaced powerfully.

'When we're working together, and in the company of our colleagues, I may from time to time call you Miss Bailey. When we're alone...' his voice lowered meaningfully '...I'll call you Anna.'

'Right.' Beneath her flawlessly satin skin, a soft pink bloomed like a summer rose.

Gratified that he still had the power to discomfit her, Dante couldn't help the smile that escaped him.

'We'll carry on then...yes?'

'Yes, all right.' She straightened her back, but her expression seemed transfixed and he had to prompt her again.

'Anna?'

She patted down her hair.

'Sorry. To answer your question—my first responsibility is to the manager...to help support him in fulfilling the hotel's promise of delivering an impeccable service to the customer.'

'And how do you and Mr Cathcart get on? Do you communicate well? Are there any problems there, for instance?'

'There aren't any problems. Jason—Mr Cathcart and I have always got on. He's kind and fair...just like his parents.'

'So you like him?'

'Yes, I like him. We work very well together.'

'Good...that's good to hear.'

Twirling his pen absently between his fingers, now it was Dante's turn to fall into a trance. Studying the arresting face before him, the face that had haunted his sleep many nights in the past, he had a hungry need to just look and appreciate. To his mind, Anna Bailey's features were perfect. The finely shaped brows above those dancing long-lashed brown eyes, the slim and elegant nose and the pensive pretty mouth—there was a serenity about her that was more than a little appealing to a man who had lived his life mostly in the fast lane.

Did Jason Cathcart enjoy that aspect of her company too? He had certainly been voluble in his praise of Anna's talents and abilities during his interview with Dante earlier. A fierce little knot of jealousy throbbed painfully under his ribs. Did the man wish they were more than colleagues? he wondered. A disturbing image of him getting cosy with Anna and Tia almost stole his breath.

'And is Mr Cathcart good at leading and inspiring his staff, would you say?' he asked, gravel-voiced.

'Definitely.' A flicker of apprehension crossed Anna's face. 'You interviewed him earlier. Surely you formed an impression of him?'

'I did,' Dante answered abruptly. 'And that, of course, will remain confidential. Now, what other responsibilities does your role entail?'

Even though he would have preferred to quiz Anna further about *her* impression of her colleague, he knew it shouldn't be in the arena of a professional conversation concerning her job. Corralling the urge to ask her outright if she had more personal feelings towards Jason, he listened intently as she described other aspects of her role as assistant manager, determinedly making himself focus on the interview at hand and not get sidetracked by emotion.

CHAPTER SIX

THE ring on the doorbell just after she'd checked to see if Tia was asleep made Anna's heart skip a beat. She knew it was Dante. He had vowed he'd return later, after going back to his apartment. They'd agreed he would drop by after she'd put Tia to bed so that they could talk in private.

Glancing at the two slim-stemmed wine glasses she'd left on the coffee table, she nervously smoothed down the multicoloured jersey tunic dress that she'd hastily donned over black leggings and cinched with a vivid green belt, praying she didn't look as flustered as she felt.

'Hi.'

She hadn't known how starved she was for the sight of his sculpted, strikingly good-looking face until she was confronted by it at the door. Her pulse went wild. In turn, Dante's disturbing gaze ran up and down her figure with equally hard-to-hide intensity, and every flicker of his glance was like lighted touchpaper to already simmering embers.

'Come in,' she invited, her voice hoarse, practically pressing herself into the wall to let him pass.

'Nice perfume,' he remarked, low-voiced, as he entered, his eyes reflecting electric blue sparks tonight, rather than the dramatic hue of stormy seas. 'Sexy.'

'Thanks,' Anna murmured, her mind going unhelpfully blank at the compliment.

'I've brought some very good Italian wine.' He placed a dark slim bottle into her hands. 'It's a Barolo. It comes from a region known as Piedmont, where they're famed for making the best wines.'

'That's kind. I've got some dry white chilling in the fridge, but if you prefer red then that's fine with me. We can have either.' Shrugging self-consciously, she shut the door behind them, adding, 'I don't mind.'

Wishing she didn't feel as if she'd been shaken hard, then stood on her head, Anna led the way into the living room.

'When we first met, I didn't know you were Italian,' she remarked lightly.

'Only on my mother's side.'

'What about your father?'

'He was British.'

'That explains why you used the surname Masterson, then. You don't have much of an Italian accent, either.'

'I stopped residing in Italy a long time ago.'

'Why? Did your parents move to the UK?'

His fascinating eyes darkened almost warningly. 'No.

They didn't. They parted company when I was very young…younger than Tia, in fact.'

'And you didn't want to stay in Italy?'

'Enough questions for now, I think.'

There was a definite tightening to Dante's perfectly symmetrical jaw, and Anna clamped her teeth down on her lip, embarrassed at the flow of curiosity that had unstoppably rushed out. But frustration niggled her—because how were she and her daughter supposed to get to know him if he was so reluctant to reveal himself?

'Why don't you sit down?' she suggested, awkward now.

Dropping down onto the couch, his expression relieved, Dante undid the single button on his tailored black jacket to reveal a midnight-blue cashmere sweater. The golden lights in his hair glinted fiercely beneath the soft glow of one of the nearby lamps, the odd silver strand here or there making him look mouthwateringly distinguished. As if she wasn't already provocatively aware of his charismatic presence, the exotically eastern tones of his aftershave sensuously made a beeline into Anna's solar plexus and caused a near meltdown.

'Open the Barolo,' he said casually, gesturing towards the bottle in her hands. 'It's a cold, rainy night outside and it will warm us up.'

His barely perceptible smile pierced her heart. Why did it seem so hard for him to relax? What was it about his past that still racked him with shadows? she mused.

'Okay...I will.'

Briefly disappearing into the kitchen to locate the corkscrew, Anna was grateful for a few moments to herself. It was clear that the inflammatory attraction that had flared out of control that night five years ago had not dimmed one *iota*. At least not for *her*. To be frank, the realisation filled her with trepidation. How could she be clear-headed and wise and do the right thing for her and Tia if all Dante had to do was walk into a room to have her temperature shooting off the scale?

In the living room once more, she gladly gave the task of pouring the wine to him. Right then her hands weren't anywhere near steady enough to do it without the possibility of spilling some. As she crossed the room to the single plump armchair, Anna felt Dante's glance track her progress.

Before raising his glass to his lips, he asked, 'Is the baby asleep?'

Charmed and taken aback that he should refer to Tia as 'the baby' with such affection in his voice, she knew her smile was unreserved. 'Yes, she is.'

'I'd like to look in on her before I go tonight.'

'Of course.'

'There's so much about her I want to know... What food she likes, her favourite colour, the book she likes the most.'

His gaze seemed to take him away to distant shores for a moment, and Anna caught her breath as a merciless stab of guilt assailed her.

But before she could comment he continued, 'We should have a toast. To Tia and her happy future.'

'Tia and her happy future,' she concurred a little huskily, her mouth drying, because she knew that the future was one of the most pertinent things they had to discuss tonight. What would it entail? Not just for her precious child, but for Anna herself now that Dante had reappeared?

Sipping at her wine, she allowed the alcohol to swim warmly into her blood for a moment, hoping it might relax her. 'This is nice...it reminds me of violets somehow.'

'You have a good nose. Barolo *does* have a bouquet of violets. You could have a new career in wine-tasting.'

'Will I need a new career?'

'Your interview wasn't *that* bad.'

'How comforting,' she quipped, unable to hide the surge of annoyance that surfaced. 'I've had no complaints about how I carry out my job so far.'

'There's no need to be defensive. You've nothing to fear from me, Anna. I certainly don't have any plans to fire you from your job.'

To her alarm, Dante set his wine glass down on the coffee table and got to his feet. Then he was standing in front of her, his nearness making her feel quite light-headed.

'Put your wine down for a minute,' he commanded quietly, voice low.

Captured by his hypnotic glance, Anna obeyed. He held out his hand and helped her to her feet.

'That dress you're wearing hurts my eyes.'

Embarrassment made her want the floor to open up and swallow her.

'I know it's a bit dazzling, but I grabbed the first thing out of my wardrobe, to tell you the truth.' She was fumbling for a foothold but couldn't find one. Had his shoulders always been this wide…his chest this broad and strong? The male heat he emanated so—so *drugging*?

'It's dazzling not because of the riot of colour but because it's on *you*. Dazzling like this glorious hair of yours.' Capturing a handful of burnished copper silk between his fingers, Dante raised the fiery strands to his lips and kissed them.

Anna couldn't move. It took every ounce of iron will she possessed not to give in to the overwhelming impulse to lay her head against his chest and wrap her arms round his waist. The intoxication of his presence almost made her forget why he was there…*almost*.

'I am so glad you haven't had it cut short since I saw you last.'

'I—I wouldn't do that… But, Dante—we—we need to talk,' she murmured, her own voice sounding like a dazed stranger's.

'We can talk like we talked when we first met. Like this… Do you remember, Anna?'

The heat of his lips touched the side of her neck,

searing the delicate skin there with an indelible brand. 'I remember,' she husked, her limbs turning to liquid silver. 'But we should— We need to...' A helpless little moan escaped her as Dante moved his lips up to her ear, his mouth planting a hot, devastatingly erotic kiss on her highly sensitive lobe. The molten heat that pooled in Anna's centre threatened to make her lose her capacity to think at all.

'What do we need to do?'

With a smile in his voice that was a seductive cocktail of fine malt whisky and luxurious honey, Dante settled his hands on her hips and firmly pulled her against him. The hard male contours encased in his fluidly elegant tailored suit and the suggestion of barely contained impressive masculine strength made Anna shiver. Mesmerised by the haze of longing in his burning gaze, she nervously swallowed. She yearned to succumb to the desire that was flowing with equal ardour through her veins, but an anguished moment of clarity returned, making her stiffen in his arms.

'What did you mean when you said you weren't going to fire me from my job? I don't like the sound of that... It makes me feel like you potentially *could* fire me if you wanted to. I can't say that fills me with confidence... not when I have a child to support, and depend on my job for a roof over our heads.'

There was a flash of impatience in his eyes.

'The point is that you don't need to depend on your job to sustain you, *or* for a roof over your heads! I meant it when I said we should marry. And when we're married I'll take care of you both.'

'You make it sound so straightforward and easy. I'm not an investment you're interested in, Dante. I'm a fully functioning independent human being with my own ideas and thoughts on lots of subjects—including marriage. It's completely wrong of you to assume that I'd instantly give up everything I've worked so hard for to throw in my lot with a man I barely know. A man who only wants marriage because he's discovered that the one-night stand that we had resulted in a child!'

He set Anna free with a muttered oath and stalked across the room, scraping his fingers through the dark blond strands of his previously groomed hair. His glare was blistering in its intensity. 'What better reason to marry someone than because you made a child together? Tia deserves to have her father in her life. I want that for her and I want that for me—and as a "fully functioning independent human being" you have no right to deny us!'

'I'm not saying I'd deny you. But marriage isn't for me. I...' She lowered her gaze to stare down at the floor, 'I like my independence... I like the fact that my hard work has finally got me somewhere and now I have opportunities... I'm captain of my own ship and it's a good feeling.'

'So you like being captain of your own ship—but do you honestly like being alone? Raising a child on your own is far from easy, no matter how many opportunities for advancing your career come your way. When the baby is ill do you welcome being her sole carer, with no one but yourself to rely upon to make the best decisions for her welfare? And when she's ill what do you do if you can't take time off work for fear of losing your job and your income?'.

Moving back across the room towards her, Dante had that faraway look Anna had seen before in his eyes.

'Once when I was five I had the measles…had it quite severely. My mother had no choice but to go out to her job in the evening—it was literally a matter of whether we ate or starved. She asked a close neighbour if I could stay with her for the evening, but the woman refused because she had five children of her own and didn't want to risk them getting infected. My mother left me in bed. The neighbour promised to regularly check up on me while she was gone. I had a raging fever, and by the time my mother came home I was convulsing. We didn't have a telephone. She ran with me through the night to a man she knew who owned a restaurant, and he called a doctor. If it weren't for that I probably wouldn't have made it.'

His tone bitterly rueful, he shook his head. 'My mother went to hell and back that night. If she had had someone to help her, someone who cared equally for my welfare, she wouldn't have suffered the torment and guilt that she did. And I have no intention of ever letting my daughter be in the precarious position I was…no matter what your assurances.'

Barely knowing how to answer him, Anna wept inside for the agony Dante and his mother must have endured that terrible night. It was the kind of nightmare scenario every mother dreaded.

Before she realised it her impulse to touch him, to comfort him in some way, overtook her, and she laid her hand against the side of his face. His skin was velvety warm, pulsing with the vibrant strength she'd detected earlier. 'I love that you care for Tia so deeply already. But I'm lucky, Dante... I may be a single mum, but I have friends—people who really care for Tia—people who would help us at the drop of a hat.'

'That may be so, but I have no intention of leaving my child's well-being to the precarious fair-weather attention of mere friends! No matter how much you might trust them, Anna. So...' He winced a little when she withdrew her hand, almost as if she'd struck him. 'There's only one solution to our dilemma, and I've already told you what that is. Now it's just a matter of arranging things. The sooner the better, I think.'

Stroking her hands up and down her arms, Anna sensed their tremble.

'I'm not getting married...I told you.'

'Then regrettably, you're pushing me into taking action I'd much rather not take,' Dante retorted. 'But I will take it if it means I can be with my daughter. I'll go to court to get full custody of Tia.'

Was it only to her own hypersensitive hearing that her heartbeat sounded so deafeningly loud? Anna thought.

She'd been musing on a mother's worst nightmare but surely this was one of the most horrendous threats a woman could face? That her child's estranged parent might sue for custody and take her away—maybe to live in another country entirely? Searching for compassion in Dante's flint-like stare, worryingly, she found none.

'No!' she protested loudly, tears stinging the backs of her lids.

He lifted an eyebrow, but looked no less resolved on his course. 'If you don't want me to take such an action, then I suggest you stop putting obstacles in the way and agree to our marriage.'

'That's so disrespectful. You'd resort to something as low as blackmail to get your own way?'

'I told you.' His broad-shouldered shrug was unapologetic. 'I'll do anything I can to be with my daughter… the daughter you have so callously denied me knowledge of for four years because my so-called reputation made you believe I didn't deserve to know about her. And you have the audacity to stand there and lecture *me* on respect!'

'I didn't keep her from you deliberately.' Wanting to cry in frustration as well as pain, Anna stared pleadingly into the heartbreakingly handsome features of the well-dressed man in front of her. 'Don't you think I would have preferred to be in a good relationship with my baby's father than be asked not to try and get in touch after we parted that night? I know it was a difficult time for you, but it didn't exactly make me feel wanted to know that you could just walk away from me and never look back. And how do you think I felt when I discovered I was pregnant? Especially when it was the first time I—' She bit her lip on what she'd been going to say and continued, 'I was shocked, lonely, scared... I experienced every one of those states—but even taken together they don't come near to describing how I felt.'

She noticed that Dante's glance was quizzical.

'It was the first time you...what, Anna?'

Backing up nervously, she reached for the glass of wine she'd left on the side-table near the armchair and drank some. She let the alcohol hit before raising her chin with a defiant air born of Dutch courage. Her dark eyes focused firmly on Dante.

'It was the first time I'd slept with a man.'

The oath he swore was in Italian, and because she was shaky after revealing her news Anna returned her glass to the table, waiting for the tirade of disbelief that she was certain would explode towards her.

But when next he spoke Dante's voice was surprisingly quiet, his words measured. 'You were untouched when I took you into my bed...that's what you're telling me?'

'I was. Couldn't you tell I was no experienced seductress who made a habit of going to bed with male guests? I'd barely even been kissed before!'

'Yet you were molten heat in my arms. Everywhere I touched you, you made me burn.'

Praying for some way to steady the deluge of emotion that tumbled forcefully through her, Anna despaired of ever feeling calm again when she saw the renewed flame of Dante's desire sinfully reflected back at her...just as if it had never gone away. With a disparaging toss of her head, she answered, 'I think I lost my mind a little that night. I would never usually behave in that way with a strange man...with *any* man for that matter.'

'We lost our minds together, Anna.' He sounded seductively accepting and non-judgmental. 'And the result was little Tia. Can you regret such an outcome?'

'Never.'

'Then we have to deal with this situation like adults, instead of feuding children, and that means our daughter's welfare takes priority.'

'You mean...' Anna surveyed him with a frown. 'You mean you still believe marriage is the only answer?'

'I do.'

'If that's the way you want to go, how about trying a trial period of living together first?'

'Too uncertain—and it hardly represents the security I want for Tia.'

'Surely that depends on how we deal with it? If we're committed to making it work, then living together could be just as secure as marriage.'

'No. That's not what I want.'

'And if I refuse? You'd really take me to court for custody?'

'I would.' His piercing glance was as unyielding as ice.

CHAPTER SEVEN

IT DIDN'T exactly enhance his self-esteem or his pride, having to potentially resort to blackmail to persuade Anna to marry him, but since he had made the earth-shattering discovery that he was a father, Dante's determination to help bring up his daughter was cast-iron. There was nothing the redheaded beauty could say that would deter him.

But in truth he was taken aback that she could so easily refuse him. He'd met plenty of women on his travels who considered him quite the catch.

Once upon a time his ex-wife Marisa had said those very words to him. *'You're quite a catch, Dante… It's a wonder that you've been allowed to say free and single for this long…'*

But that assertion by her had soon turned to ashes when she'd discovered that for her husband raw ambition came first and his most intimate relationship a very poor second. Even when his marriage had been in its dying stages he hadn't sought to rescue it, or been able to express his emotions. Marisa had walked into the arms of another man and Dante had simply let her—if he was honest, feeling nothing but relief.

Now the greatest shock that he had ever received...the news that he was a *father*...reverberated doubly on learning that Anna had been a sexual innocent when he'd slept with her. It also made him remember the flicker of apprehension in her eyes when, for a few moments as she lay beneath him, he'd sensed definite tension in her slender frame. What must she have thought when he'd asked her to spend the night and then warned her not to expect anything else? Not a phone call, not even his real name—nothing! What an introduction to the world of adult relationships she'd had.

Fast forward five years on, and Dante knew that if he'd met Anna today he would never have let her go... not for all the million-dollar real estate in the world. With her gorgeous flame hair flowing unhindered over her shoulders and her brown eyes sparkling like fire-warmed brandy she was vivacious, pretty and completely unpretentious. Her eye-catching dress with its patent green belt highlighted how tiny her waist was, and the black leggings she wore cleaved lovingly to her long, model-slim legs.

Studying her now, he acknowledged that she made the blood pound through his veins like no other woman he'd ever met. So, even if she despised him for putting her in such a compromising position, he would endeavour not to disappoint her as he had disappointed his ex. He certainly wouldn't give her cause to accuse him of ignoring her. He would also show her that he intended to be the best father to Tia that a child could have. She would not want for anything materially, and for as long as he lived Dante would dote on her. There would be no need for Anna to be lonely either, because he fully intended to keep her warm at nights and reintroduce her to the delight and pleasure of passionate lovemaking...

Having returned to the old-fashioned floral armchair, she now sat nursing her wine glass, her glance wary and resentful when it locked with his.

'I'll have to tell the Cathcarts about us,' she murmured.

'Yes, you will.' Shrugging off his jacket, Dante dropped it onto the arm of the couch. Turning back to Anna, he smiled enigmatically. 'But don't worry... they'll have plenty of time to absorb the news.'

'Why's that?'

'Because after discussing the changes that need to be implemented I'm going to suggest we close the hotel for a month while it's being refurbished and modernised. In that time we will travel to Lake Como with Tia, where you and I will marry.'

'You're intending to close the Mirabelle for a whole month?' Slamming her wine glass precariously on the side-table, Anna widened her brown eyes in disbelief. 'What about the staff? What about their jobs? They can't possibly afford to take a whole month off.'

'It will be paid leave.' An irritated muscle flinched hard in the side of Dante's cheekbone. He'd just told her he was taking her to Lake Como to marry him and all she could think about was what was going to happen to the staff! It seriously irked him that Anna's soft heart did not include fretting about *him* in such a concerned manner.

'Can you afford to do that?' she asked in wonder.

He could have replied that he could buy and refurbish the hotel and fund the staff's leave several hundred times over and still have change, but Dante didn't. The stunning house he owned in Lake Como would be a surprise and hopefully a delight to her when she saw it, and perhaps would bring home to her just how wealthy her soon-to-be husband actually was. But there was a hollow feeling in the pit of his stomach that he should take refuge in something so superficial when in truth he wanted Anna to regard him totally for himself, to see the man behind the thousand dollar suits and impressive portfolio, *not* what his money could buy.

'I have interests in several very successful businesses worldwide, Anna, so trust me…' His hand cut expressively through the air. 'Worrying about whether I can afford it is not something that even has to enter your head.'

She was puzzled that he seemed so annoyed. Had she dented his ego by querying whether he could afford to do as he'd said? But, more perturbing than that, Anna was under siege from far more unsettling concerns. Events were moving at a pace she hadn't remotely expected, and one major issue was disturbing her above all else.

Dante's insistence that they marry was making her feel as though he wanted to control and possess her, and was disturbingly reminiscent of her father's behaviour as she was growing up.

Frank Bailey had had two major passions in his life... his love affair with booze and his diminutive, too passive wife—Anna's mother, Denise. He'd been so possessive and jealous that he'd completely banned her from even having friends, because he couldn't bear her attention to be on anyone else but him. That jealousy had even transferred itself to Anna if he thought she was too demanding—which even as a small child she rarely was. But her father had been able to misread the most innocent situations, and had made his judgements with an authority that chilled the blood.

Consequently, Anna had lost count of the times she'd witnessed his rage—and that included being frequently belittled by him verbally. An occurrence that had become even more frightening and threatening to her peace of mind when he was drunk. She knew intimately that mental torment was just as destructive as physical violence. There were too many times when, upon hearing her father's key in the door, she'd sat on her bed quaking with terror, praying to disappear, praying for a greater power to make her so small that he wouldn't even notice she was there.

In agitation, she rose to her feet. 'Dante...about us going to Lake Como to—to get married...'

'What about it?'

She obviously *had* upset him, because his handsome face was fierce for a moment. But, however unapproachable he seemed, Anna refused to be intimidated by him.

'I'll go with you on one condition.'

'I have already told you that—'

'Hear me out.' Although shaking inside, her tone was unerringly firm, and there was a definite flash of surprise in Dante's light-coloured eyes. 'I don't want a wedding arranged until I see how we get on together. And I won't have you issuing me with threats of going to court for custody of Tia either. I've seen the damage it can do to a woman's spirit to have a man try to control her, and I won't accept it from anyone…not even and *especially* the man who fathered my child!'

'You're speaking from personal experience?' Although Dante's voice had turned quiet, it was underscored with shock and a sense of impatience too—as if he wanted to hear the full extent of what Anna had endured.

'Yes, I am.' She crossed her arms in front of her, knowing there was no point in keeping her past a secret. It wouldn't serve her in the long run, however painful it was to talk about it. Ghosts could only haunt a person if they colluded with them to keep them hidden. 'My father was a cruel and jealous drunk, and he made my mother's life a living hell.'

'Where is he now?'

'No longer in this world…thank goodness.' An icy shudder ran down Anna's spine.

'And your mother…where is she?'

'She's gone too.' She briefly pursed her lips, fighting hard to win the struggle over her tears. 'They said at the hospital that she died of heart disease, but I know that's not what killed her. She was simply tired and worn out… beaten down by living with my brute of a father.'

His glance glinting with anger as well as sympathy, Dante stepped towards her. 'Was he a brute to you too, Anna?' he demanded huskily.

'A man with a propensity for intimidation doesn't care who he tries to intimidate. He just gets off on the power. His children are the easiest targets of all—especially when they're too scared to answer back in case they get another verbal lashing. And the situation becomes even more horrendous when the impulse to dominate and show what a big strong man he is is fuelled by alcohol.'

Shame and despair cramped her throat for a second. 'Have you any idea what it's like to have foul beer or whisky-smelling breath right in your face, and a mocking voice yelling at you how useless you are? How worthless? Anyway, I don't want to talk any more about this right now.' She made as if to move towards the kitchen. 'I don't think I can drink any more wine, lovely as it is. I think I'll make some coffee. Would you like some?'

'No.' Dante laid his hand on her arm to prevent her from turning away, but he didn't curl his fingers to grip it. Right now he needed to tread very carefully. He could see the fear and terror in her eyes from her disturbing memories and it shook him deeply. 'We'll do as you suggest. We'll go to Lake Como and live together for a while before embarking on marriage. Does that make you happier, Anna?'

Perversely, the look of relief crossing her face was like a hammer blow to Dante. He didn't want to possess Anna—he knew that would be wrong. In the light of what she'd experienced with her bullying father it would be *doubly* wrong. Just the thought of such a man hurting her in any way brought out the most base of animal instincts in him to deal with *anyone* who threatened her or Tia. Ultimately all he wanted to do was take care of them both—to show Anna that beneath the facade of wealth and success his genuine heartfelt desire was for family and connection. He wanted the chance to prove that underneath the outward material trappings and his drive for achievement existed the good, responsible, caring man that his mother had always insisted was the *real* Dante Romano.

'Thank you,' she answered softly.

Reluctantly he let go of her arm, even though touching her through the material of her dress made him long for so much more.

'Perhaps while you make your coffee I could look in on Tia? I just want to sit beside her bed and watch her sleep for a while,' he said.

'Go ahead. Take as long as you like.'

* * *

Half an hour later, Anna opened Tia's bedroom door to find Dante comfortably ensconced in the cosy slipper chair beside their daughter's bed, his elbows resting against his long-boned thighs in his exquisitely tailored suit trousers and his body quite still. His avid gaze was transfixed by the angelic blond child who lay sleeping peacefully beneath the Walt Disney character–decorated pink duvet, one arm flung out by her side and the other clutching her favourite chewed teddy bear.

Anna needed a moment. It was as though one of her favourite made-up stories had come to startling, vivid life, and she hardly dared breathe for fear of disturbing it and making it disappear.

But Dante had heard her come in and, turning in his chair, treated her to the most disarming, knee-trembling smile she'd ever seen.

'She's so beautiful,' he breathed quietly. 'I don't want to leave her…not for a minute or even a second. I've missed so much of her growing up.'

Anna didn't mistake the catch in his voice. Advancing into the room, which was illuminated only by the soft night light glowing in the corner, she dropped her hand on his hard-muscled shoulder, silently thrilling to feel the sensuous warmth that emanated through the luxurious cashmere of his sweater.

'She's still got a lot of growing up to do, Dante…she's only four. And children quickly adapt to new situations and people. One day she'll forget there was even a time when you didn't mean the world to her.'

Covering her hand and holding it against him, Dante held Anna's gaze with a passionate heated look. 'I want her to know I'm her father. I want her to know as soon as possible. Can you understand that?'

Gripped by the pain in his voice, Anna breathed out slowly. 'I do. Of course I do. But we just—we just have to pick the right moment.'

'Tomorrow when you pick her up from school we'll take her somewhere for tea. It will give her and me the chance to get to know each other a little. But I don't want her to be kept in the dark about who I am for long, Anna.' He let go of her hand. 'I don't think I could bear that.'

'We'll tell her soon,' she said reassuringly, seeing by his expression how in earnest he was about Tia knowing he was her father.

Clenching his jaw for a moment, Dante exhaled a heavy sigh. His eyes flashed like distant lightning in a velvet midnight sky.

'Good...that's good. Now, I think it's probably time I left. We have much to do tomorrow. I'll see you in the morning, Anna.' His lips brushed briefly against her cheek as he stood up. 'Try to get some proper sleep tonight, eh?'

The sensuous trail of his cologne and the seductive warmth that was the legacy of his lips lingered on Anna's skin long after he had gone...

She asked if Anita could spare a few minutes to talk during their afternoon tea break. Expressing her usual amicable concern, the older woman kindly welcomed Anna into the office she shared with her husband—an entirely organised and *smart* office in comparison with her son Jason's. Grant had gone out to visit a new supplier and wouldn't be back until later, she confided.

She appeared much happier, Anna noticed—as if a world of worry had been lifted from her shoulders. Dante's rescue package for the Mirabelle was already making a difference, she realised. There was no doubt in her mind that he would turn the hotel's fortunes around. He was an accomplished, experienced investor, and even their sous chef Cheryl, and Amy and Linda the receptionists, were already referring to him as their 'knight in shining armour'. She didn't know why their praise and ingratiating admiration should put her back up, but it did.

'What's troubling you, sweetheart?' Stirring her tea, Anita sat back in one of the three easy chairs arranged round a coffee table, surveying Anna with concern.

'Am I that easy to read?' the younger woman quipped.

'Not always… But for some reason today I definitely sense that you're anxious about something.'

'It's about Dante,' Anna began, her fingers knotting together in her lap.

Her cheeks flamed red when Anita raised a curious eyebrow. The casual form of address had slipped out, because he'd been on her mind almost constantly since last night. Especially when she remembered that look on his face and the tremor in his voice when he'd passionately declared that he wanted Tia to know he was her father.

'I mean Mr Romano,' she corrected herself quickly.

'What's wrong? I know he's been a little...shall we say *abrasive* with you, dear—but he can be extraordinarily thoughtful of people too. He's already won friends here. And when he's talked to me and Grant about plans for updating the hotel he's consulted our opinion at every turn. There are exciting plans afoot!' Her lips splitting in a grin reminiscent of an excited schoolgirl, Anita all but hugged herself. 'We're going to call a staff meeting later, to give everyone an update, but as you're our assistant manager I may as well tell you confidentially that Dante has deemed it a good idea to close the Mirabelle for a month while the modernisation gets underway. All the staff will get paid leave.'

'How do you feel about that?'

'We're perfectly happy. Not only is it necessary, but it's a great idea too. Grant and I haven't had a break in so long. We plan to devote some time to our much neglected garden, and spend some genuine quality time together. You should think about having a little holiday, Anna...you work so hard and you and Tia deserve it.'

'Maybe I will.' Shrugging lightly, Anna wished she could hear herself think over the clamouring of her heart. 'Look, Anita...there's no way of couching this or making it sound less surprising…I've got something important to tell you.'

'You're not handing in your notice?'

'No.' Anna took a nervous swallow. 'It's something much more personal. You know I've never told you before who Tia's father is?'

Anita stared, her gaze intrigued. The ticking wall clock suddenly seemed noisily loud.

'Well, it's—'

'Yes?'

'It's Dante Romano.'

Beneath her carefully applied make-up, her boss paled a little in shock. 'Dante Romano? But how can that be? As far as I'm aware he's never been here before, so how could you two have met?'

'He *has* been here before.' Clearing her throat, Anna smiled awkwardly. 'It was about five years ago. I was working the late shift in the bar, and he—he was there having a drink. He'd just returned from Italy, where he'd been to his mother's funeral, and had stopped en route to New York, where he was living at the time.'

'And you and he…?'

Lifting her chin, because she wouldn't be ashamed of that incredible life-changing night, Anna met her boss's brown-eyed glance without flinching.

'There was an immediate attraction and we slept together that was how I fell pregnant with Tia.'

CHAPTER EIGHT

'ANNA, can I have a word?'

She was walking by Jason's office when he opened the door and beckoned to her. Having had their staff meeting, everyone was now perfectly aware of the imminent plan to close the hotel for a month while it was being modernised, but she hadn't had an opportunity to discuss it with the manager—especially the news that he'd been made project manager to oversee the refurbishments while everyone else was away. No doubt that was why he wanted to see her. It was a big step up for him, and a huge responsibility. But Anna had no doubts that Jason could do it.

Regarding her relationship with Dante, Anita Cathcart had suggested that they keep it to themselves for a while—at least until the changes were underway and the staff had returned from leave. It was cowardly, but Anna's relief that she wouldn't be the focus of curious speculation just yet was boundless.

Shutting the door behind them Jason invited Anna

to sit down. 'You look very nice,' he commented, his glance running lightly over her outfit.

'I'm collecting Tia, then we're going out to have tea.'

'Going anywhere special?'

'I'm not sure yet, but we'll find somewhere nice, I'm sure. We're spoiled for choice in Covent Garden, aren't we?'

Her heart was thudding a little at the idea of telling her little girl some time soon that Dante was her father, and her smile was uncertain. But Jason seemed preoccupied with own problems as he started to restlessly pace the floor.

When he stopped pacing to nervously return his attention to Anna his dark eyes were shining. 'I've met someone,' he said in a rush.

'You have?' He'd been single for a long time, and didn't have much confidence in blind dates or being hooked up by some well-meaning friend as a means of finding 'the one', so Anna was genuinely pleased for him.

'I won't say any more just yet, in case I jinx things, but we're seeing each other this weekend.'

'Oh, Jason, that's wonderful—and of course you won't jinx things!'

Getting to her feet, she threw her arms round him in an affectionate hug.

Someone rapped on the door and stepped into the room before Jason could invite them. *It was Dante*. Anna had no reason in the world to feel guilty, but when his frosted gaze alighted on them, radiating obvious disapproval, she felt awkward and embarrassed—like a child caught red-handed, raiding the fridge after bedtime.

'I've been looking for Anna,' he said to Jason without preamble. 'A staff member suggested I see if she was with you. Looks like I hit the jackpot.'

'We were—we were just talking.' Flashing him an uncomfortable smile, Jason stepped quickly away from the girl at his side.

'Well, if you've finished *talking*, Anna and I have to go. We have some important business to attend to.'

'Isn't she taking her daughter out to tea?' The younger man's brow was furrowing.

'I see that you like to keep completely up to date with Miss Bailey's diary, Mr Cathcart. It would be nice if you could be as diligent in looking over that list of new equipment for the hotel that I left you, and let me have your thoughts first thing in the morning. This is an absolutely vital responsibility you've accepted, becoming project manager, and the work begins right here, right now. Don't let me down.' Holding the door open for Anna, Dante was impatient. 'We really have to go,' he said firmly.

'You didn't have to be so snooty or condescending to Jason. We've done nothing wrong.'

She had to practically run to keep up with Dante's annoyed stride as she followed him out into the hotel

car park. Reaching a gleaming silver Jaguar, she heard
an electronic key open the doors. He stopped dead, and
she could see he was struggling with his temper.

'So you fling your arms round every male you work
with, do you?'

'That's ridiculous. Of course I don't! He'd just told
me some good news and I was pleased for him…that's
all.'

The resentment in Dante's mercurial eyes receded
only slightly.

'He likes you,' he said flatly.

Was he jealous? Anna let the thought swirl around
for a bit, then mentally filed it to look at later. But she
couldn't help her lips curving into a smile.

'And I like *him*. But not in the way you're insin-
uating.'

He would have liked to have quizzed her more, she
saw, but instead he glanced down at the linked gold
watch glinting on his wrist beneath his cuff and opened
the passenger door for her.

'We'd better get going if we're not going to be late
collecting Tia.'

'Where are we going for tea?' she asked lightly,
before climbing into her seat.

'The Ritz Hotel.'

Dismay washed over her.

'You might have told me that earlier… I would have
worn something smarter than this dress.'

It was a plain white linen dress that she'd teamed with

a businesslike black jacket, and the ensemble had had many outings in the past. It was perfect for a mild spring day like today, when there was just a gentle breeze blowing, but, knowing where they were heading, she was suddenly seized by the idea that it was nowhere near presentable enough for such a notoriously swish hotel.

His appreciative glance on the slender length of leg she unwittingly flashed as she sat down in her seat in a huff, Dante grinned and disarmed her completely.

'There is nothing wrong with what you are wearing, so there's no need to fret...*le guarda piu di bene a caro prezzo.*'

'And that means?'

'It means that you look more than fine.'

Dipping his head to survey Anna before closing her door, he let his light-filled gaze linger teasingly on her lips for a moment. Then it intensified. Suddenly there didn't seem to be enough air for her to breathe.

'Let's go and collect our little one, shall we?' Closing the passenger door, he moved with his usual fluid graceful stride round the Jaguar's bonnet to the driver's seat.

Tia wanted another scone and jam, and with Anna's agreement Dante leaned forward to spread the strawberry jam for her. *He'd never felt so proud.* Not one of his achievements had elicited the euphoria that poured through him now, when he surveyed this beautiful golden-haired child and knew he'd played an important part in her being.

Moving his glance across to Anna, he discovered her sherry-brown eyes were furtively studying him. With her river of auburn hair spilling unfettered down her back, and her quiet understated beauty, it was inevitable that she drew many admiring glances from the other guests taking afternoon tea. Mentally, Dante puffed out his chest. She was the mother of his child, and one day soon...*very soon* if he had his way...she would be his wife too. Yet, because of what she'd revealed about her cruel and controlling father, he needed to curb any inclination to manipulate her—even if waiting for her to say yes to marriage frustrated the hell out of him.

Her distressing childhood with such a despicable bully genuinely pained him. If Anna had been anything like their daughter, then she must have been the most exquisite, engaging little girl, and had surely deserved a man far more worthy to take care of her than the poor excuse for a father she'd had?

'This is a *golden* room,' Tia announced, licking strawberry jam off her lips as she chewed her second mouthwatering scone. 'There's a golden arch and golden tables and golden—what did you say those sparkly lamps on the ceiling were?'

'Chandeliers.'

'Yes—and golden chairs too! A king or a queen could live here. The people that own this place should call it the golden room—don't you think, Mummy?'

Reaching out to clean away some of the jam stains on her cherubic face with a linen napkin, Anna smiled. 'This is a very famous room, Tia, and it already has a name. It's called the Palm Court.'

'But,' Dante said softly, his voice lowering conspiratorially, 'from now on the three of us will always call it the golden room...deal?'

He held out his hand and Tia shook it enthusiastically, clearly delighted that the man who had brought them to such a magical place thought it was a good idea too.

'You have to shake Mummy's hand as well, Dante.'

'Of course...how silly of me to forget to do such an important thing.'

As soon as he took Anna's slim cool palm into his, the rest of the room faded away. The only thing Dante knew for sure was that his heart beat faster and heavier than it had before he'd touched her, and that if they had been alone he would have shown her in no uncertain terms that he desired her...*desired her beyond belief.* Immediately recognising the flare of heat suddenly laid bare in the liquid brown depths of her beautiful eyes, he inwardly rejoiced.

'You're meant to just shake her hand, not hold it for ages and ages!' his daughter protested huffily, pulling his hand away from her mother's with a distinctly old-fashioned look.

'Mind your manners, Tia, that was very rude.' Anna admonished her, looking embarrassed.

'I'm sorry.' The tips of the dark blond lashes that

were so like Dante's own briefly swept her cheeks in contrition, but a scant moment later her eyes shone with unrepentant mischief again. '*You're* not cross with me, are you?' She dimpled up at him.

That knock-out smile could melt his heart at a hundred paces, her father silently acknowledged. Tenderly he grazed his knuckles over her velvet cheekbone. 'No, *mia bambina*…I don't think I could be cross with you if I tried…you are far too charming and lovely for that.'

'She certainly has her moments.' Taking a sip of her Earl Grey tea in its exquisite porcelain cup, Anna replaced the delicate vessel back in its saucer before grimacing at Dante.

'Meaning?'

'Meaning that occasionally she can be a bit wild.'

'I wonder where she gets that from?' His tone was silky smooth and playful.

Surprising him with a grin, Anna tipped her head to the side.

'I can't imagine you ever doing anything that wasn't measured and considered, Dante. You just seem so organised and in charge to me—as if nothing life can throw at you could ever give you a moment's doubt about your place in the scheme of things.'

'You are wrong about that.' Feeling the need to put her right about her assumption, Dante was suddenly serious. 'Being part-Italian, passion is in my blood. Neither can I admit to never having a moment's doubt. Do you know a human being who can?'

'No,' she answered thoughtfully, 'I don't think I do.'

'What are you talking about, Mummy? It doesn't sound very interesting.'

Tia was clearly miffed at not being privy to the grown-ups' conversation. Turning her gaze to her daughter, Anna appeared to be thinking hard.

'Tia? There's something important I want to tell you.' Glancing over at Dante, she lowered her gaze meaningfully with his.

His heart pounded hard. He hadn't expected her to raise the subject on this outing, but now, realising that she was going to, he mentally began to arrange his armour—so that if Tia should protest the idea in any way the blow wouldn't wound him irreparably. Logically he knew it would take time for his daughter to learn to love him, but Dante craved her love and acceptance of him more than he could say.

'Mummy? I know you want to tell me something important, but I want to ask Dante something.' The child put her elbows on top of the white tablecloth and then, with her chin resting in her hand, studied him intently.

'What is it, sweetheart?'

'Are you married?'

Resisting the urge to laugh out loud at the uncanny aptness of the question, he endeavoured to keep his face expressionless so that Tia wouldn't think he wasn't giving her question the proper consideration.

'No, my sweet little girl...I'm not married.'

'My mummy's not married either. I wish she was. I wish she was so that I could have a daddy, like my friend Madison at school. Not all the children in my class have daddies, but she does, and I think she's very lucky—don't you?'

Powerful emotion struck Dante silent. As if in slow motion—as if time had ground to a dreamlike halt—he saw Anna's pale slim hand reach out to pull Tia's hand away from her chin and tenderly hold it.

'Darling, I want you to listen very carefully to what I need to tell you. Will you do that?'

Her blue-grey eyes widening like twin compact disks, Tia nodded gravely.

'Dante and I knew each other a long time ago—remember I told you that? Anyway, we liked each other very much. But unfortunately…because something very sad happened in Italy, where he came from…he had to go away.' Sighing softly, Anna gave him a brief heartfelt glance. 'When he left… When he left, I found out that I was expecting a baby.'

'A baby? That must have been me!'

'Yes, darling…it *was* you.'

Her innocent brow puckering, Tia swung her gaze round to alight firmly on Dante.

'Does that mean that you're my daddy, then?'

'Yes, my angel.' His throat feeling as if it had been branded with an iron, Dante attempted a smile. 'It does.'

'You mean my *real* daddy? Real like Madison's daddy is her *real* daddy?'

'Yes.'

'Then we must be a real *family*.'

Never had anyone looked clear down to his soul as his daughter did at that breathtaking moment, and he knew...*knew* beyond any shadow of doubt...that she saw him for who he really was. It was the most unsettling yet exhilarating feeling Dante had ever experienced.

'And if we're a real family then you have to come and live with us—because that's what real families do, you know. Mummy, can I have a chocolate éclair now?' Tia turned pleadingly towards her mother. 'If you don't want me to eat a whole one, in case I'm sick, can I share it with you and have just half?'

'Okay, but I think after that you should call it a day on the cake front, don't you?'

As Anna glanced at Dante with a tremulous smile, he silently formed the words *thank you*. Then, reaching towards the multi-tiered cake stand, he plucked a chocolate éclair from it and with the small silver knife by his plate proceeded to cut it in half...

It had been a day of truth-telling. Along with the relief that had followed it, an incredible fatigue rolled over Anna, dragging at her limbs and making her eyelids so heavy that she could hardly stay awake.

Having left Dante in the bedroom, watching Tia as

she drifted off to sleep after the story he'd read her, she kicked off her shoes and stretched out on the couch.

She'd told him that children quickly adapted to new situations and she'd been right. Already Tia was calling him Daddy—as if by voicing her acknowledgement of who he was gave her even more right to claim him as her own. It touched Anna almost unbearably to see father and child together, bonding as naturally as if there had never at any time been a separation. It was wonderful…a dream come true. *But where did that leave her?*

She'd been a single parent for so long. It wouldn't be easy to let go of that role, even when she knew it was probably best for Tia that her father was in her life at last. Was it wrong of her to feel so afraid? To live in fear that her autonomy over their lives would be taken away? And would it be wise to contemplate letting her loneliness be soothed by this rugged and virile urbane man to whom she'd relinquished her innocence one night five years ago, knowing that because of the wall she'd glimpsed behind his eyes more than once he'd probably never be able to love her the wholehearted way that he loved his daughter?

'How are you doing?'

Anna's eyes had been drifting closed, and suddenly Dante was there in front of her, staring down at her with his soulful light eyes in a way that would have made her knees knock together if she'd been standing.

'I'm fine, thanks. Just a bit tired, to tell you the truth.' She started to sit up, but he gestured that she stay just as she was and then dropped down to sit on the edge of the couch beside her.

The strong, long-fingered hands that she'd noticed when they first met and had privately thought poetic and artistic were linked loosely in front of him, and a lock of dark blond hair flopped sexily down in front of his forehead. His sculpted lean profile and long luxuriant lashes made him look like a movie star, and for a distressing moment Anna wondered what an outstanding male specimen like him could possibly see in someone as ordinary as her.

'It's been quite an incredible day, huh?'

And as Dante smiled at her with surprising warmth her suddenly wobbly self-esteem was completely banished beneath the breathtaking gaze that was directed straight at her...

CHAPTER NINE

'TIA loved the Ritz. She'll probably look round the Mirabelle now and think it quite shabby after being there.'

'That will be the last thing this hotel will be when we get through with all the improvements I have in mind. Did I tell you I've hired a team of designers from Milan to oversee the refurbishment?'

'Milan? Gosh.'

'This place is already in a league of its own as a Georgian building with a fascinating history. With modernisation and refurbishment it's going to be one of the most stylish and sophisticated establishments in London.'

'Anita and Grant deserve it to be. They've unstintingly lavished their love on it ever since Grant inherited it from his parents. Can I ask you something?'

He nodded.

'Talking about Milan...I was wondering...'

'Yes?'

'Does that mean you've made your peace with Italy?

It's just that you seemed reluctant to discuss it. You told me you left a long time ago, and I sensed that you had deliberately distanced yourself from it.'

'I had... But when I went back for my mother's funeral I remembered things about the place that I loved and missed. Gradually over the years I've grown to love it again. That's why I bought a house there...the house we will stay in when you and Tia return with me. Does that reply satisfy your question?'

Touching the tips of his fingers to her cheek, Dante studied her intently. Anna fell silent, hardly knowing what to say. He'd admitted that he'd distanced himself from his homeland but he hadn't said *why*. Would he ever trust her enough to disclose some of the secrets from his past? she wondered. But Lake Como was the other subject she needed to address.

'It's a big step for me to go with you to Italy. To tell you the truth, I feel a little vulnerable going there with you, Dante. I don't know the language, and I know you won't like this but I'm also wary of being pushed into something I'm not really ready for. Do you understand that?'

'It is not my intention to push you into anything or to make you feel vulnerable,' he replied thoughtfully. 'I simply want us to have a holiday together, for us to get to know one another and for Tia to get to know me. When you are ready, and *only* when you are ready, will we talk about marriage.'

'Do you mean it?'

He studied her gravely. 'My word is my bond.'

'I suppose I could do with a holiday. And, like you say...it will give you and Tia a chance to get to know each other a bit more.'

'And as for not speaking the language...I will make it my personal mission to teach you,' Dante promised. 'I will have you speaking like a native Italian before you know it! Tia too.'

'It's getting dark.' Nervously Anna glanced up at the swiftly fading evening light, evident through the room's high windows. At the same time she heard the lilting song of a lone blackbird. For some reason it made her feel a little melancholy. 'I ought to turn on the lamps.'

'Don't.' The command in Dante's tone gave her a jolt.

'It's gloomy...I'd like some light in here.'

'You're uncomfortable with the dark? There's no need when I am right here beside you, Anna. I would never let anything or anyone hurt you.'

His heated glance was in earnest, she saw. Instantly a swarm of butterflies fluttered wildly inside her.

'Yes, but I still want to... I still need some...some light.'

As she made to move, Dante slid his hand round to the back of her head, to bring her face slowly but inexorably towards his. The last thing she registered was his hot, languorous gaze before his mouth fell on hers to ravish it without restraint, his warm velvet tongue gliding and coiling sensually with hers, his breathing a grated rasp as the shadow of his beard scraped her chin.

A sea of honey lapped inside Anna. It was as though she'd been left languishing in a cold dark cave for five long years and now at last she was wildly, deliriously free again—free to breathe in pure heady oxygen and be deluged in light. The pleasure and joy that soared inside her was untrammelled as her hands pushed through the silky strands of Dante's fair hair to anchor his head as he anchored hers, all the better for their lips to meld and sup as though their hunger would never be assuaged. *Not in this lifetime...*

'No... Not—not here.' She gulped down a shaky breath as his hands tugged at the zip fastener on her dress. 'My bedroom.'

They didn't let each other go as they entered the dim, cool enclave of Anna's room. It seemed essential to keep touching, to keep holding on in case some nightmare schism should cut through their longing and keep them apart for ever.

With the heel of his Italian loafer Dante shut the door behind them. He shucked off his footwear just before falling onto the bed with her, somehow manoeuvring her on top of him as he kissed her senseless. The zipper on her linen dress was skilfully undone, the sleeves tugged urgently down over her shoulders. With dreamlike effort Anna helped Dante remove it completely, then she was astride his hard lean hips again, bending her head to give and receive drugging, passionate kisses that made her head spin and her heart gallop. Her long waving hair was a protective shield that kept the world from intruding as it drifted sensually over them both.

Cupping his face as she leant forward, Anna marvelled at the strong, chiselled contours, at the sublime slopes and plains that denoted his fascinating masculine features. But it was the vulnerable, naked look of utter longing in his eyes that undid her. Stilling in shock, she hardly registered breathing.

'I thought perhaps I'd dreamt wanting you this much…but now I see that I didn't… Or if I did the dream was just a tantalising glimpse of the incredible reality that is you, Anna.'

Finding no words that could adequately describe the force of what she was feeling, Anna began to slide the buttons through the buttonholes of his fine cotton shirt with trembling fingers. When the smooth, tanned musculature underneath, with its dusting of hair, was exposed to her, she pushed the material aside, sliding her hands over the flat male nipples and taut ribcage to explore him, to feel the throb of his heartbeat beneath her palm. She was thrilled to realise that it beat with desire for *her*. Lowering her head, she pressed her lips to Dante's deliciously warm skin.

She was following the trail of silky dark blond hair towards his belly button when he made a low, husky sound, slid his hands beneath her hair and urged her eagerly upwards again. The next thing she knew he was helping remove the scrap of plain white silk that denoted her panties and sliding down his zipper.

When he placed himself at the soft moist centre of Anna's core, easing his way inside her and then plunging upwards, she threw back her head with a whimper. The very notion of pleasure broke all its bounds. It hardly seemed an adequate description for the utterly consuming sensations that effervesced through her body. Not since she'd surrendered her innocence to Dante five years ago had such violent waves of ecstatic bliss been hers. *This* was the completeness she'd longed for—the deep connection her soul had ached to experience again. The one primal force that could drive away all melancholy and doubt.

The feeling brought it unerringly home to her why she had never wanted another man since that first time with him...why she had resigned herself to being alone for ever—because no man could possibly come close to making her feel what Dante made her feel.

Utterly losing himself in their wild, urgent coupling, Dante buried himself so deep inside her dizzying heat that he swore he would melt. Expertly opening the catch on her bra, he quickly discarded the garment to fill his palms with her perfect satin-tipped breasts, stroking his thumbs across the tender nipples. Gazing up into Anna's lovely face he saw the stunning crown of burnished hair that rippled river-like down over her pale smooth skin and knew there wasn't another woman in the world to match her for beauty and grace. *Or who could crack the frozen ice round his heart.*

He should have searched for her long before this… *why hadn't he*? Unbelievable that he'd let his fear of rejection keep him from the one woman who'd selflessly given herself to him all that time ago when he was most in need.

With urgency and passion Dante's fingers bit into the soft flesh of Anna's svelte hips, holding her to him as if he could never let her go. A long soft moan followed by her ragged breathing feathered over him as she climaxed, and suddenly he couldn't hold back the tide that lapped forcefully at the shores of his own longing, and had no choice but to let it completely sweep him away…

'Come here.' He helped her lie across his chest, then wrapped his arms around her. It was a new experience for him to hold a woman like this after making love. Not just to appease her, but simply for the sheer joy of being close—to sense the beat of her heart slowly but surely aligning with his. When they finally came to live together he would enjoy that pleasure every single day he realised. Weaving his fingers through her long flowing hair Dante kissed the top of Anna's head.

She stirred, raising her face to his. 'That was rather wonderful. But now I feel absolutely incapable of doing anything else.' She smiled.

'And exactly what did you have planned for the rest

of the evening that our enjoyment of each other has interrupted, *innamorata*?'

Her smile didn't fade. Instead it grew impish, just like their daughter's. 'Well...for starters I've got a pile of ironing to do.'

'And this is essential?'

'It might not be.' Her voice lowered seductively, and renewed desire—swift and hot as a lava-flow—made Dante bite back a groan. 'It depends what distractions are on offer as an alternative.'

'You've become a shameless temptress in my absence, I see.' In one swiftly deft move Dante took hold of Anna's arms, moved her to the side of him, then captured her beneath him. The laughter in her pretty eyes instantly died. 'As long as you haven't been practising your seductive arts on some other poor defenceless male, I won't complain.'

She looked stricken for a moment. 'I swear to you I haven't.'

The tension that had suddenly gripped him at the idea of Anna being with someone else eased.

'Then is *this* the kind of distraction you were looking for, hmm?' he enquired huskily as he firmly parted her thighs and once again hungrily joined his body to hers...

'Is that an aria by Puccini you're whistling, Anna?' Pausing in his food preparation for lunch, Luigi narrowed his gaze in surprise as he studied the hotel's slim assistant manager, who had come into the kitchen to collect the menu.

'Yes, from *Madame Butterfly*. I hope you don't think I was murdering it, or being sacrilegious or something?'

'Not at all… I am only curious as to what has made you seem happy lately?'

She could have answered *a week of nights making passionate love with the Mirabelle's handsome new major shareholder*, but of course she didn't. Only Anita and her husband Grant knew the truth about her relationship with Dante. And they had agreed that the information would stay private until they returned from the month's break they were all taking while the hotel was being modernised.

The idea of her and Tia travelling to Lake Como the following day with Dante was exciting, but Anna would be lying if she didn't admit it terrified her too. Having late-night trysts with her lover was one thing, but *living together*? That was a whole other scenario entirely. And she would be totally on his turf, so to speak—dependent on his kindness and goodwill to see her through, when she was feeling unsure about the prospect of trusting a man long-term and fearing he might want to control her.

But then he *had* given her his promise that he wouldn't try and push her into anything she wasn't ready for, she remembered.

'I suppose I'm just happy at being able to take a whole

month off to spend with Tia,' she answered Luigi, poignantly realising it was an event that had not occurred since her daughter was a newborn baby. *And if it wasn't for Dante, it wouldn't be happening at all.*

Taking a couple of steps towards the chef, she clutched the paper with the menu written on it to her chest. 'A little bird told me that you're going to Provence for a French cookery course...is that true, Luigi?'

With a dismissive flourish of his hand, he sheepishly lowered his gaze. 'Signor Romano suggested it, and is paying for me to go. If we want to get a Michelin star for the Mirabelle then of course I will do it...even if French cooking is not my subject of choice. But I am surprised that a fellow Italian can be so enthusiastic about the cooking of another nation!'

'Mr Romano is well travelled and wise, Luigi. And being able to diversify the menu will help our lunchtime trade and maximise sales, so it's great that you're going to Provence.' Anna patted his arm encouragingly. 'You'll love it, I'm sure.'

'We will see.'

After a car journey to Heathrow, then a four-hour plane journey, followed by another car ride on which they took a detour for an hour to eat at a charming restaurant Dante knew, they finally arrived at his five-storey villa in Lake Como.

It was situated in prime viewing position at the lake, on a high-banked sward where the last rays of the sun played upon the surface of the water, giving it the appearance of glinting diamonds. The scent of bougainvillaea, azalea and other heady blossoms floated on the balmy Mediterranean air, rustling through Anna's unbound hair and lightly teasing Tia's wild corkscrew curls. Both females studied the house in its fairy-tale surroundings in silent awe. Having retrieved their luggage from the boot of the Mercedes that had been waiting for them at the airport, Dante stepped up beside Anna and slid his arm around her waist. As was becoming a habit, his touch electrified her.

'It's a stunningly beautiful house, Dante,' she remarked, shyly meeting his searching blue-grey glance.

'And it will be made even more beautiful by the presence of my two beautiful girls,' he asserted warmly.

It totally made her melt when he said things like that. Her heart was already his, but when he let his guard down and spoke what seemed to be his true feelings out loud Anna honestly felt as if she would follow him to the ends of the earth and back, and not care what discomfort or challenges confronted her so long as she could confront them with him.

'Is this our new house, Daddy?' Tia piped up beside them.

For answer, Dante scooped the little girl up into his arms and planted a loud, affectionate kiss at the side of her cheek. 'This is our house in Italy, *mia bambina*.' He grinned. 'But we have other homes around the world too.'

Mentally, Anna gulped. Having called her cosy basement flat in Covent Garden home for the past eight years, it was quite some dizzying leap to realise that if she and Tia were to live permanently with Dante they would be moving around quite a lot. And if the other properties he owned had anything like the stunning architecture and formidable size of this one then Anna could possibly be feeling overwhelmed for a very long time indeed!

'Let's go inside, shall we?'

'What do you think of the place now that you've had a couple of hours to acclimatise yourself?'

Dante walked up behind her as Anna stood on the balcony off the drawing room, gazing out at the stunning lake view. With a breathtaking vista of the Alps in the distance, it was guaranteed to capture all her attention. Even breathing in the warm Mediterranean air acted like a soothing salve. It made her realise how much in need of a holiday she'd been for ages.

After kissing Tia a loving goodnight, and tucking her into bed in her new bedroom, she'd been standing here ever since Dante had gone upstairs to read her a bedtime story. Now her heart leapt as he walked onto the balcony to join her. Gesturing in disbelief at the lake, with its perfectly serene surface and the twinkling lights reflected on the water from some of the surrounding buildings now that night was falling, she slowly shook her head.

'Sometimes words are inadequate, and this is one of those times. I don't think I've ever seen a more stirring or sublime scene.'

'Well, it's yours to enjoy for however long you want… you know that.'

She fell silent.

'Come inside and sit down,' he invited—but not before Anna registered what might have been uncertainty in his eyes.

Re-entering the elegant lamplit room, which was full of stunning antiques and sublime paintings, with a huge fireplace inlaid with white marble at its head, Anna smiled.

'I feel like I'm on the movie set of a film about some sophisticated Italian noble. There's so much beauty here that I can hardly take it in.'

'You are right. There *is* so much beauty.'

His low-voiced comment was loaded with meaning—meaning that Anna couldn't fail to comprehend. She couldn't glance at him without wanting him, and knew that no matter how much she tried to contain her desire he must see it in her eyes every time their gazes met.

Gesturing, she sat on the sumptuous sofa. Dante joined her. Gathering her slender palm into his, for a while he just simply turned it over and examined it—just as if it were some priceless jewel he was contemplating purchasing.

'I don't know how you can ever bear leaving this place,' she remarked, her heart quietly thudding. 'It's like paradise on earth.'

'For a long time I couldn't see it that way. But lately I've begun to see how lucky I am being able to have a home here.'

'Is this where you're from? Como, I mean?'

He let go of her hand.

'No. I bought this house because my mother loved Como and had a home here. When I was young she always fantasised about living here one day...but the truth is that she was a very simple and contented soul, and would have been happy anywhere as long as she knew I was happy.'

'She sounds wonderful.'

Dante smiled. 'She was.'

'So where were you raised, if not here?' Anna prompted him gently.

CHAPTER TEN

'I WAS raised in a small village inland, far away from the mountains and lakes. It wasn't anything like here.' He pushed to his feet as though the memory made him restless and uneasy. 'It didn't have the cultural delights or beautiful vistas of Como, and the people who lived there were neither rich nor privileged. But there was a strong sense of community, so I've been told. However, we didn't stay. When my father walked out on her, my mother had no choice but to move to the nearest town to try and make a living.'

'Your father walked out on you and your mother?'

'He did.' Only briefly did Dante meet Anna's gaze and hold it. 'It was a long time ago. I don't even remember him.'

'So…you don't know much about him, then?'

He grimaced. 'Only that he was British and an archaeologist. He'd been working on a dig nearby, looking for Roman ruins, when he met my mother. As far as I'm aware archaeologists aren't exactly high earners. At least I've far exceeded anything my father could have made, and my mother didn't die impoverished—as *he* left her!'

The strained silence that fell after his reluctantly voiced confession made Anna's heart sore. Dante had become a man without the love or guidance of a father, or even close male relatives, and bereft of that important bond had had to forge his own way in life. He'd had to bury what must have been a deep-seated need for love and connection from his male parent, papering it over with material pursuits and the seemingly glamorous but ultimately not permanently fulfilling rewards of success.

All Anna had yearned for as a child was the unconditional love and support of her parents. No amount of money would have made her dire situation any better. It probably would have made things *worse*, because more money would have meant her father had had more income to spend on drink. But right now it was clear to her that no matter how wealthy or successful Dante had become a big part of him still yearned for the father's love he'd never had...

Moving over to where he stood, she touched her palm to the strong heart beating beneath his fine linen shirt.

'I think you've done an amazing job of turning your life around after such a challenging start, Dante,' she told him. 'But more than what you've achieved materially, you're a good man...a man any father would be proud to call his son.'

'Am I?' For a disturbing few moments his glance was tortured. 'You only say that because you don't know what I've done to get where I am today.'

Anna's dark-eyed gaze didn't waver. 'If you've done anything wrong, in my opinion it's only that you've become too hard on yourself.'

'You're just naive—that's why you say that.'

'I had to grow up too fast—just like you, Dante—and I've learned that we don't help ourselves when we constantly criticise what we've done in the past. We did the best we knew how to do at the time. How can anyone— even *you*—do more than that?'

'You learned when you started to look for me that I had a "ruthless reputation". The papers did not lie, Anna. I did whatever I could to make my fortune. I had no scruples as long as I won the deal—as long as it meant more money and power. I was so driven I didn't even care that I helped people to lose their jobs. I certainly didn't have sleepless nights worrying about how they would support themselves or their families afterwards! Even my mother started to despair of me. She warned me against alienating good people. One day I would need trustworthy friends, she said—not phoney ones who were driven by fear and greed like I was.

'Well...it took my mother's death and then meeting you, Anna, to make me wake up to the truth of my life. To make me want to work and live with more integrity... to make me want to help people instead of exploit them for what I could get. It took me a while to change things, but when I realised that the changes I had to make had to be quite radical one of the first things I did was to revert back to my Italian name. I only used my father's name because, coming from a poor background, with only the most basic education, I wanted to distance myself from Italy and all that it meant to me. Ironic, really, when I didn't even know the man and he didn't stay around for long—'

'Oh, Dante... What an incredible journey you've had to come back to yourself.' Anna's heart was so full it was hard to keep her tears at bay.

He shook his head, as if he was uncomfortable with the tenderness in her voice, as if his painful story couldn't possibly warrant it. 'There are shadows beneath your eyes, *innamorata*.'

His hand glanced softly against her cheekbone, his blue-grey eyes as hypnotically mesmerising as the moon-lit lake outside the window, and Anna wanted to lose herself in those fascinating depths for a long time.

His next words robbed her of the chance.

'We've had a long day's travelling. You really should take the opportunity of having an early night. In the morning the housekeeper I hire to look after the villa when I'm here will arrive with her daughter, who also helps out. They'll prepare breakfast for us, and also find out if there's anything we need.'

'What are their names?'

'The housekeeper and her daughter?' Dante shrugged, as though surprised by the question. 'Giovanna is the

mother and Ester the daughter. No doubt they'll immediately fall in love with Tia when they meet her—both
of them adore children, and Ester has a little son of her
own. Anyway…like I said, you look tired. You should
have a leisurely bath, then an early night. I'll join you
later.' He turned away from her.

'I hope you don't regret sharing what you just shared
with me?' Concerned, as well as disappointed that he
seemed intent on spending the rest of the evening without her, Anna restlessly coiled a long strand of her bright
hair round her finger. 'Do you?' she pressed.

'Go to bed, Anna. We'll talk again in the morning.'

'Why don't you answer me? I don't want to go to bed
and leave you brooding here on your own.'

A faint smile appeared on his fine-cut lips as he
turned to survey her.

'So you want to be my rescuer again? Just as you
tried to rescue me from my morose mood all those years
ago?'

Fielding the comment, Anna lifted her chin. 'Is it so
wrong of me to want to reach out to you? To show you
that I care about how you're feeling?'

Remaining silent, Dante looked away again.

With frustrated tears making her eyes smart, Anna
swung round on her heel and marched out of the
room…

After watching the coloured house lights reflect off
the dark lake for a long time, Dante stepped back into

the drawing room at around one in the morning. The Campari on the rocks he'd made himself was barely touched. Leaving the crystal tumbler on a rosewood table, he stretched his arms high above his head, grimacing at the locked tension in his protesting muscles.

With everything he had in him he wanted to join Anna in the stately canopied double bed. But how could he when he knew she must secretly despise him for the way he had conducted himself in the past? It had even prevented her from getting in touch with him to tell him about Tia. No, it was Anna who was good and deserving of help…not him. Fear of failure and loss had been the dark, soul-destroying forces he'd been guided by. And because his associations with Italy had been tainted with hurt from his childhood he had fled to England to make his fortune, consciously choosing to lose his accent and forget his roots to reinvent himself as the untouchable businessman, the ice man.

All in all, it didn't make a pretty picture. Bringing Anna and Tia here had raised painful spectres from his past when he'd started to believe he had let them go. What he wanted most of all was a new start for himself and his family—not to focus on his past mistakes and feel unworthy again. But could he blame Anna if ultimately she couldn't forgive him for his deplorable history?

Intensely disliking the feeling of not having his emotions under control the way he wanted, Dante scrubbed an agitated hand round his shadowed jaw. He'd be better in the morning, he told himself. A few hours' solid sleep and he'd be more like himself again. Reaching for the button on a discreet wall panel that controlled the lighting, he pressed it, lingering for a solitary moment as the room was plunged into darkness.

Tonight he *wouldn't* seek comfort in Anna's tender arms, as he ached with every fibre of his being to do. Somehow, after practically dismissing her on her first night in Como, he didn't believe he deserved it. Instead, he would retreat to one of the other palatial bedrooms and spend the night alone...

She'd left the curtains open, and in the morning, sun streamed into the room, straight at her. Anna had to shield her eyes. Her spirits plunged in dismay when she realised that Dante hadn't joined her as he'd promised he would. He'd been absolutely right about her being tired, but she was shocked at the speed with which she'd fallen asleep. She had remained in that condition up until now too. She was in a strange country, and a strange house, as well as beginning a month's trial period of living with him. You'd think any one of those things would have kept her awake...but, no.

A deep sigh of regret escaped her. She should have stayed with him last night—should have found a way to reach him, to let him know how much she cared. If she'd stayed then he would have seen that she didn't agree with his unspoken belief that he didn't deserve love and care. He would have seen that Anna was fiercely loyal to the people she cared about. Yet she was still wary of disclosing her feelings when there was the ever-present fear that he might want to take away her autonomy...

But right now she needed to see her little girl and see how she was faring. She too had slept in a strange room, in a strange bed. Glancing at the clock by the bedside, she gasped when she saw the time. What kind of a mother was she that she could blithely oversleep and leave her child to fend for herself?

Guiltily grabbing her pastel blue cotton robe from the end of the bed, she yawned—and then couldn't resist peering out at the wrought-iron balcony and the sublime view of the sun-dappled lake. A canopied boat full of early-morning tourists floated leisurely by. She caught her breath. There was a real holiday atmosphere in the air that to Anna was just like a dream. Even more so when she thought about spending her time here with the two people she cared most about in the world...

Tia had apparently long vacated her bed. Seeing clothes scattered round the pretty room, with its lovely antique furniture and tall open windows, Anna realised she had even dressed herself. Had Dante taken her downstairs for breakfast?

Laughter and the suggestion of jovial conversation drew her to the high-ceilinged oak-beamed kitchen. As she hovered in the doorway, conscious of the flimsy robe she had hastily flung on over her white cotton nightdress, she dragged the edges together and stared. Two women—one younger, and one perhaps just past middle-age, both dark-haired, with strong-boned Italian faces and bright eyes—were bustling round the kitchen, carrying plates of food to the table and beaming at Tia, who sat there with Dante just as though she was in her absolute element.

As if he intuitively knew she was there, Dante turned in his high-backed oak chair and smiled. *Any words Anna might have been going to say utterly dried up.* Bathed in the sensual sea of his storm-coloured gaze, she felt her limbs turn as weak as cooked strands of tagliatelli.

'*Buongiorno,*' he greeted her, his low-pitched 'bedroom' voice sounding slightly husky.

Flustered, all she could manage right then was an awkward nervous smile. Rising from his chair, Dante crossed the room to kiss her cheek, his lips lingering warmly at the side of her face so that her senses were crowded by his fresh clean scent and disturbingly arousing body heat. His fit lean body was encased in fitted black jeans and a loose white linen shirt, and frankly he was more sinfully tempting than any honey or sugar-laden breakfast she could think of.

Unquestioningly aware of the devastating effect he had on her, he smiled for a second time into Anna's mesmerised dark gaze and curved his arm round her waist. 'Come and meet Giovanna and Ester,' he urged, leading her across the stone-flagged floor to the long oak table where the two women had paused in their serving of food to furnish Anna with twin welcoming smiles.

They greeted her in their native Italian, but then the younger woman said in faltering English, 'It is—is so nice to see you—I mean to meet you, *signorina*.'

'Please,' Anna said warmly, taking her hand, 'call me Anna.'

'Mummy? Why aren't you dressed yet?' Tia demanded, her mouth crammed with ciabatta bread and jam. 'Do you even know what the time is?'

'Yes, I know what the time is, Tia Bailey, and I know I've slept in—but I was more tired than I realised. And by the way, Miss Bossy Boots…did you forget to say good morning?'

'Sorry, Mummy, but me and Daddy have been up for ages and ages!'

'Really?'

'The early bird catches the worm…isn't that what they say?'

Seeing the teasing glint in Dante's eyes, Anna felt a rush of dizzying warmth flood into her chest. Stooping to kiss the top of Tia's curly blond head, she felt her heart warm doubly when she detected no tension whatsoever in her child about this new unfamiliar situation. Very quickly, it seemed, she had made herself quite at home.

Glancing round at the rest of the company, she became uncomfortably conscious that she was still in her nightwear. 'I'm so sorry I got up so late. I'd like to return to my room to dress, and then I'll be back down as soon as I can—if that's okay?'

'Of course it's okay.' Dante's tone was slightly irked. 'There aren't any rules about what you can and can't do here, Anna. This is your home. Giovanna will keep some food hot for you in the oven until you return.'

By the time Anna returned to the kitchen Giovanna had disappeared upstairs to make the beds, and at Dante's request Ester had taken Tia into the gardens for a while so that she could play. The woman had beamed at him, clearly jumping at the chance to spend time with his engaging little daughter.

Staring down into a mug of strong sugared black coffee—*his troubled mind hadn't allowed him to sleep at all well last night*—he glanced expectantly towards the door as Anna appeared. She was wearing a lemon tunic dress, with sleeves that ended just past her elbows and a hemline that finished just above her knees. Her long shapely legs were bare. With her stunning auburn hair left free to tumble down over her breasts unhindered she was a vision of loveliness that put Dante's already charged senses on hyper-alertness. The mere sight of her acted as an incendiary flame on his frustrated libido, making it virtual *agony* to stay sitting and not go to her and haul her urgently into his arms.

'Tia's in the garden with Ester,' he said instead, knowing that would be the first thing that would concern her. 'Is that okay?'

'Of course.' Moving to the table, Anna briefly

squeezed her eyes shut as she leaned her arms over a chair. 'I can't tell you how good that coffee smells.'

'I'll get you some.'

'It's all right. I'm quite capable of helping myself. I don't want to disturb you when you look so relaxed, just sitting there.'

She brought a mug of the steaming beverage she'd poured from the percolator back to the table, and sat down opposite him. She looked so pretty, fresh and artless that his heart pounded with longing. Replaying their conversation of last night for the umpteenth time in his mind, he wondered if she would ever truly be able to accept him for himself and not hold his past against him.

'Tia indicated you were up early. Couldn't you sleep?'

Tumbling headlong into the liquid depths of her big brown eyes for a moment, he edged the corner of his mouth into an almost painful rueful grin. 'No, Anna… I could not sleep. Did you think I could without you in my bed?'

Blushing, she stared down into her coffee cup for long seconds. 'I would have stayed with you last night… talking downstairs, I mean.' She lifted her gaze to his. 'But you clearly didn't want me to. Whenever I try to get close to you, Dante, it seems you push me away. Do you intend on doing that for ever?'

His grin vanished. What could he tell her when his whole system was in such an agony of need? *Mental, physical, spiritual...* He could go mad with it all. He pushed his mug of coffee from him with such force that the dark liquid slopped messily over the sides. He heard Anna's shocked intake of breath even as he rose, but he was suddenly beyond worrying about anything but the powerful need to hold her, to breathe her in as though she was life-giving air in the increasing sense of claustrophobia that seized him, the prison of his past that had kept him in the dark for so long.

Hauling her out of her chair against him, Dante buried his face in her hair while his feverish hands desperately sought the warmth of her body through her thin cotton dress.

'Anna... Oh, Anna...'

Sensing her tremble, he tipped up her face and plundered her mouth until his lips ached and his heart thundered as though it would burst inside him.

'Do you want me, Dante?' As she dragged her mouth away from his, her voice sounded broken and tearful.

'Yes... Yes, I want you. I always want you! Are you going to punish me for that?'

'No, my angel.' She pushed back some of the dark blond hair that had flopped onto his brow, and her touch was so soft, so infinitely tender that Dante couldn't speak. His muscles all but screamed with the tension that built inside him, and he prayed for it to ease soon.

'You punish yourself enough without me doing the same,' she finished sadly.

Uttering a dramatic oath, he slid his arm beneath her

and lifted her high against his chest. Bereft of words, because devastating emotion had right then robbed him of the ability to speak, he carried her out through the door and up the winding staircase with its ornate wrought-iron stair-rail to their bedroom…

'What are you looking at?'

In front of the stunning cheval mirror, brushing out her long bed-tangled hair, with the balcony doors slightly ajar to allow in a delicious thermal of sultry Mediterranean air, Anna glanced over her shoulder at Dante with a smile. Bare-chested and tousle-haired, he lay back against the bank of white silk pillows with the kind of lascivious, knowing look that made her insides clench and her toes flex hard.

An impossible ache arose inside her that all but *begged* her to join him in bed for another greedy helping of wild reckless loving. She could hardly credit her own body's hungry libidinous needs. Already tingling and aching from the voracious homage her lover had paid to her in bed, Anna was seriously torn between rejoining Dante and going down to the garden to give some attention to Tia, and to thank her generous-hearted young minder for looking after her.

'I'm looking at *you*. Where else do you expect me to focus my gaze when you stand there in that thin robe that hugs every delicious curve and reminds me that I should never have let you get out of bed?'

'Well, you've got to stop looking at me like that—or

I'll be a wreck for the rest of the day because I won't be able to concentrate on anything else but you! And I want to see some of the sights of this beautiful place, Dante... For instance that medieval monastery you mentioned.'

He got out of bed, stepped into black silk boxers, then moved barefoot across the polished parquet floor to join her. Such a simple human manoeuvre shouldn't look so mouthwateringly arresting, but when a man had a body as fit and compelling as Dante Romano's, it did.

'So...a ruined medieval monastery is preferable to looking at me, is it?' he teased, his hands settling over her hips while his mouth planted a hot, sexy little kiss at the juncture of her neck and shoulder.

Anna's loosely tied cotton robe slid off one satiny shoulder as the languorous heaviness between her thighs returned.

'I—I didn't say that,' she moaned, readjusting her robe over her shoulder, then trying to disentangle herself from her lover's arms. 'What are Giovanna and Ester going to think? I already got up late, and then you persuaded me back to bed. They'll think I've got no morals or sense of decency at all!'

He laughed. It was such a spontaneous, joyous sound that Anna could hardly credit him as being the same man who had been so gripped by inner turmoil and pain earlier.

She'd cradled him in her arms for a long time after that first stormy coupling they'd fallen into when they'd come to bed, because she'd sensed he needed it. It had been all the more poignant because even a strong, powerful man like him needed the reassurance that he was cared for, she realised—even when his whole demeanour practically screamed to deny it.

'You don't have to worry about them. They are both women of the world. Besides…Giovanna put her head round the door about ten minutes after we came up here and saw that we were…busy.'

'What?' Covering her face with her hands, Anna groaned. 'Why didn't you tell me? Oh, my God…how am I ever going to look the woman in the eye again?'

'Beautiful Anna…you are making far too much of this when there really is no need. We already have a daughter. Don't you think that Giovanna and Ester have already guessed that we've been intimate?'

His teasing gaze brimmed with laughter again, and Anna lightly hit him on his toned tanned bicep. 'That's not funny!' Whirling away from him, she grabbed up her clothes from the arm of the chair, where she'd carelessly thrown them earlier, and headed for the sumptuous marble bathroom. 'You are utterly impossible—you know that?'

Dante was still grinning from ear to ear as she dramatically slammed the door shut.

CHAPTER ELEVEN

AMBLING through the quaint cobblestoned streets and alleyways of the bewitching lakeside town, Dante glanced at the titian-haired beauty beside him and wondered what he'd done to deserve the sense of satisfaction and contentment that kept washing over him.

Wearing a shift dress printed with pink poppies, her bright hair streaming loose down her back like Millais's *Ophelia*, she was the most eye-catching woman in the vicinity. More than that, the buzz he got from just holding her hand, strolling along like any other entranced tourist, couldn't be measured. All the money and success in the world couldn't match the pleasure of it. And as he walked Dante saw his home and the stunning Renaissance architecture that abounded with fresh eyes.

Another first was that for once he was simply being himself. It didn't matter who he was or where he came from. He'd shed the 'billionaire businessman' persona with alacrity, and there was such a euphoric sense of liberation about that that he almost wanted to announce it to the world. Instead, his hand lightly squeezed Anna's. In return, he received a traffic-stopping smile.

Tia was the only thing that was missing to make the day absolutely perfect. She had begged to be allowed to go with Ester and collect her son Paolo from kindergarten, after which she'd been invited to stay for lunch and to play with him for the afternoon. With Anna's consent first of all, Dante had agreed that she could go. He wouldn't have if he hadn't trusted Ester and her mother, Giovanna, completely. Giovanna had been his mother's closest and dearest friend, and that was how she and her daughter had come to take care of Dante's house for him—both when he was there and when he was away.

But although he was missing Tia already, they would all eat dinner together this evening, and he was appreciative of having some free time with Anna. This morning when they'd returned to bed she had surrendered *everything* to him. It had been as though she'd let all her carefully erected barriers down at once—even perhaps her fear of being controlled. She had simply accepted his sometimes too passionate loving with equal ardour and longing, her breathless sighs and eager exploring hands on his body letting Dante know that she was right where she wanted to be...no question.

Honestly, he had never known a woman so generous and giving—*in* bed and *out* of it. If he thought about losing her or letting her go his heart missed a beat. Frankly, it frightened him to realise how much she had come to mean to him. *Would she ever agree to marry him?* He almost felt sick at the idea she might not.

Stopping suddenly beside him, Anna pushed her huge sunglasses back onto her head to study him. 'I can hear a lot of wheels grinding and turning.' She grinned.

'What do you mean?' he asked, perplexed.

'I mean the wheels in your busy mind, Dante. What have you been thinking about?' Her brown eyes crinkled at the corners against the bright sunlight.

Pushing aside the sudden fear that arose inside him like a malevolent cloud blocking out the sun, Dante made himself smile. 'Nothing very interesting, I'm afraid. I was merely enjoying holding your hand and us being able to have this time together.'

'You weren't worrying about work? About what's going on at the Mirabelle or what million-dollar deals you're going to be making next?' Her tone was gently teasing.

'You believe all I think about is work when I'm with you?' He frowned, but then, when he might have descended into feeling guilty or frustrated that she could have such perception, he stroked his fingers across her soft cheek and followed it up with a playful pinch. 'Let me assure you, *innamorata*…my thoughts are *definitely* not about work when I'm with you. Could you doubt that after what happened this morning? There are still places on my body that throb and burn from making such uninhibited love with you. It's a wonder I can walk at all!'

Hot colour seared her cheeks and Anna lowered her gaze.

Dante chuckled softly. It was such a delight and also the biggest aphrodisiac to see her blush.

'You said there was a park that was a century old not too far away,' she commented, determinedly meeting his glance again, even though her cheeks still carried the heated evidence of her embarrassment. 'Can we go there?'

'We'll need to jump on the ferry, but why not?' he agreed, secretly delighted that he could give her such a simple pleasure.

'A ferry?' Anna beamed. 'Oh, I'd love that!'

And she did love it.

Her excitement was charmingly contagious. Dante received vicarious pleasure from travelling over the glinting blue lake on the passenger ferry with her, viewing the stunning homes that hugged the shoreline and the glimpses of medieval walls and towers in the background, even though the trip was hardly new to him and he had seen the sights many times before.

Seated on a slatted wooden bench half an hour later, in a park on the waterway that was full of Linden trees as well as a plethora of pink and red rhododendrons and white camellias, Anna swivelled round to observe Dante more closely. 'Tell me something about you that I don't know,' she urged smilingly.

Knowing there was no way of ducking out of the

question, Dante sighed, then answered quietly, 'I've been married before.'

Her beautiful smile vanished. 'Married? Not when we first met?'

'No.' His throat felt a little tight, and his voice sounded rusty. 'It was a long time before we met, Anna. I'd been divorced for about three years before I stayed at the Mirabelle that night.'

'Oh…' The relief in that breathless exhalation was tangible. 'What was her name?'

'Her name?' It never failed to astonish Dante how women always wanted to know the most inconsequential details. Another time it might amuse him. But not right now. Not when it had suddenly occurred to him that Anna might have strong reservations over marrying a man who had been divorced…especially when he told her the reason *why*. 'Her name was Marisa.'

'Was she Italian?'

'No. She came from California. I met her when I was living in New York. She worked at one of the financial establishments I dealt with there.'

'How long were you married?'

Reaching round a hand to rub the back of his neck, Dante sighed. 'Three years. She left me for someone else, if you want to know. But our marriage had hit the rocks long before that.'

'Why?'

Anna was twisting her hands together in her lap, and he sensed her definite unease. He cursed himself for bringing up the subject in the first place. To her question, 'Tell me something about you that I don't know,' he could just as easily have replied, *I'm a big fan of the opera, fine art and Italian football.* Telling her anything along the lines of the personal interests or hobbies he had would have been fine. Not that he'd ever had time for anything as normal or mundane as a hobby.

'She resented my extreme devotion to work. Whilst she loved what the rewards of that work could buy, she craved my attention too—and to be fair I wasn't as attentive of her as I could have been.'

'But it must have hurt when she left you for somebody else. Were you in love with her?'

Dante could hardly believe that he was seeing sympathy reflected in Anna's lovely dark gaze. He couldn't attest to understanding it, and was momentarily confused.

'No,' he answered honestly, 'I wasn't in love with her. Although when we first met I probably fooled myself that I was. She was vivacious, attractive and clever, and I had a couple of friends at the time who were also interested in her.' Ruefully, he shook his head. 'I suppose it was the thrill of the chase. That was the kind of thing that obsessed me then. Who could win the best deal, buy the best property, woo and win the most unattainable woman? Anyway, Marisa decided I didn't need to do much chasing after all. The wealthy lifestyle I could give her was a great incentive, you understand?'

His laugh was short and harsh. 'For a time we shared

similar aims. I was driven to succeed more and more, and so was she. She definitely wasn't the kind of woman who hankered after having a family. I suppose I kidded myself that the superficial interests we shared were enough to make our partnership work. That was until she met the young designer who came to remodel our New York apartment and had an affair with him.'

'And where is she now?'

'As far as I know she's remarried and living happily in Greenwich Village in New York, but it doesn't really concern me.' Standing up, he reached down a hand to help his silent companion to her feet. 'Let's walk on, shall we?'

Had he cared enough for his ex that he really *had* been hurt when she'd had an affair and then left him? Anna sucked in a breath, suddenly believing she knew why he seemed to have this need to take charge and control situations. Both his father and his wife had left him—it didn't matter that their marriage hadn't been a union made in heaven—and that had to have left some deep emotional scarring. It also must have pained him to learn he was married to a woman who'd seen his wealth as his greatest asset. To not be loved for yourself but instead to be wanted because of the lifestyle you could provide must be shattering.

Refusing to be downhearted because Dante had revealed he'd been married before—with his confession about his past the other night, at least now he was opening up to her a little bit—Anna smiled, sincere and relaxed. 'Yes, let's walk,' she agreed.

Walking along beside this broad-shouldered handsome man, in his sexy designer shades, with every passing female no matter what her age glancing helplessly at him, she returned her attention to the beautiful sights and scents of the park, with its plethora of flowers, ornate water fountains and sculptures. No matter what transpired between them she would never forget her month's sojourn in this magical place, nor its matchless, timeless beauty, she vowed. Even now, on only the second day into her visit, she hated the thought of leaving...

'And Paolo says I can visit him again any time I want. He speaks Italian, but his mummy told me what he said. He's so nice, Daddy. I really, really like him!'

His little daughter had scarcely paused for breath since Ester had brought her home. She'd been talking so excitedly about her visit with Ester's son that she had hardly touched the wonderful food that Giovanna had prepared for them. She'd made spaghetti Bolognaise especially because Tia had requested it.

Seated at the rectangular oak table in the woodenbeamed dining room with its huge marble fireplace, Dante had never enjoyed a meal more. Never in his life had anything felt more right than being here in Italy with Anna and his daughter.

'Well, sweetheart,' he said, beaming down into Tia's

bright eyes, 'I'm sure you will see little Paolo again very soon. But now you should try and eat something, eh?'

She took a mouthful of food, chewed it thoughtfully, then gazed back at him. 'Paolo said his daddy was dead.'

Opposite him, Anna put her fork carefully down on her plate. Dante sensed her concern. 'I know, *piccolina*,' he replied gently, laying his hand over Tia's. 'He was a friend of mine, and it was very sad when he died.'

'Does that mean that you're going to die soon, Daddy?'

Swallowing hard, Dante felt the question hit him like an iron fist in the belly. Just the thought of being separated from his child and her mother any time soon made him want to hold them in the circle of his protection with all his might—and woe betide anyone who tried to rip him away!

'Nobody knows when they are going to die, my angel… But I'm sure that heaven is not ready for me yet—especially not when I need to be here to take care of my girls!'

His throat was cramped and sore as he lifted his glance to Anna's. Just when he wanted to say more, his mobile phone rang. Glancing down at the caller ID as he took it from his shirt pocket, he saw it was from the Mirabelle.

'I'm sorry, but I really should get this. It's from Jason at the hotel,' he explained, swiftly moving away from the table and out into the corridor.

'Is everything all right?'

It wasn't the Mirabelle that was her topic of choice, Anna reflected as Dante came back into the room. What he'd said about needing to be here for her and Tia had touched her heart as nothing had ever done before, and now, setting eyes on his incredible sculpted features and winter-coloured gaze, she had an almost painfully irresistible desire to touch him and hold him. But he was holding out his phone to her, looking slightly perturbed.

'Everything at the hotel is fine... He just wanted to update me on the latest developments. Jason would like to speak with you.'

'Oh...'

Getting to her feet, and uncomfortably sensing Dante's disapproving gaze as he handed her the mobile, Anna followed his example and went out into the imposing corridor with its wall-mounted chandeliers and softly glowing lamps to take the call.

'Hi, Jason...what's up?'

'A couple of things.' His voice was friendly, but concerned. 'I heard that you were in Como with Dante. How's it going?'

'You know about me and Dante?'

'Mum and Dad told me yesterday. It was a shock, but I've had a funny feeling something's going on between the two of you ever since he showed up. Is it true that he's Tia's father?'

'Yes, it's true.'

Jason was a great colleague, and a friend, but she braced herself for his possible condemnation and hoped that if and when it came she could stay calm.

She heard him sigh. 'It must have been so hard for you, raising Tia all alone and not feeling able to contact Dante to let him know that you were pregnant. If I loved someone that much I could no more keep it to myself than fly to the moon!'

Mentally, Anna did a double-take, but her gaze was caught by the shining disc of the full moon reflecting off the dark lake outside the open casement window where the scent of heady Mediterranean blossoms floated in. Her heart squeezed with the magic of it all.

'What do you mean "if I loved someone"?'

'I can see now that you're crazy about him, that's all. You wouldn't be in Como with him if you weren't. I'm glad for you—so glad. There's nobody I know who deserves to have a happy ending more than you!'

'I *do* love him, Jason…you're right.' Acceptance and acknowledgement of her deepest feelings lapped through her like a warm velvet wave, and she crossed her arm over her waist as if to hug herself.

'So…when will the happy day be?'

'What?'

'If the man hasn't asked you to marry him then he needs his head tested.'

Chewing anxiously down on her lip, Anna glanced towards the not quite closed heavy oak door of the dining room and moved a little bit farther away from it. 'He did ask me to marry him, but I suggested we have a trial period of living together first.'

'What on earth for?'

'It makes sense, doesn't it?'

'When did loving someone ever make sense?'

To Anna's amusement, Jason sounded almost exasperated with her.

'If you love him and he loves you, and you already have the most adorable little girl together, then what's the point in having a trial period? You should be beating a path over the sun-baked cobblestones to the nearest church and sending us all invitations to the wedding quicker than I can say *la dolce vita*!'

'Should I?' she smiled. This new enthusiasm she was hearing in his voice was infectious. 'You said there were a couple of things... What else did you want to say?'

'I just wanted to let you know that included in the hotel modernisation your flat is to be converted too. I hope I haven't put my foot in it by telling you that— maybe Dante's told you about it already?'

Anna frowned. 'No, he hasn't. This is the first I've heard about it. What about all my stuff? I don't want all my belongings just thrown somewhere!'

'Don't be daft. I'll make sure everything is stored away safely—you know I will. There was just one other thing before I go.'

'Not another bombshell, I hope?'

'It's a surprise more than a bombshell. You know we were talking about romance just now...?'

The joy in his voice was hard to mistake, and Anna's curiosity grew.

'Don't keep me in suspense, Jason—tell me!'

'I think I've found my soul-mate.'

'You have? Oh, my God!' She squealed into the phone in sheer delight.

CHAPTER TWELVE

DANTE waited until Tia was in bed before confronting his fears about Anna's phone conversation with Jason Cathcart. She was sitting in front of the ornate dressing table mirror in her robe, brushing out her long fiery hair, when he walked up behind her and placed his hands on her slender shoulders. The material of the robe was thin enough for him to feel the shape of her bones, and beneath his touch he sensed her stiffen.

He wanted to say something like, *You sounded happy when you spoke to Jason,* but instead the words that came out of his mouth were sharp, bordering on accusing. 'What did Jason want? He had no business wanting to talk to you about work while you're on leave.'

Watching her expression in the dressing table mirror, he saw the satin-smooth skin between her brows pucker. 'Not even to tell me that my flat is being converted while I'm away and all my stuff is being put into storage?'

His hands reluctantly fell away as she turned to accusingly look up at him. 'I'm sorry I didn't get round to talking to you about that. With so much going on I—'

'Slipped your mind, did it? I can't pretend I'm not cross about this, Dante, because I am. That's my home that's being dismantled while I'm away.'

The subject really *had* slipped his mind since they'd arrived, and now Dante could have kicked himself. He knew how important her own place was to Anna, but there was something else he'd planned without telling her too.

It seemed now was the time to confess all.

Shaking his head slightly, he moved away across the floor. 'I owe you an apology...a big one, I know. But with the extensive refurbishment and modernisation going on at the hotel you couldn't expect your flat not to be included. However, I also want to tell you that I plan to buy a house for you and Tia—independent of whether you agree to move in with me permanently or not. A real place of your own that will come with no conditional strings attached and will be yours to do exactly what you like with.'

Without a doubt Anna was taken aback. Coiling her hair behind her ear, she didn't reply straight away, but seemed to be collecting her thoughts. When she did finally speak her expression was as touched and surprised as a small child upon whom a gift she'd never dreamt would be hers had been bestowed. 'You don't have to do that. It's an extremely generous gesture—*too* generous, really—but—'

'I want to do it for you, Anna.' Returning to stand in front of her again, Dante knew he meant it in earnest.

'I never want you to feel that your home is dependent on anyone ever again—either your employers or even *me*.'

'I don't—I don't know what to say.'

He grinned. 'Just say thank you and we'll forget about it.'

'Thank you.'

'Was the flat being converted all that Jason wanted to talk to you about?'

For some reason the question made Anna smile. 'It wasn't, actually.'

'No?' Dante sensed his irritation return. 'Then what else did he want to talk about?'

'It was a personal matter.'

'And you're his only confidante?' He was tunnelling his fingers through his hair and pacing the floor in a bid to contain his temper.

'We're good friends as well as colleagues.' Her slightly husky tone was the epitome of reason and calmness, but Dante felt his insides twist with jealousy and frustration.

'Good friends?' he said mockingly, throwing his arms wide as he came to a stop in front of her again. 'Isn't the man capable of having a male friend for a confidant?'

'Your tone suggests you think he might fancy me. Is that what's bothering you, Dante?'

'Can you blame me if it is?'

'That sounds a little possessive to me, and I don't like

it. I want to be free to talk to who I like without you being suspicious of me. I do have integrity, you know, and if I give my word that something is true then you'd better believe it.'

'If I'm concerned when you share confidences with a young, good-looking male it doesn't mean I'm trying to control or possess you. It simply means that I'm the man who has your best interests at heart, and naturally I care about who you associate with. You're the mother of my child, after all. That gives me certain rights whether you like it or not.'

Sighing, Anna fell silent for a moment, then got to her feet. 'Rights to discuss what's best for her as her father, yes,' she said. 'But those rights don't include trying to control *me*.'

'*Il mio Dio!*' He stared at her in disbelief. 'Did you not hear what I just said? I'm not trying to control you. Just because your father treated your mother like some—some possession he could do as he liked with, it doesn't mean that I'm cut from the same poor-quality cloth! I understand how the possibility of me being like that might scare you, Anna...' Moving closer to her, Dante slipped his hand onto her shoulder again, his heart pounding as though the starting pistol at a race had just cracked against his ear. 'I know you have great integrity, and I do believe you when you tell me that Jason is just a friend.' His lips stretched ruefully. 'But I can't help feeling a little jealous when I hear you being so animated on the phone with him.'

'Well, there's no need to be jealous.'

Her lustrous brown eyes had grown even darker, and her tone was soft, almost caressing. Now Dante's heart pounded hard for another reason. Dared he trust what he thought he saw in those silky warm depths?

Anna sighed. 'Jason told me that he's found his soulmate at last and he's in love.'

'Really?' Relief was like a dam bursting inside him.

'I was so happy for him, because he'd started to lose faith in finding the love of his life. I told him the perfect person was just waiting somewhere, and that when the time was right, they would appear. So all's well that ends well, as they say.'

'And do you believe that the perfect person is waiting for every one?'

'I do.'

'I didn't realise you were such a romantic.'

'There's a lot of things you don't realise about me, Dante!'

Now she had a maddeningly secret smile playing about her lips, and he was plunged into confusion again. If he lived to be a hundred he would never understand women...never! All she seemed to want to do was torment him.

'Is there something else you have to tell me? If there is, for pity's sake just come out and say it.' He scowled at her.

'First of all, Jason would never fancy me because

I'm the wrong sex, and secondly...I've found my own perfect person. Yes, and he's standing right here in front of me. So, Signor Romano...there wasn't the remotest need for you to be jealous.'

Looping her arms around him, she planted an achingly moist and provocative kiss against his lips. Desire was like a thunderbolt flashing through him. Catching her by the waist, Dante impelled Anna urgently against his already hardening body. Beneath the ridiculously thin robe she wore an equally insubstantial nightgown with shoestring straps. He was already visualising tearing off both garments and having her firmly beneath him.

'Marry me.' His lips, tongue and teeth clashed voraciously with hers as heat, want and devastating need broke all their bounds. Breaking off the kiss with a harsh affected breath, he cupped her face to stare deeply into her eyes. 'You *have* to marry me, Anna.'

'Of course I do... That's what I want too.'

Words failed him. All he could do right then was stare at her in wonder. Then, when he trusted he could speak, he raised his eyebrow and asked, 'When did you decide that?'

'The first time we were together, of course—when I saw you sitting in the lounge bar looking so handsome, indomitable and fierce. I knew the intimidating facade you projected wasn't the truth. Underneath I sensed you were hurting so bad you didn't know where to go or what to do. I suppose I grew up having a finely tuned antenna for people's pain. My mum's marriage was so hurtful and destroying, how could I help it?' Her eyes turned moist for a moment. 'But she believed in true love. I don't know how she held on to such a belief when she was married to a man like my father, yet she did. And she wanted the very best for me. She always told me that when I gave myself to a man it should be to the man I love. I want you to know that I do love you, Dante... I always have and always will.'

'And you forgive me?'

'For what?'

'For not trying to contact you and then changing my name, not knowing or *believing* that you might want to contact *me*, or that you would even *want* to see me again after my telling you we could only have one night together?'

'We've both made mistakes. If we can't forgive each other and move on then it's hopeless. That's not a message I want to give our daughter—that if she makes a mistake there'll be no forgiveness.'

'*Ti amo.*' Dante smiled, his lips visiting a series of heartfelt passionate little kisses on her eyelids, nose, cheeks and mouth. 'I love you, Anna, with all my heart and soul. Sometimes I think love is not a strong enough word to express how I feel. That evening in the hotel bar I thought I was incapable of feeling anything remotely warm towards another human being again, but you proved me wrong. Yes...' His voice grew tender. 'You reached out to me so unselfishly, even accepting my little speech about not being able to offer you anything else but that one night. And then, like an idiot, I let you go. I've had to come to terms with some hard losses in my life, but if I lost you again… If I lost Tia now that I've discovered her…I don't think I would ever recover.'

'Well, you're not going to lose either of us, my love.'

'Is that a promise?'

With her heart in her eyes, Anna nodded. 'I swear it.'

Leaving her for just a moment, Dante crossed the room to the panel beside the door and turned down the lights. A warm scented breeze blew in off the lake.

'You can turn them off completely. There's a ravishing full moon shining just outside the window. Didn't you see it?'

Going to the balcony doors, Anna pushed them opened a little wider. For a few seconds she stepped outside to stare up at the moonlit sky. A sliver of white cloud was drifting lazily across the fiercely bright orb in the inky darkness, just as if some divine artist had painted it right there, right at that moment, for her to see. The illuminating and magical scene made her shiver with delicious anticipation.

Joining her, Dante urged her back against his warm hard chest. As Anna relaxed against him he undid the belt of her robe and slipped the garment from her shoulders. The robe was immediately cast aside onto a nearby wrought-iron chair. Then, through the paper-thin cotton of her nightdress, he cupped her breasts.

The heat from his hands, the perfect weight and shape of them against her most tender flesh, made Anna arch into his palms, her nipples puckering and hardening. Catching the rigid velvet tips between thumb and forefinger, he squeezed and tugged a little, arousing a volcanic need that poured into her centre like liquid honey heated over the hottest flame. Pressing himself against her bottom, Dante left her in no doubt he was as turned on by their arousing foreplay as she was.

Turning into his arms, Anna urgently tore at the buttons on his shirt, making him smile as in her haste her fingers fumbled and missed the openings, causing her to curse softly beneath her breath.

'What are you trying to do to me, my angel?' he mocked gently, his hollowed out cheekbones emphasised even more by that devastatingly handsome smile.

'I'm trying to get you naked! What do you think I'm trying to do?'

With one fluidly mesmerising movement, Dante ripped his hand down the centre of the fine linen material and made the buttons fly off into the unknown.

Face to face with his magnificent tanned chest, the ripple of smooth sculpted muscle over a strong defined ribcage, Anna pressed a slow, loving kiss onto the warm hard flesh matted softly with dark blond hair. Then his hands were entwined in her hair, and he lifted her head up so that he could once again claim her lips with a demanding, almost savagely passionate kiss of his own.

'When you get me naked,' he said, the timbre of his voice sounding as though it had rolled over sun-baked gravel, 'what do you intend to do with me, *innamorata*?'

Looking straight into his moonlit blue-grey eyes, Anna smiled. 'I'm going to keep you awake until the early hours of the morning…and I should tell you that I've got an extremely vivid imagination. How do you like the sound of that?'

Dante nodded. 'I like it very much, you little witch. As long as you don't fall asleep on me when I take you on the little outing I have planned for us tomorrow.'

'Oh? Where would that be?'

'I'm taking you to see my mother's house.'

'You are?'

'I want to show you what I've done with it…the new use I've put it to.'

'I'm intrigued. I would love to see where your mother lived, Dante…to get a sense of the person she was. I know she meant the world to you.'

'Well, tomorrow you will. But right now…' He fixed her with the most meltingly wicked gleam she'd ever seen. Then he scooped one strong arm under her bottom, another round her waist, and lifted her high into his arms, so that she was suddenly on even more intimate terms with his eye-catching masculine chest and his drugging male heat. 'Right now I am taking you to bed...any objections?'

Anna gulped, her heart drumming hard. 'No...I can honestly say I've no objections at all, Signor Romano.'

Brimming with anticipation, along with a genuine sense of excitement, Dante hoped that Anna and Tia would enjoy the visit he had planned to the villa on the other side of the lake.

The house he had brought them to, across the water in a luxurious motorboat, sat almost majestically back from the lakeshore, its frontage a long verdant garden that ran down to its own landing stage. He was about to reveal something about himself that he had revealed to less than a handful of friends and acquaintances, and he wanted Anna to love it. Apart from fathering his lovely daughter, it was the achievement he was most proud of.

'This was where your mother lived?' Anna commented interestedly as he helped first Tia then her out of the boat. 'It's got to be one of the prettiest villas I've seen since I've been here.'

And it *was*, Dante silently acknowledged with pride, letting his gaze travel over the ancient olive trees and tubs of glorious red, white and pink bougainvillaea dotted all around. His loving glance strayed helplessly to his bewitching wife-to-be, with her dazzling copper hair, and his lovely daughter, with her sunlit blond curls, and he knew he was the luckiest man in the world.

He pocketed the motorboat key and reached for Anna's and Tia's hands. 'Let's go and take a look inside, shall we?'

'Do you have someone looking after the place?'

'Wait and see,' he answered mysteriously, urging them cheerfully onwards.

A young woman who looked like some avant garde artist, with wild dark hair, kohl-lined eyes and row of hooped gold earrings dangling from each ear, opened the door to them with a sweet-faced baby on her hip. A burst of animated Italian issued immediately when she recognised Dante, and she flung her arms around him with obvious affection and delight.

Fielding the little stab of jealousy that pricked her, Anna strove to hold on to the ready smile she'd adopted in anticipation of meeting whoever lived in the house now. Dante made the introductions, and the young woman who went by the enchanting name of Consolata hugged Anna and Tia in turn, making much of both Anna's and her daughter's eye-catching hair. Anna's anxiety dissipated.

'Come in...yes, you must come inside,' the girl urged in enthusiastic halting English.

They stepped into the most stunning glass-roofed vestibule. It reminded Anna of one of the greenhouses for exotic and tropical plants at Kew Gardens. It was so unique and beautiful that for a few moments she didn't know what to say. *What was this place? And who was Consolata?*

Glancing at Tia, whose hand was being firmly held by her handsome father, she smiled reassuringly. But her amazingly relaxed daughter was taking everything in her stride, glancing round the glass-roofed vestibule with wonder in her big blue-grey eyes, clearly loving every second of her visit already.

A warm kiss at the side of her cheek, an intoxicating drift of musky aftershave and Dante captured Anna's hand as well. 'My mother loved this place,' he explained softly. 'See that portrait over the marble fireplace? That's a picture of her that I had commissioned when she turned sixty. She was still very beautiful.'

'I can see that,' Anna murmured, gazing up at the stunning oil painting of a woman easily as bewitching as Sophia Loren—in fact, she didn't look dissimilar.

'When I returned to Italy, almost a year after her funeral, I had it in my mind to do something in memory of her—something that she would have been proud to be a part of. I spoke with Giovanna, and she told me of the problem of some of her daughter Ester's friends who are all single mothers. She then introduced me to Consolata, and some of the other young women who are struggling to raise children on their own. I donated the house to them, so that they could all live here and raise their babies knowing they were somewhere safe and secure that wouldn't be taken away from them. Giovanna manages the place, and the children and the mothers adore her. As well as five self-contained apartments in the building, there's a communal area and two large playrooms. All the women have access to local advisory and support services. Shall we go and meet some of them?'

All Anna could do was nod dumbly. Inside, she was deluged with so much pride and joy that she could scarcely contain it. She'd always suspected that the man she loved had the biggest heart, but nothing could have prepared her for *this*. What an amazing, wonderful and generous gift! What mother wouldn't be bursting with pride at having such a son? He had honoured his mother's memory in the most touching and incredible way.

Having experienced the challenges of single parenthood, Anna guessed how much such a place like this must mean to all those mothers. It also told her how deeply Dante must have been affected by his own experience of being the son of a mother who had struggled to raise him alone. But now the man had turned his childhood adversity into something positive and inspirational for the good of others.

Curling her hand more deeply into the curve of his palm, she knew what she was feeling blazed from her eyes as she gazed back at him. Instead of fearing that marriage might mean a loss of her independence and autonomy she was now actively looking forward to joining her life with this man. And when the time came to say her vows at their wedding she would utter them with absolute conviction and love...

* * *

Leaving the yacht in the harbour, the small group of well-wishers dressed in all their finery, including a couple of professional photographers, joyfully followed the bride-to-be and her groom on foot through a small network of cobbled streets to the plain whitewashed church on the hill, with its simple wooden cross.

Halfway there Anna laughingly took off her ludicrously expensive designer shoes, because the heels kept getting stuck between the cobblestones. But she didn't mind one bit. The sun was shining and the cloudless sky was a majestic azure blue—the kind of sky you dreamed of having on your wedding day. Everything was a good omen today. She couldn't have found a bad one if she'd tried.

With the straps of her cream-coloured shoes swinging from her fingers as they mounted the stone steps to the church, Anna glanced round at her daughter. Tia was holding on to the delicate tulle train of her mother's medieval-style ivory wedding dress as though guarding it from thieves or marauders intent on snatching it away from her. The expression on her angelic little face was one of intense concentration.

They stopped for a few moments on the steps as Dante gently but firmly pulled Anna into his side. On this, their wedding day, the mere sight of her husband-to-be stalled her heart. His suit was ivory-coloured linen, and beneath it his shirt was pristine white. Pushing aside some floppily perfect sun-kissed blond hair from his brow, Anna briefly bit down on her lip, then smiled.

Today his amazing eyes weren't the colour of winter. Instead they had the hue of a calm blue lake in midsummer, and here and there the glint of dazzling diamonds shone from their depths.

'You take my breath away, Dante Romano, and it's not just because you look good enough to eat.'

He brought her hand up to his lips and kissed it, avidly observing her from beneath his lashes. 'And I am in awe of your beauty and goodness, Anna mine. Today really *is* the best day of my life…so far—because from here on in it can only get better and better.'

A couple of camera flashes went off, and Grant Cathcart—bowled over by Anna's request for him to stand as father of the bride and give her away—called out, 'Hey, you two. The kissing's meant to happen *after* the wedding…not before it!'

'Yes, Mummy and Daddy—didn't you even know *that*?' Hand on hip, Tia let go of the train of Anna's dress for a moment and affected exasperation. As her parents and guests laughed, her look of exasperation was quickly replaced by one of horror as she saw the ivory train trailing over the stone steps. She grabbed it up again. 'I hope this hasn't got dirty—because if it has then I shall be *very* cross with both of you!' she declared.

'How on earth did we produce such a bossy child?' Dante laughed.

'It's got to come from *your* side.' Anna grinned. '*I*

was the personification of sweetness and light, growing up.'

His eyes narrowing, Dante tipped his head to the side, pretending to be doubtful. 'You sure about that, *innamorata*? Only I definitely recall one or two memorable occasions when the ability to be bossy seemed to come very naturally to you.'

'I'll make sure you pay for that remark later,' she whispered, her mouth trembling with humour as Dante once again pulled her towards him.

Hefting a noisy sigh, Tia turned round to the guests gathered at the base of the steps, in her ivory-coloured bridesmaid dress and pretty crown of delicate flowers, and threw up her hands. 'Everybody hurry up and go inside the church—before they kiss *again*!'

WEALTHY AUSTRALIAN, SECRET SON

MARGARET WAY

USA TODAY bestselling author **Margaret Way** was born and raised in the River City of Brisbane, capital of Queensland, Australia. A conservatorium-trained professional musician, in 1969 she decided to fulfil a childhood dream to write a book and have it published. She submitted a manuscript to the iconic publishing firm of Mills & Boon in London. To her delight, the manuscript received immediate acceptance. The first book, published in 1970, *King Country*, was an outstanding success, heralding the start of a long and very successful career. The author hopes and believes the two goals she set herself since the beginning of her writing career have been achieved. First and foremost, to bring pleasure and relaxation to her global readership; second, to open up a window to the world on her own beautiful, unique country, captivating the hearts of her readers as they identify with rural and outback Australia and the Dreamtime culture of its Australian indigenous people. An award-winning author of more than one hundred and thirty books, published in one hundred and fourteen countries in thirty-four languages, Margaret Way is a three-time finalist in the Romance Writers of Australia's RUBY Award.

CHAPTER ONE

The present

IT WAS an idyllic day for a garden party. The sky was a deep blue; sparkling sunshine flooded the Valley; a cooling breeze lowered the spring into summer heat. A veritable explosion of flowering trees and foaming blossom had turned the rich rural area into one breathtakingly beautiful garden that leapt at the eye and caught at the throat. It was so perfect a world the inhabitants of Silver Valley felt privileged to live in it.

Only Charlotte Prescott, a widow at twenty-six, with a seven-year-old child, stood in front of the bank of mirrors in her dressing room, staring blindly at her own reflection. The end of an era had finally arrived, but there was no joy in it for her, for her father, or for Christopher, her clever, thoughtful child. They were the dispossessed, and nothing in the world could soothe the pain of loss.

For the past month, since the invitations had begun to arrive, Silver Valley had been eagerly anticipating the Open Day: a get-to-know-you garden party to be held in the grounds of the grandest colonial mansion in the valley, Riverbend. Such a lovely name, Riverbend! A private house, its grandeur reflected the wealth and community standing of the man who had built it in the 1880s, Charles

Randall Marsdon, a young man of means who had migrated from England to a country that didn't have a splendid *past*, like his homeland, but in his opinion had a glowing *future*. He'd meant to be part of that future. He'd meant to get to the top!

There might have been a certain amount of bravado in that young man's goal, but Charles Marsdon had turned out not only to be a visionary, but a hard-headed businessman who had moved to the highest echelons of colonial life with enviable speed.

Riverbend was a wonderfully romantic two-storey mansion, with a fine Georgian façade and soaring white columns, its classic architecture adapted to climatic needs with large-scale open-arched verandahs providing deep shading for the house. It had been in the Marsdon family—*her* family—for six generations, but sadly it would never pass to her adored son. For the simple reason that Riverbend was no longer theirs. The mansion, its surrounding vineyards and olive groves, badly neglected since the Tragedy, had been sold to a company called Vortex. Little was known about Vortex, except that it had met the stiff price her father had put on the estate. Not that he could have afforded to take a lofty attitude. Marsdon money had all but run out. But Vivian Marsdon was an immensely proud man who never for a moment underestimated his important position in the Valley. It was *everything* to him to keep face. In any event, the asking price, exorbitantly high, had been paid swiftly—and oddly enough without a single quibble.

Now, months later, the CEO of the company was finally coming to town. Naturally she and her father had been invited, although neither of them had met any Vortex representative. The sale had been handled to her father's satisfaction by their family solicitors, Dunnett & Banfield. Part of the deal was that her father was to have tenure of the Lodge—originally an old coach house—during his lifetime, after which it would be returned to the estate. The coach house had been converted and greatly enlarged by her grandfather into a beautiful and comfortable guest house that had enjoyed a good deal of use in the old days, when her grandparents had entertained on a grand scale, and it was at the Lodge they were living now. Just the three of them: father, daughter, grandson.

Her former in-laws—Martyn's parents and his sister Nicole—barely acknowledged them these days. The estrangement had become entrenched in the eighteen months since Martyn's death. Her husband, three years older than she, had been killed when he'd lost control of his high-powered sports car on a notorious black spot in the Valley and smashed into a tree. A young woman had been with him. Mercifully she'd been thrown clear of the car, suffering only minor injuries. It had later transpired she had been Martyn's mistress for close on six months. Of course Martyn hadn't been getting what he'd needed at home. If Charlotte had been a loving wife the tragedy would never have happened. The *second* major tragedy in her lifetime. It seemed very much as if Charlotte Prescott was a jinx.

Poor old you! Charlotte spoke silently to her image. *What a mess you've made of your life!*

She really didn't need anyone to tell her that. The irony was that her father had made just as much a mess of his own life—even before the Tragedy. The *first* tragedy. The only one that mattered to her parents. Her father had had little time for Martyn, yet he himself was a man without insight into his own limitations. Perhaps the defining one was unloading responsibility. Vivian Marsdon was constitutionally incapable of accepting the blame for anything. Anything that went wrong was always someone else's fault, or due to some circumstance beyond his control. The start of the Marsdon freefall from grace had begun when her highly respected grandfather, Sir Richard Marsdon, had died. His only son and heir had not been able to pick up the reins. It was as simple as that. The theory of three. One man made the money, the next enlarged on it, the third lost it. No better cushion than piles of money. Not every generation produced an heir with the Midas touch, let alone the necessary drive to manage and significantly enlarge the family fortune.

Her father, born to wealth and prestige, lacked Sir Richard's strong character as well as his formidable business brain. Marsdon money had begun to disappear early, like water down a drain. Failed pie-in-the-sky schemes had been approached with enthusiasm. Her father had turned a deaf ear to cautioning counsel from accountants and solicitors alike. He knew best. Sadly, his lack of judgement had put a discernible dent in the family fortunes. And that was even before the Tragedy that had blighted their family life.

With a sigh of regret, Charlotte picked up her lovely hat with its wide floppy brim, settling it on her head. She rarely wore her long hair loose these days, preferring to pull it back from her face and arrange it in various knots. In any case, the straw picture hat demanded she pull her hair back off her face. Her dress was Hermes silk, in chartreuse, strapless except for a wide silk band over one shoulder that flowed down the bodice and short skirt. The hat was a perfect colour match, adorned with organdie peonies in masterly deep pinks that complemented the unique shade of golden lime-green.

The outfit wasn't new, but she had only worn it once, at Melbourne Cup day when Martyn was alive. Martyn had taken great pride in how she looked. She'd always had to look her best. In those days she had been every inch a *fashionista*, such had been their extravagant and, it had to be said, *empty* lifestyle. Martyn had been a man much like her father—an inheritor of wealth who could do what he liked, when he liked, if he so chose. Martyn had made his choice. He had always expected to marry her, right from childhood, bringing about the union of two long-established rural families. And once he'd had her—he had always been mad about her—he had set about making their lifestyle a whirl of pleasure up until his untimely death.

From time to time she had consoled herself with the thought that perhaps Martyn, as he matured, would cease taking up endless defensive positions against his highly effective father, Gordon, come to recognise his family responsibilities and then pursue them with some skill and determination.

Sadly, all her hopes—and Gordon Prescott's—had been killed off one by one. And she'd had to face some hard facts herself. Hadn't she been left with a legacy of guilt? She had never loved Martyn. Bonded to him from earliest childhood, she had always regarded him with great affection. But *romantic* love? Never! The heart wasn't obedient to the expectations of others. She *knew* what romantic love was. She *knew* about passion—dangerous passion and its infinite temptations—but she hadn't steered away from it in the interests of safety. She had totally succumbed.

All these years later her heart still pumped his name. *Rohan.*

She heard her son's voice clearly. He sounded anxious. "Mummy, are you ready? Grandpa wants to leave."

A moment later, Christopher, a strikingly handsome little boy, dressed in a bright blue shirt with mother-of-pearl buttons and grey cargo pants, tore into the room.

"Come on, come on," he urged, holding out his hand to

her. "He's stomping around the hall and going red in the face. That means his blood pressure is going up, doesn't it?"

"Nothing for you to worry about, sweetheart," Charlotte answered calmly. "Grandpa's health is excellent. Stomping is a way to get our attention. Anyway, we're not late," she pointed out.

It had been after Martyn's death, on her father's urging, that she and Christopher had moved into the Lodge. Her father was sad and lonely, finding it hard getting over the big reversals in his life. She knew at some point she *had* to make a life for herself and her son. But where? She couldn't escape the Valley. Christopher loved it here. It was his home. He loved his friends, his school, his beautiful environment and his bond with his grandfather. It made a move away from the Valley extremely difficult, and there were other crucial considerations for a single mother with a young child.

Martyn had left her little money. They had lived with his parents at their huge High Grove estate. They had wanted for nothing, all expenses paid, but Martyn's father—knowing his son's proclivities—had kept his son on a fairly tight leash. His widow, so all members of the Prescott family had come to believe, was undeserving.

"Grandpa runs to a timetable of his own," Christopher was saying, shaking his golden-blond head. She too was blonde, with green eyes. Martyn had been fair as well, with greyish-blue eyes. Christopher's eyes were as brilliant as blue-fire diamonds. "You look lovely in that dress, Mummy," he added, full of love and pride in his beautiful mother. "Please don't be sad today. I just wish I was seventeen instead of seven," he lamented. "I'm just a kid. But I'll grow up and become a great big success. You'll have *me* to look after you."

"My knight in shining armour!" She bent to give him a

big hug, then took his outstretched hand, shaking it back and forth as if beginning a march. "Onward, Christian soldiers!"

"What's that?" He looked up at her with interest.

"It's an English hymn," she explained. Her father wouldn't have included hymns in the curriculum. Her father wasn't big on hymns. Not since the Tragedy. "It means we have to go forth and do our best. *Endure*. It was a favourite hymn of Sir Winston Churchill. You know who he was?"

"Of course!" Christopher scoffed. "He was the great English World War II Prime Minister. The country gave him a *huge* amount of money for his services to the nation, then they took most of it back in tax. Grandpa told me."

Charlotte laughed. Very well read himself, her father had taken it upon himself to "educate" Christopher. Christopher had attended the best school in the Valley for a few years now, but her father took his grandson's education much further, taking pride and delight it setting streams of general, historical and geographical questions for which Christopher had to find the answers. Christopher was already computer literate but her father wasn't—something that infuriated him—and insisted he find the answers in the books in the well-stocked library. Christopher never cheated. He always came up trumps. Christopher was a very clever little boy.

Like his father.

The garden party was well underway by the time they finished their stroll along the curving driveway. Riverbend had never looked more beautiful, Charlotte thought, pierced by the same sense of loss she knew her father was experiencing—though one would never have known it from his confident Lord of the Manor bearing. Her father was a handsome man, but alas not a lot of people in the Valley

liked him. The mansion, since they had moved, had under-
gone very necessary repairs. These days it was superbly
maintained, and staffed by a housekeeper, her husband—a
sort of major-domo—and several ground staff to bring the
once-famous gardens back to their best. A good-looking
young woman came out from Sydney from time to time,
to check on what was being done. Charlotte had met her
once, purely by accident...

The young woman had left her Mercedes parked off the
broad gravelled driveway so she could take a good look
at the Lodge, screened from view by a grove of mature
trees. Charlotte had been deadheading the roses when
her uninvited visitor—brunette, dark-eyed, in a glamorous black power suit worn with a very stylish snow-white
ruffled blouse—had near tumbled into view on her very
high heels.

"Oh, good afternoon! Hope I didn't startle you?" she'd
called, the voice loud and very precise.

Well, sort of, Charlotte thought. "You did rather," she
answered mildly. The woman's greeting had been pleasant enough. The tone wasn't. It was seriously imperative.
Charlotte might as well have been a slack employee who
needed checking up on. "May I help you?" She was aware
she was being treated to a comprehensive appraisal. A
head-to-toe affair.

The young woman staggered a few steps further across
the thick green grass, thoroughly aerating it. She had to
give up as the stiletto heels of her expensive shoes sank
with every step. "I don't think so. I'm Diane Rodgers, by
the way."

"Well, hello, Diane Rodgers," Charlotte said with a
smile.

Ms Rodgers responded to that with a crisp look. "I've
been appointed by the new owner to oversee progress at

Riverbend. I just thought I'd take a look at the Lodge while I was at it."

"May I ask if you're an estate agent?" Charlotte knew perfectly well she wasn't, but she was reacting to the tone.

"Of course I'm not!" Ms Rodgers looked affronted. An estate agent, indeed!

"Just checking. The Lodge is private property, Ms Rodgers. But I'm sure you know that."

"Surely you have no objection to my taking a look?" The question was undisguisedly sarcastic. "I'm not making an inspection, after all."

"Which would be entirely inappropriate," Charlotte countered.

"Excuse me?" Ms Rodgers's arching black brows rose high.

"No offence, Ms Rodgers, but this is *private* property." The woman already knew that and didn't care. Had she tried a friendly approach, things might have gone differently.

As it was, Diane Rodgers was clearly on a power trip.

She gave an incredulous laugh, accompanied by a toss of her glossy head. "No need to get on your high horse. Though I expect it's understandable. You couldn't bear to part with the place. Isn't that right? You're the daughter of the previous owner." It was a statement, not a question.

"Why would you assume that?" Charlotte resumed deadheading the exquisite deep crimson Ecstasy roses.

"I've *heard* about you, Mrs Prescott." The emphasis was heavy, the smile *knowing*—as if Charlotte's secret was out. She had spent time in an institution. Possibly mental. "You're every bit as beautiful as I've been told."

"Beauty isn't the be all and end all. There are more important things. But may I ask who told you that?" There was a glint in Charlotte's crystal-clear green eyes.

"Sorry, that would be telling. You know yourself how

people love to talk. But being rich and beautiful can't prevent tragedy from occurring, can it? I hear you lost a brother when you were both children. Then a husband only a while back. Must have been frightful experiences? Both?"

Charlotte felt her stomach lurch. Who had this remarkably insensitive young woman spoken to? Someone she'd met in the village? Nicole, Martyn's younger sister? Nicole had always resented her. If Ms Rodgers's informant *had* been Nicole she would have learned a lot—most of it laced with vitriol.

A moment passed. "I'm sure you heard about that too, Ms Rodgers," Charlotte said quietly. "Now, you must excuse me. I have things to do. Preparations for dinner, for one."

"Just your father and your son, I'm told?"

It was more or less a taunt, and it bewildered Charlotte. Why the aggression? The expression on Ms Rodgers's face was hardly compassionate. Charlotte felt a wave of anger flow over her. "I must go in, Ms Rodgers." She folded her secateurs, then placed them in the white wicker basket at her feet. "Do please remember in future the Lodge is off-limits."

Diane Rodgers had intended to sound coolly amused, but she couldn't for the life of her disguise her resentment—which happened to be extreme. Who *was* this Charlotte Prescott to be so hoity-toity? She had well and truly fallen off her pedestal. At least that was the word. "Suit yourself!" she clipped, making too swift an about turn. She staggered, and had to throw a balancing arm aloft, making for the safety of solid ground.

Everyone appeared to be dressed to the nines for the Open Day. Filmy pastel dresses and pretty wide-brimmed hats were all the rage. Women had learned to take shelter from

the blazing Australian sun. Sunscreen. Hats. Charlotte recalled how her mother had always looked after her skin,
making sure her daughter did the same. Early days. These
days her mother didn't talk to her often. Her mother didn't
talk to *anyone* from the old days. Certainly not her ex-
husband. Her parents had divorced two years after the
Tragedy. Her mother had remarried a few years after that,
and lived in some splendour in Melbourne's elite Toorak.
If she had ever hoped her mother would find solace in her
beautiful grandson, Christopher, she had been doomed to
bitter disappointment. There had only been *one* boy in her
mother's life: her pride and joy, her son Matthew.

"Mummy, can I please go off with Peter?" Christopher
jolted her out of her sad thoughts. Peter Stafford was
Christopher's best friend from day one at pre-school. He
stood at Christopher's shoulder with a big grin planted on
his engaging little face.

"I don't see why not." Charlotte smiled back. "Hello
there, Peter. You're looking very smart." She touched a
hand to his checked-cotton clad shoulder.

"Am I?" Peter blushed with pleasure, looking down at
his new clothes. Christopher had told him in advance he
was wearing long trousers, so Peter had insisted his mother
buy him a pair. His first. He felt very grown-up.

Christopher hit him mildly in the ribs. "You know
Mummy's only being nice."

"I *mean* it, Peter." Charlotte glanced over Peter's head.
"Mum and Dad are here?"

Peter nodded. "Angie too." Angie was his older sister.
"We had to wait ages for Angie to change her dress. I liked
the first dress better. Then she had to fix her hair again.
She was making Mum really angry."

"Well, I'm sure everyone has settled down," Charlotte
offered soothingly. She knew Angela Stafford—as difficult

a child as Peter was trouble-free. "We're all here to enjoy ourselves, and it's a beautiful day." Charlotte placed a loving hand on top of her son's head. "Check in with me from time to time, sweetheart?"

"Of course." He smiled up at her, searching her face in a near-adult way. "If you prefer, Pete and I can stay with you."

"Don't be silly!" she scoffed. "Off you go." Christopher— her little man!

The boys had begun to move away when Peter turned back. "I'm very sorry Riverbend is going out of the family, Mrs Prescott," he said, his brown eyes sweetly sympathetic. "Sorry for you *and* Mr Marsdon. Riverbend would have come to Chris."

Charlotte almost burst into tears. "Well, you know what they say, Peter," she managed lightly. "All good things must come to an end. But thank you. You're a good boy. A credit to your family."

"If *he* is, so am I!" Christopher crowed, impatiently brushing his thick floppy golden hair off his forehead. It was a gesture Charlotte knew well.

She turned her head away. She had to keep her spirits up. Her father was deeply involved in a conversation with the rotund, flush-faced Mayor. The Mayor appeared to be paying careful attention. The Marsdon name still carried a lot of clout. She walked on, waving a hand to those in the crowd who had stuck by her and her father.

Her parents' separation, and subsequent divorce, had split the Valley. Her beautiful, very dignified mother had chaired most of the Valley's charity functions, opening up the grounds of Riverbend for events much like today's. She had been well respected. Her father had never approached that high level of Valley approval, though he was supremely unaware of it such was his unshakeable self-confidence.

The Tragedy had torn her mother to pieces. Her father, grief-stricken, had managed to survive.

What exactly had happened to *her*? She had grown up knowing her mother loved her, but that Matthew, her older brother, the firstborn, was the apple of their mother's eye—her favourite. Her mother was the sort of woman who doted on a *son*. Charlotte hadn't minded at all. She had adored her brother too. Matthew had been a miraculously happy boy. A child of light. And he'd always had Rohan for his best friend. Rohan had been the young son of a single mother in the Valley—Mary Rose Costello.

Mary Rose, orphaned at an early age, had been "raised right" by her maternal grandmother, a strict woman of modest means, who had sent her very pretty granddaughter to the district's excellent convent school. Mary Rose Costello, with the Celt's white skin and red hair, had been regarded by the whole community as a "good girl". One who didn't "play around". Yet Mary Rose Costello, too young to be wise, had blotted her copybook by falling pregnant. Horror of horrors out of wedlock or even an engagement. The odd thing was, in that closely knit Valley, no one had been able to come up with the identity of Rohan's father. Lord knew they had all speculated, long and hard.

Mary Rose had never confided in anyone—including her bitterly shocked and disappointed grandmother. Mary Rose had never spoken the name of her child's father, but everyone was in agreement that he must have been a stunningly handsome man. And clever. Rohan Costello, born on the wrong side of the blanket, was far and away the handsomest, cleverest boy in the Valley. When Mary Rose's grandmother had died, she'd had the heart to leave her granddaughter and her little son the cottage. Mary Rose had then worked as a domestic in both the Marsdon and Prescott residences. She'd also done dressmaking. She had, in fact, been a very fine dressmaker, with natural skills. It was Charlotte's mother who had encouraged Mary Rose to take in orders, spreading the word to her friends across the Valley. So the Costellos had survived, given her mother's continuing patronage.

Up until the Tragedy.

People were milling about on the lush open lawn that stretched a goodly distance to all points of the compass, or taking shelter from the sun beneath the magnolia trees, heavy with plate-sized waxy cream flowers. Children were playing hide and seek amid the hedges; others romped on the grass. The naughty ones were running under the spray from the playing fountain until some adult stopped them before they got soaked. Everyone looked delighted to have been invited. A huge white marquee had been erected, serving delicious little crustless sandwiches, an amazing variety of beautifully decorated cupcakes, and lashings of strawberries and cream. White wine, a selection of fruit juices and the ubiquitous colas and soft drinks were also provided. No one would be allowed to get sozzled on alcohol that afternoon.

Charlotte had a few pleasant words with dozens of people as she threaded her way through the crowd. Her smile was starting to feel like a glaze on her face. It wasn't easy, appearing relaxed and composed, given the melancholy depths of her feelings, but she'd had plenty of practice. Years of containing her grief had taught control, if nothing else. Years of going down to breakfast with the Prescotts, a smile glued to her face, after another fierce encounter with Martyn. At such times he had hit her. Lashed out. Nowhere it would show. That would have caused an uproar. Though spoilt rotten by his mother and sister, his father would swiftly have taken him to account. Domestic violence was totally unacceptable. A man *never* hit a woman. It was unthinkable. Cowardly.

Only Martyn, who had turned out to be a bully, had desperately wanted what she could never give him. Her undivided love. He had even been jealous of Christopher. Had he ever dared lift a hand to her son she would have left him. But as it was, pride had held her in place. It wasn't as though she could have rung home and said, *I'm up to the neck with this marriage. I want out. I'm coming home.*

Her mother had been endeavouring to make a new life for herself elsewhere. Her father at that stage would have told her to "pull her socks up" and make her marriage work. It was only after Martyn had been killed and the scandalous circumstances were on public record that her father had welcomed her back—lonely, and totally unused to running a house. That was women's work. He'd detested the cleaning ladies who came in from time to time. His daughter would take over and cook him some decent meals. Such was his Lord of the Manor mentality. Besides, he loved his little grandson. "Chip off the old block!" he used to say, when Christopher unquestionably *wasn't*.

He took it for granted that Charlotte would stay, when she knew she could not. But when would the right time arrive? Christopher was now seven. No longer a small child.

Everyone was agog to meet the new mystery owner. So far he hadn't appeared, but an hour into the afternoon a helicopter suddenly flew overhead, disappearing over the roof of the mansion to land on the great spread of lawn at the rear of the house. Ten minutes later there was a little fanfare that got everyone's attention. A tall man, immaculately tailored with a red rosebud in his lapel, followed by no less a personage than Ms Diane Rodgers in full garden party regalia, came through the front door.

Even at a distance one could see this was someone quite out of the ordinary. He moved with lithe grace across the colonnaded verandah, coming to stand at the top of the short flight of stone stairs that led to the garden. His eyes surveyed the smiling crowd as he lifted a hand.

Immediately, enthusiastic clapping broke out. Here was their host at last! And didn't he look the part! They were just so thrilled—especially the children, who had stared up in wonderment at the big silver helicopter with its loud whirring rotors.

How is Dad going to handle this? Charlotte thought.

Her father revealed his class. He strolled out of the crowd, perhaps with a certain swagger, to greet the CEO of the company that had bought the ancestral home. "Come along, Charlotte," he commanded, as he drew alongside her. "It's just you and me now. Time to greet the new owner. I very much suspect he's more than just a CEO."

Unfailingly, Charlotte supported her father.

"My, he *is* a handsome man." Her father pitched his voice low. "And a whole lot younger than I would have expected," he tacked on in some surprise. "I fully anticipated someone in their late forties at least. Hang on—don't I know him?"

Charlotte couldn't say whether he did or he didn't. Even with the broad brim of her picture hat the slanting sun was in her eyes. But she did manage to put a lovely welcoming smile on her face. They were on show. Anyone who was anyone in the Valley was ranged behind them—every last man, woman and child keen observers of this meeting. This was an historic day. The Marsdons, for so long lords and ladies of the Valley, now displaced, were expected to act with grace and aplomb.

Except it didn't happen that way.

"Good God, Costello—it *can't* be you?" Vivian Randall bellowed like an enraged bull.

He came to such an abrupt halt Charlotte, slightly behind him, all but slammed into him, clutching at his arm to steady herself. She saw the blood draining out of her father's face. A hard man to surprise, he looked utterly pole-axed.

She, herself, had felt no portent of disaster. No inkling that another great turning point in her life had arrived. She couldn't change direction. She was stuck in place, with such a tangle of emotions knotted inside her they could never be untied.

There wasn't a flicker of answering emotion on the man's striking, highly intelligent face. "Good afternoon, Mr Marsdon," he said suavely, coming down the stone steps to greet them. Effortless charm. An overlay of natural command. His voice was cultured, the timbre dark. An extremely attractive voice. One people would always listen to. "Charlotte." He turned his head to look at her. Blazing blue eyes consumed her, the electric *blueness* in startling contrast to his colouring—crow-black hair and brows, olive skin that was tanned to a polished bronze. The searing gaze remained fixed on her.

She was swamped by an overwhelming sense of unreality.

Rohan!

The intervening years were as nothing—carried away as if by a king tide. The day of reckoning had come. Hadn't she always known it would? Her heart was pumping double time. The shock was devastating—too excruciating to be borne. She had thought she had built up many protective layers. Now she was blown away by her own emotional fragility. She tried to get her breath, slow her palpitating heart. She felt as weak as a kitten. She raised one trembling hand to her temple as a great stillness started to descend on her. She was vaguely aware she was slipping sideways...

No, no—don't give way! Hold up!

"Rohan!" she breathed.

He was as familiar to her as she was to herself. Yet he had never given a hint of warning—right up until this very day. It was cruel. Rohan had never been cruel. But it was abundantly clear he wanted to shock her far more than he wanted to shock her father. He wanted to stun *her* to her very soul. She read it in his dynamic face. Revenge, smoothly masked. But not to her. She knew him too well. So long as there was memory, the past lived on. One might long to forget, but memory wouldn't allow it.

Her pride broke.

"You do *this* to me, Rohan?" She knew she sounded pitiful. The immediate world had turned from radiant sunshine to a swirling grey fog. It smothered her like a thick blanket. Her ears seemed stuffed with cotton wool. She was moving beyond complete awareness, deeper into the fog, oblivious to the strong arms that shot out with alacrity to gather her up.

A little golden-haired boy ran out of the crowd, crying over and over in a panic, "Mummy...Mummy... Mummy!"

His grandfather, beside himself with sick rage, tried to catch him. The boy broke away, intent on only one thing: following the tall stranger who was carrying his beautiful mother back into the house.

This was the new owner of Riverbend! By now everyone was saying his name, turning one to the other, themselves in a state of shock.

Rohan Costello.

Fate had a way of catching up with everyone.

CHAPTER TWO

Silver Valley, summer fourteen years ago

IT WAS one of those endless afternoons of high summer—
glorious months of the school vacation, when the heat sent
them racing from the turquoise swimming pool in the mansion's grounds into the river. It meandered through the
valley and lay in a broad glittering curve at Riverbend's
feet. They knew they were supposed to keep to the pool
that afternoon, but it wasn't as though they weren't allowed
to take frequent dips in the river. After all, their father had
had a carpenter erect a diving dock for their pleasure. Prior
to that they had used a rope and an old tyre, fixed to stout
branches of a river gum to swing from.

She was twelve, and very much part of the Pack of Four,
as they had become known throughout the Valley. She
didn't feel honoured to be allowed to tag along with the
boys. She *was* one of them. All three boys were inseparable
friends: her older brother Mattie, Rohan—Mrs Costello's
son—a courtesy title insisted on by their mother, because
Mrs Costello was really a miss, but who cared?—and
Martyn Prescott, young son of the neighbouring estate,
High Grove. Charlotte was their muse.

Although she would have died rather than say it aloud,
Rohan was her shining white knight. She loved him. She

loved the burning blue looks he bent on her. But these days
a kind of humming tension had cut into their easy affection. Once or twice she'd had the crazy desire to kiss him.
Proof, if any were needed, that she was fast growing up.

Rohan easily beat them into the water that day, striking
out into the middle of the stream, the ripples on the dark
green surface edged with sparkles the sunlight had cast
on the river. "What's keeping you?" he yelled, throwing a
long tanned arm above water. "Come on, Charlie. You can
beat the both of them!"

He was absolutely splendid, Rohan! Even as a boy he
had a glamour about him. As her mother had once commented, "Rohan's an extraordinary boy—a born leader,
and so good for my darling Mattie!" In those early days
their mother had been very protective of her only son.

"Won't do him a bit of good, wrapping him in cotton
wool." That irritated comment always came from their
father, who was sure such mollycoddling was holding his
son back.

Perhaps he was right? But their mother took no notice.
Unlike her young daughter, who enjoyed splendid health,
Matthew had suffered from asthma since infancy. Mattie's
paediatrician had told their anxiety-ridden mother he would
most likely grow out of it by age fourteen. It was that kind
of asthma.

That fatal day Charlotte remembered running to the
diving dock, her long, silver-blonde hair flying around her
face. It was Martyn who had pulled her hair out of its thick
plait. It was something he loved to do. Most of the time she
rounded on him—"How stupid, Martyn!" was her usual
protest as she began to re-plait it.

"You look better that way, Charlie. One day you're going
to be an absolute knockout. Mum and Dad say that. Not

Nicole, of course. She's as jealous as hell. One day we're going to get married. Mum says that too."

"Dream on!" she always scoffed. Get married, indeed! Some husband Martyn would make.

Mattie always laughed, "Boy, has he got a crush on you, Charlie!"

She chose not to believe it. She didn't know then that some crushes get very crushed.

Rohan never laughed. Never joked about it. He kept silent on that score. The Marsdons and the Prescotts were the privileged children of the Valley. Certainly not Rohan Costello, who lived with his mother on the outskirts of town in a little cottage hardly big enough to swing a cat. Their mother said the pair would have to shift soon.

"Rohan is quickly turning into a man!"

At fourteen, nearing fifteen, it was apparent the fast-growing Rohan would easily attain six feet and more in maturity. Mattie, on the other hand, was small for his age. Rohan was by far the strongest and the best swimmer, though she was pretty good herself—but built for speed rather than endurance.

Totally unselfconscious, even with her budding breasts showing through her swimsuit and her long light limbs gleaming a pale gold, with Rohan—her hero—watching, she made a full racing dive into the water, striking out towards him as he urged her on, both of them utterly carefree, not knowing then that this was the last day they would ever swim in the river.

Years later she would shudder when she remembered their odd near-total absorption in one another that summer afternoon. A boy and a girl. One almost fifteen, the other twelve.

Romeo and Juliet.

Martyn appeared angry with them, sniping away. Jealous. Mattie was his normal sweet self. At one stage he called out that he was going to swim across to the opposite bank, where beautiful weeping willows bent their branches towards the stream.

"Stay with us, Mattie," Rohan yelled, cupping his hands around his mouth.

"What's the matter? Reckon I can't do it?" Mattie called back, sounding very much as if he was going to take up the challenge.

"'Course you can!" she had shouted, always mindful of her brother's self-esteem, undermined by his sickness. "But do like Rohan says, Mattie. Stay with us."

Mattie appeared persuaded. He turned in their direction, only then Martyn yelled, his voice loud with taunt, "Don't be such a cream puff, Marsdon! Are you always going to do what Mummy says? Are you always going to stick by Rohan's side? Rohan will look after Mummy's little darling. Isn't that his job? Go for it, Mattie! Don't be such a wimp!"

"Shut up, Martyn!" Rohan roared, in a voice none of them had ever heard before. It was an adult voice. The voice of command.

Immediately Martyn ceased his taunts, but Mattie confounded them all by kicking out towards the opposite bank, his thin arms stiff and straight in the water.

"Perhaps we should let him?" Charlotte had appealed to Rohan, brows knotted. "Mummy really does mollycoddle him."

"You can say that again!" Martyn chortled unkindly. Everyone in the Valley knew how protective Barbara Marsdon was of her only son.

"I'm going after him." It only took a little while of watching Mattie's efforts for Rohan to make the decision. "You shouldn't have taunted him, Martyn. You're supposed to be Mattie's friend. He's trying to be brave, but the brave way is the safest way. Mattie doesn't have your strength, or mine. He isn't the strongest of swimmers."

"He'll make it." Martyn was trying not to sound anxious, but his warier brain cells had kicked in. Rohan was right. He shouldn't have egged Mattie on. He went to say something in his own defence, only Rohan had struck out in his powerful freestyle while Charlotte followed.

Martyn chose to remain behind. He thought they were both overreacting. Mattie would be okay. Sure he would! The distance between the banks at that point wasn't all that wide. The water was warm. The surface was still. There was no appreciable undercurrent. Well, not really. The waters were much murkier on the other side, with the wild tangle of undergrowth, the heavy overhang of trees, the resultant debris that would have found its way into the river. For someone like Rohan the swim would be no more than a couple of lengths of the pool. But for Mattie?

Hell, they could be in the middle of a crisis, Martyn realised—too late.

One minute Mattie's thin arms were making silver splashes in the water, and then to their utter horror his head, gilded by sunlight, disappeared beneath the water.

All of a sudden the river that had taken them so many times into its wonderful cool embrace seemed a frightening place.

"Oh, God—oh, God!" Charlotte shrieked, knowing in her bones something was wrong. "Get him, Rohan!" she cried hysterically.

"Come on, don't be stupid, Charlie. He's only showing off," Martyn shouted at her, starting to feel desperately worried. The traumas of childhood had a way of echoing down the years. Martyn felt shivers of prescience shoot into his gut.

Charlotte ignored him, heart in her mouth. Martyn never was much good in a crisis. It was Rohan who knifed through the dark green water with the speed of a torpedo.

She went after him, showing her own unprecedented burst of speed. "God—oh, God!" Tears were pouring down her face, lost in river water.

There was no sign of Matthew. She knew he wouldn't be playing games. Matthew was enormously considerate of others. He would never frighten her, never cause concern to the people he loved. He loved her. He loved Rohan, his best friend. He wouldn't even have caused dread to Martyn, who had taunted him either.

"Mattie…Mattie *Mattie…!*" She was yelling his name at the top of her lungs, startling birds that took off in a kaleidoscope of colour.

Rohan too had disappeared, diving beneath the dark green water. She followed his example, fear reverberating deep within her body. Lungs tortured, she had to surface for air. As she came up she thought she saw something shimmering—a *shape* moving downstream. She went after it. Rohan beat her to it. She was screaming in earnest now. Rohan was cradling a clearly unconscious Mattie like a baby, holding him out of the water in his strong arms. A thin runnel of blood was streaming off Mattie's pale temple.

Fate could swoop like an eagle from a clear blue sky.

"I'll tow him to the bank," Rohan shouted to her. His voice was choked, his handsome young face twisted in terror. 'I'll try CPR. Keep at it. Charlie—get help."

But Mattie was gone. She *knew* it. Lovely, laughing Mattie. The best brother in the world.

A swim across the river. She could have done it easily. Yet Mattie might have plunged into a deep sea in the blackness of night. There was no sign of Martyn either. He must have run back to the house for help. She thought she might as well drown herself with Mattie gone. There would be no life at Riverbend now. Her mother would most likely go mad. She knew her father would somehow survive. But her mother, even if she could get through the years of annihilating grief, wouldn't stay within sight of the river where her adored Matthew had drowned. She would go away, leaving Charlotte and her father alone.

Except for the gentle shadow of Matthew Marsdon, who would always be fourteen.

The whole tragic thing would be blamed on someone. Her inner voice gave her the sacrificial name.

Rohan.

Rohan the born leader, who would be judged by her parents, the Prescotts, and a few others in the Valley resentful of the Costello boy's superior looks and high intelligence over their own sons, to have let Matthew Marsdon drown.

Such an intolerable burden to place on the shoulders of a mere boy. A crime, and Rohan Costello was innocent of the charge.

The present. The garden party.

Rohan Costello had returned to the scene of his childhood devastation. That showed passion and courage. It also showed that the cleverest boy in the Valley had become extraordinarily successful in life. Matthew Marsdon's tragic death had locked the daughter, Charlotte, and Costello even more closely together. Eventually they'd gone beyond the boundaries, but that had never been known, or if suspected never proved. What *was* known was that the Tragedy had never driven them apart—even when Charlotte's parents, in particular her mother Barbara, had burned with something approaching hatred for the boy she had in a way helped nurture.

There had only been one course left to the Costellos. Mother and son had been virtually driven out of the Valley, the sheer weight of condemnation too great.

The brutality of it!

People could only wonder if Rohan Costello had returned to Silver Valley to settle old scores? The past was never as far away as people liked to pretend.

Charlotte's faint lasted only seconds, but when she was out of it and the world had stopped spinning she was still in a state of shock, her body trembling with nerves. She was lying on one of the long sofas in the drawing room, her head and her feet resting on a pile of silk cushions. Her hair had all but fallen out of its elegant arrangement. She was minus her hat and, she noted dazedly, her expensive sandals.

Rohan was at her head. Christopher was at her feet. Diane Rodgers and a couple of her mother's old friends stood close by. Her mother's friends' watching faces were showing their concern. Not so Ms Rodgers, whose almond eyes were narrow. There was no sign of her father, but George Morrissey, their family doctor, hurried in, calling as he came, "Charlie, dear, whatever happened?"

Morrissey had brought the Marsdon children into the world, and Charlotte had always been a great favourite.

"How are you feeling now?" He sat down beside her to take her pulse. A few more checks, and then, satisfied there was nothing serious about the faint, he raised her up gently, while Rohan Costello, the new owner, resettled the cushions as a prop at her back.

"The heat, George," she explained, not daring to look up at Rohan, who had so stunningly re-entered her life. What she wanted to do was seize hold of her little son and run for her life. Except there was no escape. Not now. "I must be going soft."

"That'll be the day!" the doctor scoffed.

"Mummy?" Christopher's lovely olive skin had turned paper-white. "Are you all right?"

"I'm fine, darling." She held out a reassuring hand. "Come here to me." She tried hard to inject brightness into her voice. "I love you, Chrissie."

"Mummy, I love you too. You've never fainted before." He clutched her hand, staring anxiously into her face.

"I'm fine now, sweetheart. Just a little dizzy." She drew him down onto the spot Dr Morrissey had readily vacated, putting a soothing arm around him and dropping a kiss on the top of his golden head. "I'll get up in a minute."

"Give it a little longer, Charlie," Morrissey advised, happy to see her natural colour returning. He very much suspected extreme shock was the cause of Charlotte's faint. Incredible to think young Costello had become so successful. Then again, not. Rohan Costello *had* been an exceptionally bright lad.

"This *is* a surprise, Rohan," he said, turning to hold out his hand.

Rohan Costello took it in a firm grip. The doctor could hardly say, given the circumstances of Rohan Costello's departure, *Welcome back to Silver Valley*!

"It's good to see you again, Dr Morrissey," Rohan answered smoothly. "You were always kind to my mother and me."

"You were both very easy to be kind to, Rohan," Morrissey assured him with genuine warmth. "And how is your mother?"

"She's doing very well, sir," Rohan responded pleasantly, but it was obvious he wasn't going to be more forthcoming.

"Good, good! I'm very glad to hear it. Do you intend to spend much time in the Valley, Rohan?" Morrissey dared to ask. "You must have become a very successful businessman?"

Rohan gave him a half smile that bracketed his handsome mouth. "I've had a few lucky breaks, Doctor."

"I think it would have more to do with brain power. You were always very clever."

George Morrissey, the keeper of many secrets, turned back to take another look at Charlotte and her precious boy. What a beautiful child Christopher was, with those glorious blue eyes! One rarely saw that depth of colour. He had delivered Christopher Prescott, Charlotte's baby, who had come a little early. He was sure everyone had believed him. He was the most respected medical doctor in the Valley. After the tragic death of Charlotte's young brother Matthew, and the flight of her mother from the "haunted" Valley, he had become very protective of Charlotte Marsdon, who had gone on to marry a young man who in his opinion had simply not been worthy of her. Martyn Prescott—who himself had met a tragic fate.

Christopher too wanted to talk to the tall stranger—the man who had carried his mother so effortlessly into their house. Well, *his* house now. And it seemed to suit him just fine. Christopher was very thankful the *right* person would have ownership of Riverbend. He looked just the sort of man to look after it.

Christopher stood up, wondering why his mother was trying to grab hold of his arm. He held out his hand, as he had been taught. "Hello, I'm Christopher. We used to live here."

"I know that, Christopher," the man answered quietly, moving in closer.

The man's blue eyes made contact with his own, and Christopher felt transfixed. "Do you know Mummy?" He didn't see how the man could, yet those vibes he seemed to have inherited from someone told him this man and his mother knew one another well. It was a mystery, but there it was!

Charlotte put her feet to the floor, unsure if she could even stand, still not looking at Rohan but acutely aware that the full force of his attention was focused on her and her son. "Mr Costello is a very busy man, Chris," she said. Christopher was so sharp. "We mustn't keep him from mingling with his guests."

"No, Mummy." Christopher nodded his head in agreement, but continued with a further question. "*How* do you know my mother?" It seemed important he find out. Perceptive beyond his years, he felt the tension between his mother and the tall stranger. He couldn't figure it out. But it was *there*. Mummy was nice to everyone, yet she wasn't being exactly nice to Mr Costello. Something had to be worrying her.

"Your mother and I grew up together, Christopher," Rohan explained. "I left the Valley when I was seventeen. I'm Rohan. No need to call me Mr Costello."

"Oh, I'd like that," Christopher said, his cheeks taking on a gratified flush. "We thought you were going to be pretty old. But you're *young*!"

"Your mother has never mentioned me?"

Christopher shook his blond head. "Did you know my dad died?" He edged closer to the man. It was like being drawn by a magnet. It sort of *thrilled* him. He felt he could follow this man Rohan like the disciples in Bible stories had followed their Master. It both pleased and puzzled him.

"Yes, I did, Christopher. I'm very sorry." Rohan's voice was gentle, yet his expression was stern.

"There's just Mummy and me now." Christopher felt the sting of tears at the back of his eyes. He had loved his dad. Of course he had. One *had* to love one's dad. But never like he loved his mother. What was really strange was that he cared for his grumpy old grandfather more than he had cared for his dad. "And Grandpa, of course," he tacked on. "You must have known my dad and Uncle Mattie?"

"Oh, darling, not all these questions!" Charlotte spoke with agitation. He had sussed out enough already. Something had happened to Christopher of late. He was picking up on vibes, on looks and words that appeared to him laden with meaning. He was growing up too fast.

For once, Christopher didn't heed her. "Uncle Mattie is still around," he told Rohan, staring up at him. He was really surprised by the way he felt drawn to his man. "I often *feel* Uncle Mattie around."

Rohan didn't laugh or deride his claim. "I believe it, Christopher," he said. "I feel Mattie too, at different times. He would have *loved* you."

"Would he?" Christopher was immensely pleased. Uncle Mattie would have loved him! He was liking Rohan more and more. "Mummy said I looked like him when I was little." He continued to meet Rohan's amazing blue eyes. They glittered like jewels. "Do I?"

Rohan considered that carefully. "You might have, Christopher, when you were younger. But not now."

"No." Christopher shook his blond head, as though his own opinion had been confirmed. "I don't look like anyone, really," he confided.

Oh, yes, you do!

Charlotte kept her head down, her heart fluttering wildly in her breast. Christopher's face had changed as the baby

softness had firmed and his features became more pronounced. Heredity. It was all so *dangerous*.

It was Diane Rodgers who located Charlotte's expensive
sandals, then passed them to her in such a manner as to
suggest a hurry-up. There was a faint accompanying glare
as well. Charlotte bent to put her strappy sandals back on,
then made an attempt to fix her hair. She felt totally dis-
orientated. And there was Christopher, chattering away to
Rohan as if he had known him all his young life. It almost
broke her.

"Here's your hat, love." A familiar face swam into view.
Kathy Nolan—a good friend to her mother and a good
friend to her. "It's beautiful."

"Thank you, Kathy." Charlotte took the picture hat in
her hand.

"Feeling better now, love?" Kathy Nolan was very fond
of Charlotte.

"Much better, thank you, Kathy. I'm so sorry I embarrassed you all. The heat got to me."

Kathy, a kindly woman, let that go. A beautiful breeze
was keeping the temperature positively balmy. Charlotte
had fainted because Rohan Costello was the last man in
the universe she would have expected to buy the Marsdon
mansion, Kathy reckoned. To tell the truth she felt a little
freaked out herself. Rohan Costello, of all people! And
didn't he look *marvellous*! Always a handsome boy, the
adult Rohan took her breath away. Many people in the
Valley—herself and her husband certainly—had been unhappy when the Costellos had left after Rohan had completed his final year at secondary school. Later they had
learned he was their top achiever. The highest category.
No surprise.

Poor Barbara had never made allowances for the ages

of the other children when Mattie had drowned. It had been a terrible accident. With all the care in the world, accidents still happened. Yet Barbara had gone on a bitter, never-ending attack. So very sad! Loss took people in different ways. Bereft of her son, Barbara Marsdon had been in despair. That inner devastation had brought about the divorce. The marriage had been beyond repair. Barbara had told her she'd doubted her ability to be a good mother to Charlotte. She wasn't functioning properly. That had been true enough. Charlotte was to remain with her father.

Yet here was Rohan Costello, back in the Valley. Not only that, taking possession of Riverbend. Fact is far stranger than fiction, Kathy thought.

Diane Rodgers, looking very glamorous in classic white, with a striking black and white creation on her head, spoke up. "Would you like me to help you back to the Lodge, Mrs Prescott? No trouble, I assure you."

At the sound of those precise tones, Christopher swung back. "Mummy has *me*," he said, not rudely—he knew better than that—but he didn't like the way the lady was speaking to his mother. It didn't sound gentle and caring, like Mrs Nolan. It sounded more like teachers at his school when the kids weren't on their best behaviour.

"Wouldn't you like to stay on, Christopher?" Rohan suggested. "I'm sure you have a friend with you. I'll run your mother home."

Christopher considered that for a full minute. "I won't stay if you don't feel well, Mummy," he said, his protective attitude on show. "Peter will be okay."

Charlotte rose to her feet, hoping she didn't look as desperate as she felt. "Sweetheart, I don't want you to bother about me. I don't want *anyone* to bother about me. I'm fine."

"You're sure of that, Charlie?" Morrissey laid a gentle hand on her shoulder.

"You mustn't let me keep you, George." Charlotte gave him a shaky smile. "I know you and Ruth will love wandering around the grounds. They're in tip-top condition."

"That they are!" George Morrissey agreed. He turned back to the tall authoritative figure of the adult Rohan Costello. "I'd be delighted if you'd say hello to my wife, Rohan. She'd love to catch up."

"It would be a pleasure." Rohan gave a slight inclination of his handsome dark head.

The doctor lifted a hand in general farewell, then walked off towards the entrance hall.

"You must allow me to run you back to the Lodge at least, Charlotte," Rohan said, with a compelling undernote she couldn't fail to miss. "I'll make sure Chris gets home."

"Thank you, Rohan," Christopher piped up. "Can't take the helicopter, I suppose?" he joked, executing a full circle, arms outstretched. "Whump, whump, whump!"

"Not that far." Rohan returned the boy's entrancing smile. "But I promise you a ride one day soon."

Christopher looked blown away. "Gee, that's great! Wait until I tell Peter."

"Maybe Peter too," Rohan said.

"That'd be *awesome*! So where's Grandpa?" Christopher suddenly asked of his mother. "Why didn't he come into the house?"

"He may well be outside, Christopher," Rohan answered smoothly. "Why don't you go and see? Your mother is safe with me."

"Is that all right, Mummy? I can go?" Christopher studied her face. His mother was *so* beautiful. The most beautiful mother in the world.

"Of course you can, darling." Charlotte summoned up a smile. "I want you to enjoy yourself."

"Thank you." Christopher shifted his blue gaze back to Rohan. "It's great to meet you, Rohan." He put out his hand. Man to man.

Rohan shook it gravely. "Great to meet you too, Christopher," he responded. *At long last.*

Many things in life changed. Some things never did.

CHAPTER THREE

THEY were quite alone. It was terrifying. Was she afraid of Rohan? That simply couldn't be. But she was terrified of the emotions that must be raging through him. Terrified of the *steel* in him. Where had her beautiful white knight gone? A shudder ripped through her. This was a Rohan she had never seen.

The village ladies had gone back outside, to enjoy the rest of the afternoon. Diane Rodgers had hovered, but Rohan had given her a taut smile and told her in his dark mellifluous voice to go and take a look at the roses. They were in magnificent full bloom. Ms Rodgers looked as though she had been planning something entirely different. One would have had to be blind to miss Ms Rodgers's keen interest in Rohan. And who could blame her?

The pulverising shock had not worn off. Nor would it for a long time. Now she felt an added trepidation, and—God help her—the old pounding excitement. He looked wonderful. *Wonderful!* The man who had loved her and whom she had loved in return.

Rohan.

She saw how much she still loved him. No one else had ever mattered. But now wasn't the time to fall apart. She had to keep some measure of herself together. "I can walk back to the Lodge," she said, although her voice was reduced to a trembling whisper. "You don't have to take me."

"*Don't* I?"

The slash of his voice cut her heart to ribbons.

God—oh, God!

Recognition of the trouble she was in settled on her.

He took hold of her bare slender arm, pulling her in to his side. "He's *mine*, isn't he?" he ground out. His tone was implacable.

She wasn't up to this. She was a lost soul. She was acutely aware of the pronounced pallor beneath his golden-olive skin. He was in shock too. She wanted to touch his face. Didn't dare. She felt sorrow. Guilt. Pity. Remorse. Her heart was fluttering like a frantic bird in her breast. She had to try to evade the whole momentous issue. She needed time to *think*.

"I don't know what you're talking about, Rohan." She allowed a fallen lock of hair to half-shield her face.

"Is that why you're trembling from head to foot?" he answered curtly. "Christopher is *mine*. My child—not Martyn's."

She tried to disengage herself, but didn't have a hope. He was far too strong. "Are you insane?" Her voice shook with alarm.

"God!" Rohan burst out, his breathing harsh. "Don't play the fool with me, Charlotte. He has *my* eyes. My nose. My mouth. My chin."

Your beautiful smile. The habit you had of flipping your hair back with an impatient hand.

"He's going to get more and more like me," Rohan gritted. "What are you going to do then?"

"Rohan, *please*," she begged, hating herself.

He took no pity on her. It was all he could do not to shake her until her blonde head collapsed against his chest.

Despite himself, he was breathing in the very special scent of her—the freshness, the fragrance. He could breathe her in for ever. He was that much of a fool.

"How could you do this, Charlotte? It's unforgivable what you've done. No *way* is Christopher Martyn's child."

"Please, Rohan, *stop*!" She shut her eyes tight in pain and despair. She was still light-headed.

"You made the decision to banish me from your heart and your head," he accused her. "You know you did. No love in a cottage for Charlotte Marsdon. God, no! Poor Martyn was always crazy about you. You were the ultimate prize, waiting for him. Did he *know* the child wasn't his?"

Years of unhappiness, pain and guilt echoed from her throat. "How *could* he know?" she shouted. "*I* didn't."

"What?" He took a backward glance through the mansion, then led her away into the splendid book-lined library.

Her father had taken his pick of the valuable collection of books. Even in her highly perturbed state she could see their number had been replaced.

"You mean you were having sex with us *both*?" Rohan asked, looking and sounding appalled. "Oh, don't tell me. I don't want to know," he groaned.

She had to turn away from the anger flashing in his blue eyes. "It wasn't like that, Rohan. You were lost to me. Forever lost to me.'

His brief laugh couldn't have been more bitter or disbelieving. "You're lying again. You *knew* I would never let you go. I had to make something of myself, Charlotte. I had to have something to offer you. All I needed was a little time. I told you that. I believed you understood. But, no, you got yourself married to *Martyn* in double-quick time. Poor gutless Martyn, who went around telling everyone who would listen that *I* had goaded Mattie into trying to swim the river. Martyn was the golden boy in the Valley, not me. I was Mary Rose Costello's bastard son. Yet I thought the world would freeze over before *you* ever gave yourself to Martyn."

"Maybe he *took* me, Rohan. Ever think of that?" She threw up her head in a kind of wild defiance, though she was on the verge of breaking down completely.

"What are you *saying*?" There was fire in his eyes.

Rivers of tears were threateningly close. "I don't know *what* I'm saying." Her heart was labouring in her chest. "I never thought I would lay eyes on you again."

"Rubbish!" he responded violently. "You *knew* you would see me again. With Martyn gone. I've given you enough time to recover.'

"There would *never* be enough time." Her green eyes glittered. "What do you expect me to say? Welcome back, Rohan?"

A great anger was running in his veins. Whatever he had expected, it had never been *this*. He had learned early that she and Martyn had had a child—a boy. The agony of it, the pain of loss and betrayal, had nearly driven him mad. Day and night, month after month, year after year he had fought his demons. Charlotte and Martyn. Now he was confronted by the staggering truth. Christopher wasn't Martyn's at all. Christopher was *his*.

How terrible a crime was that? And what about the precautions she was supposed to have taken? "You're a cheat and a liar, Charlotte," he said, low-voiced and dangerous. "And I fully intend to prove it. You told me you loved me. You promised to wait for as long as it took. Why not? We had plenty of time. You were only eighteen. I hadn't even turned twenty-one. *I'm* Christopher's father. Don't look away from me. Don't attempt more lies. I *will* push this further."

"A threat?"

"You bet!" he said harshly, even though to his horror the old hunger was as fierce as ever. Would *nothing* kill it? She was even more beautiful—her beauty more pronounced, more complete. Charlotte who had betrayed him. And herself.

"Please, Rohan, I don't need this now." There was anguish in her face and in her voice. "I can walk back to the Lodge."

"Forget it. I'm driving you. Has your father the faintest clue? Or is he still hiding his head in the sand?" He compelled her out of the comfortable elegance of the library and back into the arched corridor, making for the rear of the house, where a vehicle was garaged and kept for his convenience.

"Dad loves Christopher very much." There was a trembling catch in her voice.

"Not what I asked you," he said grimly.

They were out in the sunshine now. The scent of the white rambling rose that framed the pedimented door and climbed the stone wall filled the air with its lovely nostalgic perfume. More roses rioted in the gardens, and lovely plump peonies—one of her great favourites.

"Chris did have a fleeting look of Mattie for a few years," she offered bleakly. This was the age of DNA. There was no point in trying to delude Rohan. What he said was correct. Christopher would only grow more like him. Hadn't she been buffeted by the winds of panic for some time? "Now that he's lost his little-boy softness the resemblance has disappeared. He has our blond hair."

"Isn't that marvelous?" he exclaimed ironically. "He has the Marsdon blond hair! God knows what might have happened had his hair been crow-black, like mine. Or, even worse, *red* like my mother's."

"I loved you, Rohan." The words flamed out of her.

In response he made a strangled sound of utter disgust. "You must have wept buckets after you decided to drop me. But there's intense satisfaction in my being rich. Daddy turned out to be a real loser with his lack of financial acumen. I had nothing. Too young. Martyn stood to inherit a fortune. Must have ruined your day when you lost him. How come you're living with your father? Didn't Martyn leave you a rich woman?"

"Sad to say, no. It's none of your business, Rohan."

"I beg to differ. It's very much my business. Martyn's father was too smart to let go of the purse strings. And your mother? The self-appointed avenger?"

"My mother has settled—or tried to settle—into a different life. I don't see much of her. She has little interest in my beautiful Chrissie."

"*Our* beautiful Christopher," he corrected curtly, usurping her as the single parent.

"He's not Mattie, you see," she continued sadly. "Really there was no one else for my mother."

Rohan's striking face was set like granite. "She loved you in her way. Of course she did."

"Not enough," she answered simply.

"I think I might find that a blessing," Rohan mused. "Your mother keeping her distance from my son. Your mother is deeply neurotic. She would never accept *me* in any capacity. Not in a hundred lifetimes."

She couldn't deny it. Rohan had been chosen as the scapegoat. She had been the daughter of the family—a girl of twelve. Martyn Prescott the only son of close friends. It had to be Rohan Costello—Mary Rose's boy. "My mother has been steeped in grief, Rohan. Dad has soldiered on."

"Good old Vivian!" Rohan retorted with extreme sarcasm. "The fire's not out in the old boy either. Did you hear the way he bellowed my name?"

Charlotte flinched, defending him quickly. "It was cruel not to let us know."

"Cruel?" Rohan's brilliant eyes shot sparks. "The hide of you to talk of cruelty! I can't believe *your* treachery! I've missed out on the first seven years of my son's life, Charlotte. First words. First steps. Birthdays. The first day at school. How can you possibly make it up to me for that?"

"I can't. I *can't*. I'm so sorry, Rohan. Sorry. Sorry, sorry. Do you want me to go down on my knees? I've raised Christopher as best I could. He's a beautiful, loving, clever child. He's everything in the world to me."

"So that's okay, then, is it? He's everything in the world to *you*. What about *me*? I never held my newborn son in my arms. I was robbed of that great joy. Tell me, how did you manage to put it across Martyn? Or didn't you? It's common knowledge he had a young woman in the car with him. It's a great mercy she wasn't killed or injured as well. Tell me—did he fall out of love with you? Or did he get sick of what little affection you could show him? You didn't love him. Don't tell me you did."

"I married Martyn and what came of it?" she said. "He's dead."

"You weren't responsible for that." He reacted to the pain in her face.

"Wasn't I?"

"So he had a tough time? Why did you do it, Charlotte? The money, the position?"

"I was *pregnant*, Rohan."

"By *me*!" he exploded. "Why didn't you contact me? God knows, I had the right to know."

"I wasn't sure whose child I was carrying, Rohan." Her voice was that of the frightened, isolated young girl she had been.

"Oh, poor, poor you! It couldn't have taken you all that long to find out!"

"Too late," she acknowledged, remembering her shock. "Martyn never did find out. Christopher has changed quite a lot in the past eighteen months."

"I'm not getting this at all," he frowned. "What about the Prescotts?"

"They have their suspicions. Nicole hates me. Always did, I think. We don't see much of them."

"Another plus! So when did you decide to seduce Martyn? I mean have sex with him. Clinch your position in his life."

"I don't want to talk about this, Rohan," she said, in a tight, defensive voice. "It's all over and done with."

"Not by a long shot. I can see you're badly frightened, and you should be. I have every intention of claiming my son."

She stood paralysed. "You can't do that to me."

"Can't I? I *can*, by God!" There was strain and a world of determination in his striking face.

"You can't take him from me, Rohan. You can't mean that. He's my life. I adore him."

"Who would take any notice of *you*? You were supposed to have *adored* me, remember? I don't intend to take our son from you, Charlotte. Unlike you, I do have a heart. *You* are part of the package." He let his eyes rest on her. Beautiful, beautiful, unfaithful Charlotte. "I want you *and* our son. Our boy can't be separated from his mother."

Jets of emotion shot through her. "In the same way you needed to have Riverbend?" she challenged.

"Perhaps I hated to see such a magnificent estate go to

rack and ruin." He shrugged. "I have plans for Riverbend, Charlotte. Plans for the vineyards, a winery, olive groves."

She accepted he had plans without hesitation. "You own the estate—not the company Vortex?"

"I *am* Vortex—and a couple of other affiliated companies as well. And I own Riverbend, lock, stock and barrel. Your father has done virtually nothing in the way of improvements since your grandfather died. I don't particularly dislike your father. I never did. It was your *mother* who was truly horrible to us. You know—your mother—the *great* lady." His eyes glittered with blue light.

"There are big turning points in life, Rohan," she said in a pain-filled voice. "My mother was never the same person after we lost Mattie. Feel pity for her. I do. Mattie's death blasted her apart. God knows how *I* would continue if anything...if anything—" She broke off in deep distress.

"Oh, stop it." He cut her off ruthlessly. "Nothing is going to happen to Christopher."

"God keep him safe. I've loved and protected him. Taken care of him all these years."

His voice carried both anger and confusion. "Martyn—how did he feel? Of course you always could twist him around your little finger."

"I can't talk about Martyn, Rohan." She focused her gaze on the massed beds of Japanese hybrid petunias—white in one, rosy-pink in another.

"You couldn't have let him down worse than you did me," he said bleakly. "He had *no* suspicions?"

She brought her green gaze back to him. Was he aware she was *devouring* his marvellous face, feature by feature, marking the changes, the refinements of maturity. *Rohan. Her Rohan.* "I told you. I can't talk about this."

"Maybe not today, but you will," he insisted. "You saw

Christopher with me, Charlotte. He accepted me on sight. I won't let him go. You either."

She took in his unyielding expression. "You want to punish me?"

"Every day," he admitted with a grim smile. "My perfect captive—my golden Charlotte, Martyn Prescott's *widow*." His tone was quiet, yet it lashed out at her. "Now, there's no need for you to go into a mad panic. I realise we've both had a tremendous shock today. I'll handle this from now on. You don't have to do or say a thing. I'll be making frequent trips in and out of the Valley. Plenty of time to establish a truly poignant renewal of our old romance. The whole Valley knows how close we were at one time. This will be our second chance. Isn't that wonderful? A second chance. I'm certain you'll have the sense to fall into line."

She found the strength to launch her own attack. "It doesn't really look like I have an option. And Diane Rodgers? What about her? Will you keep her on as your mistress?'

His black brows drew together. "Don't be so ridiculous. Diane is a highly efficient PR person. Nothing more."

"Perhaps you should tell *her* that." She stared at him directly—only he didn't appear to be taking on board what she said.

"God, isn't it *good* to be back in Silver Valley?" he enthused with great irony. "Let me return you to Daddy, Charlotte. We'll take the Range Rover. You've got an awful lot to think about, haven't you? Don't worry about *our* son. I'll bring him safely home."

Of course he would. She trusted him. "All I want is Christopher's happiness," she said.

His magnetic smile turned deeply mocking. "I think I can guarantee that. As for *us*—we're just going to have to work very hard at our respective roles."

"You won't say anything to Christopher?" In her agitation she grasped his arm.

He looked down at her elegant, long fingers. "What do you take me for? I won't be telling him our little secret until I'm sure—*we're* sure—he can handle it."

"Thank you, Rohan." She removed her hand—she knew he wanted her to—overcome by relief and gratitude. Rohan had suffered so much as a boy it would have been impossible for him to heap grief on any child, let alone his own son.

It was her own actions that gave her the most pain. What she had done to Rohan was beyond forgiveness. There was little comfort in the knowledge that she had believed at the beginning she was carrying Martyn's child. She had been taking the pill when she and Rohan had been together, that first year at university in Sydney. A necessary precaution against her falling pregnant. They'd both been so young. Rohan had begged her to give him time to make something of himself he would be in a position to offer marriage. Growing up as he had, with the social stigma of not knowing who his father was, he'd been intent on doing everything just right.

Yet despite that she *had* fallen pregnant. And by Rohan. She had been certain for some years now. It had taken her over-long to realise the contraceptive pill's efficacy could be put in jeopardy if a woman experienced a bout of sickness like a bad stomach upset. That had happened to her around about that time. A chicken roll at a campus picnic. She and a girlfriend had been very sick for twenty-four hours following the picnic. One had to be so careful in the heat. Chicken was about the worst food there was.

As for Martyn! Even now she couldn't bear to think about that night when he had totally lost his head. All these years later she was still left with mental bruising—far

worse than the physical bruising Martyn had left on her unyielding body. The monstrous reality of it was that Martyn,
her friend from earliest childhood, had taken her against
her will. There was a word for it. She studiously avoided
it. But she remembered the way she had thrashed about as
she'd tried to stop him. It had only excited him further—as
though he'd believed she was playing a game. The comforting arm he had initially offered her had turned swiftly into
the arm that had so easily overpowered her. Afterwards he
had begged for forgiveness in tears, citing that he'd had too
much to drink.

He *had*. But into their marriage he had told her, with
triumph in her eyes, that her pregnancy had been a sure
way of getting her away from Rohan.

*"You know Rohan will never be in a position to reinvent
himself. I mean, he's really poor. It'll always be a long,
hard hike for him to get ahead. Probably twenty years.
What you need is the life you were born to. A guy like me
to lean on."*

How could she have leant on Martyn when he hadn't
even been able to stand up for himself?

It had been the worst possible start to a disastrous marriage that should never have happened. Only in those days
she had been literally terrified of bringing further trauma
to her already traumatised parents. Facts were facts. She'd
been pregnant. Martyn was the father. They'd been too
young, but he'd adored her. In a way she had brought it all
down on herself.

Her father had given them a lavish wedding at Riverbend.
He had spent a fortune. The Prescotts had been over the
moon at that time, with the union of the two families.
She'd been seen, even then, as a steadying influence on
Martyn.

Many times she had thought she would go to her grave

not telling anyone the truth of what had really happened that awful night. She had so trusted Martyn, and he had been obsessed with taking control of her body. What was going to happen now was quite another matter. Rohan was back. Rohan was indisputably in charge. Christopher would not remain very long not knowing who his real father was. Not that much longer and everyone in the Valley would know. Had Christopher inherited Rohan's raven locks instead of the Marsdon blond hair they would know already. Christopher was fast turning into a dead ringer for his father.

Her father stormed into the entrance hall of the Lodge just as she stepped inside the door. Rohan had dropped her off outside. He knew about the side entrance to the Lodge, of course. It had been an excruciating short ride. Both of them utterly silent, yet unbearably aware of each other. She couldn't even find the courage to ask about his mother. Mrs Costello had always been lovely to her. They had embraced in tears the day she and Rohan had left the Valley.

"Not your fault. Never your fault, Charlotte."

Getting herself married to Martyn Prescott was. It had wrecked their friendship. It had wrecked lives.

So there she was, on what was supposed to have been a picture-perfect day, with her heart slashed to ribbons.

"That was Costello, wasn't it?" A great helpless anger seemed to surround Vivian Marsdon like a cloud.

"You know it was, Dad." She moved past him into the living room, sinking dazedly into an armchair. Her father followed her, remaining standing. He would think that gave him the advantage. "No point in working yourself up. It's not going to do a bit of good. And, really, you can't yell at Rohan. Not ever again. You'll get more than you bargained for. We *all* will. The old days are over—the days when you and Mum attacked Rohan and Mrs Costello at every opportunity.'

"That fire-eater!' Vivian Marsdon snorted, his expression tight.

"And good for her!" Charlotte felt her own anger gather. "All Mrs Costello did was defend her son."

"*Miss* Costello, thank you."

"Don't be so sanctimonious! Maybe she was like a tigress defending her young? Good on her! I admired her immensely for taking on my high and mighty parents. She was driven to it. You were both so cruel. Mum was by far the worst."

"Your mother was off her head, Charlie. I mean she was completely out of it. We had lost our only son. What *did* you expect of us?" he asked, his voice a mix of shame and outrage.

"I expected wisdom, Dad. Compassion, understanding. Not a blind allocation of the blame. It was a terrible freak accident. We're not the only family to have lost loved ones in tragic accidents. Families suffer all over the world—the rich and the poor alike. Please sit down, Dad. Better yet, calm down. Can I tell you, not for the first time, it was Martyn who was at fault? It was Martyn who goaded Mattie into swimming the river. Rohan and I called him back. He *was* coming back. But Martyn wanted to wind Mattie up. Throw down a challenge. Rohan went after Mattie, but Mattie wouldn't stop. He was trying to prove something."

Vivian Marsdon recoiled in near horror. "What *is* this?"

"The *truth* of that terrible afternoon, Dad. The truth you and Mum wouldn't listen to. But you surely heard the version Martyn, coward that he was, put about."

"I—don't—believe—you." There was a kind of delirium

in Vivian's deep, cultured voice. "You worshipped young Costello. You would always be on his side. You would lie for him if you had to."

"What does it matter now, Dad? I give up. Let's say the fault lay with Fate." Charlotte put a hand to her pounding head. "You've only ever believed what you wanted to anyway."

Her father panted with outrage. "To think you would malign your late husband! Poor, dead Martyn! You're still looking to clear Costello, of course."

"You're right about that!" she declared. "All those years ago you and Mum turned on us with deaf ears. You had your own agenda. Martyn was a Prescott. Rohan was a nobody. Only that was far from true, wasn't it? Rohan was always destined to be somebody. Even Mum said it when she was still sane. The two of you made him your scapegoat."

Vivian Marsdon's chin quivered with rage. "He was the ringleader of your silly Pack of Four. You were just a girl. Martyn always played the fool. It was Costello who had to pay for his extreme negligence, his lack of supervision."

"How brutally unfair! Mattie, Martyn and Rohan were all of an age. Why should *Rohan* have to pay?"

"Because we'll never get our son back—that's why," her father thundered. "Don't you understand that? Losing Matthew broke up our marriage. Your mother couldn't bear to stay here. She couldn't bear to be with me though I shared her pain."

"Of course you did, Dad, but never to the same degree. Mum will rake over the ashes of that terrible day until she dies. I wonder how Reiner copes? Sometimes he must feel like he's in prison."

Her father slumped down heavily. "Who cares about Reiner? God knows how your mother married the man.

We'll never get Matthew back. I'll never get *her* back. But
we have our splendid little Chrissie. Where is he, anyway?"
He stared around, suddenly becoming aware his grandson
hadn't yet come home.

"Settle down, Dad," Charlotte begged wearily. "He's
with Peter. I'm not going to chain him to me, like Mum
did with Mattie. Christopher and Peter are sensible boys.
They're only down the drive. "

"He should have come home with you, none the less,"
Vivian maintained.

He was very seriously disturbed by Rohan Costello's
shock return to the Valley. And that wasn't the only reason
for his sense of anxiety. What was the effect it was going
to have on Charlotte? He wasn't such a fool he didn't know
Rohan Costello had once been everything in the world
to his daughter. Was Rohan Costello's desire *now* for
revenge?

"Chris is enjoying himself, Dad. Don't worry about him.
And whatever you do," she added with heavy irony, "don't
worry about me—the child who survived. Mum told me in
one of her black fits of depression she wished *I* had been
the one to die."

Vivian had to steady himself by gripping the sides of
his high-backed armchair. "She didn't. She *couldn't*." He
was sincerely shocked.

"Sorry, Dad. She *did*. She didn't have to say it anyway.
We both knew Mattie was the light of Mum's eyes."

"But, Charlie, dear, she loved you." He was shaking his
fair head as though he couldn't believe her disclosure.

"Only as long as Mattie was around." Charlotte took
the last clip out of her hair and shook its gleaming masses
free.

Vivian Marsdon's tanned skin had gone very white.
"Well, *I* love you, Charlotte. *You* were my favourite. I loved

Matthew, of course. But you were my little girl—always so clever and bright and full of life. Your mother wrapped poor Matthew in cotton wool. It was a big mistake, but Barbara would never listen to me."

"She listened to no one when it came to Mattie. It was Rohan who encouraged Mattie to be more outgoing. And look where it got him."

Her father flinched. "It will be impossible to make peace with Costello. Too much history, Charlotte," he said. "I'm tormented by the past. Only the young can spring back from tragedy."

She exhaled a long breath. "If you *can't* make peace, Dad, you will have to learn to be civil. We're going to be seeing a lot of Rohan. He's staying in the Valley for some time."

"So what did he say?"

"That he's going to make Riverbend, its vineyards and the olive groves, the best in the Valley. He's going to produce fine wines and the finest olive oils. He's got big plans."

"Good luck to him, then," her father said, sounding hollowed out. Vivian Marsdon knew Costello would achieve everything he had ever wanted. And didn't that include Charlotte, his daughter? "Oh, God, I feel wretched," he mumbled. "I started my married life with such high hopes. I wanted to be loved and admired like my father. I wanted to be a great success. I thought I had inherited his business brain. I didn't, sad to say. I've had to come face to face with the cold, hard facts. I never listened. I made terrible mistakes. It cost us all. And I had to live with your mother's chronic obsession with Mattie and his health."

"Don't upset yourself, Dad. We won't talk about Mattie any more. It's too painful."

"Indeed it is. But we have our Chrissie—the best boy in the world. He's amazingly bright."

Like father. Like son.

"I know *you* were always a top student, Charlie," her father continued, "but Martyn definitely wasn't. He couldn't even get a place at university. He was spoiled rotten—born lazy. Unlike Gordon. Christopher has an exceptionally high IQ. I was thrilled when he was classed as a gifted child."

"And you've brought him on wonderfully, Dad," she said gently. "I'm so grateful you take such an interest in him."

Her father's thick eyebrows shot up. "Good God, girl, he's my grandson."

"Please remember that, Dad," she said very quietly. "Mum has little or no time for him."

Vivian Marsdon moaned in distress. "Her loss, my dear. Chrissie used to look like Matthew, but he doesn't any more. Still, he's a Marsdon. My eyes have faded somewhat, but they used to be very blue. Did you ask Costello how he's made his money? He owns the place outright, doesn't he?"

Charlotte nodded. "He *is* Vortex. I wasn't about to question him, Dad. I don't have the right."

"Blasted revenge—that's what it is." Vivian Marsdon was back to railing. "He's lived to get square. I tell you, I was shocked out of my mind to see him."

"And *I* wasn't?"

"The arrogance of him!" Marsdon fumed. "Always had it—even as a boy."

Charlotte expelled a long breath. "Not arrogance, Dad. Rohan was never arrogant. Rohan *is* what he is. Someone truly exceptional. By temperament a born leader."

Vivian Marsdon drew a deep sigh. Who could deny it? Many a time he had wished for a son like Rohan Costello, at the same time feeling guilty at the very thought. It was as if he were brushing his own son Matthew, a beautiful, sunny-natured boy, aside.

"Well, Costello—unlike me—obviously knows how to make money," he said finally. "But doesn't that prove how little he actually cares about you? You were supposed to be such great friends. Inseparable at one time. He surely could have notified you? Let you know beforehand. Not shocked us both. If that isn't revenge, what is?"

She had absolutely no comeback to that.

CHAPTER FOUR

MONDAY morning. School. The same primary school they had all attended as children. She followed her normal routine, picking up Peter Stafford and his scratchy little sister Angela along the way. Angela was such an unpleasant child sometimes it was hard to believe the two were related.

As always, Charlotte arrived in comfortable time, allowing the boys to settle before classes began. There was welcome shade beneath a flowering gum twenty yards from the front gate. She moved her Mercedes smoothly into the parking spot left by a departing Volvo. The driver, her friend Penny, wiggled a hand out of the window. Penny's little one, Emma, was only in pre-school. Charlotte had been the first to marry and fall pregnant. Or rather the other way about. She wouldn't be the first or the last. But it certainly made her the youngest mother of a Grade 3 child.

"Thank you, Mrs Prescott." Dear little Peter never forgot to thank her, while his sister dashed away without a backward glance.

She watched the boys shoulder their backpacks. "It's always a pleasure, Peter." She smiled affectionately at him. "Now, you two have a good day and I'll see you this afternoon." She touched a farewelling hand to Peter's shoulder, dropped a kiss on her son's head.

"See you, Mummy," Christopher said, his face lighting up with his wonderfully sweet smile.

It tore at her heart. Rohan had smiled at her like that. Once. Christopher's hair was a gleaming blond, like hers, but he didn't have her creamy skin. He had Rohan's olive skin. In summer it turned a trouble-free gold.

She stood watching a minute more as they ran through the open double gates, meeting up with a group of their friends. All weekend Christopher had been as happy and excited as any young boy could be at having met Rohan, who now owned Riverbend. Things might have been a little different had he taken a dislike to the new owner. As it was, he appeared thrilled. It had been Rohan said this; Rohan said that.

She had thought her father might fly off the handle, but oddly enough he'd listened to his grandson with an attentive smile. He would be thinking Christopher was missing his father. That was Martyn. So far her father suspected nothing. She knew her father would always love Christopher, no matter what. But the inevitability of Christopher's real paternity coming out scared her to death. There had never been a scandal attached to the Marsdon name. Martyn had blotted the Prescotts' copybook. She wasn't thinking of herself. She was thinking, as always, of her son. And her father. God knew what her absent mother would make of it! She shuddered to think.

She was about to return to her car when she became aware that a tall, lean, stunning young man, wearing jeans and a navy T-shirt with a white logo, was heading straight for her. Only now could she see the estate's Range Rover a little distance down on the opposite side of the road. He must have been waiting for her.

She stood stock still, willing her heart to stop racing. Her body, which had been calm enough, was now assailed by tingles. She watched him swiftly cross the road. Rohan had always been graceful, beautifully co-ordinated. He hadn't just excelled in the classroom, he had been the Valley's top athlete. Many of the boys had been gifted young sportsmen—Martyn had been a fine swimmer, tennis and cricket player. He had wanted to study sports when he finished high school, but he hadn't had the marks. Poor Martyn. His father had put him to work. Well, in a manner of speaking. Martyn had wanted for nothing.

Except *her*. Unrequited love did terrible things to a man.

"Good morning, Rohan." She knew she sounded very formal, but she was concentrating hard on marshalling her strength. "You wanted to see me?"

"I thought we could have a cup of coffee." He was studying her as intently as she was studying him.

"I really don't have the time."

"I think you do. A cup of coffee and a friendly chat. Won't keep you long. I've checked out the village. Stefano's?"

She nodded. "It's the best."

"So I'll meet you there?"

Her nerves were drawn so tight they were thrumming like live wires. "I can't imagine not doing what you want, Rohan." She turned away before he could form a retort.

At that time in the morning it was easy to find a parking spot in the main road, outside the popular coffee shop with its attractive awning in broad white and terracotta stripes. Stefano's was owned and run by an Italian family who really knew their business. Coffee was accompanied by selections of little cakes, mini-cheesecakes and pastries. Stefano's also served delicious light lunches. Charlotte and the friends who had remained loyal to her had been frequent customers since the café had opened almost a year before.

This morning she was greeted with a beaming, *"Buon giorno*, Carlotta—Signor Costello." Stefano was a large man, almost bear-like in appearance, but very light on his feet.

"Buon giorno, Stefano."

It only then occurred to Charlotte that the de Campo family would have been invited to the Open Day. Obviously Stefano, the grandfather and head of the family, had met Rohan that day. Hence the big flashing smile and the use of his name.

Stefano took their orders after a few pleasantries: long black for Rohan, cappuccino for her, and a small slice each of Signora de Campo's freshly baked Siena cake—a great favourite with the customers.

Charlotte looked across the table, set with a crisp white cloth and a tiny glass vase containing a single fresh flower—a sunshine-yellow gerbera, with an open smiling face. "So, how can I help you, Rohan?"

He just looked at her. He wanted to keep looking at her. Never stop. Her beautiful blonde hair was drawn back from her face, a section caught high with a gold clasp, the rest of her shining mane hanging down her back. She was dressed much as he was, but in a feminine version: jeans—white, in her case—with a pink and white checked shirt, white trainers on her feet. She was wearing no make-up apart from a soft pink lipgloss, so far as he could see. She always had had flawless skin.

"How's Christopher?"

So many emotions were cascading through her. "Full of his new best friend. It's been Rohan this, Rohan that, all weekend," she told him.

"How did your father take that?" His gaze sharpened.

"To be honest—"

"For a *change*," he cut in.

She gave a small grimace and looked away from him into the sunlit street. Two of the school mothers were going into the bookshop opposite. Other villagers were strolling past the coffee shop, one commenting on the luxuriant potted golden canes that flanked the front door.

"Dad loves Christopher," she said, turning her head slowly back to him. "I told you that. He listened and smiled."

"Good grief!" Rohan leaned back in his comfortable chair, eyes sparkling with malice. "Maybe there are miracles after all!"

"One likes to think so. Here comes Stefano."

"Gosh, why the warning?" he asked sardonically. "I thought we looked perfectly relaxed—not raring for a fight."

"*You* might feel relaxed. I don't."

"Charlotte, you look perfectly beautiful and quite normal. A good actress, I guess."

Stefano set the tray down on an adjacent empty table, then unloaded their coffee, placing it before them. The panforte followed, heavily dusted with white icing sugar and showing roasted nuts and a succulent mix of candied peel.

"*Grazie*, Stefano." Rohan nodded in acknowledgement. "This looks good."

"*Altro?*"

"*Nient'altro, grazie.*" Charlotte answered this time, giving the courtly proprietor a warm smile.

It was the first genuine smile Rohan had seen from her in a very, very long time. It wasn't directed at him. He saw Stefano flush with pleasure. Charlotte had never been fully aware of her own beauty and its power.

The coffee was excellent. Stefano glanced back and Rohan gave him the seal of approval with a thumbs-up. Stefano was a great *barista*, and it wasn't all that easy. He savoured another long sip, then leaned back. "I'm having a few guests this coming Saturday. Probably they'll all be here by late afternoon, and will stay over until Sunday. Ten of us in all. Counting you, of course."

She hoped her composed expression didn't change. "Who needs *my* acceptance?" She turned out her palms.

"Come on," he jeered softly. "In the old days you were someone very special in my life. You're about to be reinstated."

She saw the glint in his eyes. "I'm absolutely rapt about that, Rohan. This is blackmail, you know."

His voice hardened. "You'd do well to remember the reason. Try the cake. It looks delicious."

"So what am I supposed to *do*?" she asked after a moment.

"Nothing too onerous. I've given my housekeeper the night off. Ms Rodgers will be looking after the catering. All you have to do is look beautiful and come to dinner Saturday night."

"That's all?" Part of her wanted to tell him she didn't much like his PR woman. She hoped Ms Rodgers wasn't going to play hostess at Riverbend. She didn't think she could take seeing Diane Rodgers sitting where her mother had always sat.

"That's all—apart from an impromptu little after-dinner concert." He raised a black brow at her.

"I'm sorry, Rohan. I'm out of practice." She wasn't. She loved her piano. She was a very good pianist—just like her mother. She had started teaching Christopher the very day he'd shown interest. He'd been five. "Besides, there's the little matter of a piano."

"Solved," he said. "I've had a new Steinway installed. "Even out of practice—which I doubt—an hour or two on that would set you right.'

She had a flashback to the Open Day, when she had fainted. Used to seeing a concert grand in the Drawing Room, in her bemused state she had thought it hers.

"Just a couple of party pieces?" he suggested. "I want to show you off. I intend everyone to know we're back to being *very good friends*!"

Very good friends? "Aren't you rather rushing it?" There was a defiant look in her eyes.

"Not at all." He shrugged. "My friends know I grew up in Silver Valley. They will learn it was your father who sold me Riverbend."

"They don't know now?"

"Only Diane."

"Of course—Diane. Sounds like she runs your life. Am I to take it she'll be a guest at dinner?"

"You know the rules, Charlotte. Even numbers." His tone was sardonic.

"So you have someone for me?"

"I have someone for Diane," he corrected. "*You're* my certain someone, Charlotte. God knows, I've waited all these years, never considering for a moment what you'd been up to."

"Formal or informal dress?" Stoically she ignored his taunting.

"Why, formal—what else? Your parents' dinner parties were always formal. My mother—you know, the hired help—used to tell me how everyone dressed up. How beautiful your mother always looked, the splendid jewellery she wore. In those days my mother thought the world of Mrs Marsdon, the Lady of the Manor."

It gave Charlotte an opening, if nothing else. "How *is* your mother? I wanted so much to ask."

"So why didn't you?'

"I knew right off to exercise extreme caution around you. You've changed, Rohan."

"Alas, I have!" he drawled. "Let me see. Who could have changed me? Changed my life?"

"Fate is as close as I can get." She picked up her coffee before it went cold.

He gave her an insouciant smile. "I have to return to Sydney this afternoon. Back Friday night. I have business meetings lined up."

She gave him an enquiring look. "Dare I ask what line of business you are in?"

"Why not?" He leaned forward. "You remember I was a computer whiz kid?"

"Absolutely. You were a whiz kid at everything," she admitted wryly.

"You might also remember I was searching desperately for a way to make money so I could offer marriage to the girl I *then* loved." The steely glint was back in his eyes. "I was always into computer science, I had a special flair for it. Then it struck me that the quickest way to make money was to try to break into entertainment software. I'd done well enough with educational software, but decided to take the risk of moving to games. Sometimes they don't take off. Mine did. I've never looked back. In no time at all the money started to flow in. I have three companies now that handle multiple software programs. I hire the right people. My employees are all young and brilliant at what they do. I've built businesses around what I and my staff enjoy. They also have the opportunity to buy shares in our companies—share in the profits. They all want to get rich too."

"So you've made millions?" she asked, not at all surprised. He had energy and enterprise written all over him.

"The *reason* I wanted to make millions," he told her tersely, "was to keep *you* in the style you were accustomed to. And, of course, to make life much better and easier for my mother. Which, needless to say, I have."

"And I'm glad, Rohan. Truly glad. Your mother deserves her slice of good fortune. But why ever did you want Riverbend?"

He gave an elegant shrug of his shoulder. Whoever his father was, he must have been a fascinating man. "Simple. I'm always on the lookout for something else. I got started on real estate investing. Real estate, as you know, is one of the best ways to create wealth. Better yet hold on to it for the family I intend to have. Christopher is our *first* child. Hopefully I'll get to hold our second-born child in my arms. It was a dream of mine to have our child."

"It was *our* dream, Rohan." There was no mistaking the injured look in her lustrous green eyes.

"Odd way you went about it."

They were so utterly engrossed in each other they failed to notice the small, dumpy young woman who strode with single-minded purpose to their table.

"Well, well, well!" Nicole Prescott said, her tone coated with layer upon layer of meaning they were obviously meant to guess at.

Charlotte realised at once that Nicole's seeing them together had greatly upset her. Every muscle in her own stomach clenched, as though steeling for the blows that might come. Rohan stood up, looking perfectly self-assured, and at six-three towering over the diminutive Nicole. Nicole could easily have looked so much better, but Charlotte had learned to her cost that Nicole much preferred her image of messy, prolonged adolescence.

"Mind your own business, Charlotte. We can't all look like you!" How many times had she heard that?

"Well, well, well, to you too, Nicole," Rohan said suavely. "Tell me—were you after coffee, or did you see us through the window?" He gave her a brilliant look that fell short of contempt. He had never liked Nicole Prescott. Had little reason to.

A tremor shook Charlotte's whole body. Nicole had always been such an abrasive person, with an oversized chip on her shoulder. It had made her very hurtful. Over the years Nicole had developed such a badly done by expression it had set like cement. Did she intend to make a scene? Nicole was given to hurling insults. She was even cruel. She had done her best to blacken Rohan's name—though, knowing her brother, she must have had serious doubts about Martyn's version of events that fatal afternoon. It all went back to Mattie.

"You just never could keep away from each other," Nicole hissed, literally seething with resentment.

Rohan pitched his voice low, but it carried natural authority and the capacity to act on it. "I would advise you not to make an enemy of me, Nicole."

"That's right—you're *rich* now," she sneered.

"And I have big interests in this valley."

Nicole blinked. *Big interests?* Hadn't her father hinted at some such thing? Not just Riverbend, then? She forced herself to look away from Rohan Costello's burning blue gaze. It transfixed her. Bluer than blue. She heard her mother's voice in her head, *"We don't know. We don't know."* Always handsome, Rohan Costello had matured into the sort of man women couldn't take their eyes off. She had to concentrate now on Charlotte—the weak link.

She had hated beautiful Charlotte Marsdon all her life. So unfairly blessed. Beauty, charm, brains. She had the lot. Everyone loved her. Well, *she* hated Charlotte. Had hated her even when she'd followed Charlotte down the aisle to join her besotted brother in unholy matrimony—she the shortest and the plainest of the bridesmaids. Beauty gave a woman such power. Martyn was the one who had inherited all the looks. As a kid he had nicknamed her Mousy. It still stuck in some quarters. But she had triumphed over her nondescript looks by developing a tongue sharp enough to cut.

They hadn't been invited to the garden party. She and her mother had fumed over that. They were the Prescotts. Not a family to be ignored. Small wonder they were furious. Her father had simply made the comment, "What did the two of you expect?"

It was like that these days. Two against one. She and her mother against her father. He was so unbelievably *tolerant*. And he had never had much faith or pride in her adored brother. She would never forgive him for that.

"You knew about all this, didn't you?" She rounded on Charlotte with the barbed accusation. "You knew he'd bought Riverbend. You knew he'd had us barred from the garden party."

"Wrong on both counts, Nicole," Charlotte said. It was news to her. There was no guarantee Nicole wouldn't start spewing venom any moment now. Out of the corner of her eye she could see Stefano, looking their way rather anxiously.

"I *know* you," Nicole spat. "I know the two of you. Your history. I know how you broke my brother's heart."

"And we know *you*, Nicole," Rohan responded in a warning voice. "You and Martyn. *Unfortunately*. If you want a cup of coffee I suggest you consider going elsewhere."

There was a daunting edge to his voice. "We've only just settled in, and Stefano is looking this way with concern."

"Forget him!" Nicole snapped out, but the hard challenge was causing her to crumple like soggy tissue paper. "How's my nephew, by the way?" She shot Charlotte a look of utter loathing.

Charlotte thought her heart might go into spasm. Christopher had to be protected at all costs. She looked beyond Nicole with her puffy cheeks to Rohan, who had made the slightest move forward. "Why don't *we* go?" she suggested quickly. "Nicole is beyond hope."

"*I'm* beyond hope?" Nicole's face took on high colour. She was the one to do the taunting, launch the insults. Not lovely, ladylike Charlotte.

"Probably you know it," Rohan suggested suavely. "I'd go now, Nicole, if I were you. Remember you're a *Prescott*!"

That stopped Nicole more effectively than a jug of cold water. She backed off abruptly, saying scornfully as she went, "Your poor mother—the *cleaning lady*—never did teach you any manners, did she?"

Rohan laughed, as though genuinely amused by the comment. "I've never heard my mother swear—yet *your* mother drops the F-word in every other sentence. I bet you do too."

For once Nicole had no reply. She spun about, and then took off like a bat out of hell.

Rohan sat down again with an exaggerated sigh. "What a gentle little soul she is! A helicopter could spot that chip on her shoulder. All in all, the Prescotts were blessed with their children, wouldn't you say? Nicole's jealousy of you is downright pathological.'

"That's what makes her dangerous, Rohan."

He looked across at her, seeing her distress. "It's okay. Stop worrying. What can she actually do?"

"She's already seized on Christopher's resemblance to you," she said in a deeply concerned voice.

"Christopher's relationship to me *must* come out." His tone hardened.

"But you promised!"

"And I meant it." Frowning, he looked truly formidable. "Nicole and her dreadful mother—how in God's name did you ever live with them?—can suspect all they like. They don't *know*."

"They could offer to take him for a weekend. This is the age of DNA testing." Fear was lodged like a heavy stone against her heart.

"Isn't that good?" he countered with the utmost sarcasm. "Tell them *no*. You've already said they've seen little of you since Martyn's death."

"I like Gordon—Martyn's father. He's the nice one of the family."

"Wasn't Martyn nice enough to marry?"

"Martyn's dead." She veiled her eyes.

"Well, his death is one less cross for you to bear," he pointed out rather callously. "I'm sorry Martyn had to die so young, Charlotte. Once we were friends, until he turned on me with a vengeance. Anything to protect himself. He really was gutless. We both know he had a foolhardy streak that was always going to get him and sadly other people into trouble. You could have divorced him."

"Then I really would have been in trouble." She reacted with an involuntary shudder.

He sat forward, staring at her in consternation. "What is *that* supposed to mean?" His eyes blazed.

She didn't answer. She had said too much already. Did

anyone get through life unscathed? Women particularly? Vulnerable women with children to protect?

"Were you afraid of Martyn? What he might do?"

She shook her head.

"If you ever try to leave me, I'll kill you and the boy."

Martyn's final words to her had played over and over in her head. By now they were driven deep into her psyche. "I must go, Rohan," she pleaded. "There are things I have to do at home."

"You're going to have to talk to me some time." He rose to his splendid height, extracting a couple of notes from his wallet.

She stood up more slowly. "There are some things you don't need to hear, Rohan."

His steely determination—the determination that had turned him at under thirty into a multimillionaire—was well in evidence. "That, Charlotte, is an answer I don't accept."

Life for Charlotte had become an endless series of hurdles.

CHAPTER FIVE

SOMEONE on Rohan's staff was to pick her up at ten to seven. Drinks in the library. Dinner in the formal dining room. Diane Rodgers was handling the catering. Diane Rodgers would be sitting down to dinner. Swanning around Charlotte's former home.

"Why are you doing this?" her father asked, for the umpteenth time.

It wasn't as though she had a choice. "Rohan insisted."

"And you jumped?"

"Only some of the time." She had no protection from Rohan.

"You look *beautiful*, Mummy." Christopher caught his mother's fingers. He didn't like it when Grandpa had words with his mother. "I love it when you let your hair down." He looked up admiringly at his mother's thick golden hair. He was used to seeing her hair tied back, but tonight it fell in lovely big waves around her face and over her shoulders. "I love the dress too," he enthused. "I've never seen it before." It was a long dress of some shiny material. It deepened the colour of his mother's green eyes and made her lovely skin glow.

"You love *everything* about your mother," Vivian Marsdon said with an indulgent smile. He too loved seeing his daughter looking her best. As a boy, like Christopher, he had taken great pleasure in seeing his own mother dress up for an occasion. "You *do* look beautiful, Charlotte." He paused for a moment, considering. "Why don't you wear your grandmother's emeralds?"

"Goodness me, Dad, I don't want to overdo it!" she exclaimed. Her mother had taken the beautiful jewellery her husband had given her, but Grandma Marsdon's jewellery was off-limits. It was to remain in the family.

"Well, I *want* you to," Vivian Marsdon decided. "Damned strangers swanning around in our house." Eerily, he echoed her thoughts.

"You swore, Grandpa," Christopher turned to look at his grandfather. "You know the rules. Swearing isn't allowed." He figured it was time to get one back at Grandpa.

"I'm sorry, son," Vivian apologised. "I'm a bit upset. I'll take the emeralds from the safe, Charlotte. I'd like you to wear them. Keep the flag flying, if you like. I'm sure the other women will be wearing their best jewellery."

"Probably, Dad," she conceded. "But it might be a mite hard to top Gran's emeralds."

"Well, you have the beauty and the style," he said, already moving off to his study, where the safe was installed. "Besides, they'll go perfectly with that dress. Green is your colour."

Rohan, looking devastatingly handsome in black tie, greeted her at the door. "Ah, Charlotte! You look a vision of beauty!"

She brought herself quickly under control. It wasn't easy when she was on an emotional see-saw. Fear. Elation. She couldn't get over having Rohan back in her life. It was like some impossible dream. Her love for him had never lost its intensity, even through the unhappy years of her marriage. She had given up the love of her life for Martyn, whose

actions had determined the course of all three of their lives.
She rarely let her mind travel back to Martyn's unwitting
part in Mattie's tragedy. She had never, ever upbraided
Martyn for it. Only for his part in denouncing Rohan to
anyone who would listen. Martyn hadn't been a strong
character. He had known that and suffered for it.

Now Rohan's brilliant eyes glittered over her and touched
on the emeralds, no more dazzling than her eyes. He bent
his dark head to brush her cheek. Her heart turned over.
The clean male scent of him! He took the opportunity to
murmur in her ear. "Ah, the famous Marsdon emeralds.
They look glorious! But no more than you!"

"Why, thank you, Rohan." She had become fairly adept
at pretending cool composure. "That's what Dad was hoping for. 'Fly the flag' were his exact words."

"And how triumphantly it's unfurled! Come on in."
He took her hand, his long fingers curling around hers.
Electricity shot up her arm, branched away into her throat,
her breast, travelled to the sensitive delta of her body. She
felt the impact of skin on skin at every level. "Meet my
guests," he was saying smoothly. "I'm sure you'll like them,
and they you. Still think losing Riverbend is tragic?" His
downbent head pinned her gaze.

"Not any more. I only wanted it for Christopher anyway."

"Then your prayers have been answered," he returned
sardonically.

Diane Rodgers had marked their entry. Immediately
she was seized by a jealousy so powerful it was a wonder
she didn't moan aloud. She felt so completely engulfed by
it, it was like drowning in mortal sin. If there was such a
thing. They looked *perfect* together. Stunning foils for each
other. Charlotte Prescott looked *beyond* glamorous—and
looking glamorous was her own crowning achievement. Up

until now she had thought she looked terrific in her short mesh and sequin dress. Hell, she *did* look terrific. But Mrs Prescott looked *fabulous*—a walking, breathing, real-live beautiful woman. The long dress, clinging and dipping in all the right places, put her in mind of the emerald silk number Keira Knightley had worn in the movie *Atonement*. If that weren't enough, a magnificent diamond and emerald necklace was strung around her neck like a glittering tie, caught by a big dazzling emerald clasp of God knew how many carats. The full length of the separate strands dipped into her creamy cleavage.

Hell!

Diane looked furtively about her. She had an idea she might have exclaimed aloud.

She couldn't have. No one responded. Not that they were looking in her direction. They were staring at the beauty on Rohan's arm. One thing offered a grain of consolation. Mrs Prescott's late husband—a bit of a playboy, she'd heard—had been having an affair at the time of his fatal accident. A young woman had been with him in his luxury Maserati. The miracle was she hadn't joined her boyfriend. So the beauteous Mrs Prescott hadn't been able to hang on to her husband! She had lost him. Diane half believed that gave her hope.

The only other times she had seen Charlotte Marsdon, her long hair had been confined. Now it billowed away from her face, revealing matching diamond and emerald earrings. Who the hell could compete with that? It was utterly demoralising. Her mood turned from super-confident to darkly brooding.

"Geez, isn't she *fan-taas-tic*!" Sam Bailey turned his smooth brown head to give her a cat-like grin.

Diane Rodgers was tempted to crack him on the nose;

instead she met his look head-on. "Gorgeous!" she agreed, feeling as if she was under siege.

She had never much liked Sam Bailey. Now she hated him and his playful little taunts. At least she *thought* they were playful. She'd been certain she'd been keeping her wild infatuation with the dead sexy Rohan under wraps. Apparently not. Rohan Costello had got right under her skin at first sight, and she prided herself on her street cool. Were they all laughing at her? God, that would be catastrophic! She couldn't ask Sam—he was making a bee-line for his boss and the exquisite Mrs Prescott. What a hell of a pity the husband was dead. But playboys given to driving fast cars sadly tended to die young.

Diane had done an impressive job of handling the arrangements. Charlotte awarded her top marks. If she hadn't exactly done things herself, then she had the knack of gathering together the right people. The flower arrangements in the entrance hall and the main reception rooms were stunning. A quartet of sumptuous yellow roses, their lovely full heads massed in crystal bowls, were set at intervals along the dining table. She had never seen the impressive gold and white dinner set before, but she recognised Versace. The dinner plates were flanked by sterling silver flatware. Georgian silver candlesticks marched apace. Trios of exquisite crystal wine glasses were set at the head of the dinner plates.

Food and drink turned out to be superb, as did the efficient and unobtrusive service from two good-looking, nattily uniformed young waiters. Perfectly moulded smoked salmon and prawn timbales topped with a slice of cucumber and a sprig of coriander for starters; a choice of beef fillet with wild mushrooms and a mushroom vinaigrette or chicken with peaches and vanilla; crêpes with walnut cream and butterscotch sauce or chocolate cherry liqueur cake. It was a truly elegant and satisfying feast.

Conversation flowed easily, ranging over a number of interesting and entertaining topics—all non-divisive. Charlotte found it much easier than she had anticipated. She had never been to Riverbend as a guest. Rohan presided at the head of the table, she to his right. The guest of honour. She wondered what they all thought. Curiously, she felt relaxed—even with Diane Rodgers shooting her many a burning look of appraisal that bit hostile.

She had attended countless dinner parties over the years, but she found herself enjoying Rohan's quick-witted and amusing guests more than most. It was obvious they thought the world of him. Their friend as well as their boss. They were all of an age. Three of the young men and two of the very attractive young women, not including Diane Rodgers, worked for Rohan. Two of the young men were computer whiz kids and had brought their girlfriends along.

Rohan's guests knew better than to start asking leading questions. Except for Diane who, over coffee and liqueurs in the Drawing Room, decided it was high time to throw the cat among the pigeons. For starters there was the enthralling subject of their shared childhood. Charlotte's and Rohan's.

"I bet Rohan was an A-grade student," she said, setting down her exquisite little coffee cup so she could lap up the answer.

Charlotte smiled, wondering where this was going. "The cleverest boy in the Valley," she said, without looking at Rohan. "We all knew he was going to make a huge success of himself."

"Whereas you settled for being a wife and mother?" Diane said, her voice full of womanly understanding. "Possibly the best job of all. You must have been very young when you had your gorgeous little boy. He's—what? Seven?"

"Yes, he is. And he *is* beautiful," Charlotte agreed, hoping Diane would stop. Rohan might look perfectly at ease, lounging back in his armchair, but she knew him so well she could sense a growing turbulence.

"You married another one of your childhood friends— Martyn Prescott, I believe?" Diane pressed on where angels would fear to tread. "Isn't that right? What were you called again? The Gang of Four?"

Charlotte's heart plunged. She was certain Diane Rodgers had talked to Nicole Prescott. "The *Pack* of Four, Diane. But I think you already knew that."

Rohan broke in crisply. "I'm sure Charlotte doesn't want to continue the interrogation, Diane. But *I'm* rather interested to know who told you about the Pack of Four."

Diane's colour deepened. "Gosh, I can't remember," she said, with an innocent blink of her heavily made up dark eyes. "I thought it was a lovely story, anyway. I'm sorry if I've upset you, Charlotte. I just wasn't thinking." Her voice dripped apology.

"That's quite all right, Diane." Charlotte maintained her cool calm. Maybe Diane was on the level? Anything was possible. "I lost my husband eighteen months ago," she told the table. They murmured their sympathy, all of them embarrassed by Diane's insensitivity. At least three of the guests could have told Charlotte that Diane Rodgers could be obnoxious.

"Sorry. So sorry." Diane pressed a hand to her mouth, then thought she had nothing to lose. "I know you've had more than your fair share of tragedy."

Down the table, Sam Bailey rolled his eyes. "Is that silly bitch into annihilation? If she doesn't shut her mouth soon she could just find herself out of a well-paid job," he muttered to his girlfriend, who was in total agreement. They all knew Diane Rodgers was highly effective—she was devoted to their boss and very capable—but the dumbest person on the planet could diagnose an attack of monster jealousy when they saw it.

Some time later, Charlotte took her place at the piano—to delighted applause.

"Do you want the lid up?" Rohan asked, aware Diane had upset Charlotte. Which meant she had upset him, too. Anyone would think he'd been sleeping with Diane, so apparent was her jealousy.

"Not right up," Charlotte said. "I don't want to rocket my audience out of the room." Spacious as the Drawing Room was, this was a nine-foot concert grand.

"This just gets better and better!" Sam exclaimed, settling onto one of the sofas beside his girlfriend and taking her hand. He was blown away by the magnificence of Riverbend. For that matter blown away by the beautiful daughter of the former owner. There was quite a story there.

"I'm a little out of practice," Charlotte turned on the long piano seat to confess. "I've chosen the lovely 'Levitski Waltz'. You may not know the name, but I'm sure you will know the melody, and a couple of shortish pieces from Albéniz's *Suite Española*."

"*Olé!*" Irrepressible Sam essayed a burst of flamenco clapping. Rohan's Charlotte was simply sensational. Why not? So was his boss.

Charlotte waited until they were all seated comfortably, Rohan at their centre. Then she turned back to the Steinway. She was certain Rohan would have had it tuned to perfect pitch after it had been shifted into the house.

To be on the safe side she made a short exploration of the beautiful instrument's dynamics.

"What the hell is she doing?" Diane had to ask the question, feeling a stab of dismay. She wasn't into classical music. She fluffed out her shiny bob. "Is that it?" she whispered to the young woman beside her.

"Get real!" was the astonished response. "Charlotte is just warming up."

"Yeah—I was just having a little joke," said Diane, trying to prove she was as clued-up as the rest of them. She knew Rohan loved classical music. She had seen many of his CDs. Piano, violin, opera singers, symphony orchestras. You name it. Difficult when she had a passion for rock. Something *hot*!

When at last the beautiful, talented Mrs Prescott's little recital came to an end Diane muttered to herself, *"Thank you, God!"* She felt sure Charlotte had been showing off. Closed eyes. Bowed head. That business with her raised hands. *Showing off.* The waltz hadn't been too bad. But she'd had no compulsion to tap her toes at the Spanish numbers. Needless to say that smart alec Sam the sycophant had. It had really pained her to mark the expression on Rohan's handsome face. It suggested he had been transported to some celestial plain. Okay, he adored classical music. Probably that was his only fault.

The party broke up around twelve-thirty. Rohan's guests started to make their way upstairs, having told Charlotte how much they'd enjoyed meeting her and congratulating her on her lovely performance at the piano. Rohan's Charlotte was a true musician.

Last in line, Diane bit her lip so hard she very nearly drew blood. "I hope you enjoyed yourself, Charlotte?" she said, with a bright hostess look.

"Very much so." Charlotte smiled. "I must congratulate you on arranging everything so beautifully, Diane."

"All in a day's work!" Diane's expression turned suitably modest. "I'll say goodnight, then. Will we be seeing you tomorrow?" It wasn't as though the Prescott woman didn't have plenty of time to squander, she thought.

"I doubt it," Charlotte replied lightly. "Goodnight, Diane."

"Goodnight." Diane revved up a smile even though she was so angry. "Goodnight, Rohan."

God, he had to be the sexiest man on the planet. Maybe too sexy for his own good? She had an overwhelming urge to grab him and press him to her throbbing bosom. She had convinced herself she was worthy of Rohan Costello, although she knew he came with a warning. This was a guy who broke hearts. Not intentionally, was the word. But he hadn't been serious about any one of the highly attractive young women he had dated in the past. It distressed her terribly to have Charlotte Prescott, the widow, re-emerge.

Rohan gave her the smile she adored. Did he have any idea how sexy he was? "Goodnight, Diane. Everything went very well."

"Why, thank you!" Diane saw herself as the very image of indefatigable efficiency. She waggled her fingers, then started to move off towards the grand staircase, carrying the heavy weight of jealousy. She paused and turned back for a moment, focusing her gaze on Charlotte. "Look, why don't we catch up some time, Charlotte?" she suggested, making it sound as though they had hit it off wonderfully well. Kindred spirits, as it were.

"You want to keep her under observation?" Rohan asked suavely.

Diane wasn't sure if that was a joke or not. Rohan was such a man of mystery.

Charlotte was kinder. "I'll keep it in mind, Diane."

"Lovely!" Diane threw in another brilliant hostessy smile.

They remained silent until they saw Diane moving gracefully up the staircase on her very high heels.

Charlotte felt rather sorry for Diane. She didn't blame her for falling for Rohan. He was magnetic enough to draw any woman. She had caught Sam Bailey in particular having little snickers at Diane's expense. Diane wasn't liked, it seemed. But she *was* efficient. And very vulnerable where her boss was concerned.

"Now, there's a woman who would like to own you," she said wryly.

"Good thing she hasn't told *me*," was Rohan's brisk reply. "Will we walk back to the Lodge, or won't your evening sandals take it?" He glanced down at her beautifully shod narrow feet. "We can go through the garden. Or I can drive you."

"The drive might be safer."

"Oh, don't be ridiculous!" His tone was derisive. "Nobody said anything about sex," he taunted.

"But you're planning on having it soon?" She rounded on him, lustrous green eyes sparking a challenge.

"Well, we always were compatible in that area," he said, taking her arm. "So—a walk, or the Range Rover?"

"The garden," she said. "It's quickest and the easiest."

His brilliant gaze moved searchingly over her, as though he could uncover her every thought, her every secret. "I can't promise I'll make a point of sticking to the paths."

She put a hand to her throat, as though her heart had suddenly leapt there. Punishment she deserved. The day of reckoning wasn't far off. And then there was Rohan's mother, Mary Rose, deprived of her only grandchild.

Mea culpa!

* * *

A lovely soothing breeze lapped at her hair and her skin, at the fluid long skirt of her evening gown. It wrapped her body and caressed her ankles. The familiar scents of a thousand roses and creamy honeysuckle hung in the air. Above them the stars glittered and danced in a sky of midnight blue velvet. This wasn't wise. But then she had never been able to command wisdom. An aching throb was building up fast in her body.

"Shouldn't you have brought a torch?" she asked, afraid she was revealing too much of her inner agitation.

"For *you*? For *me*?" He gave an edgy laugh. "We know every inch of this place. Don't twist away from me."

"Ah, Rohan!" She gave vent to a deep tremulous sigh that managed to be incredibly seductive. For all their time apart, she was still in thrall to him. Once married to Martyn, she had tried very hard to exorcise Rohan's powerful image. Only it had haunted her every day of her life. And then, as her adored little son had grown older, Rohan's features and mannerisms had begun to emerge! The *fear* she had felt when that occurred! The outright panic. God help her—she had married the *wrong* man! Martyn wasn't the father of her child.

How horrendously rash she had been. She hadn't allowed herself enough time. Only back then she hadn't known what else to do. So young. Pregnant. And she couldn't think Martyn, her friend from childhood, wicked for having physically overcome her. She'd known before they had started out to a rock concert that evening how badly Martyn wanted her. For years he had wanted to be more than just her friend. Only there had always been Rohan. Rohan—who couldn't offer the financial security and the lifestyle he could.

So Martyn had watched and waited for *his* moment.

When she'd realised she was pregnant how she had longed for a wise, loving mother to turn to—a mother full of unconditional love, full of advice as to which course she should take. Her father hadn't been ready for any more shocks. Her escape routes had all been cut off. There had seemed no other course than to pay for her mistake.

Rohan's hand on her tightened, startling her out of her melancholy. "You know it's cruel in its way," he began conversationally. "One can kill trust, respect, write off the crime of betrayal, but one can never kill sexual attraction. I want you very badly—which you damn well know. But then, ours was a very passionate relationship, wasn't it, Charlotte? While it lasted, that is."

Even as he spoke, he could feel the hot blood coursing through his veins. How could he punish Charlotte? Countless times he had longed to be in a position to do so. He had even bought Riverbend, putting in an outrageous offer almost as soon as it came on the market. Revenge on the Marsdons? Revenge on Charlotte who had betrayed him with Martyn, of all people? The only massive impediment was that he wanted her no matter what she did. Charlotte had taken possession of the deepest part of his being.

They walked through a tunnel hung with lovely wisteria towards the summer house, designed as a small Grecian-style temple portico. It glowed whitely ahead. The four classical columns that supported the stone structure were garlanded with a beautiful old-fashioned rose that put out great romantic clusters of cream and palest yellow fragrant blooms, with dark green glossy leaves. Her mother had used to call it the Bourbon rose.

She had a feeling of being inwardly lit up with desire—languorous on the one hand, on the other highly alert. The radiance she felt was so intense it surely must be showing in the luminescence of her skin. She stumbled just a little in her high-heeled sandals. He gripped her arm.

"Oh, Lord!" came from Rohan under his breath. "You were the *world* to me." He hauled her very tightly into his arms. "I lived for you. For our future together."

She was desperate to make amends. "Rohan, I thought—"

He cut her off. "I *don't* want to hear. Remember how we used to come to this place? In secret? This was our shrine, remember? The place of our spiritual and sexual exploration."

"Rohan, I loved you with all my heart."

"Yet you betrayed me."

"I told you. I deserved punishment." She was trembling so badly she needed his tall, lean body to balance her. So much she'd had to endure over the past years. She wanted to cry her heart out. Swear that what she would confess would be the truth, the whole truth, and nothing but the truth.

His grip was fierce and unrelenting. "Well, I have you *now*," he breathed, taking a silky massed handful of her hair and tilting her face up to him. "Come on, Charlotte. Kiss me like you used to."

It was a taunt, a torment. Never an invitation. As in everything he took the initiative. "You're never going to go away, Charlotte."

"No." She was breathless.

"Say it."

"I'm never going to go away. I'll never leave you."

"As if I haven't heard that before." His voice was unbearably cynical. "Only this time we have our son."

Oh, Rohan, hold me. Hold me.

It was an old, old prayer for when she was in a hopeless, helpless situation.

He let go of her long hair, his hands moving to cup her face, his fingers pressing into the fine bones of her skull.

His kiss fell intently on her mouth. Only she confounded him by opening it fully, like a flower to the rain, admitting his seeking tongue to the moist interior. There was no end to sensation, the rush of desire, the rediscovery of rapture. No end to the richness, the incredible *lushness* of sensual pleasure. She reached up naked arms to lock them around his neck. Their darting tongues met in an age-old love dance. She could feel his hands on her, trembling. This had to be a dream from which she never wanted to wake. The first time since the last time she had come blazingly alive. More extraordinarily, the bitterness she knew she had caused, the torture of years of thinking himself betrayed, were nowhere. Not in his mouth. Not in his hands. Profound passion came for them at an annihilating rush.

His hand sought and found her breast, forefinger and thumb stimulating the already tightly budded nipple.

She moaned in mindless rapture, throwing back her head as he kissed her throat.

Oh, the depths of passion! Not even suffering could blunt them.

She could feel herself dissolving. He her captor; she his. She yearned for him…yearned for him… This was her once-in-a-lifetime great love. Desire beat like a drum. It gained power. Surrender would come swiftly behind it. Soon all sense of place would vanish with their clothes. Passion demanded flesh on flesh.

Somehow she found the strength to put a restraining hand over the caressing hand that was palming the globe of her breast. Another second of this and she would be lost to the world.

He must have felt the same way, because he stopped the arousing movement of his hand, letting his hot cheek fall against hers, encountering the wetness of her tears. He savoured them, licking them off with his tongue. They had both been moving with tremendous momentum towards the point of no return.

"All right," he acknowledged, trying to subsume his own near-ungovernable arousal. "I want you for the *night*. Not just minutes out of time."

"Rohan, I can't—"

He cut her off. "You'll have to come to *me*," he said, his voice picking up strength and determination. "Not here. Not Riverbend. I realise the difficulties. But Sydney. Next weekend I've been invited to a big charity function. You'll come as my partner. I'll leave it to you to explain it to your father and Christopher."

She tried to focus on rearranging the bodice of her beautiful silk gown. The flesh of her breast still tingled from his touch. At the very portal of surrender she had pulled back, though she knew her sex-starved body would have no peaceful rest that night.

"It would upset Dad quite a bit," she managed after a while.

"Do you think that bothers me?" His answer was full of disdain. "Your fine, upstanding parents gave my mother and me hell. The only person I'm concerned about is Christopher. I'm only guessing, but I think he'll take it rather well. You're a beautiful young woman, Charlotte. You can't go the rest of your life alone. Or were you planning on living with Daddy for ever?"

"I don't deserve that, Rohan," she shot back. "It's been very difficult. Martyn's death. Dad so sad and lonely. He needed me, Rohan. I couldn't refuse him. I went on to finish my Arts degree externally. I didn't give up. I know I could get myself a halfway decent job in the city, but here in the Valley it would be difficult. No teaching jobs, for instance. All taken. Then there's the fact Chrissie loves the Valley. He loves Dad. I'd hate to uproot him, and I'd have the difficult job of finding a suitable minder for holidays and after-school hours. Not easy!"

"No." He saw the difficulties. "But you don't have to worry now. That's all been taken care of. Our son needs his father."

"I can't let you browbeat me, Rohan." Out of the blue Martyn and his treatment of her popped sickeningly into her mind.

But Rohan was no Martyn.

"*Browbeat* you?" He looked down at her, aghast. "As if I would or could. You want me as much as I want you. That was always the way. Who do you think you're kidding, Charlotte?"

She could feel the tears coming on again. "I've had no *self*, Rohan! Do you understand? No *self.*"

He was shaken by the very real agony in her voice. "Did you think you could learn to love Martyn?" He was trying desperately to understand.

"I *loathed* him!" She thrust away. This was dangerous. She had to get home.

"Loathed him?" Rohan was stunned. "What did he do to make you loathe him? Martyn was mad about you. You *loathed* him? Come on, now. I need to know why."

She tossed back her long mane that tumbled in gleaming disarray over her shoulders, struggling hard to come up with an answer that might stave off a confrontation. "You know Martyn wasn't the strongest of characters. His mother pampered him all his life. Rendered him useless. I don't want to talk about Martyn. He's dead, and in some way I am to blame."

He stood stock still, wishing she were under a spotlight so he could look deep into her eyes. "You couldn't possibly have been frightened of Martyn?" He was forced to consider what he had never considered before. Martyn had adored Charlotte. He would never have hurt her. Would he? "I know he could be a bit of a bully, but you could always handle him. Remember how he bullied that little Thomas kid? I threatened to knock the living daylights out of him if he didn't lay off the kid. First and last time I ever threatened anyone. When you married Martyn you put yourself in the Prescotts' power. And Martyn's father was always a decent man."

"The past is past, Rohan," she said, low-voiced. "Neither of us can change it."

"So you *won't* talk?"

"There's nothing to talk about any more," she insisted. "If I could undo the past I would."

Rohan groaned like a man desperate for peace of mind. "I'm not following this at all. If you seriously believed Martyn was Christopher's father—and that's *your* story— you were having sex with both of us."

"I was so *alone*." *Unprotected. Isolated.* "You took that computer job in Western Australia. It couldn't have been further away. I know they offered you a lot of money, but that meant you were gone for the entire summer vacation. I was without you for the best part of four months. I can't talk about this any more, Rohan. I betrayed you. I betrayed myself. I made a terrible mess of my life. But I'm begging for a ceasefire. You've told me what you want. I understand. I want to make it up to you for your suffering."

Rohan raised a staying hand. "Oh, be damned to that, Charlotte!" he said, very sombrely. "Thing is, you *can't*. I understand your wanting the continuation of your privileged lifestyle. Pregnancy would have made you very vulnerable. You were so young. But I can't forgive you for depriving me of my son, depriving my innocent, hard-working mother of her grandson. You do well to cry. Now, I'd better get you home. Daddy will be waiting up for his golden girl."

CHAPTER SIX

Just as she feared, her father made strenuous objections to her spending the following weekend in Sydney.

"You've always been in Costello's power!" he ranted. "You'd think the boy was some powerful sorcerer. He's always had your heart and your mind."

How true! She and Rohan had connected from early childhood on some profoundly crucial wavelength. "He's not a *boy* any longer, Dad," she pointed out. "He's very much a man. I'm twenty-six, remember? I want a life."

"Not with Costello." Vivian Marsdon violently shook his head. "Never with Costello. The idea is *monstrous*! What would it do to your mother?"

Charlotte's caught her father's eyes. "Do you mean the mother who so cherishes me and my little son?" she asked with considerable pain. "Mum took herself out of our lives. Why should I now worry what *she* thinks?"

"Because you always did and you always will. We both care. I still love Barbara. And you still love your mother, no matter how badly she let us down."

"What about Christopher, Dad?" Charlotte asked heatedly. "*You'll* always love him? No matter what?"

Vivian Marsdon frowningly picked up on her words. "No matter what? What are we talking about, here? Have you formed some new understanding with Costello?"

"There's so much you don't know, Dad. At the heart of it is the sad fact you never *wanted* to know. If Rohan could get me at the snap of a finger, why do you suppose I married Martyn?"

Vivian Marsdon's thick sandy blond eyebrows drew together in a ferocious frown. "Because he loved you. God, Charlie, he was *madly* in love with you. You were all things to him. I scarcely need mention he was in a position to offer you far more than Costello ever could. Security counts with a woman."

"You mean what he could offer *at the time*? It wasn't Martyn's money anyway. The truth is, Dad, Martyn and I lived off his father. They wanted it that way. I wasn't allowed a job outside organising social events. And there was nothing, absolutely nothing, I could do."

Vivian Marsdon stumbled back into his vast armchair. "I don't believe this."

"That's because you've spent your life hiding your head in the sand. It's safer down there."

"It's what I *believed*, Charlie, but I see now I was wrong. I was fearful for your mother's sanity. I couldn't bring myself to take a stand against her. God, I loved her. She was my *wife*. We were happy in the old days. Before our darling Mattie died."

"I know, Dad." Charlotte bowed her head. Nothing good had come out of Mattie's tragic death. But for years of her childhood up until that point it *had* been a magic time. And most of that magic had been due to Rohan Costello.

"But *you* don't have to be alone, Charlie. You're a very beautiful, highly intelligent young woman. You're *my* daughter. A Marsdon. That name still carries a lot of clout. I could name a dozen young men in the Valley desperate to pound their way to your door."

She laughed. "Not a few of them you didn't frighten off, Dad. Good thing I wasn't interested in any of them."

"Why would you be?" he snorted. "Ordinary. Ordinary young men. Costello *isn't*, whatever else he is. He's bought Riverbend on *your* account!" He said it as though he had hit on an invisible truth.

"Rohan bought Riverbend because he's a very astute businessman. It's prime real estate, Dad. The most beautiful estate in a beautiful prosperous valley. Rohan has big plans."

"And they surely include you," Vivian Marsdon said with a sinking heart.

"That upsets you so dreadfully, Dad?"

He looked across at her mournfully. "I couldn't bear to lose you and Chrissie, Charlotte. I have no one else."

"But you won't be losing either of us, Dad," she said, with a burst of love and sympathy. "As long as that's what you want, I would never deprive my boy of his grandfather. He *loves* you."

"He does. God has blessed me. And I love my grandson with all my heart. He's a wonderful little boy. He's going to make his mark in the world. And I didn't think much of Costello's trying to buy the boy's affection by taking him and young Peter for that helicopter ride."

"Oh, come on now, Dad. They were absolutely thrilled. Chris had all the kids madly envious when he told them about it at school. Chris went with Rohan very willingly."

Vivian Marsdon sighed. "I ask you—how did it happen? You'd think Christopher had known him all his life," he added with amazement. "Of course a helicopter ride is a sure way to get to a seven-year-old's heart."

"See it as Christopher learning new things, Dad. He's

only a little boy, but he's a good judge of a person's character. Children see very clearly."

"Especially the latest in helicopters," Marsdon grunted. "It sounds very much to me as though you and Costello have an agenda of your own. How did it happen in such a very short time? I mean, he's only just back in your life. You fainted when you saw him, you were so distressed. Are you really over your husband? What will the Prescotts think if you two get together?"

Charlotte's clear voice hardened. "The only Prescott you have any time for, Dad, is Gordon Prescott. Don't pretend you respected Martyn."

Her father shifted uncomfortably. "I truly believe the only reason he was unfaithful to you, Charlie, was because you didn't love him as he wished."

"Dad, you could be right." Her expression was a mix of self-disgust and sorrow. "I have to tell you I never loved Martyn. It was all a big cover-up. I was pregnant when I married him."

Her father gave vent to another deep sigh. "Yes, well… All the more reason for you to have tried very hard to make a go of it."

"I *did* try, Dad. Not easy pretending you love someone when you don't."

Vivian Marsdon sat with a mournful expression carved into his handsome face. "Your mother didn't beat about the bush with me. She took off."

"It was Riverbend—the river, Dad." She tried to console him.

"Yet we still see Mattie walking by the river, don't we?" He lifted his head to give her the saddest smile. "The river doesn't torture us. In mysterious ways it comforts us. Mattie is close by. Our Chrissie feels Mattie's presence. I never thought much about a *soul* until we lost Mattie. But now

I'm certain we do have one. Never thought much about God. Unlike your mother, I now know there is one. Mattie's *spirit* is here. And it's not a sad one. Wherever he is, Mattie is happy. Remember that strange woman who came to stay outside the village some years back? Always dressed like the old idea of a gypsy? She stopped me once to ask the name of the other child who was with little Christopher and me."

"I remember your account of the incident vividly. The woman claimed she saw a blond boy, on the frail side, aged about fourteen, walking along with you."

"That's right." Vivian Marsdon covered his face with his hand. "It shocked me at the time, but then I realised someone must have told her about Mattie in the village."

"That *could* have happened, Dad, but I don't think it did. She'd only just arrived. Besides, it would have been very cruel to approach you in that way, and you saw no sign of her being anything like that. She kept herself to herself while she was living in that old cottage that had belonged to a relative, and the very last thing people did was bring up our family tragedy. Everyone knew the grief and suffering it had brought down on our heads. Who knows? Maybe she did have a genuine gift. I'm open-minded about such things. You are too. We all *see* Mattie. He's not a trillion miles away. Some part of him is still here, in the place where he lost his mortal life."

"Your mother couldn't bear the thought," Vivian Marsdon said. 'But it comforts me to think that woman might have been saying it the way she saw it."

"Me too." Charlotte reached out for her father's hand.

"You're a good girl, Charlie. *My* girl." He took his handkerchief from his pocket, then strenuously blew his nose. "So, you're going to Sydney for the weekend?"

"I am."

"Have you told Chrissie?"

"Not before I'd spoken to you."

Vivian sank further into his armchair. "I have the feeling he won't have any objection. There could be another helicopter ride in store for him."

Charlotte waited until she had dropped off Peter and his little monster of a sister at their front gate. Peter stood and waved. Angela, as was her custom, ran inside without any acknowledgement of the ride. Then she waited until Peter too was safely inside his front gate. They watched him walking up the short drive.

"Gosh, she's an awful kid!" Christopher made a funny whooping noise. "The rudest kid I know." He was amazed by Angela's behaviour. "Do you suppose she's going to spend her whole life in a bad mood? Peter tells his mother how rude she is, but even Mrs Stafford doesn't seem able to get Angie to say thank you."

"Hopefully it's just a phase." Charlotte patted her son's small hand. The shape of it was Rohan's. "I've something to ask you," she said, keeping her eyes on the road. Safety was all-important. Martyn had been such a careless driver, even when he'd had her and their precious child on board. "Rohan has asked me to be his partner at a big charity function in Sydney this coming Saturday night."

"Really?" Christopher's radiant blue eyes grew huge. "Gee, he's a fast worker," he said, with real admiration.

"If you don't want me to go, I won't." Charlotte meant it.

Christopher laughed. "Don't be silly. I think it's great! I really like Rohan. I want him to be our friend. He's so clever. He'd make a great teacher. He knows tons of things. More than Grandpa, I think. I'd never say that to Gramps, though. Rohan knows all about vineyards and olive groves too. He has lots of plans for Riverbend. He told me I could be in on all of them. Honestly, Mum, I can't think of anyone better than Rohan to go out with. It's sad, the way you're always stuck at home. You looked so beautiful the other night. Rohan thought so too."

"Did he tell you?" She felt the heat in her cheeks.

"Sure he told me. He told me all about when you were kids. You were the greatest friends. He told me really, *really* nice things about you and Uncle Mattie."

She bit her lip. "And about your—father? About Daddy?"

"No, not about Daddy," Christopher admitted. "But Rohan is so easy to talk to I nearly told him I didn't think Daddy liked me."

"What?" Charlotte felt her every nerve in her body stretch to breaking point.

"I *didn't* say anything," Christopher swiftly reassured her, suddenly looking upset. "But Daddy didn't like me much, did he? Not like Grandpa loves me. Nothing like *you* love me. You love me to bits!"

"You can bet on that!" Charlotte spoke with great fervour. "But Daddy did love you, Chrissie," she said, deeply distressed.

"No, Mum." He shook his head. "I don't want you to tell a big fat lie to make me feel better. None of them seemed to care about me. Maybe Grandfather Prescott did. He was always nice. But Grandma Prescott and Nicole—they sure weren't very nice to me. Especially Nicole. I reckon Angela will grow up to be a person just like Nicole. Then there's Grandma Marsdon. She doesn't want to see me. Maybe she thinks you shouldn't have had me in the first place?"

"Christopher, my darling boy! You've been thinking all these things?" She was shocked and appalled. Her son was only seven years old, but already he was weighing up things in his head like an adult.

"Don't worry about it, Mummy." His expression turned protective. "I don't actually care about them any more. Some of the kids tease me about how you and I live with Grandpa. They say things like, 'Why doesn't your mum get married again?' That sort of thing. It annoys me a bit, but it makes Pete *really* angry. He's my friend."

Charlotte's heart gave a great lunge. "You've never told me any of this before. I thought you told me everything?" She felt very sad.

"I didn't tell you because I knew it would upset you. But Rohan's *great*!" Enthusiasm was renewed. "I'm wishing and wishing you two hit it off."

So without even trying Rohan had found a powerful ally.

In his *son*.

Charlotte found as much excitement in the helicopter ride as Christopher would. It was fantastic to see the beautiful rural landscape become a cityscape unfolding beneath them. With the helicopter's wraparound glass the visibility was everything one could wish for, and the Harbour looked magnificent on that special Saturday morning.

It was impossible for her not to feel a surge of pride at the first sight of their beautiful capital city and the iconic "Coathanger"—which was what Sydneysiders called the Sydney Harbour Bridge. The world's largest steel arched bridge, it linked the Sydney CBD and the South and North Shores, with their famous beaches. And down there, jutting out into the sparkling blue waters of Bennelong Point, was one of the great wonders of the modern world: the Sydney Opera House, its famous roof evocative of a ship at full sail.

It couldn't have been more appropriate for the Harbour City, Charlotte thought, though the distinguishing "sails" had cost a great fortune and a whole lot of heartache. But there it was today, in all its splendour. Probably the nation's most recognisable image.

Their pilot Tim Holland, a very experienced and highly respected pilot, was retained by Rohan for personal *and* company use. On Rohan's instructions he took them on a short joyride to increase Charlotte's pleasure. Yachts were out aplenty. The Harbour bloomed with a profusion of white sails. Below them a crowd swam and frolicked in the legendary Bondi surf. Others lay out on the golden sand, sunbaking. Charlotte hoped they were slathered in sunblock. Sydney was Australia's oldest, largest and most culturally diverse city. It was also the most exciting, with an unmatchable *buzz*. She could feel her spirits, for so long down, soaring.

Rohan used his state-of-the-art headset with its voice-activated microphone to speak with her and their pilot, Tim. The headsets enabled them to easily communicate.

"American Airmen during the Second World War flew a couple of Kittyhawks under the Bridge. Not to be outdone, the following year a *flight* of RAAF Wirraways did their own fly-under. These days tourists and locals love climbing it. I've made the Bridge Climb three times. By day, at twilight, and by night."

"It can't be for the faint-hearted?"

"Well, there are safety precautions, of course. One has to give a blood-alcohol reading, for a start. Then there's the Climb Simulator, to get an idea of what one might experience. But the view is worth it a million times over. It's absolutely breathtaking."

"Like now!" she replied. "Christopher would find this the most marvellous adventure."

"He'll see it." Rohan spoke matter-of-factly. He might have issues with her, but he had bonded with his son on sight. Such was the power of blood.

A company limo was standing by to take them the short distance to her city hotel, beautifully positioned between the Opera House and the Harbour Bridge. She had insisted on checking into a hotel, even though she knew she would be spending the night with Rohan at his Harbourside apartment. That was their agreement. But she had promised Christopher she would ring him from her hotel when she arrived, and tell him of all the excitement of the helicopter flight. Plus there was the fact she wanted to offer at least token resistance to Rohan's command of events.

He accompanied her to her luxurious room, looking around him as if to assure himself everything was up to scratch. "You know as well as I do, Rohan, this hotel has a reputation for excellence," she protested mildly. "But I suppose as you've paid for it you're entitled to check out the mod-cons."

"Thank you for thinking of that, Charlotte," he returned suavely. "I have a little trip planned for us this afternoon after lunch."

"It can't top the flight. That was wonderful. I'm going to ring Chrissie in a minute. He's the main man in my life."

"He's now the main man in *my* life as well. What I have in mind, my beautiful Charlotte, is to take you on a visit to my mother."

She was taken by complete surprise.

"Remember, I do have one?" he said, sardonically. "One of these days I might even go in search of my father."

She slumped onto the bed, staring up at him. "Have you found out who he is? Your mother told you?"

"Miraculously, *yes*. A huge step for mankind. She

hadn't told a soul—including the grandmother who reared her—but..."

"But, what?"

He lowered his lean length into an armchair, facing her. "I'm surprised you haven't guessed, Charlotte. You were always so intuitive. I was in rather a mess when I found out you'd married Martyn. But that was nothing to finding out you'd borne him a child. My mother was very worried about me. She decided at long last she was going to tell me what had happened to her when she was very young."

"Are you going to share it with me?"

Tension snapped and hummed as if overhead electricity wires were strung across the room.

"Why not? My father is Italian. Who would have thought it? I had always assumed he was Australian. But my birth father was born and lived in Rome. He and a few of his well-heeled student friends were tripping around the world, enjoying a university vacation. The Opera House, apparently, was a must-see for him. He was an architectural student, and the Opera House is a magnet for architects as well as millions of people from around the world. It was Jorn Utzon's *tour de force*, after all. He met my mother while the two of them were wandering around the plateau. He was taking photographs for his own records. They got to talking. That was the start of it! He was something of a polyglot, which no doubt helped. Apparently he spoke fluent English, French—and Italian, of course. My mother thought him the most fascinating human being she had ever met in her life. She fell for him hook, line and sinker. Whether he was just taking advantage of a pretty girl in a foreign country, I don't know. She says *not*. But she knew their romance couldn't last. Too much against it. He was from another country and a totally different background, obviously wealthy."

"Yet she took enormous risks?"

"A lot of us make mistakes when we're young, Charlotte," he said dryly. "I don't have to tell *you* that. He swore he would write to her, but he never did. Once he was home again among his own people his holiday romance would soon have faded away. Happens all the time." He gave a cynical shrug.

"But you know his name?"

There was a slight flare to his nostrils. He looked every inch a man of high mettle. "I do. He's most likely married, with grown-up children. He wouldn't be all that happy to discover he'd left an illegitimate son in far-off Australia. It would upset the apple cart. No, Charlotte, I'm the product of a short, sweet encounter. Maybe he remembers my mother now and again. She must have been very pretty. She still is."

"I believe it!" Very pretty, with lovely Celtic colouring that hadn't got a look-in with Christopher. "You're upset, Rohan?"

"Am I not supposed to be?" he challenged. "You're so good at analysing people, Charlotte."

"I'm good at analysing *you,*" she returned with some spirit. "Don't be bitter."

"My dear Charlotte, I'm *managing* my bitterness. You know, in some ways you and my mother are alike. Both of you have lived your lives withholding vital information. Both of you took it upon yourselves to decide the outcome of your pregnancies. My mother told no one. You decided to go with a great lie."

She flushed at the hardness of the gaze. "So you're going to take it out on me for ever?"

"No. Let's forget about it." He rose lithely to his feet. "Worse things have happened at sea. I have a couple of things I need to attend to. I'll pick you up in an hour.

Remember me to my son, won't you? Tell him I'll organise another trip for him. His friend Peter too, if he likes. Mattie always thought of me whenever there was a trip on offer."

"Mattie worshipped you."

He sighed deeply. "Matthew should have been allowed to run wild when we were kids, but your mother insisted on cooping him up. I find that truly sad."

Neither of them spoke for a moment, both lost in the past. Charlotte was the first to recover. "I must tell you something that now appears not all that amazing. Christopher says he wants to be an architect when he grows up. He's seen the Opera House many times. We've been out on the Harbour. He thinks the sails are like the rising waves of the Pacific. He used to draw them over and over, lamenting he could never get them right. Dad's been happy to buy books for him. He's told him all about the brilliant young Danish architect who had no computer to work with, no internet, just a drawing board. Christopher is very good at art. His skills are way beyond his peers, according to his art teacher."

"Good grief!" Rohan looked surprised. "I can draw myself. You'll remember that? But these days we have all the technology we need to hand. I never thought of becoming an architect, even if we'd had the money. But *Christopher*!"

"I guess blood will out," she said quietly.

"Then we have to see he realises his dream." Rohan turned brisk. "We'll have lunch, then we'll go and see my mother. I bought her a very nice apartment at Point Piper." He named one of the most sought-after areas to live in Sydney. "It has everything going for it. The best north-facing Harbour views, easy access to the city, exclusive shops and restaurants, ocean beaches nearby."

She caught him up at the door, laying a detaining hand on his arm. "Does she know about Christopher?" Her green eyes were huge with concern.

"Don't panic," he said quietly. "She *would* if she ever laid eyes on him. But no, Charlotte, I'm not cruel. My mother knows I've bought Riverbend. She knows I went after *you*, seeing as I don't seem capable of staying away," he said with a degree of self-contempt. "And I've told her we're back together again."

"What did she say to that?" Her expression grew more anxious.

His strong arms encircled her waist as he drew her to him. He dropped a light kiss on her mouth—not soft, but subtle—lingering over it as though there were no better way for the two of them to communicate. "What makes me happy makes my mother happy," he said when he lifted his head.

"But she knows how much I hurt you. She must know that I..." Her voice faltered, gave out.

"Unquestionably it will be a great shock to her to find out Christopher is *my* son, not Martyn Prescott's. But you can be sure of one thing. She will welcome Christopher, her *grandson*, with open arms."

"If not me?" There was great sadness and regret in her tone. Mary Rose of the flame-coloured hair had adored her son, her only child. She would feel very strongly about what had been done to him to this day.

"Lucky for you, my mother has a very loving heart, Charlotte. A great blessing when *your* mother gave herself up to obsession."

"She didn't know how to control it!" she responded, with a show of heat. "She didn't know how to properly *love*! She's not the only one."

"Indeed she isn't." He dropped his encircling arms, his face grim. "Some of it must have rubbed off on you."

She swung away, her body quaking with nerves. Once she had been a very spirited young person—full of life, full of a bright challenge. But all the stuffing had been knocked out of her. "I'm having second thoughts about staying, Rohan," she warned him.

He glanced very casually at his handsome gold watch. "I'll pick you up in the foyer. We might as well have lunch here. The restaurants are very good. Then on to my mother's. All that has happened you'll find she'll forgive you, Charlotte. After all, like you, she's a woman with a past."

"The last word as ever, Rohan?" she countered.

He spun back, his low laugh sardonic. "It was *you* who had the last word, Charlotte. But times have changed." He reached only a few inches to pull her back into his arms. "What about letting yourself go for a minute?" he challenged, his blue eyes alight. "See it as practice, if you like. *Kiss me, Charlotte.* The sort of kiss that will carry me right through the day." His hands slid gently down her shoulders. "Remember how we used to sleep together naked, our limbs entwined? My arms around the silky curves of your body. The scent of your skin was wonderful! Peaches and citrus and something subtly musky too. God, how I loved you! I could never get enough of you. So kiss me, Charlotte. It's a simple thing."

Only it wasn't simple at all. It was as terrifying as taking a leap off the edge of a cliff. She *wanted* to kiss him. Kiss him deeply. She wanted to hold his dark head with her hands. She wanted to express her profound sense of loss and grief. In the end she lifted herself onto her toes, touching her lips to his. It was a feather-light kiss, so gentle, her hand caressing the side of his face. His darkly olive skin had a faint rasp from his beard.

He opened his mouth slightly to accommodate her. Immediately she slipped the tip of her tongue into the cavity, brushing it over his fine white teeth and the inside of his upper lip. He tasted wonderful. Her body was reacting very strongly. The kiss deepened into something *real*. The fever of it, the never-to-be-forgotten rapture… The time they had *wasted*!

His hand slid down the creamy column of her neck, pale as a rose, closing on the small high mound of her breast. The sensitive coral-pink nipple was already erect, like a tiny budding fruit.

"Is this kiss *real*?" he drew back a little to ask. To taunt? "It seems real to me."

"Rohan, don't let's fight. I only want us to become closer."

"Well, we do have tonight." His handsome head descended and he began to kiss in earnest. So deeply, so ravenously, that after a while she fully expected both of them would simply topple to the floor, captives of passion.

It was beautiful. It was agonising. It was a language both of them spoke perfectly…

Then suddenly his hands on her shoulders were firm. He was holding her away, male supremacy absolute. "Some things can't be crushed, can they?" he muttered ironically. "It's the same as it used to be, our lovemaking."

"You sound like it's a curse." She could barely speak for the thudding of her heart and the turmoil in her flesh.

"Some curse!" he said with a twisted smile. He dropped his hands, becoming businesslike. "I'm sure you've brought a dress to wear this afternoon. Not that I don't love the jeans and T-shirt. You have a great body. But a dress, I think. I'm sure my mother will agree you're even more beautiful now than you were as a girl. God knows, your grace and beauty turned me inside out."

Charlotte touched him with a trembling hand. "Let's try to be kind to one another, Rohan."

He thought that over for a tense moment, then flashed his white smile. Their son's smile. "Why not? For old times' sake, if nothing else."

They were actually outside the door of Mary Rose Costello's luxury apartment. Charlotte was in a daze of apprehension, trying to grapple with the speed of recent events. The force of her beating heart was stirring the printed silk of her dress. She was seeking forgiveness, but she didn't know how she could begin to deserve it. She wasn't the only one haunted by the events of the past. So was Rohan—and his mother. If Mary Rose Costello even suspected she had a little grandson who had been denied to her...

Dear God!

Rohan took her hand, his long fingers twining with hers. "Just like the old days," he said sardonically, standing back a little as his mother opened the door to them. Her expression was composed, but it had to be said a shade austere.

Charlotte just escaped making some little exclamation. Mary Rose Costello, a woman well over forty, looked a good ten years younger—as pretty and polished a woman as one could hope to see. Her former shock of copper-red hair was cut short and beautifully styled. Her complexion was the genuine redhead's classic alabaster. Not a wrinkle in sight. She looked rich and cared for down to her pearly fingertips. Petite and slight as ever, she was wearing a lovely cool maxi-dress—white splashed with small flowers.

Mary Rose Costello looked back at Charlotte keenly. There was no welcoming smile on her face. No big hello. *Maybe she might flatly refuse to let me in?* Charlotte

agonised, worried her treacherous knees might buckle.
Maybe Mary Rose would start to vent her stored-up rage?
Charlotte half expected it. Perhaps would have *preferred*
rage to a false welcome. Still, she made the first move.

"Mrs Costello." She held out her hand. "I only learned
from Rohan of this visit today. You don't have to ask me
in if you don't want to." She wasn't going to cry, but she
felt very much like it. Instead she bit the inside of her lip.

Mary Rose took a few seconds to respond. "You and
my son have reunited, Charlotte. It's only natural I should
agree to his request to invite you." A moment's hesitation,
then she stepped forward, drawing the taller Charlotte into
a short hug. "Come in, my dear. You must remember I was
always very fond of you."

"I'm so grateful, Mrs Costello." Charlotte didn't look
back at Rohan.

"My son looks after me in style, as you can see." Mary
Rose flashed a proud loving smile in Rohan's direction.
"But I do own and run a successful boutique in Double Bay.
I was always very interested in fashion, if you remember?
I'll show you over the boutique one day soon."

"Thank you. I'd be interested to see it. I remember all
the lovely dresses you used to make." She was in peril of
mentioning her mother, who had been so good and then
so very vengeful towards the Costellos. She was feeling
unreal. It was getting to be a constant state of mind.

"Come along, darling," Rohan said with the greatest
show of affection, taking hold of Charlotte's nerveless arm
and guiding her into the living room.

All for his mother's benefit, of course. Charlotte was
fully conscious of that. They needed to present a united
front. This was the first step. The more difficult ones were
to follow.

"Please do call me Mary Rose, Charlotte." Mary Rose

indicated they should both take a seat on one of the richly textured cream sofas. The seats were separated by a long black lacquer coffee table holding several coffee table books and an exquisite arrangement of pure white hippeastrum heads, packed into a simple but elegantly-shaped white porcelain vase.

"How very beautiful!" Charlotte remarked, loving the purity of the arrangement.

"We have a wonderful young florist in the area, fast becoming known." Mary Rose had expected Charlotte to notice. "She really brings the beauty of even a few flowers to life. I must show you her beautiful white butterfly orchid in a pot. She put the pot into a bed of bright green moss inside a glass vase like a large tumbler. I love white flowers."

"As do I." Charlotte looked around the living room, grateful for a little breathing space. How did one go about having a conversation when all the important issues had to be avoided like the plague? The living room was spacious, and elegantly decorated, with many imaginative touches and a small collection of very fine art. "I recognise the work of that artist," she said, naming a painter famous for her abstracts. One of her large canvases hung above the white marble mantel—dramatic, but beautifully calm.

"Rohan bought it for my birthday," Mary Rose said, with the sweetest smile she reserved for her son.

How would she smile at her grandson? *Would* she smile?

"It makes a balance for the panoramic views, don't you think, Charlotte?" Rohan was acting lover-like to the hilt. "I had a landscaper come in to make a little green oasis on the balcony."

"What I can see of it is stunning." Small-talk was going a little way to helping her relax. Through the open sliding glass doors she could see many beautiful plants growing in planter troughs. An eye-catching green flowering wall had been integrated into the design.

"My lovely lush sanctuary." Mary Rose smiled. "It's amazing what they're doing these days with apartment balconies. You look very beautiful, Charlotte." Mary Rose took a seat on the opposite sofa.

"Thank you." Charlotte responded quietly. She had never been comfortable with comments on her physical beauty. It was all in the genes anyway. There were many other things besides regular features.

"The last thing Charlotte is is vain." Rohan caught Charlotte's hand, carrying it to his mouth. He did it so beautifully he might well have meant it. Only they were putting on a show for his mother.

"May I say how wonderful *you* look?" Charlotte offered, in a sincere compliment. She didn't dare withdraw her hand from Rohan's. No telling what he might do next.

"I have to admit to a little hard work. I go to a gym twice a week. My son likes me to look my best. And of course I have to look good for the boutique. My clients expect it."

"Not a lot look as good or as youthful as my mother," Rohan said.

"That I well believe."

Was it going to be this simple? Charlotte thought. On the face of it it appeared to be accepted and forgiven. But then Mary Rose didn't know she had been deprived of her grandson—shut out of his early life, the precious infant and toddler years.

Inevitably the conversation, just as she'd dreaded, had to come around to Martyn. "I was very sorry to hear of his premature death." Mary Rose's face contorted slightly. "He was your husband. It must have been awful for you and for little Christopher. Rohan has told me what a remarkable little boy he is. Would you have a photo with you? If so, I'd love to see it."

Heart hammering, Charlotte opened her handbag, taking out her wallet. She had been meaning to replace the small photo of Christopher at age five with a current one. Now she was glad she hadn't. Christopher's blond curls clustered around his head. He was smiling. He looked like an angel. "This was taken a couple of years ago," she said, removing the photograph and handing it across to Mary Rose—her son's paternal grandmother.

Mary Rose started forward to take it. Her gaze rested on it for quite a while, then she lifted her copper head slowly. "You won't believe this, but he looks a bit like my Rohan when he was younger. Rohan didn't start out with dark hair, you know. It was fair for a few of those early years. Of course your boy has inherited the Marsdon blond hair," Mary Rose said, retaining her searching expression. "He's as beautiful as you are. He must be a great joy to you. But I can't see he looks much like you at this stage, Charlotte. Or Martyn." She frowned.

"He keeps changing." Charlotte felt the pulse beating in her temple.

"I must meet him." Mary Rose handed the photo back. "And your mother and father? How are they?"

"Didn't Rohan tell you?" Charlotte turned her head to look into Rohan's fire-blue eyes.

Rohan didn't answer. He waited for his mother's response.

Mary Rose shook her head. "I never really wanted to go there, Charlotte," she said. "Those years after you lost your brother and my son lost his dearest friend were very hard on all of us. The way my son was blamed by your mother broke my heart. But as a mother I understood she was out of her mind with grief. Still, it was a very painful time. Thank God my son has moved on. So have I. And here you are again, back in my son's life—as I often felt you would be, despite all the odds. Rohan tells me you and he are planning to get married very soon?"

She fixed her hazel gaze on Charlotte's face, with no attempt at lightness. This was the young woman who had broken her beloved son's heart. She had rejected him so she could have it all. Or so it had seemed. But even then, Mary Rose realised, some part of her had questioned Charlotte's motivation. Charlotte Marsdon had never been one to cause pain. The daughter of privilege, she had always been her lovely graceful self with everyone. Social standing hadn't come into it.

"Yes." Charlotte sat, her slender body taut, a whole weight of emotion in her eyes. "I want you to forgive me, Mrs Costello—Mary Rose. We need your blessing. *I* need your blessing. Finally I get to do the right thing." She stopped before she burst into tears.

"Then you *have* my blessing." Mary Rose Costello was herself holding back tears. "You need to get a life for yourself, Charlotte. For yourself and for your son. It's terrible, the loss of all the good years. Take it from someone who knows."

CHAPTER SEVEN

CHARLOTTE recognised any number of people as she entered the huge function room on Rohan's arm. From somewhere a small orchestra was playing classical music. It was barely audible above the loud hum of conversation and laughter. The glassed-in walls, the lighting, the profusion of flowers and green plants, the women's beautiful evening dresses all lent the grand ballroom of one of Sydney's most glamorous venues for social and charity events an exotic look—rather like a splendid conservatory. Tonight's function was to raise funds for a children's leukaemia foundation, and there was a heart-warming turnout.

Many people had marked their arrival. She was aware that heads were turning in all directions.

"Ah, there's Charlotte Prescott back on the scene. You remember her husband? A bit of a scandal there. And isn't that the new mover and shaker she's with? Rohan Costello?"

Charlotte acknowledged the people she knew with a little wave and a smile. Her mother had been a great fundraiser.

A woman's face stood out in the crowd—if only because of the cold distaste of her expression and the rigidity in the set of her head and shoulders. It was Diane Rodgers, looking very elegant in black and silver. Her dark eyes focused quite alarmingly on Charlotte and then moved on to Rohan. But Rohan had his head turned go the side, saluting a colleague.

Thank God Ms Rodgers wasn't seated at their table, Charlotte thought, wondering if Rohan had anything to do with it. Diane Rodgers was an assertive go-getter. It was painfully obvious she had convinced herself she had a real chance with Rohan, and her bitter disappointment over the destruction of her daydreams had turned to loathing of her perceived rival. Unrequited love could be a terrible business.

Rohan knew everyone at their table, and swiftly and charmingly made introductions. Charlotte was greeted warmly. Waiters appeared with champagne. The evening was underway.

Charlotte gazed around her with pleasure. The ballroom, which had one of the most spectacular views of Sydney Harbour, was a glitter of lights. The circular tables placed all around the huge room had floor-length cloths of alternating pastel blue, pink and silver. The chairs were tied with broad bands of silver satin. Small arrangements of blue hydrangeas or posies of pink roses acted as centrepieces. Massed clouds of pink, blue and silver balloons were suspended from the ceiling. The huge screen up on the dais showed the logo of the charity in the familiar colours.

Guests had really dressed up for the occasion. Men in black tie, women wearing the sorts of gowns one saw flipping over the pages of *Vogue*. Everyone had the sense this was going to be a most successful evening, for a very deserving charity. Charlotte was pleased to see some of the richest and most powerful men in the country seated at tables not far from them. That could only mean a great deal of money would be raised.

Hours later, after a very successful evening, it was time to go home. Just as Charlotte had expected, Diane Rodgers, dark eyes glowing like coals, was lying in wait for Rohan.

"Won't be a moment," Rohan told Charlotte with a wry smile.

"That's okay."

A beaming, portly elderly man was making for Charlotte, calling her name in a delighted voice. Charlotte held out her hand to ex-senator Sir Malcolm Fielding. "How lovely to see you, Malcolm." She held up her cheek for his kiss. Malcolm Fielding had gone to school and university with her grandfather. They had always remained good friends. In the old days Malcolm and his late wife had been frequent visitors to Riverbend.

"Your mother is here, dear—did you know?" Malcolm Fielding looked about, as though trying to locate Barbara in the moving throng.

"No, I didn't," Charlotte answered, calmly enough, though her feelings were rapidly turning to blind panic. *Her mother!* She was lucky if her mother ever answered one of her calls.

"An impressive lady, your mother," said Malcolm. "And still a handsome woman. A bit chilly though, dear. Even her smile, wouldn't you say? Terrible tragedy about young Mattie, but Barbara might be reminded she still has *you*. I was totally blitzed when your parents separated. But tragedy can sometimes do that to people."

He looked over Charlotte's shining blonde head. "Oh—a bit early, but there's my ride!" he exclaimed. "Can't keep them waiting. A flawless event, wouldn't you say, Charlotte? All the more because we met up." He kissed her cheek again. "I couldn't help noticing the young man you're with," he added roguishly. "Costello is making quite a name for himself. No relation to our ex-treasurer. Don't forget to remember me to your father, now. Tell him to give me a ring. We'll have lunch at the club."

"Will do, Sir Malcolm." Charlotte smiled, although a feeling of alarm was invading her entire body. Had her mother seen her with Rohan? Why was she so surprised her mother was in Sydney? She had spotted many a Melbournite who had flown in to attend this big charity function.

To calm her agitation she started walking along with the happy, chattering crowd towards one of the arched door-ways that led onto the street. She knew Rohan would follow fairly soon. Outside, limousines were starting to cruise, picking up their passengers. The headlights picked up the multi colours of the women's dresses and the brilliance of their jewellery.

Charlotte was just slowing her steps so she wouldn't get too far ahead of Rohan when a woman's firm hand caught her from behind.

"One moment, Charlotte."

Charlotte turned back to face her mother.

I'm scared of this woman, she thought. *Scared of my own mother. Or of the bitter, backward-looking woman my mother had become.*

She wanted to run, but knew she had to stand her ground. "Good evening, Mother," she said courteously. "Is Kurt with you?" Kurt Reiner was a decent enough man. Very rich, of course.

"Forget Kurt!" Barbara Reiner snapped explosively. "He's somewhere. At the moment I don't give a toss where." Barbara Reiner's haughty face with its classic features had become marred over the years by a perpetual expression of malcontent.

"I didn't see you. It was such a big turn-out. Malcolm Fielding told me you were here. You look very well." Her mother wore vintage Dior, black lace, with a double string of South Sea pearls around her throat and large pearl pendant drops.

"The emeralds, I see!" She showed bitter disappointment that they weren't hanging from her own neck.

"Dad gave me permission to wear them."

"Well, he would, wouldn't he? He always did indulge you." Barbara's narrowed glance darted back to where Rohan was standing with the Premier and his wife. They were about to enter the back seat of a Rolls-Royce. "Tell me that's not Rohan Costello?" Fury streaked across Barbara's cold, distinguished face.

"Why ask a question when you know the answer?" Charlotte replied quietly. "You know perfectly well it's Rohan. Does anyone else look like him? Besides, you must have taken note of his very generous donation."

"So he's done well for himself." Barbara gritted her teeth. "He's got himself a *life*. Unlike my dead boy."

They would never rise above their family tragedy. "Nothing but Mattie. Nothing but Mattie," Charlotte moaned. "It's about time you pulled out of your tortured state of mind, Mum. Matthew would never have wanted it."

Barbara lifted a hand as though about to strike. "Don't you *ever* tell me how to live my life, Charlotte. I will mourn my son until the day I die. The agony will never go away."

"I understand that, Mum." Charlotte hastened to placate her. "But Dad and I grieve too. We loved Mattie."

"No one grieves like a mother," Barbara shot back.

"What would you do if you lost your boy? Go on—tell me. Losing a child is the worst blow a woman can ever suffer in life."

"You don't have to tell me that, Mum. I adore my son. But I can never forget that you once told me it was a pity it wasn't me who'd drowned instead of Mattie." Charlotte gave her mother a look of incurable hurt. "You don't have any deep regrets over that? You'd have got over *my* death, wouldn't you? Probably completely. Please let go of my arm."

Barbara had the grace to comply. "I've only just heard Costello was behind the purchase of Riverbend." She said it as though a monstrous deal had been done.

Charlotte began to walk away from the crowd. Quite a few people had been looking their way. Her mother was forced to follow. The breeze off the water caught at Charlotte's long blonde hair and the hem of her exquisite white chiffon gown. "Please keep your voice down, Mum. It's very carrying."

"Of course it is. Clarity and resonance has stood me in good stead. What I really feel like doing is screaming my head off." Barbara was visibly struggling for self-possession. "You're back with him, of course. The boy's his, isn't he? Your father might be a fool, but you can't fool me, Charlotte. I've always had my suspicions. You were pregnant by Costello, yet you married poor Martyn. What a terrible injustice! Did you ever get around to telling him his son was really Rohan Costello's child?" Barbara's demeanour showed frightening aggression.

"No, I didn't. Never!" It was hard to maintain control. "It might shock you, but I believed when I married Martyn he *was* the father of my child."

"I didn't come down in the last shower!" Barbara gave a contemptuous laugh. "You chose to marry *money*,

Charlotte. I understand that at least. Only a foolish woman thinks she can live on love alone—or what passes for love. A driving lust was all you had for Costello."

"Lust?" Charlotte was compelled to swallow down her anger. "What *is* to become of you, Mum? You're deeply neurotic. You need help."

Even in the semi-dark it was possible to see Barbara's flush. "Don't go too far, my girl," she warned. "What would have happened had your husband lived?" There was challenge in her voice. "When you think about it, you were cheating on both of them. Fancy that! Your father's saintly *angel*, with her long blonde hair, having sex with two young men at the same time. I can only marvel!"

"Marvel away!" Charlotte invited, chilled to the bone though the night was warm. She leaned in close to her mother. "I didn't have sex with Martyn, Mum. He *forced* sex on me." It was a measure of her upset that she revealed what she had never revealed before.

Her mother, who had been glaring at her, drew back with a fierce bark of laughter. "I—don't—believe—you."

"Why not, when you're so smart?" Charlotte was close to despair. She had just confided what she'd thought wild horses wouldn't drag out of her. "Things got out of hand. I begged him to stop but he wouldn't. *Couldn't.* I had to live with him. So I learned to think of it that way."

"As well you might!" Barbara drew further back in disgust. "Martyn was totally in love with you, you little fool! It's clear to me you must have led him on," she raged. "You know what you are?"

"Do tell me." Charlotte stood fast. It seemed as if mother-daughter love had gone for ever.

Rohan, unnoticed by both of them, was now only a few feet away. "Charlotte!"

"Don't attempt to drag Rohan into this," Charlotte warned, able to gather herself now Rohan was returning.

"I can and I *will*," Barbara stated forcefully.

Charlotte's heart pumped double-time.

"Good evening, Mrs Reiner," Rohan said.

He looked the very image of a staggeringly handsome and highly successful young man about town, but Barbara stormed towards him as though he were a deadbeat. "You two deserve one another, you know. Do you think I'm a fool?"

Rohan answered with complete self-control. "I certainly don't think you're a fool, Mrs Reiner. So what's the point of acting like one? I'm sure you don't really want to draw attention to yourself. *You're* the one with the fine reputation, after all."

Barbara's coiffed head shot back. "Kindly treat me with respect, Costello," she said, with shocking arrogance.

"Maybe I'll do that when you do the same for me," Rohan replied suavely. He took Charlotte's trembling arm, aware of just how much punishment Charlotte had taken over the years. Barbara Marsdon had been unbelievably cruel to her daughter. "We'll say goodnight, Mrs Reiner. I see you've been giving Charlotte hell. Nothing new in that."

Barbara's stare was malignant. She took in his impressive height and physique, the way he held himself, the self-assuredness, the cultured voice, his stunning good-looks. And those *eyes*! Mary Rose Costello's illegitimate child had come a long way. There was no sign of remorse in him—no plea for forgiveness. Didn't he know Mattie's death had nearly killed her? There was no reality any more. No normal life. Sometimes she thought it would have been best had she drowned with her son. And to think Rohan Costello was back into their lives! He still wanted

her daughter! That couldn't be allowed. As for the boy…
A bitter resentment rolled off Barbara in waves.

"So confident," she said icily, as though he had no right
to be. "And haven't you grown inches? But you'll be hearing more from me, Rohan Costello. That I can promise."

"Then please do keep it civil, Mrs Reiner." Rohan retained his low, even tone. "I wouldn't want to take action
against you."

Barbara didn't deign to answer. She turned away, trying
to get her ravaged face in order before she went back to
her husband. How she wished something horrible would
happen to Rohan Costello! So arrogant, so challenging, and
far, far too confident. As for her daughter! She was going
to reserve a little time and place for Charlotte…

"God, I think we could do with a couple of major tranquil-
lisers after that brush with your mother." Rohan put out his
hand to signal his approaching limousine driver. "What do
you suppose she knows about hiring hit men?"

"Don't laugh, Rohan." Charlotte's beautiful face was full
of upset. She was bitterly regretting her admission about
Martyn. She knew she would have to pay for it somewhere
down the line.

"So what do you want me to do? Buy a suit of armour?
Your mother ran out on you and your father. She should
not be allowed to interfere in your life. And she had better
consider that *your* life is *my* life."

CHAPTER EIGHT

THEY were inside Rohan's penthouse apartment up in the clouds within twenty minutes. This was the second time Charlotte had been inside. As she'd promised to stay overnight she'd left her suitcase there before they had gone on to the function.

"I'm going to pour myself a stiff Scotch." Rohan reached a hand to a bank of switches. "What about you?"

He looked back at her. She looked supremely beautiful, but with a *fragile* overlay that didn't surprise him. He felt rattled himself. Some women were born martyrs. Barbara Marsdon-Reiner was one of them. The incredible thing was that in the pre-Mattie Tragedy days Barbara had been a nice woman. Obviously her whole mode of thinking had altered drastically after the terrible experience of losing her son. Her loathing of *him* hadn't gone away. It still held sway.

"I'll have a brandy." It was all Charlotte could think of. "A good French cognac, if you've got it."

"Which one of them *isn't* good?" he asked with a touch of humour.

They moved through the entrance hall with its stunning gold and white marble floor. An important seascape hung above an antique black and gold commode. The large living room beyond matched up with the hall in its refined opulence. Very European.

"Go sit down while I take a look." He walked away to a well-stocked drinks trolley, with an assortment of crystal decanters, and bent over it, checking. "You're in luck. I've the best of the best Hennessy and a Rémy Martin. One or the other should do the trick. Both nearly sent me broke."

"The Rémy Martin." Her father's choice. Budgeting, so far as her father was concerned, didn't include fine wines and brandies.

She felt shot through with desolation. The awful way her mother had attacked Rohan! Unforgivable. By her mother's lights Rohan Costello should have been one great big failure in life. Instead he had made an outstanding success of himself.

Unable to settle, she drifted about the living room. "If I hadn't thought it before, I think grief has unhinged my mother," she offered sadly.

"You only *think*?" Rohan's dark head lifted. "Did she seem dangerous to you?" He wasn't entirely joking.

"Oh, don't say that!" She gave an involuntary shudder.

"Then what would you say?"

"Dad's lucky to be out of it?" She managed a wry laugh.

"You bet he is." Rohan continued fixing their drinks, fighting down the powerful urge to simply go to her, sweep her up in his arms and carry her into the bedroom.

How many times had Martyn Prescott swept her up in his arms? Hundreds? He couldn't bear to think about it. Not now.

"*You're* lucky too," he said. "And don't let me start on how lucky our son is. It's a good thing Grandmama doesn't want to see him. You'd have to think very seriously about that, Charlotte. I sure do. After tonight I wouldn't want her around him. Up until your mother's appearance it had been a brilliant night. We didn't really need her to mess it up."

She sighed deeply, turning to face the floor-to-ceiling sliding glass doors. The apartment had stupendous views of the Harbour and city on three sides. Glorious by day, it was absolutely breath-taking by night. A wonderland of glittering multi-coloured lights. This was very much a *man's* apartment. It had the feel of an exclusive gentlemen's club. She ran her hands appreciatively over the back of a black leather armchair. A custom-built sofa nearby was upholstered in a knobbly black and gold fabric of striking design. So easily did Rohan fit into these luxurious surroundings they might have been his heritage.

"My mother is one of the despairs of my life." She sank into the sofa. "She defeats me. I've loved her throughout all our traumas, but I can no longer cope. My mother still hates you. Can you believe it?"

"Charlotte, do please pay attention. Some old hatreds never die. Let's forget about your dear mother. I have it in my heart to spare a thought for poor old Reiner. He can't be a happy man."

"Maybe he drinks himself into oblivion when Mum sinks into one of her moods."

Rohan had to laugh, though he was deeply affected by the sadness in her face. Charlotte's *blondeness* and the pure white chiffon of her dress made her a vision of femininity against the lushly dark background of his sofa. She was removing the glorious Marsdon diamond and emerald earrings, putting them down on the coffee table. He watched her shake out her hair.

"Lord, those earrings are heavy," she sighed. "So is the necklace."

"Leave it," Rohan ordered, as she put up her hands to the clasp.

Adrenalin made a mad rush into her veins. "Why? Have you something erotic in mind?'

"Haven't *you*?" His blue eyes glittered. "We're so good at it."

"Old history, Rohan."

"Really?" His handsome mouth curled. Her cool touch-me-not look was incredibly sexy. "You still enjoy being kissed." He handed over a crystal brandy balloon, containing a good shot of cognac. "There's the same old excitement."

"So why don't *you* feel better about the whole thing?"

He didn't answer. Her beauty made its own light, he thought. She didn't need diamonds and emeralds. "I'll feel better when I know the whole story," he said eventually. "Mind if I sit beside you?"

"Oh, Rohan!" She was searingly aware of the devilment in his eyes.

"Relax, Charlotte." Instead he took an armchair. He had undone his black tie, letting it dangle against the snow-white of his dress shirt. He looked like a man one could only dream about.

"I love where you live." She took a slow sip of the cognac, feeling the subtle fire.

He flicked a careless glance around the living room. "It cost a good deal of money. But I'm happy with it."

"So how much time are you going to be able to spend at Riverbend?" She fixed her gaze on the contents of her brandy balloon as though it contained the answer. "Is it your intention to instal me there with Christopher?" Her eyes swept up to study him. The slant of a downlight gilded the planes and angles of his arresting face. Her heart turned over with the endless love she couldn't find the courage to put voice to.

"You mean do I intend to instal my wife and son there?" he asked dryly. "The answer is yes. *I* have no heritage. No background I can speak of. My biological father is a mystery man. He has played no part in my life. My mother and my grandmother had nothing. Mum had to work hard to survive. I was smart enough to gain scholarships and bursaries to secure my education. I want Christopher to retain his Marsdon heritage."

"Only *you* have made it possible," she told him quietly. "Life is very strange. Matthew should have inherited Riverbend. And his children, had he lived to have them. Now you say my son—"

"*Our* son," he corrected firmly.

"Will inherit?"

"Isn't that a comfort, Charlotte?" There was a tautness in his voice.

"Beyond comfort, Rohan. My poor father raced through his inheritance. I think he still doesn't quite know how it happened. Losing Mattie blighted all our lives. But Dad would have continued to make his ill-advised investments even if Mattie had lived. So in the end Mattie would still have missed out."

"I'm certain Matthew would have approved of his little nephew as heir."

"He would." Charlotte was assailed by what might have been. "Mattie would have loved him."

"Mattie would have given his life for you, Charlotte. You were very close. I never heard a cross word pass between you. Yet you used to tell Martyn off left, right and centre."

"He deserved it." Charlotte curled her fingers tightly

around her crystal glass. "It only takes one tragedy to affect so many other lives."

"Undoubtedly—but it doesn't come close to explaining how you came to choose Martyn over me. Every teacher, every tutor, all my classmates voted me the one most destined to succeed. You know. You were there. All I needed was a little time. As it turned out, *very* little time. I hit on a huge money-maker. It wasn't going to be my be-all and end-all. No way! But my every thought was for *you*, for our future together."

"Not all dreams have happy endings, Rohan," she said with a melancholy expression.

How could she ever tell Rohan that Martyn, their friend from childhood, had raped her? Such a hideous word she hesitated to think it, let alone give it voice. It was all too degrading. Rohan would be speechless with anger—some of which would have to fall on her for having given Martyn opportunity.

"Even now, my mother will do her utmost to break us up," she added.

"She won't succeed," he said, with absolute belief in himself. "I'm thinking an April wedding. We'll honeymoon in the European spring. Five months will give you time to get back into practice for loving me. It's a lifetime when a man wants a woman as desperately as I want you. You led me down the garden path, Charlotte, from when we were kids. We might not get the happy ending we talked about, but we do get another chance. We'll be together with our son."

She should have told him there and then that he was all she had ever wanted. Why didn't she? What was stopping her from saying, *Rohan, I love you. I've never stopped loving you. I was in despair when I had to marry Martyn. I truly believed I was carrying his child.* But she knew

Rohan's mind was focused on very different reasons. Getting back what he had once had was all that mattered to him now.

"What are you thinking about?" Rohan's voice brought her out of her reverie.

Her poignant smile tore at his heart.

All the awful stuff locked up inside her. The years with Martyn.

He'd *had* to have her. But oddly he'd never got her pregnant. She hadn't always taken precautions, believing she had a moral duty to give him his own child and his parents a *real* grandchild.

"I was thinking one has to pay for past sins," she said, bitter tears at the back of her throat.

"Not surprising, when the past is where it all began," he said quietly. "Come to bed."

The note in his voice, the look in his eyes, turned her limbs liquid. There was a *burning* along her veins. She didn't think she could move at all, or even draw breath, though her heart was soaring, lifting on wings.

Come to bed.

Could they really reclaim what they'd had? Passion was ravishing. Trust was something else again. Any relationship would flounder without trust.

"Finish your cognac if you think you need it."

She looked back at him across the space of seven years. The times they had been in each other's arms. The secret meetings. The secret language they'd used to communicate with one another. She thought of the passionate lovemaking, the delirious lovemaking, the soft, sweet lovemaking, of the times they'd been content to make each other laugh. They had been so *young*.

He had taken her virginity, himself a virgin. The first time for one had been the first time for the other. Only they had been quickly done with the kissing and the teasing. They had been driven to move on. Unfulfilled rapture was one thing, but there was too much physical pain involved if overwhelming desire couldn't find release.

How, then, could he believe for a moment she had sold herself to Martyn? How could he think her capable of such treachery? Shouldn't he be working his way through to some answers?

You're not helping him, chided the voice in her head.

How could she help him? My God, Martyn had done a job on her. She couldn't speak for the shame.

"Charlotte? Are you coming?" He held out his hand.

Her answer was little more than a whisper. She picked up her crystal balloon, took a last fevered gulp. Heat coursed down her throat, past her breasts into her stomach, then into the delta between her legs. That was where she wanted him—to make her cry out in rapture. She wanted other children. *His* children. Siblings for her darling Christopher.

He went to her, drawing her to her feet. Then his arms closed around her as if they were going to dance. Maybe he had some romantic ballad in his head? He must have, because he danced her around the quiet room, all the while staring down into her face.

She made an aching sound in her throat. There had been such heartbreak. But there was always *hope*. How could the intense love they had shared ever go entirely away? The space between them was throbbing with a sexual desire that had only picked up momentum.

"I want you so badly," he said, in an overpowering rush.

"*Want* is one word. Please tell me another."

"I *need* you." He kissed her cheek very softly.

"Can't you keep going?"

He was clasping her so tightly their bodies seemed

fused—his hard with desire. "What is it you want to hear? That I'll love you for ever and a day?"

"You used to tell me that." Her sadness was immense.

"The past is another country, Charlotte." He kissed the dip behind her ear.

"But you know how unpredictable life is." She lifted imploring green eyes. "Good things happen. Bad things happen. Life-altering things."

"We were supposed to face them together. I used to *dream* I would get you pregnant."

An incredible intimacy bonded them. "You *did*," she said softly.

"But you married Martyn."

"My mistake. I had to live with it." The opening was there again. A brave woman would have taken the hurdle. Only once more she balked. "Those years are over, Rohan. They were full of pain."

Frustration caught him by the throat. He wanted to shake the truth out of her. He had difficulty not doing it. "So why can't you *tell* me the whole story? Don't I have a right to know? Were you frightened of how your parents—your mother—would react? Knowing them, I can appreciate that. Was there *safety* and *security* in marrying Martyn? Pleasing your parents?"

Charlotte swallowed painfully. "Does it matter now?" The trouble was he was judging Martyn by his own standards. Martyn fell far below them. Martyn had been ill-equipped for not getting his own way, even by force. He had thought taking her was his right. Would the truth help her here?

"Okay. I'm done with talking."

Rohan's voice echoed his tension. He released her abruptly, so hard with desire he wanted to pull her down onto the rug and cover her there and then. His hunger was so strong. He wanted his body over hers. He wanted to forget those years when he'd thought his life had been smashed. If they had any chance at all he had to forget his bitterness, clamp down on his frustration. He had her now. He could so easily spoil things. Martyn had won her. But Martyn was gone.

She was a lightweight in his arms.

He carried her down the passageway to the master bedroom, cool from the air-conditioning. He let her body fall gently onto the luxurious bed. She bounced against its springiness before half rolling away from him.

He lowered himself onto the bed beside her, one hand on the slope of her bare shoulder, turning her back to him. "'While the one eludes, must the other pursue.' Browning, I think." He stared down into her river-green eyes. "I'm not looking for the right wife to live with, Charlotte. I've had other women. Nothing easy about being celibate. But I've never been able to wipe you out of my mind. Never lost my vivid memories of you. Attractive women came and *went*. All because of *you*. I found I didn't want a woman I could live happily enough with. I want a wife I can't live *without*. And that, Charlotte, is *you*. I know you never loved Martyn."

Her long hair glittered against the mix of gold, chocolate and black silk cushions that adorned the bed. That much she *could* admit. She *had* never loved Martyn.

"I'm trying so hard to understand."

"Then you'll use up all your understanding." Her defensive walls had been too long in place. "Make love to me, Rohan." She pressed a hand to her aching breast. "At least you *want* me."

"As you want me."

It was a statement not to be denied.

"Maybe we should let go of the past?" he suggested quietly.

"I want that too."

He turned her over, putting a hand to the long covered zipper on her evening dress. His nimble fingers unzipped her in one smooth movement before turning her back to him. "One thing, Charlotte." There was severity in his expression. "Never, *never* lie to me again."

A flush travelled all over her flawless skin. "I have never lied."

He dismissed that with a wave of his hand. "*Promise* me. Say it. *I'll never lie to you again, Rohan.*"

"Then you must say that to me too." Her eyes glowed as green as the ocean.

He didn't say a word. Neither did she.

Instead he began slowly to lower the bodice of her gown, revealing her small breasts, the white of roses. "Having our son hasn't changed your body," he said very quietly, his eyes gliding all over her as she lay on his bed. "Your breasts are still as perfect, the nipples coral-pink. See how they swell to my fingertips? Your waist is as narrow..." He began to peel the white chiffon dress further down her body like a man enthralled, listing his observations as he went. "Your stomach just as taut." He palmed his hand over it, circling and circling, moving lower, until he let his long fingers sink into the triangle of fine blonde hair at her core. "Remember all the crazy things we used to do?" His eyes were a perfect electric-blue. "Your body was my body. My body was yours. Two bodies. One beating heart. One soul."

She shivered to his touch. Beyond answering. She would picture how they'd been when she was dying. So young. Alone together. Without inhibition. Heat was sizzling up through her skin. Her whole body went into spasm as his fingers sought and then touched on an acutely sensitive spot. Her trembling legs fell apart. She wanted to lift them, wrap them around him, bind him to her. She wanted to make it up to him for every moment of those years of heartbreak.

His mouth came down on hers with a ravenous hunger, opening it up fully to his tongue. "Good," he muttered into the brandied sweet honey of her mouth. "Because we're going to do all of them again."

Love could bring either agony or ecstasy. Sometimes it brought both entwined.

The last time he had made love to her they had made a baby. A beautiful baby. Christopher.

Only she hadn't told him that momentous thing. It was beyond making sense of.

Within a week of that most memorable night Barbara Reiner decided it was high time to pay her daughter a visit. Vivian would most probably be at Riverbend—at the Lodge, of all places. Talk about a headlong fall from grace! Vivian was such a fool—always hiding his head in the sand. And to think he had sold the Marsdon ancestral home to Rohan Costello! It defied belief. But then Vivian was notorious for making horrendous decisions.

Silver Valley was only a few hundred miles from Sydney, but she certainly didn't intend to drive herself. She commandeered Kurt's Bentley and his chauffeur for the afternoon. Kurt had dared to rumble a tiny protest. Apparently he needed the car. But she had raised her eyebrows and told him to call a cab. She was looking forward to the trip. She knew Costello was in Sydney. She had rung his office, pretending she was a friend. No way did she want Costello anywhere on the scene. She didn't want him around to back up her daughter.

The boy would be at school. Rohan Costello's son. She could remember the precise moment when she'd first had her suspicions. She had been trying to give Charlotte some advice, and the boy—way too protective of his mother—had turned and given her such a piercing look of appraisal, with near-adult intelligence, she had been truly astonished. She had been judged and found wanting. It had suddenly dawned on her that she had seen that very look before. And those *brilliant blue eyes* didn't fit into the family, did they? Vivian had blue eyes, of course, but even as a young man they had never had that depth of colour, never mind the intensity of regard. She didn't actually *know*. She'd just had a gut feeling.

That was when she had started ignoring the boy. Others might find that extremely harsh, but they hadn't suffered like she had. And there was her daughter—the survivor. Charlotte hadn't learned her lesson. Costello was back in her life. There was going to be a scandal, but she had gone beyond caring. Anything to get back at Costello. He might have passed himself off in society, but his very humble beginnings were bound to come out. And there was the way poor Martyn had been treated! The only thing that would guarantee her silence was for Charlotte and Costello to split up. She presumed he didn't know the child was his. Any woman could pull the wool over a man's eyes. Men missed so much!

Charlotte couldn't remember the last time Christopher had had a day off school, but he—like a number of children and adults in the Valley—had caught a twenty-four-hour bug that had been doing the rounds. Mild enough, she had nevertheless decided to keep him at home for the day. Rohan had picked out some suitable computer games, so that would keep him occupied in his room.

It was a room any boy would envy. It housed his computer, a television, and a bookcase packed with a range of books on subjects that interested him. Not many boys Christopher's age shared his wide-ranging interest in learning and getting "the facts", but that was the way his mind worked. She had nearly fainted when his headmaster had made the chance remark, "The only other child I can remember as extraordinary as your boy, Mrs Prescott, was Rohan Costello."

One day Christopher would have to know the truth. But she recognised with gratitude that Rohan was as committed as she to giving their son time.

Christopher was actually the first to spot the Bentley sweeping up the driveway. It was after lunch. He ran back down the stairs, calling out excitedly to his mother, "Mummy, Mummy—I think maybe it's Grandmother in a Bentley."

Vivian Marsdon strode into the entrance hall. "Good God, surely not!"

"That will cost you, Grandpa!"

"Well, knock me down with a feather." Vivian changed tack, a huge frown on his face. "What do you suppose she wants?" he asked of his equally transfixed daughter.

"Maybe she's dropping in with goodies?" Christopher burst out laughing at his own joke.

Goodies, indeed. Charlotte felt only alarm. "Go back upstairs, darling. Stay in your room like a good boy."

"Can't I stay here?" Instinct told Christopher his mother and grandfather were preparing for trouble. They might need his help.

Vivian Marsdon confirmed his hunch. "There's something wrong with this. Why didn't she ring? I hope she hasn't got that b—husband of hers with her."

"Another fifty cents, Grandpa," Christopher reminded him, as the swear words started to come thick and fast.

"All right, all right. I'll pay up. Your mother is right. Go upstairs, Chrissie. Please don't come down until I come to get you."

Christopher took his mother's hand. "Won't it make you feel better if I stay? Grandmother doesn't worry me. She has no feelings for me."

Vivian Marsdon was aghast. "My dearest boy, your grandmother *loves* you. She just doesn't know how to show it."

Christopher gave his grandfather a kindly look. "It's okay, Grandpa. I don't miss her either."

"If I hadn't given up smoking I'd consider lighting up a cigar."

"Cigars are for celebration, aren't they?" Christopher asked.

"They're also an excellent way to soothe a man's nerves."

Charlotte smiled down on her son. "Do as I say, darling. Go back upstairs. Grandpa and I will take care of this."

Obediently Christopher turned away. "How do you know you can?" he paused to ask. "Grandmother is a serious pain in the a—"

"That will do, Christopher," Vivian Marsdon held up a warning hand. "I've told you not to use that crude expression."

"Sorry, Grandpa. By the way, she's by herself in the back seat. A chauffeur is driving. He's wearing a uniform with a hat."

"Dear Lord!" Vivian Marsdon rolled his eyes heavenward as Christopher disappeared up the stairs. "This is like waiting for a bomb to go off. Barbara has developed such a taste for doom and gloom, all she has left is her dark side."

Charlotte bowed her head in silent agreement. Her own concerns were intense. Today of all days, when Christopher was by chance home from school, her mother had arrived.

Barbara took tea before she launched into the reason for her unscheduled visit.

"It's about the boy," she said, setting down her fine bone-china cup.

"His name is Christopher," Vivian reminded his ex-wife testily. "The boy…the boy…I very much resent your calling your grandson that."

"So what do *you* call him?" Barbara asked, with a wild flash in her eyes.

Vivian stared back, utterly perplexed. "What on earth are you talking about, Barbara?"

Barbara's eyes shot to her daughter, who was looking very pale. "I see you haven't told your father?" she said, totally without sympathy.

"No one tells me a thing—how would I know?"

"Why are you doing this, Mum?" Charlotte asked. "Have you absolutely no compassion? No love in your heart?"

Barbara's tone was hard. "Don't try to turn the tables on me, Charlotte. I can't bear to be part of this…this… conspiracy," she cried, looking the very picture of self-righteousness.

Vivian Marsdon, provoked beyond measure, suddenly gave vent to a roar. "What the hell is this? Is it supposed to be some sort of trial, with you the judge and the jury, Barbara?"

She glared back at him. "Your golden angel betrayed us all," she said, riding a bitter wave. "She married poor

Martyn Prescott, knowing she was carrying Rohan Costello's child."

Vivian Marsdon's handsome face turned purple. *"W-h-a-t?"*

"Doesn't that make you feel good?" Barbara hurled at him. "Charlotte—your perfect girl—was having sex with both of them. She might have thought at the beginning it was Martyn's child—got her dates wrong—but it wouldn't have taken her long to wake up. The boy is enormously bright, I grant you. And poor Martyn was an idiot."

"You be very careful with what you're saying." Vivian Marsdon looked formidable. "If this is some vicious scheme from an old woman—"

"Old? *Old!*" For a moment Barbara looked as if she was going into cardiac arrest. "Why, you silly old man—I'm three years younger than you."

"And you're not looking good, Barbara. You're taking on the persona of the Wicked Witch of the West."

To Barbara it was a hard slap in the face. "For you of all people to say that! You loved me madly."

"And how much did you love *me*?" he countered, his mood abruptly shifting. "You never loved me, Barbara, did you? It was the Marsdon name. The Marsdon money."

Barbara gave him a vicious smile. "Which you promptly lost."

"Just like it's now the Reiner money—poor old fool," Vivian continued, as though she hadn't spoken. "By now he must know you're crazy."

Barbara threw up her hands in frustration. "We were supposed to be talking about your daughter and the things she got up to."

Vivian gave her a look of utter contempt. "You surely can't think you can turn me against my daughter? You can't think you can turn me against my beloved grandson? I don't give a damn who Chrissie's father is. My daughter Charlotte is his mother, and *I'm* his grandfather."

"Costello is his *father*!" Barbara shouted. "So that's your answer, is it? You don't mind that Rohan Costello is the boy's father? Rohan Costello—who let *our* boy drown?"

"Oh, Mum!" Charlotte moaned in despair, thanking God Christopher was far away in his room.

Vivian Marsdon was so angry he was temporarily unable to speak. "I should have stopped you, Barbara," he said grimly after a few moments. "I shouldn't have let you crucify young Costello and his mother—a struggling young woman you had once helped. Losing Mattie has deranged you. You desperately needed counselling at the time. I should have seen you got it. Instead I let you wreck your mental health and the Costellos' lives. Rohan was *not* to blame for Mattie's death. It was a tragic accident. I've long since accepted that."

"So he's not so bad. Is that it?" Barbara asked, breathing heavily. "You can adjust?"

"I may need a little time." Vivian turned to his daughter. "It's true, Charlie?"

"Of course it's true," Barbara cut in. "I don't go around making up stories."

"Keep out of this, Barbara," Vivian Marsdon warned. "I'm running out of patience with you."

Barbara gave a shriek of horror. "Patience? I just got here."

Charlotte ignored her mother. "Yes, Dad. But I believed when I married Martyn I was carrying his child."

"What else do you need, Vivian? A blasted DNA report?"

"Shut up, woman," Vivian Marsdon thundered, shocked

at his ex-wife's vindictiveness. "If you can't shut up then I'll show you the door." He had never sounded so authoritative.

Barbara Reiner reeled back in her chair. "I—beg—your—pardon?" She could scarcely believe her ears.

"Please…please stop. Both of you," Charlotte begged. "Marrying Martyn was a huge mistake, but I didn't know what else to do at the time. It wasn't as though you were here for me, Mum. I didn't have the guts to tell Dad I was pregnant. I didn't have the guts to go it alone."

"Go it alone?" Barbara repeated with scorn. "You took all the comfort you could from poor Martyn, though, didn't you? So much for your endless love for Costello!"

Charlotte met her mother's hard, accusatory gaze. "I *did* go to Martyn for comfort. I was missing Rohan terribly. We'd been friends all our lives."

"And you used him," Barbara condemned.

"I suppose I did." It had never for a second entered her head to abort her child. But she couldn't have turned to Rohan when she was carrying Martyn's child. There'd be no way out of it. She'd married Martyn.

"That's it. That's enough, Barbara," Vivian Marsdon said sternly. "How could Charlie go to you? Her mother? You were never the soul of comfort at the best of times. You spent all the years of Mattie's life dancing attendance on him."

"Because he was delicate, you ignorant fool!"

"The bitter truth was you spoonfed him. You would never listen to me—"

Charlotte cut in. "Please keep your voices down. I couldn't bear for Christopher to hear you."

"He won't hear us, Charlie." Vivian reached out to pat her hand. "His bedroom is too far away."

"Just as well." Charlotte shuddered. "What did you hope to achieve, Mum, by coming here?"

Barbara straightened her shoulders. "I need your word, Charlotte, that you won't marry Costello. I couldn't live with that. If you give me your promise there's no more to be said. You can carry on with your charade."

Charlotte stared back at her mother in wonderment. So wonderfully elegant on the outside, a total mess within. "I'm afraid there's no question of that. Rohan recognised his son the instant he laid eyes on him."

"Did he really?" Vivian Marsdon turned to his daughter, showing his shock.

"As per usual, Vivian, you've had your head in the sand," his ex-wife said contemptuously. "The boy will grow into the image of him. Those blue eyes, for a start. One rarely sees eyes like that. Are you *really* prepared to create a great scandal, Charlotte? For Costello? He's making quite a name for himself in the city. An illegitimate child won't help. Or the mother of his child marrying his childhood friend. What about the Valley? The news would shock the entire district. God alone knows what the Prescotts will think, let alone *do*."

"They'll do nothing," Vivian Marsdon said, his eyes on fire.

"They won't have to. There are few things Nicole and her mother like better than airing their suspicions," Charlotte said. "Rohan and I are prepared to wear it all. One can't hide the truth for ever."

"Just another nine-day wonder," Vivian Marsdon said with a hopeful smile. There would be a scandal. No question. But it was high time he came out on the side of his long-suffering daughter. "Good God, woman, Costello has bought Riverbend. He has big plans for it. Christopher is his son and heir. Christopher will one day inherit his birthright. Think of that. The wheel of fortune has turned full circle. Marsdons planted the first vines in the Valley, the first olive groves. We won't just be selling our harvested crops. I've heard Costello is planning to build a new winery. Bring in all the best people. I believe he's already having talks with the von Luckners—father and son. Remember old Konrad predicted young Rohan would have a splendid future?"

That was true. The von Luckners were members of a very posh clan from Germany, who had migrated shortly before the First World War to get away from Europe.

"Who told you, Dad?" It was no secret the von Luckners were in need of a big inflow of cash to expand and continue the late Erich von Luckner's bold vision.

"My dear girl, people tell me things. Always have. I am a Marsdon—a community leader."

"So, you're all going to finish up *friends*?" Barbara cried out in disbelief, appalled that things weren't going as she'd planned.

"There are worse things than friends, Barbara. Like ex-wives." Vivian glanced down pointedly at his watch. "Shouldn't you be getting back to poor old Reiner? I suppose he let you have the Bentley without a whimper?"

CHAPTER NINE

AFTER Barbara had left, acting as though she was cut to the quick by their refusal to heed her warnings, father and daughter returned to the living room, their hearts heavy.

"This is my fault," Charlotte said, her psyche so wounded by years of blame she sought not one ounce of sympathy for herself.

"Of course it isn't," groaned her father. "Was that *really* the woman I married?" he asked in genuine wonder. "What's bugging her most, do you suppose? The fact that you're going to marry Rohan Costello? That's he's Christopher's father? Or that you slept with poor old Martyn too? She always did take his side, you know. She believed Martyn's version of events over yours. Rohan never defended himself."

"He didn't have to, Dad. Rohan was an innocent victim. I was only with Martyn *once* before we were married." She turned her beautiful eyes on her father. There really had to be something wrong with her. Post-traumatic stress? That was a popular diagnosis. Terrible things happened, yet they were never mentioned. Abuses of all kinds. Perhaps she should get a big sheet of cardboard and write *Rape* on it? It wasn't going to trip off her tongue.

"What awful luck! It's women who pay the price, isn't

it? Women who get hurt the most. We weren't there for you, Charlie. And you were so young."

She couldn't bear to talk about it any more. Had she been able to depend upon a loving, wise mother, her life might have turned out differently.

Charlotte turned her head, as though her son might suddenly appear. "It's a wonder Chris hasn't come downstairs," she said, with a puzzled frown. "He would have seen the Bentley leave."

"We did tell him to remain in his room. He's a good boy, and a highly intuitive one. He knew there was going to be trouble. Barbara doesn't care how many casualties there are in her one-woman war."

"I'm so sorry, Dad."

"Oh, for God's sake, Charlie! It's your parents who should be sorry. You've had some very difficult episodes in your life. Mostly because we failed you—your mother and I. We failed the Costellos. We failed Martyn. He should have been made to retract his damaging statements. It's a wonder you have any love left for me."

Did one ever lose the capacity to love a parent? Even a bad one? "Plenty of love!" Charlotte rose to her feet, dropping a kiss on her father's silver-streaked blond head. "I'll look in on Chris, then make us both a strong cup of coffee."

"I'll get things going." Vivian stood up. On the surface he was calm enough; underneath he was full of intense regrets about his own past behaviour and horror at his ex-wife's lack of compassion. "Did you hear the way that woman spoke to us?" he huffed. "I'll tell you this: she won't put a foot inside the door again."

"Try to put it out of your mind, Dad," Charlotte advised.

"With Mattie gone, love is something Mum *cannot* provide. I think of her as not being in her *right* mind."

"One wonders if she ever was."

All was quiet inside when Charlotte knocked on her son's door. "It's me, Chris. You can come out now, darling. Sorry it took so long."

She waited for him to come to the door, full of questions. Gifted children had many advantages. They also suffered disadvantages. They recognised too much, too early. Maybe he was taking a nap? He hadn't been feeling one hundred per cent, but as usual he made no complaints.

"Chrissie?" She knocked again, and then when she got no response, opened the door.

The room was empty. She sucked in her breath. He had to be in the bathroom just down the hall. Maybe he'd been sick again? She hoped not. She had thought the short bout of vomiting the night before was over.

"Chrissie, love?" She knocked on the bathroom door. "Are you sick again?"

Again no response. She opened the door, taking in the empty white and turquoise tiled bathroom at a glance. Where was he? It was too early for her to be worried, yet she felt a chill run right through her body. Was it possible Christopher had crept down the stairs to listen in on the adult conversation? Would he do that? Had he heard his grandfather's lion-like roar? That would have put him on the alert. Christopher was a great one for knowing the facts. Why had his grandmother come visiting? They rarely saw her. Why had his grandfather shouted in that angry voice?

It was possible—more than possible—her son had decided to find out. Christopher was no ordinary child.

Oh, God! Oh, God! Was it happening all over again? A missing child? A mother's worst nightmare short of a child's confirmed death. Swiftly she got a hold on herself, trying to think things through. She had to accept now that he *had* listened in. Made the choice to run. Run where? Could he have gone to Peter's place? Could he have sought the comfort of his best friend? She hurried away to put a call through to Peter's house. Pray God he was there. Peter would be home from school by now.

Rohan's secretary, Shona, appeared at the door, her pretty face without its usual dimpled smile. "I know you told me to hold your calls, Rohan, but I think you'll want to take this one. It's Charlotte. She sounds very distressed."

"Right, put it through." He was scheduled to meet up with one of his more important clients, but if there was anything wrong with Charlotte he would cancel.

Under fifteen minutes later he was in the air, the company helicopter heading for Riverbend. Children were life itself to their parents. He had found Charlotte. He had found his son. Nothing would be allowed to put their future in jeopardy. He knew Charlotte's fears were gaining momentum with every passing hour, but what he had seen of his son gave him hope. A boy under tremendous stress, he had gone off on his own. Maybe he should have told his mother first. But he had needed to do some thinking alone. He had a strong feeling Christopher had inherited his temperament.

The instant she heard the *thrump-thrump* of the rotors Charlotte was flying out through the door, feeling as though if anyone could find Christopher it would be Rohan—his father. She hurled herself at him, the bone-deep stabs of fear abating to a level she could bear. It was torture to think her seven-year-old son had had to run away to counteract the shock and the grief he must have felt as powerful deceptions were exposed. Would she ever be the same for him again? Would his great love for her, his faith in her, change?

Rohan caught her up, pulling her close into his body. Her anguish couldn't have been more visible. "I spotted the police car and the scouters from the air," he said, his cheek against her thick curtain of hair. "There are a lot of people out there, all up and down the riverbank."

The river.

A half-forgotten poem sprang disturbingly into his head.

Whoever said happiness is the light shining on the water?
The water is cold and dark and deep.

There could *never* be another drowning. That was his belief, and it was strong. He wasn't about to panic. Mattie wouldn't allow it. Mattie who had ceased to be and yet lived on.

"Practically the whole village is out." Charlotte's willowy body was shaking like a leaf. "Where *is* he, Rohan?" She stared up into his brilliant eyes as though he alone knew the answer.

He took her firmly by the shoulders. "Wherever he is, Charlotte, he's *safe*. He loves you far too much to do anything silly. He's a clever, thoughtful child. He wants to be by himself right now. He wants to sort everything out in his own mind. I used to go off by myself, remember?"

"Yes, you did." She felt a flutter of hope.

"I can tell you one thing," Rohan said grimly. "Your

mother will never be allowed near Christopher again. Where's your father?"

He put his arm around her waist, leading her back into the house. She was trying so hard to be brave. That was the thing! Charlotte *was* brave. And she had never been one to tell even the smallest lie. It wasn't a matter of degree with Charlotte. A lie was a lie was a lie! Even now her inexplicable action in marrying Martyn brought him to near breaking point. Only he didn't have the time now for all the convolutions of his mind.

"Dad is out searching," Charlotte said. "He's tremendously upset. I shouldn't say this, but I'm feeling near hatred for my mother. She provoked this thing. Dad went off in a sick rage. He loves Christopher."

"I know. There are too many people searching the riverbanks. Christopher isn't there."

She lifted her eyes to him, tears welling. "But how can we be sure of that, Rohan? What Chrissie learned would have destroyed all his certainties about life. About me—his mother. About *you*—his real flesh-and-blood father. He's only a little boy, no matter how intelligent. What he overheard would have been shocking to his ears. Who knows what a child in shock will do?"

He bent to stay her quivering mouth with a kiss. "Mattie won't let Christopher fall in the river."

Her expression totally changed. "You're saying that as though Mattie is still alive and breathing."

"So what if he isn't? He's still out there. Somewhere. Parallel universe—who knows? I continue to feel a spiritual connection to my childhood friend. I don't go around analysing it. It just *is*. Christopher wouldn't do anything so radical, anyway. He knows Mattie's story. He's a child with deep feelings. He's trying to understand what he heard. Weigh it up. I'll get the Sergeant to direct more searchers to the vineyards and the olive groves. But somehow I don't think he's there. The old winery?"

"It's been searched. The house has been searched from top to bottom." She meant the Riverbend mansion.

"Right—well, I'm off!" He spoke with immense purpose.

"I'm coming with you." A tear ran down her cheek. She dashed it away. She would search until she dropped down dead.

Only Rohan wasn't having it. "I know how hard this is for you, Charlie, but you must stay here," he said with quiet authority. "For all we know Christopher could work his way back. We don't want him returning to an empty house."

"But, Rohan—he must have heard all the commotion." She was ready to argue, her nerves strung taut. This was her son. *Their* son. "The noise of the chopper arriving. I'm so frightened. I've spent so many years of my life frightened."

No time either for him to question *that* shock admission. *Years of her life frightened?* He knew next to nothing about her life with Martyn. She wouldn't tell him. "Well, I'm here now." He let her body slump against him, feed off his strength. "And I won't be back until I find our son. Trust me, Charlotte."

"With my life!" She looked up at him, her heart in her eyes. "With our son's life. Forgive me, Rohan. I've made so many mistakes. And now our son knows them." A sound of agony escaped her lips. "He thought me perfect. He won't any more. Rohan, he mightn't even *love* me any more. The thought is too dreadful!"

He took her beautiful, agonised face between his hands. "Christopher can no more stop loving you than I can." He spoke not gently, but with some force. Enough force to close out certain fears from her mind. "What you have to do is remember you're at the very *centre* of our lives. Hold the thought close. I'll find him." He bent his head and kissed her hard.

It had been dark for well over an hour. Wherever Christopher was, he surely must have heard their raised voices. The whole area was ringing with the echoes of his name. People, truly chilled by the turn of events, were loath to return home. Even Gordon Prescott, deeply distressed, had called in to the Lodge to express his concerns, then set out with Charlotte's father, friends from childhood. The searchers would come out again at first light, but the darkness was complete.

Were the Marsdons jinxed? For that matter the Prescotts?

Both families, so closely entwined, had suffered tragedies, and that was the question people were asking themselves. The atmosphere all along the riverbank had struck many a soul as extremely spooky. They all knew Matthew Marsdon's tragic story. They had been given instructions where to search. Every last man and woman hoped they would be the one to find the boy safe. But the more time that elapsed, the more fearful the searchers became. A seven-year-old child in peril! It struck at the heart of every parent.

Why had the boy taken off? All they had been told was that he had most probably overheard a family argument and become upset. Quite a few people had seen the big Bentley driving through the area, the ex-Mrs Marsdon sitting regally in its back seat, a uniformed chauffeur up front. Once a very highly regarded woman, Barbara Reiner as she was now had taken a nosedive in the popularity stakes. The love and attention she had lavished on her son had left her only daughter out in the cold. Small wonder

Charlotte Prescott's marriage hadn't worked. The feeling at the time had been that it was a marriage of convenience. And some reckoned she'd just *had* to be pregnant when she walked reed-slim down the aisle. What did it matter anyway? Charlotte Prescott was a beautiful young woman. Inside and out. Her son had to be found.

Alive.

Rohan didn't know the moment the answer to the question of Christopher's whereabouts came to him. Was it Christopher's guardian angel whispering in his ear? Or Mattie? Or maybe Mattie had been elected for the job?

He commandeered one of the search vehicles, a utility truck, and sped off. It didn't make a lot of sense, but that didn't matter. He had the strong conviction Christopher had headed off to the cottage where Rohan and his mother had lived. He thought now he had made some comment about it to Christopher—about the place where he and his mother had lived for the first seventeen years of his life.

As if a button had been pushed, there was a shift in his thinking. He remembered how he had pointed out his grandmother's old cottage to Christopher from the helicopter. The cottage had long been empty. He knew the land—not valuable—had been bought for future development, but so far nothing had happened. The timber structure appeared to be settling down into the earth. The white picket fence had a great many broken teeth. The corrugated iron roof, once a bright red, was thickly sown with dead foliage from the overhanging canopy of trees. What had been the small front and back gardens were overrun by long grass and vegetation gone wild. It was a veritable jungle now. The old cottage where he had grown up on the wrong side of the tracks was an abandoned old derelict.

There was no moon tonight. It was as black as only

country black could be. No street lights to pierce the darkness. He had a heavy-duty torch with him on the passenger seat. Would his boy be shrinking from the darkness? Would he be sitting frozen with fear of snakes? Would he be desperately regretting what he had done?

Rohan drove the utility truck right through what had been the front gate, jamming on the brakes at the base of the short flight of steps. He swung out of the vehicle, leaving the headlights on.

"Christopher!" he shouted, running up onto the verandah, hoping the old boards would take his weight. "It's me. It's Rohan. You must come out. You're a responsible boy. Your mother is sick with worry. So is your grandfather. People have been searching for you for hours. Come out now. You're quite safe. I'm here now. I'll never leave you again. That's my solemn promise, Christopher. Come out, son. We need to get you home."

The front door lay open, hanging on its hinges. Vandals? Or simply years of no one caring what happened to the place. Having accomplished so much, Rohan was having difficulty accepting he and his mother had ever lived in such a place—but then his mother had kept the cottage spotlessly clean. He had helped her put in a vegetable garden at the back. He had cut the grass while his mother had looked after the beds of perennials around the picket fence.

He moved into the house, shining the torch down the hallway that ran from front to back. God! He could cover it in less than half a dozen paces.

"I know you're here, Christopher," he called, gentling the urgency of his voice. "I know you're frightened. But there's nothing to be frightened about. I used to run off myself when I was a boy and things got too much for me to handle. I know how you feel. But your mother and I want you to come home. Please, Christopher. There are always things in life we have to face. We have to swallow our fears. Find our courage. Come out now. Let me see you. We can confront what is worrying you together."

Rohan didn't even consider he was talking to an empty old house. Christopher, his son, was here somewhere.

A moment later a small boy stumbled out of what had been the kitchen and into the hallway, vigorously rubbing his eyes. "I'm a real sook," he announced, in a quavery voice he tried hard to make stronger. "I've been crying."

Rohan thought he would never forget this moment. Huge relief bubbled up in his chest. He moved towards his son, feeling such a rush of love he couldn't begin to describe it. "Grown men cry, Christopher," he said, unbearably touched by the way this small boy was trying to hold himself together. "There's no shame in shedding a few tears. Come here to me."

"I wanted to see where you'd lived," Christopher explained, starting towards the wonderful man he had been drawn to on sight. "Are you my *real* dad?" he asked, realising with a pang of sadness that he had been having difficulty remembering the man he had once called Daddy for some time.

Rohan reached for his son, fragile as a bird in his strong grip. He lifted him high in his arms. "I *am* your father, Christopher," he said. "I am so very, *very* sorry for the confusion that's gone on." That surely couldn't be the best way to put it to a child? Rohan agonised. *Confusion?* He could hardly say he hadn't even known he existed until very recently. "I *want* to be your father. I want to do everything I can for you and your mother. How does that feel?"

Christopher had already reached his decision. He buried his hot, sweaty little face in his father's neck. "Real *good*!" he said.

* * *

Rohan used his mobile to have the search called off. News that young Christopher Prescott had been found safe and sound flew around the network. And Rohan, in a matter of days, was to make a sizeable and very welcome contribution to the Valley's Search and Rescue Team.

All's well that ends well—was the general view. One had to keep a close eye on kids. They created problems without meaning to. Sometimes awful things happened in communities. This, by the grace of God, wasn't one of them. Lots of people believed in guardian angels. Young Christopher Prescott obviously had one. And Rohan Costello, absent so long from Silver Valley, had managed to channel that guiding light.

They were safe. Both of them were safe. Christopher and Rohan. The joy of it swamped her. The exterior lights lit up the garden, and the Jeep had barely come to a stop when Christopher opened the door and jumped out onto the gravel.

"Mummy!" he cried, as though the sight of her had put his world right.

The love in her son's voice, the expression on his dirty, tear-streaked face, told Charlotte that whatever she had done her seven-year-old son was one person who wasn't going to hold her to blame.

"Chrissie!" She caught him to her, hugged and patted him hard, folded him into a mutual display of love. "Thank God you're safe."

Christopher pulled back a little, tilting his head. "It was Rohan who found me." He slanted his rescuer, who stood leaning against the Jeep, a beaming glance.

"Of course it was." Charlotte breathed in air. Breathed, *breathed*. Of course she'd known her little son would come back to her. Hadn't she?

She turned her head, binding Rohan to her with a glance. He had made the decision to remain on the periphery, clearly giving them a minute together. Her father, who had been positioned behind her at the front door, anxiously awaiting their arrival, had joined in the reunion, his long arms now making a cocoon around his daughter and his grandson.

"Christopher, you must never run off and scare us again," he scolded, making a sudden change of direction now the boy was safe. "We're endlessly grateful to you, Rohan," he called to the tall, handsome, self-contained young man standing apart. "It's a miracle you thought of the old cottage. Christopher could have been out all night. Come in, come in," he invited, with the warmth of a man who had decided to put the traumas of the past behind them. "Let me get you a well-deserved drink."

"It was so dark I couldn't see a thing," Christopher announced. "Rohan said I have to apologise to everyone who came out to search for me. Of course I will. But I never thought people would be going to look for me. Only you and Grandpa, Mummy. Rohan wasn't coming back until the weekend. He told me before he went away."

"God only knows—" Vivian Marsdon started in exasperation, then stopped. "There was a good chance your mother wouldn't have been able to contact Rohan, Christopher," he said after a moment.

"Let's drop it for now." Charlotte tapped her father's shoulder. "Chris needs a nice long shower, and when he's done he can have something to eat. Then bed."

"My stomach is groaning. I feel really hungry. There was no water at the cottage either. I'm sorry everyone was worried, but I wanted to go somewhere I could think."

His grandfather frowned. "You might have had to spend the night there, my boy."

"I think I fell asleep, but I can't be sure."

"Well, no harm's done." Rohan intervened smoothly. "I'll have that drink, Mr Marsdon, if it's okay?" He moved into the pool of light.

"Please, please—it's Vivian," Vivian Marsdon insisted, waving a welcoming hand. "I'll join you."

Charlotte and Rohan exchanged wry glances at her father's dramatic turnaround. "I'll take Chrissie off," she said. "Could you make him a sandwich, Dad? He can have a glass of milk with it."

"Put some Milo in it, please, Grandpa?" Christopher requested.

He turned his blond head to address his saviour, who just happened to be his father. He didn't know how it had happened, but he was sure his mother would explain it properly to him. He had a feeling Rohan wanted to hear too. Was it *confusion* that had put his grandmother into such a terrible spin? He hadn't waited on the stairs to hear all she had to say. The awful grating sound in her voice had made him feel sick. He had just wanted to get away from the house.

"You're going to wait for me, aren't you, Rohan?" He held his small body very still, awaiting his hero's answer.

"Yes, I am, chief!" Rohan gave his son a reassuring smile.

Christopher beamed. "Oh, good! Rohan and I are mates, Mummy. I'm his mate. He's my mate." He turned to Rohan, giving him a confidential man-to-man look. "I'll keep calling you Rohan for a while—just like you said, Rohan."

"Good thinking!" Rohan touched his fingertips to his forehead in a tiny salute.

Christopher burst out laughing, then sobered abruptly. He shot his mother an apprehensive look. "Grandmother's gone, hasn't she?"

"Too right she has!" his grandfather answered, his deep

voice rising, the vein in the middle of his forehead twitching away. "And she won't be coming back in a hurry."

"Does she know I ran away?" Christopher asked as his mother led him off.

"She will when she checks her e-mails." Vivian Marsdon smiled grimly. "Go along now, Christopher. You've worn us all out."

Charlotte and Rohan walked into Riverbend's entrance hall hand in hand, although both were aware of the intense strain between them. Christopher had been found. The danger was over. But she knew there were many questions that were going to be asked. The problem was she didn't know how she was going to answer Rohan, let alone find acceptable answers for their son. Highly intelligent Christopher might be, but he was still only a boy of seven. Plenty of time for him to find out how babies were made.

He had fallen asleep almost as soon as his head hit the pillow. Her father, who had put in some deeply harrowing hours searching for his grandson, had joined Christopher with his sandwiches, substituting a nice drop of Laphroaig for milk and a couple of teaspoons of Milo. Rohan had accepted a single malt whisky, but declined a chicken sandwich. He had contacted his housekeeper at the house, he explained. Dinner would be waiting. He had turned his dark head to invite Charlotte to join him—a naturally commanding young man, who wasn't going to accept a refusal.

She'd had absolutely no idea what response her father would make. He was a man of the old school who regarded himself as the head of family, to be deferred to no matter what one's age or status in life. Would he say it might be best if she remained at home? As it was, she had every intention of returning to the Lodge late. Christopher might very well awaken during the night. He had, after all, suffered his own trauma.

Instead Vivian Marsdon now walked them to the front door, where he paused to look at the younger man, his expression that of a man who had set aside time to put a nagging concern in order. "I want to tell you, Rohan, I deeply regret what has gone before." He fetched up a great sigh. "I can't, of course, change anything. None of us can. But I allowed my wife to control the whole terrible situation surrounding Mattie's death. Like a fool, I couldn't see what was under my nose. I'd very much appreciate it now, Rohan, if we could be friends?" He held out his hand, the tone of his deep, rich voice absolutely sincere.

This was the moment when Rohan would be well within his rights to reject an overture that had come far too late. Instead, without a moment's hesitation, he took Vivian Marsdon's hand in a brief, firm grip. "I'd like that, sir."

"Good. Good." Vivian coloured, fiercely pleased. He bent down to kiss his daughter's cheek. "Go along now, Charlie. Enjoy dinner. Relax your nerves. I'm sure you two have lots to talk about. I'll leave the light on for you."

"Thanks, Dad." Charlotte gave her father a lovely tender smile. "Chris was pretty much exhausted, but I'd like to check on him during the night."

"Hungry?" Rohan led the way past the grand reception rooms to the state-of-the-art kitchen.

"Not really, thank you, Rohan." Hours of the most intense anxiety had shocked hunger out of her.

He studied her intently, noting the haunted expression in her green eyes, the way she held her slender body taut. "Better have something all the same." He was reminded of the way she had looked on that long-ago terrible day at the river. Both of them had suffered more than their fair share of grief.

"I shouldn't stop too long." Her eyes were stinging. What must he think of her? Rohan had always been her greatest friend. He had made her happier than anyone else in the world. He had been her truly glorious lover, was the father of her child. But she couldn't rid herself of the thought that she had lost his trust for ever. That weighed very heavily on her.

Louise Burch, the housekeeper, came bustling through the swinging kitchen door, leaving tantalising aromas in her wake. "Good evening, sir. Good evening, Mrs Prescott. I should have met you at the door," she apologised, sounding a little short of breath. "I was just coming to check."

"Don't worry about that, Louise. Roy not home yet?" Roy Burch had been one of the searchers.

Louise's face lit up with a smile as she turned to Charlotte. "All of us are so happy and relieved young Christopher has been found, Mrs Prescott. Boys are such scamps. Roy went off with some of our friends to have a celebratory drink. I was going to join them."

"Then you mustn't wait," Rohan said immediately. "Charlotte and I can manage."

Louise Burch adopted her professional manner. "Thank you so much. There's roast chicken just out of the oven. Pesto and mascarpone sauce. Little chat potatoes, beans, and baby peas from the garden. I'll wait and serve up."

"No need for that, Mrs Burch," Charlotte intervened with a smile. "You go off now. My father and I are enormously grateful to all the good caring people in the Valley. I will be telling your husband that when I see him. There's no need for you to look after the two of us."

"Well, if you say so." Louse Burch glanced from one to the other. What beautiful young people they were!

"We *do* say so, Louise." Rohan gave her an easy smile.

Louise blushed. Talk about sex appeal! "Then thank you so much. That's very good of you."

"Not at all. And we'll clear away afterwards, so you're not to worry," Charlotte said.

Moments later, apron folded away, Mrs Burch took her leave. "By the way, I made a plum cake with plum syrup," she told them with a bright smile. "One of my specialities. Plenty of ice cream and whipped cream in the fridge."

"Thank you, Louise," said Rohan. "I'll probably have a very large slice."

Louise Burch went off beaming. She and her husband were more contented than they had ever been, looking after Mr Costello. He was the best boss in the world, and their bungalow in the grounds couldn't be more comfortable. Silver Valley was absolute heaven after their last job, with a demanding old matriarch. They had made friends in no time.

Charlotte Prescott, a widow, was so beautiful—and so young to have a seven-year-old child to rear alone. Wouldn't it be wonderful if she and Mr Costello made a match of it? A grand house like Riverbend needed a lady like that. Apparently Mrs Prescott's father had fallen on hard times and had had to sell the estate. If those two beautiful young people got married Charlotte Prescott would never have to leave her old home…

"Let's eat in here," Rohan said.

"Rohan?"

"No talk. I need to feed you first. Sit down before you fall down. I can get this."

He pulled out a chair for her at the long granite-topped table before moving away, super-efficient in everything he did. She watched him walk over to some impressive-looking refrigerated wine-storage cabinets, the contents on full view through the glass doors. He pulled out a bottle of white wine, showing her the label.

"Fine. Fine…" She glanced at it, looked away. It was an award-winning Chardonnay. She was trying hard not to let the tension inside her break the surface. "Not much dinner for me, Rohan." Under his smooth control, he too had to be fighting powerful feelings.

"When did you last eat?" He found glasses, then poured the perfectly chilled wine, passing a glass to her.

"When did *you*?" she countered.

"Around seven this morning. I don't often get a chance to stop for lunch, so at the moment I'm hungry. Charlotte, you didn't answer *my* question."

She stared up at him with troubled eyes. "I can't seem to find the right answers to your questions."

"That's because you're hiding so much."

She was wearing a soft georgette top of pastel colours, with an ankle-length matching skirt. The top had a low oval neckline that allowed just a glimpse of cleavage. The fabric clung to her small high breasts and showed off her taut torso and tiny waist. She looked like a top model—especially with her long blonde mane loose. He didn't think he could ever let her cut her hair. It was too beautiful.

"You don't trust me," she said sadly.

"I *half* trust you." He softened it with a smile.

"Well, that's better than nothing. But lack of trust ruins relationships, Rohan. Anyway, I made afternoon tea for my mother. I don't remember eating anything, but I did have a cup of tea."

"We won't talk about your mother." He was busy cutting

slices of tender white chicken breast. "Not for the moment anyway."

She had to be content with that.

As it turned out, he didn't appear to have an appetite either—though they had no difficulty finishing the bottle of wine. Both ate little of what otherwise would have been a delicious meal.

"Well, we can't disappoint Mrs Burch," Rohan said later, eyeing the plum cake. The table was cleared, dishes rinsed and stacked in the dishwasher. "You'll have to join me in a slice. It looks good."

"She's a good cook. Very good."

"I wouldn't have hired her otherwise. She's rather passionate about food. I like that." He cut a large slice and then, before Charlotte could voice any protest, cut it in two, giving Charlotte the narrow end, and pouring a little plum syrup over both sections. "All right. *Eat* that."

"You're ordering me about?"

"Yes," he said crisply, then sat down again.

She took hold of her cake fork. "You want to talk to me, don't you?"

"Charlotte, my love, I've *tried* talking to you." The expression in his eyes was hard; a mocking smile curled his mouth.

"You must think I'm pathetic."

He laughed without humour. "Would you like some cream?" He stood up.

"No, thank you."

"Well, I'll have some. I need sweetening up." He went to the large stainless steel refrigerator standing side by side with a matching freezer. "Second thoughts—ice cream. Seriously—won't you join me?"

"You're enjoying this in a weird sort of way, aren't you?"

"The hell I am! We've both had a shock. I'm trying my level best to be kind." He pointed to her plate.

"Okay, okay." She handed it up to him. It might even make her feel better.

He laid a nicely turned dessertspoonful of vanilla ice cream on it.

Charlotte made herself eat. Actually, it was lovely.

When they were finished he took the plates and cutlery from her, rinsed them, then put them in the dishwasher, turning it on. Finally he disposed of the empty wine bottle.

"You're very useful in the kitchen." She gave in to a wry little laugh.

"Just one of my many talents. I'm pretty useful in the bedroom as well. And you don't hold back there, do you, Charlotte? Believe me, you're the best of the best. The cool, cool, touch-me-not is an enormous turn-on. Charlotte hiding her passionate nature."

The passionate nature only you unlocked, she thought. What a tremendous burden would be lifted from her if she could give voice to her heart!

You must help me, Rohan. I'm a damaged woman.

Seriously messed-up, too young, and with no one to turn to, to ease her out of it. It happened so much in life. She'd thought she didn't have a choice. She'd taken the wrong direction. She had married the wrong man.

"Would you like coffee?"

Rohan was desperate to make some breakthrough.

He loved this woman. Nothing could change that. Not even the fact she had rejected him for Martyn Prescott, who'd been able to give her every material thing in life. Her decision had troubled her deeply. Unfortunately one always paid in the end for bad decisions. He still wanted Charlotte very badly, and wondered whatever had happened to something called pride. Maybe love and pride didn't go together? He had been committed to Charlotte Marsdon from childhood. They were the legendary childhood sweethearts.

She stood up, her graceful body set in determined lines. "I should go."

"In a little while. You might consider *I* won't be able to rest until I hear what your mother had to say. What my son overheard."

"He didn't tell you?" She bent her shining head, almost as if in prayer.

"I didn't like to question him. It was enough to have him safe. If you must know, I think Christopher is as confused as I am. That was the fool word I had to use with him. *Confusion*. Isn't that a sick joke? There was *confusion* over who exactly was his father. Well, at least he knows now—and he seems pretty happy about it. So thank God for that! Let's go back into the living room. You're going to have to open up a little, Charlotte. If only for our son's sake."

He came around to her, taking her firmly by her upper arms.

For a split second she was elsewhere. A different time. A different place. A very different man. Bad memories surfaced, caught her up so strongly she visibly cringed. Then, realising what she had done—this was *Rohan*—she took a great gulp of air.

Rohan stared at her, astounded. "I can't possibly be hurting you." Nevertheless he slackened his grip. "For God's sake, Charlotte, what's *that* all about?"

She put her hand to her mouth. She was a mere heartbeat

away from telling him the whole shocking story. Only then she would lose his respect.

"You just *cringed* from me." Rohan tried very hard to speak gently. "Surely you didn't think I was about to hit you?"

"Of course not." She cursed herself for her involuntary action. "To tell the truth, I don't know what I'm doing."

"Charlotte, I wouldn't *dream* of hurting you."

"Rohan, I know that." She gave a desperate little moan, spent with emotion, letting her head fall forward against his chest.

"What am I going to do with you?" He began to rock her light body as if she were an inconsolable child. He'd used to think it quite possible to die of love for Charlotte. He still did. "You can't put me off, Charlotte." He lifted her chin, seeing his reflection in her eyes. "Tell me exactly what Christopher heard. Only then will I take you home. It's up to you. I need to be able to combat the fears my son has. We can't keep our history under wraps for much longer. Your father might have had blinkers on, but anyone with a sharp pair of eyes in their head will recognise me in Christopher. We both know that. It's all going to come out."

"I know." There was absolute certainty in her voice.

"You say that like you're in despair." He was grappling with the sexual hunger that had started to roar through him. "Don't you *want* the world to know Christopher is my son?"

She pressed her fingers against his mouth. "Rohan, the news will shock so many people. I don't really count my ex-in-laws among them—" she laughed raggedly "—but I must tell you I'm *elated* Chrissie has taken the revelation you're his real father in his stride. It has to be some deep primal recognition. But he must be wondering how it all happened. How I married Martyn. How we are Prescotts. And there's Martyn's tragic accident. Sooner or later someone is going to tell him there was a young woman in the car with the man he thought was his father. God, *I* can't handle it all. How can *he*? He's seven years old."

"Well, he's doing fine so far," Rohan pointed out tersely. "Come into the living room. We can work it out together, Charlotte. Life is full of revelations. People have to live with them every day. Betrayed people. I want to marry you. I'm going to marry you. Christopher should never be parted from his mother, and he's my son. We can't go our separate ways. That's not possible. I want to look after you both. Maybe it isn't happening the way I always planned, but it *is* happening. And soon."

He didn't say a word until she had finished telling him of her mother's visit. "She couldn't have been more unpleasant—"

"Vicious, don't you mean?" His fire-blue eyes blazed.

"She didn't know Christopher was at home." Of all things, she was now defending her indefensible mother. "The *one* day he misses school, my mother turns up."

"Christopher said he ran off before he heard the lot."

"He heard more than enough," she said painfully. "He heard my mother say I had sex with you *and* Martyn."

"Well, you did, didn't you?" he challenged bleakly. "Does he know what 'having sex' means?"

She was so upset she averted her face. "The things he knows *amaze* me. I don't know if he's got right down to the *'hows'*. Dad is very involved in his education. They do a lot together. But Dad would never get into that particular area. He would regard Chrissie as far too young. It's all history, geography, the moon, the stars, the earth—things like that."

"Oh, Charlotte!" He felt close to defeat. "What happened to us?"

A great swath of her hair fell forward against her cheek. "I'm not proud of myself, Rohan. But I have to ask you to take pity on me. I can't take any more tonight. Tomorrow, maybe."

"Okay. I'll take you home. I have to go back to Sydney in the morning. I have an important meeting I had to cancel today. You'll be all right? I'll come back as soon as I can. We have to decide what's best to do. Your father has had a big shock too."

Charlotte gave a little sob. "There's no accounting for reactions. He did get a shock, but he's over it already. My mother's *performance* guaranteed that. You know, he's wasted years pining for her."

His mouth twisted at the irony. "Well, now he's seen her true colours. Your father is a handsome, virile man. He should remarry."

"Maybe he might now. Lord knows there are several very attractive eligible women in the Valley who would jump at the chance of becoming the second Mrs Marsdon. The years that one wastes!" She lifted her eyes to his. They were full of tears.

"Charlie, don't do this," he groaned, his voice deepening with emotion. "I hunger and thirst for you. I want to keep you here, but I can't. Don't cry. *Please*. You cry, and I warn you my feelings will get the better of me."

"So take me home," she burst out wildly, and yet she surged towards him.

He caught her as she all but threw herself at him, trying to suppress the raging fire of desire before it got totally out of hand.

"Rohan, I'm so *afraid*!"

"Of what? *Tell* me." He felt overwhelmingly protective.

"Of the things that might happen."

"So we've got a fair bit of explaining to do?" He thought that was what she meant. Gently he smoothed damp strands of her hair from her face. "We'll do it together. We speak to the Prescotts together. You clearly think they've had suspicions for some time. Did you love Martyn? Just a little? It's okay to tell me."

Once she'd had a good deal of affection for Martyn. As had he. Martyn Prescott had been an integral part of their daily lives.

"Who said anything about my loving Martyn?"

She'd shocked him with her throbbing answer. The *sob* in her voice. The sheer force of *repugnance* in her face. The stormy expression that swept into her lustrous green eyes took him totally unawares.

He stared down at her. "You blamed him for all the women? Martyn wasn't *really* a womaniser. He was obsessed with *you*. Perhaps he went after comfort elsewhere when you couldn't give him what he wanted?'

"Don't think I didn't try!" Her response was fiery. "I married him. I told you—I thought my unborn child was his. I thought I had a duty to marry him. You were thousands of miles away, on the other side of the continent. Four months can be an eternity. You thought money was important to me. It wasn't. *You* were. You have the mind-set of a man who thinks his main job in life is to offer the woman he loves security."

"Well, isn't it?" He caught her beautiful face in his two hands, her hair a golden cloud around her face.

"No—no!"

He'd had enough. More than enough. Heart hammering,

he stopped her mouth with his own, taking a firm and desperate hold on her as though he would never let her get away. Only she returned his deep, passionate kiss, pressing her body ever closer against his, her own hunger, longing, love, hot and fierce.

"Charlotte!" At the fervour of her response, his hand moved to her breast. He knew the flimsy top would come off easily. Next the skirt. He belonged to this woman and no one else. She belonged to him.

Both of them had caught fire. Their mouths remained locked until they had to draw apart just to catch breath. There was no question of stopping. No question of saying *no* to the ecstasy on offer. They only had to come together for the fires of desire to crackle, burn, and then within moments turn into a raging inferno.

He drew her down onto the rug where they stood.

CHAPTER TEN

CHRISTOPHER, surprisingly none the worse for the traumatic events of the day before, insisted on going to school.

"I have to tell everyone I must have been delirious to do anything so stupid." He had worked out his explanation in advance. "I *did* have a high temperature, didn't I. Mummy?"

"Well, it didn't get to the scalding stage, but, yes, your temperature *was* higher than normal for some hours."

"Then that will have to do." He could never tell anyone the things his dreadful grandmother had screeched. He was still trying to figure them out.

"I'll come into school with you," Charlotte said. "Your headmaster turned out to search for you. So did the other teachers. I won't ever forget that."

Christopher looked more mortified than gratified. "I never knew people were going to search for me," he said unhappily. "I'll never do anything so stupid again."

She had to see the very calmness of his reaction had a great deal to do with his extraordinary emotional bond with Rohan. Rohan had come for him. Rohan had found him when no one else could. Rohan was now established as his *real* father, and that greatly reinforced Christopher's support base. Whatever the shock waves, they clearly hadn't overwhelmed their son. Christopher, a male child, saw

Rohan as supremely strong and capable. A father he could look up to. Two parents clearly *were* better than one. She agreed with that at every level.

The big dilemma actually centred around *her*. She had to go to her ex-in-laws and tell them exactly how it had been. She would not expose Martyn. She had no wish to bring extra pain on the Prescotts who, apart from Gordon, had never really treated her as "family". Every one in the Valley knew of the intense bond between her and the young Rohan Costello. Martyn came in second best. It didn't sit well with Mrs Prescott or Nicole, who had grown up un-wavering in her jealousy of the young woman who became her sister-in-law. Charlotte always had the feeling Nicole would have been hostile towards her even if there had been no Rohan. Perhaps she had made Nicole feel wanting in the femininity stakes.

Mrs Ellory, the Prescotts' long-time housekeeper, greeted her at the door, remarkably pleased at seeing Charlotte again. She had been told when Charlotte was due to arrive, as Charlotte had rung ahead to ask if it would be convenient if she called in.

The answer from Mrs Prescott couldn't have been more direct. "Yes," she'd said, and hung up.

"And Christopher? He's all right this morning?"

Charlotte smiled, remembering how kind Mrs Ellory had been to her little boy. "Insisted on going to school."

"Amazing what children get up to," Mrs Ellroy said. "But all's well that ends well. Mrs Prescott and Nicole are waiting for you in the Garden Room, Charlotte. Go through. I'll be bringing morning tea directly. Lovely to see you, Charlotte. I've missed you and young Christopher."

"We've missed you too, Mrs Ellory." It was perfectly

true. Sometimes she had thought "Ellie", as Christopher had called her, was her only real friend in the house.

When Charlotte walked into the Garden Room, with its beautiful display of plants and hanging baskets, neither her ex-mother-in-law nor Nicole spoke.

So that was the way it was going to be.

It was extremely unnerving, but she had to steel her resolve. If she and Rohan were to marry in a few months' time there were facts all of them had to contend with. No matter how badly she wanted to be away from here, she had no option but to pay the Prescotts the courtesy of letting them know of her plans. Though nothing had been said, Charlotte felt in her bones Mrs Prescott had come to realise Christopher wasn't her grandson. But at the beginning Martyn had been so obsessive about her. It had been as though she was the only girl in the world who could make him happy. And what Martyn wanted, Martyn got.

Rohan concluded his meeting much earlier than expected. A successful deal had been struck, with big gains for both sides. There were other pressing matters that needed his attention, but he was feeling uncommonly anxious. He knew he and Charlotte had to confront the Prescotts. They had a need and a *right* to know what he and Charlotte had planned. Charlotte believed the Prescotts already knew Christopher wasn't Martyn's child, but it would have to be stated at their meeting. Secrets might take years to come out, but they rarely remained secret for ever. In their case, with Christopher so closely resembling Rohan, discovery was imminent.

He picked up the phone, requesting that the company helicopter—on stand-by—be ready for a return flight to the Valley. He needed to be with Charlotte. He felt deep inside him that life with Martyn had damaged her. That the once highly eligible and attractive Martyn Prescott, admired by many young women in the Valley, while full of fun and good company, had apparently not matured into a strong character. He had never apologised to him or his mother for the damaging scenario he had come up with for that tragic day on the river. That was the problem with Martyn. He couldn't accept responsibility for his actions. Martyn had made life far harder for Rohan and his innocent mother. He had turned Charlotte's mother against them. The outright lies and the half truths had left unresolvable griefs.

The Prescott housekeeper, Mrs Ellory, was passing through the entrance hall of High Grove as Rohan approached the front door. Vivian Marsdon had directed him there.

"Charlotte wanted to assure them Chrissie is safe. Also to thank Gordon, if he's around, for his efforts," Marsdon had said.

That piece of news had hit Rohan like an actual blow. "You shouldn't have let her go, sir. I told Charlotte when she decided it was time to talk to the Prescotts I would go with her. How long ago did she leave?"

"Not five minutes." Vivian had been thoroughly flustered. "That's why I'm so very surprised to see *you*. We thought you were staying in Sydney."

"I had concerns. Intuitions. Anyway, I can't stop. I'm going after her. Could I borrow your car?"

"Of course. I'll get the keys."

"Well, this *is* a day for nice surprises." Mrs Ellory came to the door to greet him. "You look marvellous, Rohan. I couldn't be more thrilled you're back in the Valley. People are quite excited by your plans. More jobs. More prosperity."

"I'm glad to hear that, Mrs Ellory," Rohan said, and, getting to the point, "Do you know where Charlotte is?"

"They're in the Garden Room—at the back of the house." She looked into Rohan Costello's blazing eyes. The boy Christopher had eyes like that. "I probably shouldn't say this, but I'm glad you're here. Charlotte needs support in this house. Do you want me to take you through?"

"I'll go the back way, Mrs Ellory. It's shorter."

"And you'll be able to gauge how things are going," she whispered back. "I only stay for Mr Prescott, you know. Mrs Prescott has turned into a very bitter woman. As for Nicole...!" She rolled her eyes.

Rohan gave her quick salute, then ran down a short flight of stone steps. He could hear raised voices as he rounded the side of the house.

Nicole. Such a difficult creature, Nicole. Martyn had inherited all the looks and the charm in the family.

"You're the very *opposite* of the way you look and sound!" the jealous and insecure young woman was lashing out.

"Oh, Nicole, do be quiet," her mother cut in sharply, as if to a child. "You brought nothing but suffering to my son, Charlotte. You couldn't face the world pregnant and unmarried, and Costello was nowhere around. But Martyn *was.* Martyn adored you. God knows why, when you were so involved with Costello. And Costello was dirt-poor. He had nothing. His mother struggled just to put food on the table. I paid her more than she was worth."

"Are you *serious*?" Charlotte countered, in a clear, firm voice.

Rohan knew perfectly well the right thing to do was to go in and announce himself. Instead he stood frozen, able to hear perfectly but unable to be seen. Maybe in staying where he was he could make some sense of everything that had transpired. Charlotte was keeping so much from him. It might advantage him to stay where he was until it became obvious she needed his help.

"You never overpaid *anyone*, Lesley. A plain statement of fact. You were tight-fisted with everyone but Martyn. Nicole missed out. You owed her far more time and attention. Gordon was the kind, generous one—"

"None of your business any more," Lesley Prescott cut her off, affronted. "So, you and Costello intend to marry?"

"That's what I've come to tell you, Lesley. You have a right to know."

"Oh, how simply wonderful that you think so!" Lesley Prescott crowed. "May I ask when the great day is to be?"

"Early next year."

"No doubt with your son as pageboy?" she sneered. "You take comfort where you can find it, don't you, Charlotte? Costello has made quite a name for himself now."

"You know he's Christopher's father?"

There was a terrible note in Lesley Prescott's voice. "We didn't *know* at the beginning. We knew you and Martyn were dating when Costello wasn't around. You used my son."

"I didn't *use* Martyn," Charlotte said sadly. "I thought he was my friend—"

"And threw in a little sex," Nicole broke in with malice. "You'd been getting plenty with Costello. You must have missed it when he was away. Martyn was there. He was stupid enough to stay in love with you. That's what you do, isn't it? *Use* men."

High time to announce his presence, Rohan decided— only Charlotte's answer riveted him to the spot.

"It was Martyn who used *me*, Nicole."

No mistaking the utter gravity of her tone.

"Which means exactly what?" Lesley Prescott barked out. "You got caught out, didn't you? You never meant to fall pregnant by my son. It was always Costello you wanted."

"Always," Charlotte agreed. "How could I possibly have turned to Martyn after Rohan? Martyn was a liar. Lying was part of his nature. And it started early. It was Martyn who challenged Mattie to swim the river."

"Oh, yeah!" Nicole burst out, ample chest heaving.

"You knew your brother more than you care to admit, Nicole. You *know* he hit me. Not in the early years, but towards the end, when he was so unhappy. You *know*, but you don't dare speak the truth in front of your mother."

Lesley Prescott's face, like Charlotte's, was showing the depth of her upset. "Now it's your turn to lie," she cried. "My son would *never* do such a thing. I never saw any evidence of abuse. It wouldn't have been tolerated. Martyn adored you, even when he was off with women hardly more than prostitutes."

"It doesn't matter now, Lesley. I'm sorry I told you." Charlotte gave vent to a weary sigh.

"If my son struck you, you must have deserved it." Lesley Prescott launched into mitigation. In truth, she was shocked by the idea Martyn might have struck his beautiful wife. "You were withholding your marital obligations. You weren't a proper wife to him. Did you never consider he had saved you from a scandal? He *married* you. He thought the child was his. We all did.'

"I did too, Lesley," Charlotte responded soberly. "I was so ill-informed in those days I made a huge mistake. Rohan remains the love of my life. I was on the pill when I was with him. We couldn't afford for me to fall pregnant. I didn't realise at the time things can go wrong. I had a bout of sickness that interfered with the efficacy of the pill. I didn't know then. I know now."

"So you didn't take the pill with Martyn? Is that it?" Lesley scoffed, unable to abandon the pretence that her son had been perfect.

"With Rohan away, I stopped. There was no reason to keep on taking it until Rohan returned."

"What a risk you took with Martyn, then!" Lesley said bitterly. "You fed off his admiration and love. You seduced him, didn't you?"

"You were missing all that hot sex." Nicole, who had never had sex—hot or cold—laughed crudely.

"Do shut up, Nicole. Get a life. *Do* something about yourself," Charlotte told her—not without pity. She turned to her ex-mother-in-law. "I'm truly sorry, Lesley, for all the tragic things that have happened. I grieved for Martyn too, you know."

Lesley glared at her darkly. "Rubbish! In the olden days, Charlotte Marsdon, you would have been burned at the stake."

Something in Rohan snapped. He moved swiftly, the heart torn out of him.

"Look me in the face and tell me you're lying!" Lesley Prescott was crying. "You seduced my son. You probably got a huge kick out of it. After all, he worshipped the ground you walked on. You had to have *him* too."

Charlotte spoke so quietly Rohan could barely hear what she was saying. Then it hit him with horrified amazement.

"Martyn raped me."

He staggered as if at a king hit.

Martyn, their friend from early childhood, had raped her?

Inside the room Lesley Prescott was going berserk, also

horrified by *that* word. "Liar!" she shouted, waving her arms wildly in the air.

"What do *you* think, Nicole?" Charlotte gave the younger woman a chance to redeem herself. "You're the *one* person who knows what Martyn was like. Rohan doesn't know. I was too ashamed to tell him."

"Good!" Nicole actually looked a little crazy. "Why didn't you watch out for him, you fool?"

Lesley Prescott made a yelping sound, rounding on her daughter, astounded. "What in God's name are you talking about?"

"Wake up, Mum," Nicole said with undisguised contempt. "You and your Martyn. Your can-do-no-wrong son. Martyn was a bastard. I *knew* he was hitting Charlotte. It must have been awful for her. I *knew* he'd forced sex on her. He *told* me. He boasted about it. How else was he going to get her away from Rohan Costello?"

So there it is, Rohan's inner voice said. *The direst of secrets revealed.*

Hot blood rose like a tide, forming a red mist before his eyes. *His beautiful Charlotte.* He hadn't been there to protect or defend her. She would have trusted Martyn. If Martyn weren't dead, he thought he would kill him.

Eyes ablaze, Rohan rapped hard on the glass door with his knuckles, startling all three women. They turned their heads in unison, all three appalled.

"What a contemptible creature you are, Nicole," he said. "In your own way you're as guilty as your cowardly brother. Time to go, Charlotte." He issued the command. "I told you not to come here without me. These people have never done you any good."

Lesley Prescott felt intimidated to the bone. When exactly had young Rohan Costello become such a commanding figure? "How dare you come into my home unannounced?" she asked hoarsely.

"That wasn't my intention, Mrs Prescott. Only one never knows what one might learn by staying out of sight. I'd intended to announce myself—only in following your riveting conversation I have been able to learn the truth. Charlotte was protecting your sick bully of a son, Mrs Prescott. Think of the nobility of that. She kept silent. A mother herself, she didn't want to hurt *you*. You can only blame yourself for provoking her now. And I'm glad. Because now we have the truth of why Charlotte married Martyn. She believed herself pregnant by him. She believed marrying him was the proper course to take. Her parents failed her. *I* failed her—going so far away, leaving cunning, manipulative Martyn to seize his moment. It was always his way. Charlotte provided a few clues along the way, but I was so self-involved I was blind to them. Martyn was a coward, and a traitor to our lifelong friendship."

As Rohan moved further into the room both Prescott women stumbled back.

When exactly had Martyn turned bad? Lesley Prescott asked herself. How much of it was her fault? "Martyn is dead," she said, her face contorted with pain.

It took everything Rohan had to fall back on forgiveness. For the mother. Not the son. "Despite all the pain Martyn inflicted on us, Mrs Prescott, Charlotte and I *are* saddened by that. Come here to me, Charlotte." He held out an imperative hand.

Charlotte rushed to him, desperate for his comfort.

"The Valley will never accept you," Lesley Prescott told them heavily.

Rohan returned her a cool, confident look. "You're wrong about that, Mrs Prescott. I have big plans for the Valley. My enterprises will be creating a lot of jobs, and the von Luckners have come on board with their great expertise. Charlotte Vale will be producing ultra-premium wines. I have plans for the olive groves as well. Plans for a first-class restaurant. I think you'll find the Valley more than happy about it all after they absorb the initial shock that Christopher is my son. But then, I think a lot of people already know. We really should present some sort of a united front, Mrs Prescott. Charlotte and I want no enmity. The *one* person you should be angry at—the *one* person who betrayed us all—is Martyn. And your daughter definitely needs counselling. Jealousy is a cancer. She needs treatment. Neither of you should want to make an enemy of me," he warned, his hand tightening on Charlotte's. "Time to leave, Charlotte. It's over now."

"Are you okay to drive?" Rohan asked as they walked to her car. She was as pale as a lily.

"I'm fine, Rohan. Don't worry about me." She looked away to her father's Mercedes. "Dad lent it to you?"

"No problem. I took the chopper from Sydney. I was anxious about you. What time do you pick up Christopher?" He opened her car door, waiting for her to get behind the wheel.

"I'm always there ten minutes early, so two-fifty."

"I'll come with you. Follow me back to Riverbend."

She should have felt as if a great burden had been lifted from her shoulders. Instead she wondered what Rohan thought of her under his mask of gentleness and concern. However much he understood, his respect for her would have plummeted. She had never intended to tell him what Martyn had done. She had wanted to keep her self-respect.

It was well-documented the world over that innocent victims of abuse—physical and mental—can feel an irrational, yet powerful sense of guilt.

Charlotte had been one of them—much like an abused child. But the dark cloud that had hung over her for so long was about to be totally dispersed.

Mrs Burch opened the front door. She looked surprised to see them, noting with concern that both of them looked what she later described to her husband as "traumatised".

"Tea, thank you, Louise." Rohan kept a steadying hand on Charlotte. "We'll have it in the library."

Mrs Burch hurried away. All sorts of strange things were happening in the Valley. Beautiful Charlotte Prescott was clearly in shock. But if she was in any kind of trouble she had come to the right man.

Mrs Burch soon returned, wheeling a trolley set with tea things and a plate of home-baked cookies. She withdrew quietly, shutting the library door after her.

Rohan poured Charlotte a cup of tea. He added a little milk and two teaspoons of sugar, even though he knew she didn't take sugar in her tea. "Drink it down."

She responded with a quiet little smile.

Rohan took his tea black, but at the last moment added a teaspoon of sugar. "I need it," he said laconically, sinking into one of the burgundy leather armchairs that surrounded a reading table.

He allowed Charlotte to finish her tea in peace, then took the cup and saucer from her, leading her to the sofa.

"You're in no way to blame, Charlotte." He covered her hands with his own. "As I said to Mrs Prescott, we all failed you when you desperately needed help. I should accept the blame as I never considered for a moment that Martyn would force himself on you. My trust in him was woefully misplaced. Martyn always had his problems, but

I never believed he would hurt you. What a fool I've been!"
He sighed deeply. "The closest friends have been known to
turn into aggressors, even murderers. But Martyn! What a
catastrophe! You didn't think to let me know?"

She didn't lift her head, though relief was intensifying
in her.

"You didn't think to go to my mother?" he continued,
stroking her hand. "I know you couldn't go to *yours*!"

Charlotte spoke up. "I began to experience morning
sickness very early on, Rohan. I knew what was happening
to me. I believed I was pregnant by Martyn. How could I
let *you* of all people know? I had betrayed our love. How
could I go to your mother, tell her I was carrying Martyn
Prescott's baby? I could never put voice to the fact he had
forced me. I was suffering such shame. I *did* know Martyn
had always been in love with me. I felt I *should* have foreseen the danger. Afterwards he couldn't have been more
contrite. More sad and sorry."

"They *all* are!" Rohan said grimly.

"I suppose… Martyn broke down in tears, begging me
to forgive him. I tried hard, but I *did* keep some part of
myself remote."

"The sad and sorry bit doesn't jell with Nicole's damning
comments."

"No. But he *did* need my love, Rohan. He begged for it.
I tried to enter his world. It was a disaster. As time went
on his attitude changed. Became belligerent."

"He began to hit you." Rohan was barely holding down
his rage. "How low can a man sink? But then he wasn't a
man, was he?"

"In many ways he was like a greedy child who needed
instant gratification. But what he did weighed very heavily
on him I think."

Rohan couldn't conceal his disgust. "Stop making excuses for Martyn, Charlotte."

She looked into his blazing eyes. "Maybe it lessens *my* guilt."

"*No* guilt." Rohan gave his verdict.

"Any number of girls and women are brave enough to go it alone."

"And any number *aren't*. Not at eighteen, without support. I realise how frightened you must have been. How trapped. You had to endure years of being victimised by Martyn. You couldn't tell your father? Even Gordon Prescott? He would never have countenanced abuse. Nicole shouldn't have either. That woman needs a good psychiatrist."

"Maybe I do too."

"So does anyone who suffers abuse in silence." His voice was as gentle as any man's could be. "Forgive me for making moral judgements, my love. You were trying to tell me. I was too full of my own griefs. I love you, Charlotte. I've never stopped loving you. I gave you my heart. I don't want it back. We created our monster. His name was Martyn. Time now to lay poor Martyn to rest."

Rohan drew her to her feet. "Let's stroll down to the river. I feel like being out in the clean fresh air."

They walked hand in hand through the gardens, past the beds flushed with flowers, right down to the edge of the river. It sparkled in the sunshine, the glassy surface mantled with thousands of dancing sequins.

"If we could only go back in time," she said softly. "Mattie would be alive. You and I would be happily married. You would have asked Martyn to be your best man."

"A terrible irony in that!" He gathered her into his

embrace. "Don't let's speak of Martyn any more. Not in this place. We can never go back, however much we want to. What we *can* do is take control of our future. We're going to live it the way it would have been. Only better. We have one another. And we have our beautiful son. We're blessed. Do you love me, Charlotte?" He turned her face up to him, blue gaze intent.

"Heart and soul!" Her lovely smile was like a sunburst. "I've been so *alone* without you."

He held her to him. "We're together now. You have nothing and no one to fear. The sad years are over. A few hurdles won't go away like magic, but we'll contend with them. Believe me?" he asked.

"My belief in you has never wavered, Rohan," she answered without hesitation. "I can handle anything with you by my side." She paused, then added a little shakily, "I thought I would die of shame if you found out."

"Ah, *no!*" he groaned. "I love you, Charlotte. I'll always take care of you." He bent his head, touching his forehead to hers, then he kissed her so sweetly, so deeply, so passionately, the tormented element within her broke like a severed twine. "We have peace now, Charlotte," he murmured. "We have our whole lives. Ready to marry me?"

The world seemed bathed in a gorgeous brightness. It was as though the sun, moon and stars had come out together. *"I can't wait!"* she cried ecstatically.

Above them in the trees an invisible bird began to sing. The sound was so beautiful, so flute-like, so poignant, so far-carrying it seemed to travel the length and breadth of the river.

"Do you suppose that's Mattie?" Rohan asked, lifting his head.

Charlotte too was filled with such a sense of wonder she was nearly weeping. She stared above her into the green density of leaves. Hard to see a bird, but there was such a *glow*. It was spilling out of the trees. Pouring over them. "Why not?" she breathed.

Mattie wasn't really dead. He was an angel.

"Who knows what forces are at work in this universe?" Rohan mused, putting his arm around her slender shoulders. "We should be getting back, my love. It's almost time to pick up our son."

Its song completed, the invisible bird rose up into the sky on opalescent wings. It made a full circuit around Charlotte and Rohan before it disappeared.

Had it even been there?

HER PRINCE'S
SECRET SON

LINDA GOODNIGHT

CHAPTER ONE

PRINCE ALEKSANDRE D' GABRIEL took one look at Dr. Konstantine's long face and knew the news was bad.

"I'm sorry, Your Majesty, there is nothing more I can do." The royal physician, either unable or unwilling to meet his prince's eyes, stared down at the gleaming marble floor. "Your son is dying."

The softly spoken words pierced Aleks's soul like a bayonet. His boy, his reason for living, lay just beyond the thick, ancient castle wall dying, while his father stood in the long, ornate corridor of Carvainian Castle wishing to die in his stead.

Aleks was a ruler, a warrior prince, a man of wealth and power, and yet he was helpless against the infection that was destroying his son's internal organs.

He clenched his fists against the rising tide of fear, stifling the urge to pummel the stone walls in frustration and despair.

His mother, Queen Irena, touched his arm. "There must be something more we can do. Perhaps another physician?"

Dr. Konstantine's head jerked upward. "Your Highness, we've consulted every hepatology specialist in the world. The only answer is an organ donation. A tiny piece of organ from the right person will save his life. Nothing more, nothing less."

Queen Irena's face, still lovely though she was nearing sixty, had aged in the past weeks of Prince Nico's illness. The lines around her mouth deepened as she said, "My apologies, Doctor, I didn't mean to imply anything less than the best on your part. It's just that—" She lifted one hand in a helpless gesture.

Aleksandre understood exactly what she was feeling. The queen doted on the motherless boy she'd carried in her arms from America nearly five years ago. Without his mother's help, Aleksandre would never have known his son.

Fate and determination had given him Nico, and he would not give up his child without a fight.

"There must be a match somewhere," he said. "We will continue our search."

"Thousands have been tested, Your Majesty."

His people, loyal Carvainians, had lined the streets and clogged the telephones and computers in their sincere desire to save the adored little prince. But not a single person was a suitable match for the child whose blood was not one hundred percent Carvainian.

Aleksandre fought the sickness churning in his gut and the memory of an American woman who still haunted his heart. The child's mixed blood was his fault, just as the illness was, and yet Nico would not be Nico without Sara Presley's blood.

"I have a suggestion." Dr. Konstantine's gaze skittered away only to return with a fresh boldness. "May I speak frankly?"

The prince gave a bark of mirthless laughter. Dr. Konstantine had tended him for years, through childhood illnesses and wartime wounds. He trusted the man implicitly. "I have yet to quell your propensity for doing so. And we now are at a point of desperate measures. Say your piece."

"Nico's birth mother."

"No!" At the queen's outcry, both Prince Aleksandre and

the physician turned to stare. Her face had gone white, and the long, graceful fingers pressed against her lips trembled. Aleks understood her reluctance for it matched his own, and yet, had he not just been thinking of Sara Presley?

"She won't agree." A deep and dreadful knot formed in his chest at the thought of the woman who had jilted him and abandoned their child. She had no love for either the father or the son. She had not cared then. She would not care now if Nico lived or died.

The physician pressed. "You have no other choice but to contact her, Your Majesty. She is the little prince's last hope."

The queen regained her voice. Her nails scraped against Aleksandre's sleeve. Almost feverishly she said, "Listen to me, Aleksandre. The woman has a heart of stone. She will never agree. Contacting her can only bring trouble that we do not need. Our burdens are heavy enough to bear. Think of the consequences. Think of what she might require of you. Of your son."

Aleksandre knew his mother was right. Sara Presley had damaged him before, but now, with Nico as a pawn, she might try to exact a price he was unwilling to pay. And yet, what choice did they have?

Dr. Konstantine was like a dog with a bone—or a man with no other recourse. "If she is a match, she could be the answer to our prayers."

"*If* she is a match, and *if* she would agree," Aleksandre said grimly. So many ifs. A woman who would abandon her newborn was not likely to go through surgery on his behalf… unless she had a strong incentive.

Queen Irena paced to the sunlit patch at the end of the hallway. She spun toward him, her agitation showing in jerky movements and the rapid rise and fall of silk over her breasts. "I won't have her here, Aleksandre. She's poison. She'll hurt us. Hurt you. Hurt Nico. I can't bear to watch that happen again."

The prince held up a hand. "Stop. This is my decision. Let me think."

Both his companions bowed slightly and grew silent. His mother's soulful black eyes watched him, reproachful. A twinge of guilt niggled at his conscience.

If not for the Queen Mother, Carvainia would have no Crown Prince Nico, and he would have no son. No one, other than himself, understood the treachery of Sara Presley as well as Mother. She was trying to protect both of her princes as she always had.

Aleksandre closed his eyes tightly for a brief moment to calm his raging spirit. He'd learned in battle to shut out the noise and horror around him and go deep inside to a place of peace where wisdom lived. He did that now, weeding out his own anguish at the thought of seeing Sara Presley again and concentrated instead on saving his child.

Vaguely, he could hear the quiet hush of servants moving about the castle and of nurses moving in and out of Nico's room. He listened deeper, imagined the sounds of the sea just outside the castle walls.

The sea was his solace and when time allowed he walked the beach to taste the salt spray on his tongue and smell the wind blowing across the great water. Someday he would teach Nico to sail and fish and race his speedboats. He would tell his son stories of the generations of Carvainians who had used the sea for defense and trade and livelihood.

But first, his son must live. And to live, he must have an organ donation. And that could only come from his biological mother.

He took a deep, cleansing breath and opened his eyes, certain now of what he must do.

"You are correct, Mother, when you say that the American woman will not come willingly. I also agree with you, Doctor, that she is our only hope. She must come." His jaw hardened with resolve. "She *will* come."

Queen Irena tossed her head. "You cannot force her. She is not under Carvainian jurisdiction."

"Not yet." A sly smile touched his bitter-tasting lips. "But she will be."

The queen's eyes widened. "Aleksandre, whatever are you thinking?"

"The American woman will not come to Carvainia for me or even for her son, but she will come if the incentive is great enough."

"And you will see that it is?"

"I know exactly what matters most to Sara Presley."

As a prince who'd led men into battle, he knew the importance of strategy and of knowing one's enemy.

And so a battle plan was forged.

"If something sounds too good to be true, it probably is," Sara Presley said with a laugh as she unpacked a box of novels for the romance section of The Book Shelf.

"But what if the prize is real, Sara?" Penny Carter, her friend and business partner waved the letter beneath Sara's nose for the umpteenth time in two days. "What if you've really won a fabulous trip to a European health spa—in a castle, no less?"

Sara scoffed. "To win, I would have to enter, right?"

"Well, maybe, but we own a bookstore. What if one of our vendors is rewarding us for outstanding sales?"

"Then you would be included in the trip. And you're not." Sara held a new book to her nose and sniffed.

"I love that smell," she said, trying to direct Penny's thoughts somewhere besides the goofy award letter. It couldn't be real. The prize was either a joke, or when she called, they'd ask her to send thousands of dollars or to provide her credit card number. She wasn't that stupid.

But as she'd done all morning, Penny stayed after her. "What about those contests you signed up for at the fair last month?"

Sara paused in thought, gazing down at a book cover. A shirtless cowboy gave her a sexy grin but she didn't feel a thing. No matter how sexy or how nice, no man had gotten past her defenses in over five years. She was a strong advocate of "once burned, twice warned."

"Cassie Binger won a blender at the fair last year," she mused, "so I guess that's possible."

Penny let out a whoop, pounding her index finger at the letter. "Call this number, right now, before I die of curiosity." She patted a hand over her heart. The letter crinkled against her plaid shirt. "Castle-by-the-Sea Health and Beauty Spa sounds so romantic."

"The only place I'll find romance is between the covers of the books we sell. The letter is a scam, Penny. It has to be. My luck ran out a long time ago." She quickly turned to the wall-high bookshelves.

Penny marched around to her side. Hands on her hips she said, "Sara, listen to me. You've spent five years living in the past. Five years haunting the Internet in hopes of finding out who adopted your baby. Five years getting over the jerk who left you."

Tears welled in Sara's eyes. Her belly gnawed with emptiness now as it did every time she thought of the infant son she'd lost. And she thought of him constantly. A TV show, a book cover, a child on the street or in the store could send her into a tailspin for days. "Don't, Penny."

Penny grasped Sara's upper arms and pulled her around, her face wreathed in compassion. "Honey, I'm not trying to hurt you. You're my best friend and I love you like a sister. But I've watched you beat yourself up for too long. When life offers sunshine, don't hide in the shade. You have to move on."

"I can't, Penny." She sniffed. "My baby is out there somewhere. Is he happy and healthy? Does his adoptive mother love him the way I do?"

"You made the right choice. You did what was best for him at the time. Let it go. Move on. Let yourself live again."

They'd hashed this through hundreds of times and Sara knew Penny was right. Penniless, without family to turn to, and still in college on scholarship, she'd done what she had to in order to secure her baby's future. "I'm haunted by the thought that if I'd kept him, something would have worked out."

"If that Aleks jerk had stuck around and been the man you thought he was, things would have worked out. But he didn't. That's my point. Life happened. It sucks but it happened. Now, life is happening again in a good way." She shoved the letter at Sara. "Take a chance, Sara. Go for it. Just this once, let yourself be happy."

Sara shook her head but took the letter in hand. Penny's insistence was starting to wear her down. She did need a change. She needed to shake loose from the guilt and loss and depression that had plagued her for too long.

In a feeble attempt to resist, she muttered, "It can't be true. I wish it was, but I'm not the kind of person who wins fabulous trips to Europe."

A male voice intruded. "I beg to differ, Miss Presley. If you are indeed Sara Presley, you are our grand prize winner."

Both women spun toward the tall, imposing figure who had entered the shop. Dressed in a business suit with hair graying at the temples and the smell of intellect coming off him in waves, the man reminded her of a slick television lawyer.

"Who are you?" Sara blurted. "And how do you know about the prize?"

"I am here as executor of the contest, Miss Presley. Since you have not yet called to claim your prize, the owner of the spa felt an official visit was in order to assure you that everything is in order and that our staff eagerly awaits your arrival."

Sara looked from the man to Penny. Her friend's eyes were as round as saucers.

"Are you serious?" Sara gestured to the letter. "This is for real?"

"Indeed." The man moved into the small space behind the cluttered counter and offered Sara a manila envelope. "Inside you will find a brochure detailing the prize, a round-trip ticket and your cash prize."

"Cash?" Sara squeaked. "Ticket?"

With hands now trembling, she removed the items from the envelope one by one. Penny leaned over her shoulder. "That stuff's real, Sara."

"I can't believe this." She read over the brochure and saw photos of pampered women getting massages and facials, of a fabulous castle standing proud and ancient by a perfect blue sea, of rooms so beautiful they stole her breath. She checked the airline ticket. Her stomach jumped into her throat. "First class?"

"A vacation unrivaled by any other awaits you, miss, a once-in-a-lifetime opportunity." The man tilted his head. "Do you believe it now?"

"I'm beginning to."

"Excellent. I will tell the owner of Castle-by-the-Sea to expect you. He will be delighted to greet you on Thursday."

Sara trailed him as he moved toward the door. "Thursday? This coming Thursday? That's only two days away."

"Why, yes, madam. Is that a problem?"

Penny popped up behind them and gave Sara a little whack on the shoulder. "No problem at all. She'll be there."

Two days later Sara was still in delighted shock as she waved goodbye to a jubilant Penny and boarded a plane for London. Once there, she was whisked aboard a private jet that took her to Castle-by-the-Sea.

As she disembarked, she breathed in the scent of sea spray, warm and salty and so different from the landlocked aroma of Kansas.

At the bottom of the steps, a line of attendants waited, tidy and professional in red uniforms. The castle itself sprawled before her, a stunning old stone structure complete with spires and cupolas and towers that had no doubt once housed European royalty. In the distance, below the hill was a blue sea that would have provided protection for the castle inhabitants. Today a handful of people reclined on the white sand or cavorted in the crystal waters.

The butterflies in her belly fluttered. "This must be a resort for the rich and famous."

She pinched herself. Surely there was a mistake. She was a nobody. Surely she would be sent packing by nightfall.

But that was not the case. She was escorted to a private suite high in one wing of the castle, and for the rest of the afternoon she was fed and massaged, pampered and waited upon so that when night came she fell asleep in the canopied bed with a smile on her face. Maybe her run of bad luck was finally over.

* * *

"Miss Presley. Miss Presley." A woman's accented voice penetrated the fog in Sara's brain.

"I'm Sara. Just Sara," she muttered, though her throat was froggy with sleep. She snuggled deeper into the smooth, silken sheets and pulled the down comforter up to her ears. She'd been having the loveliest dream ever.

"Well, 'Just Sara.' The intruding voice sounded amused. "I take it you slept well."

Sara sat up straight and stared around the luxurious room and then at the young woman whom she recognized as Antonia, her personal attendant. "I wasn't dreaming. This is real."

"Yes, miss. Very real. Would you care for breakfast before we begin the day?"

"Coffee please."

From a pretty tray, the round-figured Antonia poured the fragrant coffee and handed it to Sara. "Not a very healthy beginning to a busy day. Some melon perhaps? Or strawberries and cream? That seems to be a favorite with our guests. We grow our own, you see."

"The strawberries or the cream?"

"Both." The young woman giggled.

Feeling a little like Cinderella, Sara laughed with her. "What's on the agenda for today?"

Something shifted through Antonia's soft brown eyes. Sara noticed the slight hesitation and wondered. But before her thoughts could wander too far, the attendant smiled and the expression disappeared. "A very special treat awaits you. The owner of Castle-by-the-Sea wishes to see you."

"I was hoping you'd say that. I really want to thank him."

Antonia gazed at her a second longer before turning away. Within the hour Sara was dressed and standing outside an enormous pair of ornate double doors inside a palace of such breathtaking beauty, it must be a tourist attraction. From the looks of this particular wing—one of many from what she'd observed so far—and the scurry of suit-clad men and women going in and out of offices, this was the business section of the spa. Apparently behind these white and gilded doors fit for a king was the owner himself.

A nervous jitter danced down her arms.

One of the doors opened inward. A butler uniformed in red and gold gave a slight bow. His perfect posture made her want to stand up straighter. "Miss Presley, Prince Aleksandre will see you now."

Sara started to follow the man, then stopped. "Prince? As in a real prince?"

The butler inclined his head. "But of course." He motioned her forward with one hand. "If you please. His Majesty is waiting."

His Majesty? Oh my gosh. She was in a real castle with a real prince. Wait until Penny heard about this!

Knees quivering and curiosity driving her, Sara stepped into the room—a very large, regal office—and got her first glimpse of her benefactor.

The dark-haired man was standing with his back to her, gazing out at a panorama of green land and aqua sea. Legs spread, hands clasped at his back below a trim waist, his posture was as stiff as the butler's, his shoulders wide and exuding strength. Though he didn't appear much older than herself, an air of authority and power emanated from him. Dressed in a perfectly tailored suit, something about his well-honed physique looked eerily familiar.

The butler cleared his throat. If such a thing was possible, the servant's carriage grew more erect and perfect as he snapped to attention. "Your Majesty, may I present Miss Sara Presley. Miss Presley, His Majesty Prince Aleksandre d'Gabriel."

The name struck a chord of alarm in Sara as the prince turned and leveled an empty stare in her direction.

"So Sara," he said quietly. "We meet again."

CHAPTER TWO

"ALEKS!"

The woman before him clutched her chest, her mouth open in shock. She had gone as white and still as the alabaster statues lining the palace staircase. Aleks fought down the unexpected and disturbing urge to cross the Persian rug, take her in his arms and offer reassurance. Only the stern mental reminder of her ruthlessness kept him standing rigidly behind his desk, his heart thundering in his chest. Though he had once loved her enough to give up anything to have her, that love had long since turned to loathing. She was here for one reason and one reason only. Nico.

"You are surprised to see me." The sentence was a statement. He knew she'd be surprised. A surprise attack on one's enemies always worked best.

"Aleks," she said again and started toward him, one hand extended.

Aleks braced himself. Was that hope flaring in her sea-colored eyes?

He took a step back and forced a dark and forbidding expression. The woman paused. Her hand fell to her side. She looked lost and uncertain, and Aleks again fought the need to comfort her.

She was as beautiful to him now as she had been before, but he noted a subtle change, as well. The light had gone out in her. Where before she'd been vibrant and joyous, she now appeared older...sadder. Regret perhaps? Guilt? Or had life been unkind to Sara Presley?

He'd thought the terrors of war and near death added to the years of loathing had hardened him enough to face her. But he knew without a doubt he could not let her touch him. At least not now while his insides canted toward her like a seasick sailor.

"Welcome to Castle-by-the-Sea," he said. "I trust your accommodations are satisfactory."

Sara's look of bewilderment was exactly what he'd hoped. He'd caught her completely off guard.

"You're a prince?"

He inclined his head. "Ruler of Carvainia."

It was imperative she understand his power and place and forget about the lovesick youth he'd once been. He must be in control, and now that he'd seen her again, this was going to be more difficult than he'd thought.

"You never told me," she said. One hand went to her forehead and then fell to her side. "Why didn't you tell me?"

Considering her cruel abandonment, he was glad he hadn't. "Would it have made any difference?"

"No, of course not, but—"

He didn't believe her. "My country has enemies. To protect my friends and myself, I chose to attend college without fanfare, though I always had bodyguards at hand."

"You did?"

She seemed genuinely stunned by his royalty. Would she have been less treacherous, less likely to abandon him and his son if she had known the truth? Or would she have used the information to her advantage? "Remember Carlo and Stephan?"

"I thought they were students like you. Friends from your country."

"They were both." The knot in his stomach twisted. Though the difference in stations had separated them to some degree, he and his bodyguards were friends, as well. And Carlo had paid the ultimate price for his loyalty.

Sara Presley, the woman who held Nico's life in her unsuspecting hands, shook her head. Hair the color of cinnamon rustled against the shoulders of a simple yellow sundress—a dress that rose and fell with the rapid in and out of her anxious breathing.

"I don't understand." The tip of her tongue flicked out to moisten peach-colored lips. Aleks averted his gaze. No doubt her mouth had gone as dry as his, though for far different reasons. "What is this all about, Aleks? Why am I here?"

Though he felt no humor whatsoever, he offered an amused tilt of his head. "You are our grand prize winner. Remember?"

She scoffed. "Don't give me that. Something else is going on here."

He was not quite ready to reveal everything. "Sit down please. You seem…disturbed."

"Disturbed? I've never been so confused in my life. You disappeared five years ago and now suddenly I'm whisked out of my bookstore and into a castle. *Your* castle. And I didn't even know you *had* a castle. After all this time, I never expected to see you again."

He could believe that. If not for Nico, she wouldn't have. He almost said as much but knew he must be careful. His son's future rested with this woman. He must proceed with great caution. The battle plan was working well so far. He must not become reckless like a new recruit and ruin everything.

Sara moved to the chair he indicated, and he noticed the slightest tremor in the hands she placed on the armrests. He turned his attention to her face. Even there he saw again the vulnerability. She was nervous and uncertain…and perhaps a bit scared. She was angry, too, though she had no right to be, all things considered.

She reached for her earring—a long chain of silver—and her fingers trembled. They were cold, too, he was certain, for he remembered the subtle nuances of her emotions. He didn't need to touch her to know she was anxious, maybe even afraid. Memories of her had tortured him enough.

He hardened his heart. Any weakness she displayed would be used to his advantage.

"If you think I've brought you here because I couldn't bear to be without you any longer, think again."

A deep rose color flushed her pale skin. "After what you did, that much is a mercy."

After what he'd done? "I don't equate a white lie about my royalty with outright betrayal, particularly when that white lie was intended to protect all concerned."

Eyelashes as lush as sable blinked at him. "I have no idea what you're talking about."

He quelled the memory of his lips against those eyelids and the feel of her lashes tickling his skin. "Oh, I think you do."

Her chin hitched up. "No, I don't. All I know was that your father fell ill and you had to return home. You promised to be in touch, but I never heard from you again."

Had he not known the lengths to which his mother had gone to contact this woman, he would have believed her lies.

"Nor did I hear from you."

You didn't even bother to contact me about the child you were carrying. My child. But he left those last words unspoken. He would let her lies continue while she backed herself into a corner. Then, when she met Nico, she would be forced to admit her transgression and agree to his demands.

"How could I contact you? You weren't even honest enough to tell me who you were or where you lived. I thought you lived in Italy. I thought your name was Aleks Gabriel."

He stepped down from the raised dais where his desk was situated. "Enough!"

"Don't 'enough' me, Mr. Prince. I'm not one of your subjects. I demand to know what's going on. Why the outlandish ruse to get me here?"

"Ruse?"

"Don't play dumb. I didn't win any all-expense-paid vacation to a health spa."

"Are you certain of that? Have you not been treated well by my staff? Did the masseuse and hairdresser not visit your rooms? Do you not have a personal attendant at your beck and call?"

"Well, yes, but…"

"And this treatment shall continue for the duration of your stay. Whatever you need is at your disposal."

She blinked again, confusion warring with the need to assert herself. Aleks felt victory at hand. A confused enemy was easy to defeat.

Feeling in total control now, his emotions ruthlessly in check, he moved to her side and reached for her hand. The skin was incredibly soft and silken and every bit as cold as he'd known it would be. As cold as her soul.

Sara snatched her hand away and glared at him.

Teeth tight, he took her elbow and forced her to stand.

"Come. I want you to meet someone."

"Who?" She tried to pull away again but Aleks held tight to her arm, propelling her to the door.

"I think," he said through gritted teeth, "you will be greatly surprised."

Sara's knees trembled as Aleks's strong fingers dug into her skin. She recalled all the times he'd placed his hand exactly there, guiding her with such courtesy and grace across campus, into a movie or a restaurant, into a car. But today, his hold was impersonal, even cruel.

Her head spun with the impact of the last few minutes. She could hardly take everything in. For a brief moment, she had entertained the hope that Aleks had brought her here to set the past straight. As furious as she was that he would contact her now when it was too late, and as much as she wanted to hate him for all the anguish she had gone through, Sara could not deny that she was still very much attracted to the man who even now rushed her past stiff-backed guards, over marbled floors and down a furnished hallway to an elevator.

Everyone they passed stopped working to pay respects to their ruler, and Sara felt the curious stares of each one fall on her, as well.

Saints alive, the man who'd left her pregnant and penniless was a prince. She couldn't take it in. Her Aleks, the man she'd loved, the man she'd given her innocence to, was a wealthy, powerful prince. He could have easily cared for her and their baby even if he had no longer wanted her. Surely, he would have wanted his son.

Why, oh, why had he left without a word?

The bitter taste of gall rose in her throat. It was too late now. Her baby was gone and Aleks would never know what he'd thrown away. Her stomach rolled with nerves and fear and loss. She wanted to stop at a restroom and throw up.

But Aleks seemed mercilessly unaware of her distress as he thrust her into a gleaming brass-and-mirrored elevator. The door pinged shut and he loosened his grip to push a number.

She'd dreamed of him for so long and now here he was, in the flesh. But oh, that flesh was hard and unyielding, not warm and loving as she remembered.

He loathed her. That much was evident. But why? He was the one who'd abandoned her.

She longed to ask, but right now she was still in shock and if she admitted it, more than a little unnerved. Something was very wrong here and until she understood, she would play her hand very close to the vest.

During the entire elevator ride, Aleks stared straight ahead at the closed doors, avoiding eye contact, and said not a word. He was as stiff and cold as an icicle but still as handsome and dynamic as ever.

But the years had altered him. Where he'd been a charming, carefree college student, engrossed in getting his master's degree while embracing sports and cars and the American college life, today he was a solemn man with hard eyes.

He was so near, this man who'd broken her heart that she could feel the tension in his frame and smell the fabric of his navy blue jacket. But he was also as far away as her bookstore.

She should be demanding her release, filing a kidnapping complaint, or at the least, slapping his royal face. But here she was noticing the added lines around his mouth, his beautiful, dark skin, and remembering the time he'd buried them in autumn leaves and they'd kissed and cuddled in their leafy hideaway, content to be together and so completely in love.

Or at least, she had been.

"I never knew you at all, did I?" she whispered, surprised that she had spoken aloud.

Aleks slowly turned his head and stared at her with those icy eyes. "Ours was a brief romance. A fling I think you Americans call it."

A fling. The word seared her heart like a hot iron against tender flesh. She'd given him everything she had to give. And he called their love a fling.

How could she have fallen for a man who had deceived her so badly? He had not only walked out with little explanation but he'd never been honest with her from the beginning.

He was a royal prince, but she was a royal fool.

The elevator eased to a stop and the doors slid open. Aleks stepped aside, holding the door with one hand while motioning with the other for her to exit. She did so, her mind reeling.

Who could he possibly want her to meet? Why was she here? And why didn't he just tell her what was going on?

The floor they stepped out on was similar to the one where her suite of rooms was situated. A long, carpeted hallway lit by sconces and new lighting—a fascinating mix of old and modern—was guarded by a pair of uniformed men. Stunning murals graced the vaulted ceilings. Tapestry and gilded paintings lined the walls above elegant furniture groupings. At one end an arched window looked out at the sunlit day. Sara had never seen a place of such over-the-top wealth and splendor.

Aleks seemed impervious to it all as he reclaimed her elbow.

Two people, a man and a woman both dressed in white uniforms, sat outside a closed door but quickly stood to attention when they saw Aleks approach. They turned curious gazes in Sara's direction.

Aleks glanced toward the closed door. The cold mask slipped from his face. For the briefest moment, Sara was certain she saw tenderness…and fear.

"How is he?"

Something in his voice gave Sara pause. She stared at the side of his face, trying to comprehend the undercurrent flowing between him and the others.

"He's sleeping, Your Majesty."

The news seemed to bring relief to Aleks. Some of the tension flowed out of him.

"Excellent." He occasioned a glance at Sara. The frosty glare was back. "We will go inside."

Whoever resided inside that room held special meaning to the Prince of Carvainia. But what did this have to do with her?

"Who—" she started, but Aleks shot her a warning glance as if daring her to make a noise and wake the sleeper. Sara fell silent.

He pushed the door open. Sara's pulse rate elevated with an inexplicable nervousness as they tiptoed inside.

Sara's first impression was a smell. Though the overriding scent was antiseptic, another odor that she couldn't quite place lingered, too. This was a medical ward, not a bedroom.

The large room was semidarkened with enough light to see and work by but not enough to disturb the sleeper. An array of medical equipment looked out of place next to a stunning iron bed canopied in blood-red draperies trimmed in gold and black. The quiet was broken only by the *shoosh* and *burr* of those machines.

At the sight of Aleks, the attendants hovering near the bed bowed and backed silently away, but not before their eyes flicked over Sara, all with the same identical and troubling expression. Sara's nervousness increased. Her palms began to sweat.

Following Aleks's lead, she approached the enormous, raised bed.

A handsome little boy rested against the pillows, his long eyelashes startling black against his pale cheeks. He was thin and his skin color was an odd gold-over-olive. The scent she'd noticed rose from the bed, the odor of fever.

"Is he sick?" she whispered.

A muscle jerked in Aleks's cheek. "Very."

"Poor little child. I'm so sorry."

Aleks gave her a strange look. "As am I."

They stood in silence, staring down at the sleeping child. Looking at the small boy was a powerful reminder and Sara ached both for him and for herself. Her child would have been near the age of this little boy. She prayed that wherever he was, her son was well and that no sickness ever befell him.

"What's wrong with him?"

"A virus has attacked his liver."

"Will he be all right?"

Aleks glared at her, his expression so bewildering and strange that she grew afraid.

"We will know soon."

A sense of silent anticipation hovered in the room as if the people standing in the shadows held their collective breath.

"Who is he?" she whispered.

The mask of coldness seemed to slip for a moment, and Sara could have sworn he was hurting. "He is my son."

"Your...son?" The words nearly choked her.

She placed a hand over her womb. She felt so empty. Aleks had moved on without a backward glance, marrying and producing a son. He had a child. She had nothing but an empty ache.

Did her little boy, wherever he was, look like this? Did he have Aleks's black eyelashes and aristocratic nose?

Against the lump of regret and longing that clogged her throat, she said, "Your son is very beautiful. He deserves to be well."

Aleks took both her elbows and turned her to face him. He stared at her long and hard and without mercy. She swallowed, the sound loud in a room where only the breath of a small boy and his incessant machinery broke the silence.

His fingers tightened. "So does yours."

She frowned, puzzled. An erratic beat of something she couldn't name started deep inside, shouting a warning that she did not comprehend.

"My son?" she asked, voice trembling with dread. "What do you mean?" And how did he know? How could he possibly know about her son? About their son?

Aleks's black eyes held hers as if peering into her soul. Then slowly, slowly, they slid away to the sleeping child.

In a voice of ice and steel, he said, "Meet Nico, or as he is officially known, Crown Prince Domenico Emmanuel Lucian d'Gabriel…the child you abandoned."

Every ounce of strength left Sara's body. Her knees buckled. And the world went black.

CHAPTER THREE

PRINCE ALEKSANDRE STOOD beside Sara's bed waiting for her to regain consciousness. The fainting spell had come as a surprise. One minute she'd been staring at him in horror and the next she'd crumpled like tissue paper.

He was still pondering the meaning of her reaction.

In an effort not to disturb Nico, he'd swept her into his arms and carried her here to the guest wing. Halfway to the suite, he'd been tempted to hand her off to one of the guards trailing them. Not because she was too heavy. She weighed nothing. But because the feel of her curves pressed against him stirred more than memories.

Now as he glared down at her, willing her to awaken, he couldn't help noticing the way her red hair spilled over the white pillow like fire on snow. Nor could he miss the gentle curve of her mouth or the tiny scar above her lip that he'd once found particularly tasty.

She moaned softly. He steeled himself with a stern reminder than his attraction to this woman had already cost him enough.

She opened her eyes and looked around, her expression clouded. He waited, silent while she regained her bearings.

With a gasp of awareness, she sat up.

Aleks pressed her back. "Lie still. You've had a shock."

She slapped at him. "Get your hands off me."

In a flurry of movement the two bodyguards flanked him, hands on their weapons. He waved them off. "Leave us."

"But Your Majesty—"

"Leave us. This woman poses no threat." At least not physically.

Sara swung her legs over the side of the bed and stood. "That's what you think."

Had this been another woman or another time, Aleks would have laughed. Sara barely came to his chin and even with fists tight at her sides and eyes shooting sparks, she was no match for his size and strength.

The guards looked from Sara to Aleks, ever vigilant, but they followed his command and backed from the room. He knew very well they were both standing with ears pressed against the closed door, anxious because he was out of their sight with a fiery woman.

The moment they disappeared, Sara stormed toward him, long hair flying wildly around her shoulders. "Is Nico my son? Are you telling me the truth?"

"Nico is *my* son and mine alone. You gave him away."

All of the fight went out of her. Her shoulders slumped. She pressed both hands to her stomach and bent forward so that Aleks wondered if she might faint again. He started to her but stopped when she groaned. "Oh, God, I did. I gave him away."

This was the truth he'd dreaded hearing but the truth as he already knew it. Though he'd loved this woman, he'd never really known what she was capable of until she had abandoned their child.

"Did you hate me that much, Sara?"

He hadn't intended to ask the question nor to sound quite as vulnerable as he feared he did.

"I never hated you, Aleks. I loved you." Disturbingly haunted eyes implored him. "I longed for you."

He glanced away. "You will forgive me if I don't believe that."

"You promised to come back. I waited."

His lips curled in distaste. "Not for long."

"I was pregnant with your child, alone, scared out of my mind, with no means of support. What was I supposed to do?"

Not sell my son to the highest bidder, he thought. If not for the queen's intervention, someone else would have paid the price for the handsome male child with royal bloodlines, though another family would not have known the boy was a crown prince, and the prince of Carvainia would never have had a son and an heir. The fury of that near disaster raced through his blood with the sting of alcohol on an open wound.

Seething, he turned his back to stare blindly at a dressing table littered with feminine jars and a silver hand mirror. "The past does not matter to me. *You* do not matter to me."

"Then why did you bring me here after all this time? To punish me? To let me know how much you despise me for putting our son up for adoption?"

"I never wanted you involved in his life. Let me make that clear." Slowly, he pivoted, jaw tight enough to crack a bone. "You are here because I had no other choice."

She didn't need to know about the stir her presence had caused, both among the staff and within the royal family. As it was, the queen had taken to her bed with a migraine the moment Sara Presley entered the castle. He regretted that deeply.

Without his mother's help and guidance during that terrible

time five years ago, he wasn't sure he could have survived. First, he'd lost his father. Then an old enemy, the greedy king of Perseidia had perceived a weakness in the new Carvainian government and had invaded their northern borders. Like the warriors of old and as he'd been trained, he'd led his men into battle and had come out the victor. But at what price? Wounded, and heartsick at the loss of fine young men, he'd been further shattered by the news that his former love had given birth to his son and was offering the baby to the highest bidder.

Though the queen had expressed serious doubt, Aleks was convinced the child was his. Sara had been an innocent when they'd first come together, so shy and eager and loving. He could not imagine her with another man.

She'd likely had several men by now, but he refused to care.

"How did you learn about the baby?" she asked. "How did he get here?"

"Money and power have their advantages."

"Why didn't you contact me? Where were you?"

"At war, fighting for my country's independence where I belonged." He chopped the air in impatience. "None of this matters anymore, Sara."

"It matters to me! I've missed four years of my baby's life, four years of wondering if the wealthy family that adopted him loves him, wondering if he's all right. Then suddenly I'm whisked away from America without explanation to discover he's been here with you all along. Why have you contacted me now when you didn't then?"

Aleks grabbed her arm and stared down into her face with all the will he had inside him.

"Let me explain as clearly as I know how." He swallowed, hating the words to come. "Nico…is dying."

"No!" Sara shrank away from him, a hand to her throat. "Please no."

The stark despair in her expression would have shaken him had he not been braced for it. She had ignored her child since birth. A pained cry and a few tears would not convince him that she cared.

"His only hope is a liver transplant."

Sara slid onto a chair and buried her face in her hands. Once again, Aleks battled back an urge to go to her. He stood with rigid military discipline, reminding himself that this woman was the enemy. This woman had no scruples. This woman had tossed his child away like a stray dog.

When she lifted her tearstained face, his gut spasmed. She'd looked this way on the day he'd gotten news that his father was dying. She'd cried for him.

He'd been a fool then. He wouldn't be again.

"Is he on a transplant list?" she asked. "I don't know how things like that work here in your country. What can be done?"

"The best hope for Nico is a living donor. His body would then regenerate the donated segment into a full-sized body part while the donor's body would also fully recover. But Carvainia is a country of genetically similar people. No one we can find shares his blood type."

"AB negative," she murmured.

"Yours, I assume."

She nodded. "Yes."

"Nor does anyone, including myself, my mother, nor any of the royal family share the specific blood markers that he requires." Impatient, he chopped the air again. "I don't pretend to understand the medical details. I only know that Nico is dying and his only hope is a living donor who matches him as exactly as possible."

Perched on the edge of the chair, she bent forward, forearms against her thighs, hair falling over her shoulders as she looked up. "And that's why I'm here, isn't it? To be his donor."

Aleks tensed. His heart galloped in his chest like one of his racehorses. If he was to gain Sara's cooperation, he must proceed with extreme caution.

"You needn't worry. I will pay you well."

A soft gasp escaped her. "You'll…pay me?"

Though she sounded less than eager, Aleks was confident she would agree once she understood the terms. Greed was a powerful incentive. A baby, a body part, it was all the same to a woman like Sara. "One million American dollars."

Something hard shifted through her features. "No."

Aleks blinked once, slowly, certain he had heard wrong. "No?"

Her lips tightened. "I said no."

Sickness churned in his belly, and for the first time, he began to doubt his plan. What if he failed? What if Sara Presley was even more heartless than he'd expected?

The muscles in his neck tightened to the breaking point. "Then name your price. Whatever you want is yours."

Sara stared back at him with eyes that had turned the color of a stormy sea. They were eyes that had beguiled him when he was young and foolish. Eyes that had promised so much and then had forgotten him. Eyes that now defied him.

With a near-regal grace, she rose, fists clenched at her side, her chin thrust upward. "Then here's the deal, Prince Charming. I want to spend time with my son and get to know him. I want to be his mother."

She wanted to be Nico's mother? Cold fear sliced through Aleks. "You should have thought about that a long time ago,

Sara. Nico is mine and mine alone. You will have no part in his life. None ever."

"A little late for that, don't you think? You've brought me here. I'm involved."

"As a hired body part. Nothing else."

She blanched and rocked back, biting down on her bottom lip.

Aleks refused to be moved by her wounded reaction. He would do anything to protect Nico, particularly from the woman who had abandoned them both.

In clipped tones with barely suppressed anger, he said, "Presenting a sick child with a long-lost mother is not in his best interest. Have you no compassion whatsoever? Think of the questions he'd ask! Do you want him to know that he was given away at birth? Do you want him asking why he's never known about you? His health is far too fragile for that kind of revelation."

Sara made a tiny noise of dismay and began to move around the room. She twisted her fingers together, worrying a small gold ring on her pinky. The hem of the yellow sundress swished softly against her thighs as curvy hips swayed below a slender waist.

Aleks didn't want to notice her lush body or to remember the silk of her thighs against his palms. With firm resolve, he focused on the coldness of her heart and on his plan.

Now, while Sara was still in a state of shock, he had to press his advantage. "I'm prepared to pay you a million if you are a match and another million after the surgery."

He was prepared to pay her far more than that should she balk. Everyone had a price.

Like a wounded tigress, Sara whirled on him. "Get this

through your pig head, Aleks. I don't want your money. I want my child."

"He is not yours to want."

On a sharp inhale, she drew up to her full height, shoulders high and tight as she contemplated him.

While Aleks held his own breath, she exhaled in a rush of words. "Then I won't cooperate. You'll have to search elsewhere for your donor." She marched to the door and yanked it open. "You'll also have to excuse me, *Your Majesty*, I must pack. I'm leaving in the morning."

Aleks was stunned by the woman's audacity. She was showing him out?

When he didn't move, she said, "I never had the chance to know my son. I don't want your money. I want to spend time with Nico. That's the deal, Aleks. Take it, or I'm going home."

Aleks could scarcely believe this was happening. She was bargaining with Nico's life. But why? He didn't believe for one second that she would turn down a million dollars in the end. Why the pretense of belated maternal feelings? Did she despise him enough to hurt him through Nico?

Whatever the reason, Sara was worse than he'd dreamed.

"Close the door."

He had no wish for this conversation to be carried by the servants to his mother's ears. She was upset enough. She would be livid to learn of the bargain he was about to strike.

The door snapped shut. Sara stood with one hand on the pull, facing him as calmly as if they were trading automobiles. Only the quiver of pulse above her collarbone indicated distress. "Do we have a deal?"

What choice did he have? He wanted Nico alive and well, and Sara was his only chance.

"You may visit his rooms, but either I or the queen must be present at all times."

She cocked her head. A silver earring glinted against the pale skin of her neck. "You don't trust me."

About as much as he trusted the king of Perseidia. "Not in the least."

A small skirmish went on behind sea-blue eyes but finally she said, "Okay, agreed, as long as I can see him as often as I like."

"Done." He reached for the door handle and paused. "One thing, though, Sara, is not negotiable."

She regarded him warily. "And that is?"

Calling upon four years of festered anger and bitterness, he said, "Nico is never to know you are the bitch that whelped him."

The color, which had drained from her face, now surged forth, setting her delicate skin aflame. She raised a hand as if to strike him. He caught her wrist. "I think not."

Long after Aleks left her alone, Sara sat at the window staring out at the magical country of Carvainia. Aleks's country. Her baby's country.

Emotional exhaustion made her limbs heavy so she could hardly lift her hands to swipe at the tears flowing down her cheeks.

Her baby was here. After the years of guilt and regret, she'd found him. All this time of worry and he'd been right here with his natural father. She was glad for that, though still astonished by the turn of events. Nothing Aleks said in explanation had made any sense. He claimed to have contacted her but she knew he hadn't. And yet, how could he have known about the pregnancy? How could he have gotten custody of Nico?

Joy at finding her son intermingled with the loss of years and the fear that he was deathly ill. Now that she'd found him again, she couldn't bear the thought of losing him.

She longed to go to his rooms and stay with him every minute of every day. But she knew without a doubt that if she tried to see him now, without Aleks's permission, a host of staff would block her way.

And so she waited for him to return with the contract he insisted she sign. A contract. Dear heaven. What had happened to the man who'd claimed to love her?

She reached for a tissue and rubbed at eyes gone raw and hot. A sob slipped from her lips. Aleks had offered her money to help her own child. How low she had fallen in his eyes that he would believe such an offer was necessary. She would do anything to see Nico well. Her demands to see him were nothing more than a bluff though she'd been praying the entire time that Aleks would fall for it. Even if he'd refused, she would never have left this castle without doing all in her power to save her child's life.

Part of her didn't blame Aleks for despising her. Didn't she despise herself for letting go when she might have found a way to keep their child? Wasn't she haunted by a host of what-might-have-beens?

The door opened and Antonia entered carrying a tray. "You must eat something, Miss Sara. Lunch is long past."

The young woman set the tray on the small round table at Sara's elbow. Sara took one glance at the array of beautifully prepared finger foods and shook her head. "Thank you, Antonia. I'm not hungry."

Antonia studied her with compassion. "You are upset, miss. Let me get some cucumber slices for the swelling in your eyes. And perhaps I could arrange a soothing massage and a spa treatment?"

Sara shook her head. No amount of pampering could soothe the ache in her heart. "Not now."

Clearly wishing to provide service, but at a loss, Antonia lingered. Except for the attendant's fidgety movements the suite was quiet, the sounds of activity outside the door silenced by the thick stone walls.

"A refreshing candle, then," Antonia said.

The rasp of match against striker sawed at Sara's raw nerve endings. A teardrop flame flared, and then the smell of sulfur mingled with the clean scent of vanilla.

"If you are certain you don't require anything—"

"Nothing." Sara lifted a limp hand, but the effort was too much and she let it fall to her lap. "Thanks."

"If you should change your mind, please ring. Prince Aleksandre left specific orders that you are to have everything you desire."

Yeah, right, anything but her son. Sara gave a short, joyless laugh. "Your Prince Aleksandre is a royal jerk."

Antonia gasped and with a polite bow made a hasty exit, apparently disturbed that anyone would speak ill of the prince. Sara supposed she should be more careful. After all, this was not America. For all she knew, she may have just committed a crime punishable by stoning.

No, Aleks wouldn't hurt her. She knew that for certain, not because of the love they'd once shared, but because he needed her.

She reached for a strawberry but didn't eat it. How could she eat with this enormous wad of hope and fear and longing filling up her insides? When she could touch her son and hear his voice and see him smile, then she would be filled in a way that had nothing to do with food.

If only Aleks would hurry, but she knew he would not. He

was no longer the kind and playful and fiercely protective man she remembered. He was a ruling prince, unyielding and cold. Perhaps the war had done that to him. She'd been shocked to hear that he'd fought beside his men, and yet her Aleks would have done exactly that.

Her Aleks. A bitter laugh escaped her, sounding loud in the large, quiet room. This Prince Aleksandre was not her Aleks.

Her Aleks had loved her, and she had loved him.

But she had to face the truth and her own culpability. She had killed his love by putting his son up for adoption.

She picked at the strawberry's leafy cap.

A new fear crowded into an already overwhelmed mind.

Aleks had agreed to let her spend time with Nico now. But what would happen after the surgery, after Nico was well again?

Aleksandre d'Gabriel was the absolute law and ruler of Carvainia. She, a simple bookshop owner from Kansas, had no legal rights in this place. Once Aleks had what he wanted from her, would she ever see her son again?

CHAPTER FOUR

SARA SAT ON A PLUSH CHAIR at Nico's bedside, waiting for her son to awaken. After two impatient hours with the doctors and a miserable thirty minutes hashing over the details of Aleks's contract, she'd insisted on coming to Nico's room.

"He sleeps most of the time," Aleks had said, obviously trying to forestall her visit.

She'd hitched her stubborn chin. "Then I will watch him sleep."

"I have a nation to run."

After four years and thousands of miles, Sara was not about to let Aleks's reluctance keep her away from her baby. He'd promised and he would deliver.

"The decision to be present was yours."

Finally, he'd conceded and escorted her to this wing, which Sara understood to be a medical floor fully staffed for the royal family.

Both thrilled and terrified, but utterly determined to make up for lost time, she gazed at the sleeping baby face and waited. She may have appeared calm with her hands resting serenely in her lap, but her heart hammered and she could barely breathe.

The tension was magnified by the imposing ruler who stood like a stone sentry at the foot of Nico's bed. Sara's gaze flicked briefly to him. Jaw rigid, Aleks never even glanced her way. He treated her with cold courtesy and little else. She was grateful that his staff was more inclined toward friendliness. Though none of them voiced their knowledge of her unique situation, she was certain they at least suspected the reasons for her presence. Antonia knew Sara was the hoped-for organ donor. Beyond that, Sara had no idea what Aleks had told his employees about her.

Having only seen Nico briefly at birth, it was surreal to realize this was the baby she'd carried beneath her heart, the baby she'd mourned and hunted and prayed for. Over the years, she'd imagined what he would look like. She'd dreamed of finding him again, certain she would recognize her own son. She wouldn't have. He was all Aleks and nothing of her.

And yet he was everything she'd dreamed and more.

At a movement from the pillows, Sara's heart, already pounding out of her chest, galloped even harder. He was waking. She would meet him. Finally. She pressed her hands into her knees to keep from leaping from the chair and rushing forward.

Nico's thick lashes fluttered upward. Glazed, feverish eyes locked on the man at the end of the bed. His thin face brightened. "Papa."

That one small, breathy word held such power. Sara's whole being heaved toward the sick child. And the hard and mighty ruler of Carvainia melted like butter left too long in the sun.

Aleks tweaked the boy's sheet-covered toe. "Ah, the great and lazy Prince Nico has awakened."

The joke must have been a familiar one for the child offered a feeble grin, his sick eyes twinkling. "A growing boy needs his rest."

Aleks laughed softly. "Indeed. A growing boy also needs food. Maria tells me you refused your meal."

"Food tastes nasty, Papa." His tone apologized as though he was aware of his father's worry and sad to make it worse.

Aleks moved to the boy's side. "I know, son, but you must try." He touched Nico's cheek. "Promise Papa you will try."

Sara shared the pleading despair in Aleks's voice. Nico was far too thin. His arms, resting along the sides of his body on top of the damask coverlet, were like sticks and his cheekbones stood out above the hollows of his face.

The small handsome head nodded. His tongue flicked over dry lips. "I promise."

Carefully perching on the bed's edge so that the mattress barely shifted, Aleks reached for a glass of water. "Have a drink for Papa."

Gently cradling Nico's head, the prince raised the boy enough for a few sips. Then he brushed a hand over Nico's temple, smoothing bed-tumbled hair. "Do you feel like playing a game?"

"I'm a bit tired, Papa." For indeed, he seemed to have expended all his energy on a simple drink of water.

Aleks's chest rose and fell in a heavy sigh. He patted the child's fragile chest and sat back in the chair, shoulders angled toward Sara. Her pulse leaped.

"I don't want to tire him," she murmured through dry lips. Her son was desperately ill and conversation took so much out of his frail body.

Aleks's gaze, so warm and tender with Nico, frosted over. "Come."

As she stood, her knees trembled in tandem with her emotions. "Maybe we should do this later. I'm content to watch him sleep."

His Majesty didn't look as though he bought that. He turned back to the boy. "Someone has come to say hello."

Sara stepped closer and with the movement brushed Aleks's knees. Once upon a time he would have pulled her onto his lap, and she would have gone willingly for kisses and laughter. Today, he shifted away as though her touch was poison. Shoulders tense and mouth grim, animosity flowed from him. Surely, Nico would feel the tension and be put off by it.

She longed to touch him, both of them, and to make them understand how sorry she was for everything. She'd made a terrible mistake in letting Nico go, but she'd also paid a terrible price. Couldn't Aleks see that? She'd lost everything that mattered—him, her baby.

The beautiful little prince was flesh of her flesh and yet she did not know him at all. The pain of that truth would burn forever.

"Hello, Nico," she said, amazed to sound so normal. "My name is Sara. I'm—"

As though afraid of what she'd say, Aleks interrupted. "Sara is someone I knew in America."

Nico's dark eyes swung up to hers. "You were my father's friend at university?"

So sweet. So innocent. So unaware of the painful alliance between his father and herself.

A lump formed in her throat. She cleared it. "Yes."

"Papa, did you tell me about Sara? I don't remember her in your stories."

Aleks shifted uncomfortably, but he kept his tone light.

"Remember the girl who capsized the boat and dumped me into the river?"

Sara stared at him, stunned. He'd spoken of her to Nico? But Aleks's expression was as hard as his jaw. If he remembered the time fondly, he wasn't about to let her know.

Nico giggled. "That was you?"

"Yes, that was me," she said, delighted to have found common ground. "I wasn't the best swimmer."

"And Papa had to save you." Nico's voice was weak, but he seemed to relish casting his father as a hero.

"Yes. You should have seen him. We were both laughing so hard, I think I nearly drowned him."

"Papa said you spilled the picnic basket, too."

"I'm afraid so. Your poor Papa went without lunch except for the chocolate bar we shared."

They'd shared a great deal more than chocolate that weekend. A master boatman, Aleks had wanted to canoe the mighty Mississippi River, so they'd driven to St. Louis for the day and wound up spending the weekend. Sara had often wondered if she'd gotten pregnant during those magical two days before Aleks suddenly and completely disappeared from her life.

Overtaken by nostalgia, she turned to look at Aleks.

Abruptly he pushed up from the bed's edge and stepped away. "This little trip down memory lane has been fun, but I think we should let Nico rest now."

The interruption shouldn't have come as a surprise, but it did sting. That Aleks despised her and any memory of their time together was painfully clear.

But he was also correct. The boy was visibly fading. With no forethought, Sara touched Nico's forehead. He was too warm, but touching him was a salve for her soul. This was her baby. Her son! She couldn't get over the thrill of it.

"Your Papa is right. You must rest and get well so you can someday have your own wonderful adventures."

Nico's eyelids drooped but he struggled to keep them open.

"Will you be here after my nap? And tell me about America? Papa liked America very much."

Sara looked to the man in charge and held his frigid gaze in challenge. If his feelings about America had anything to do with her, she would never know. "I will be back, Nico. I promise."

Aleks glared at her for one long moment, then bent low to kiss the boy's forehead and softly murmur something. By the time he straightened, Nico's eyes were closed.

Still the ruler prince did not move. He stared into the face of his son with an expression of love and sorrow and longing.

Prince Aleksandre loved their son. There was no denying that.

What he didn't understand was that she loved him, too. And she would do anything, even die on the operating table, to make him well.

She glanced at the stiff-backed man who'd broken her heart, and remembered a time she would have done the same for him.

And yet, to him, she'd been nothing more than a fling.

Without a doubt the day of Nico's surgery was the hardest day of Aleks's life, harder even than the day he'd been wounded and nearly died, harder than the day word had come of Sara's betrayal. Every dream and hope of the future hinged on the outcome of today's surgery.

Twice he had gone down to his office, but his mind refused to think about anything except the transplant taking place here in the especially constructed surgical wing of the castle. For once, duty to his country took second place.

He gazed at the unconscious Sara Presley, her surgery

complete. He didn't know why he'd come here to the recovery suite to see her. Gratitude, he supposed.

She'd kept her promises thus far though she'd driven him to distraction with her demands to see Nico. He was trapped by his own design, a poor tactic that put him in frequent contact with the enemy of his heart. Regardless of his oath to ignore her, she'd been on his mind constantly and in his presence so often that her subtle perfume seemed to linger in his nostrils long after they parted.

Queen Irena was utterly terrified of this American. Perhaps he was, too, though for different reasons.

With tubes running from her body and her lips swollen, Sara Presley looked fragile, vulnerable and utterly alone. Other than some distant relatives, she had no real family to rally round her. According to his staff, she had friends in Kansas, in particular a co-owner of a book store who she telephoned frequently, but here she was alone. Alone and at his mercy.

He'd expected to revel in the victory, but instead, he felt the troubling urge to comfort her. It was an urge he'd battled from the moment she'd entered his world a week ago, full of fire and fury and lies. He clenched his fists at his sides. It was the lies that kept him from touching her.

He knew what she'd done. No amount of talking would change it.

"When can she return to America?" Queen Irena had asked the moment Sara was wheeled out of the operating room.

"She has done us no harm, Mother," he'd answered, too weary and worried to dwell on the dangers the American woman presented. Today she brought only good.

"But she could at any time. She is not to be trusted."

How well he knew.

To make matters worse, in the days leading up to the

surgery, Sara had hardly left Nico's bedside. She'd read to him, played quiet games or, most often, simply sat at his side watching while he slept. More than once, Aleks had been forced by his own unsettled emotions to leave the room, something he'd sworn not to do.

The innocent, affectionate Nico had quickly—too quickly—come to welcome her company.

Aleks squeezed the bridge of his nose.

To this point, Nico accepted Sara's presence as a friend willing and able to help him get well. He was too small and too ill to understand more than that.

"Aleks." The word was a husky whisper that drew him back to Sara. Her puffy-lidded eyes were opened the slightest bit. She swallowed hard as though her throat was raw. It probably was. "Nico," she rasped. "Is Nico okay?"

"I'm still awaiting word."

Her head moved up and down once before she closed her eyes again. A nurse moved in to read the monitors. "Miss Presley, do you need something for the pain?"

Red hair swished against the stiff linen pillow. "Nico. Is Nico okay?"

The nurse looked to Aleks and he shook his head. "I'll let you know if she complains."

He didn't know why he'd said that. He had no intentions of remaining here with Sara.

The door to the room opened and Dr. Konstantine, attired in green operating scrubs, entered. Though specialists had done the transplant, the royal physician had been present at Aleksandre's request.

"I have news, Your Majesty."

Aleksandre spun to face him, gripping the bed rail in desperate hope. "How is he?"

The doctor's tired face wrinkled with a smile. "Exceptional. The transplant is complete, Prince Nico came through very well, and already the tiny liver has begun to function. Barring unexpected complications, the prognosis, according to Dr. Schlessinger and all involved, is a full recovery and a long and healthy life."

An exultant cry of relieved joy rose in Aleks's throat. It was all he could do not to shout it out.

Behind him, a cold hand found his and squeezed. He looked back to see Sara, forehead wrinkled with emotion as tears flowed down her face.

He carefully slid his hand from beneath hers, but not before something strong and troubling bloomed in his chest.

Sara awoke to the sound of Nico's cries. Her side ached and she still felt as wobbly as a flat tire, but neither mattered at the moment.

Bracing her tender incision with one arm held tightly against her side, she slipped from the bed and hobbled, bent forward, across the dimly lit hallway. Her knees trembled from the effort.

She had no idea what time it was, but from the dark quiet, the hour must be late.

At Nico's doorway, an attendant blocked her entrance. "I'm sorry, Miss Presley, we have our orders."

She ground her teeth in frustration. How many times had she repeated this scenario in the last few days?

"He's crying. Please. He needs me."

"I cannot let you inside without the queen or His Majesty Prince Aleksandre."

"Then call one of them."

"It's midnight. They're asleep."

"Nico is not asleep. He's crying."

The attendant remained firm. "He has a nurse."

A nurse was not the same as a mother who adored him, whether the child knew her or not.

Sara tired to peer around him. "Who is the nurse?"

"Maria is with him tonight."

Maria. Regardless of her smiling face, the woman bothered Sara. Nonetheless, she could see the attendant was not going to give in, and there was little she could do until the morning.

A niggle of an idea came to her. Perhaps there *was* something she could do.

Heedless of her bare feet and nightgown, she hobbled to the elevator; leaned, breathless, against the interior; and rode up to the family wing. The floor was quiet and devoid of staff, lit only by sconces along each wall.

In the time she'd been in the castle, she'd learned the power of talking to the castle employees. Because of Antonia especially, Sara knew exactly which room belonged to Prince Aleksandre. Normally, Nico, too, slept in this wing, near his father.

Hurrying now, lest a security camera spot her, she made her way to the door and knocked softly.

"Aleks," she called. Annoyingly fatigued from the journey, her breath came in small puffs.

The door opened so quickly she could have sworn he'd been standing just inside. Yet, his disheveled appearance said he'd been asleep—and restless.

Sara's pulse skipped a beat.

Wearing only pajama bottoms, the prince looked as he had that one fabulous weekend long ago. Strong, masculine, and oh-so sexy.

She hadn't considered *this* before rushing up here.

Sara!" He ran splayed fingers over his head. "What are you doing?"

"Nico."

Suddenly coming to attention, he grasped her arm.

"What's wrong? Is he worse?"

"No, no. I don't know. They wouldn't let me in. I need to be with him. You promised—"

Eyes narrowing, Aleks yanked her closer. Her side ached but she hardly noticed. Aleks's naked chest was warm and muscular and brushing the front of her thin nightgown.

His Royal Majesty was unfazed. "Are you telling me that you've come up here to my room and awakened me, because you want to pay Nico a visit in the middle of the night?"

She tossed her chin up. "Yes."

In the dim lighting his black eyes glittered. "No. He has round-the-clock nurses. Isn't Maria with him?"

"I don't trust that woman."

Aleks scoffed.

"You have no idea what you're saying. Maria is a trusted and loyal friend. Her son died—" He stopped, pain flickering through his eyes. He pressed his lips into a line and glanced down the hallway before tugging on her arm. "Come inside. I do not want everyone in the palace gossiping about the two of us in our nightclothes. You've caused enough gossip already."

"I want to see my son."

Pulling her inside, he shut the door and snapped on a lamp. Though they were in a small entrance, she could see through to a bedroom. The large room was dominated by a massive bed, rumpled now by the prince's fitful sleep. The air was redolent with the scent of warm, somnolent male.

She crossed her arms, suddenly a little too aware of her

state of undress and of the partially clad man standing too close for comfort. Her eyes flicked up to his and she saw him swallow. A glimmer of awareness danced between them, as unwelcome as a skunk in church.

Her breath became shallow and quick, nerves she hoped, and not attraction.

But oh, Prince Aleksandre was most definitely attractive. The cover models on her romance novels couldn't begin to compare to this man. She didn't want to stare, but she couldn't help it. He was a beautiful male specimen. Her gaze roamed over his honed shoulders and chest and down to the hard ridges of his belly. What she saw there made her gasp.

"Aleks!" Without a thought to the impropriety, she touched the thick, ragged mass of scars along the left side of his belly. "You've been hurt. Badly."

In a steel grip, his hand trapped hers against his hot skin. "It's nothing."

"Don't lie." She looked up at his hard face. No wonder he'd changed. "What happened? Tell me."

His nostrils flared.

"War is ugly, even for those who lead. My men and I were hit by a grenade." Briefly, his eyes squeezed shut as if the memory was too much to bear.

She studied his face, wondering what other secrets lay behind the aloof facade of Prince Aleksandre. He had suffered, too. He'd been hurt, badly wounded in war. A war that had occurred while she was pregnant with Nico. The ramifications of that were something she needed to think about.

A powerful desire to kneel at his side and kiss the wounds set her to trembling.

"I should go." But her fingers were trapped beneath his, and the feel of his hot flesh was a powerful aphrodisiac.

"No." His lips barely moved but his eyes glittered like onyx in sunlight.

She had to get out of here before she did something totally inappropriate. She tugged. He held on.

"Am I under house arrest or something?"

A short laugh escaped him, dispelling some of the tension. He lifted her hand from his side but didn't release it. "You wouldn't make it back to your room right now. Sit down. You've overdone. You're shaking."

She most certainly was. "My side hurts a little."

The incision was as good an excuse as any.

He motioned to a chair and guided her down. The heat from his hand burned into her skin long after he stepped away.

"You shouldn't have come up here."

He was right about that.

"I need to see my son."

A hint of a smile lifted his mouth. "You are a single-minded woman."

She'd thought so, too, but five minutes with Aleks had her brain scrambled. Here, alone in his apartments, without the trappings of royalty around him, he was so much more approachable, more human, and much more the Aleks she'd loved.

"I will never do anything to hurt Nico. Let me see him at will. Whether you believe me or not, I love him. I would willingly give him my heart if that's what he needed."

"For compensation."

"Let's not have this argument again. I do not want your blood money." She touched her side. "My intentions should be clear by now."

And if he hadn't figured out that those intentions were good, there was nothing she could do about it.

He said nothing for several beats of time, but his glittering eyes watched her like a cat deciding if a mouse was worthy of his attention. She could see the wheels turning, thinking of the payment he'd promised, as though that mattered to her.

"Is this invasion of my bedroom a ploy to upset me or are you truly concerned for Nico? My mother suspects you have ulterior motives—beyond the payment, of course."

"She doesn't like me."

One eyebrow rose imperiously. "For good reason."

Sara bent forward in the chair, cradling her side, though perversely glad for the aching reminder that she had finally done something right for her child. "I made a terrible mistake."

"Indeed."

"Regardless of what you believe, Aleks, I didn't think you were coming back. I never received any messages from you. Nothing. I lost hope." And now she wondered, had the warrior prince been too ill to contact her? But if so, how had he gained custody of Nico?

Again, that pensive silence and then in a faraway murmur, he said, "I wish I could believe that."

So did she.

"You said our relationship was nothing but a fling."

He went still, his gaze somewhere in the distance. When he spoke, the word was soft and held no rancor, but it cut just the same. "True."

Regardless of his fury at her for putting Nico up for adoption, the prince himself had never intended to return.

"I'll go." She stood and headed for the door. Aleks remained where he was.

As she started out, she heard him sigh.

"Go to Nico," he said. "I'll be there as soon I've dressed."

CHAPTER FIVE

"She was seen coming from your rooms, Aleksandre. What are you thinking? You've fallen under her spell again, haven't you?"

"Don't be foolish."

Last night had rattled him, but his mother was already distressed enough. He would certainly not tell her as much. Sara in her white gown and flowing red hair had stirred his desire as well as his memory. When she'd touched his scars and looked at him with wide, compassionate eyes, he'd been sorely tempted to pull her into his arms and tell her every place inside him that hurt.

Thank heaven, he hadn't. Her nearness was like a drug that addled his senses. In the light of day, he could better recall the myriad reasons for remaining impersonal with the lovely Miss Presley.

But more than this, he'd been rattled by her dogged devotion to Nico. Within hours after surgery, she'd insisted on sitting at his bedside, one hand touching his limp fingers, her eyes brimming with tears.

He didn't understand this. He didn't understand her. Why would a woman discard a baby and four years later behave this way? Guilt?

Once she'd breached Nico's sickroom last night, she'd refused to leave until dawn. The boy was restless, she'd said, and needed her. He suspected Maria was partly the reason for her determined stay. Sara didn't trust Carlo's mother, an ungrounded reaction, and more proof of how misguided he'd been to fall for the American in the first place. She was the untrustworthy one, not Maria.

Maria was the most loyal person in his castle. Like mother, like son. Because of Carlo's heroic sacrifice, the Prince of Carvainia would care for Maria all the days of her life.

The memory of Carlo, his best friend and bodyguard, brought both pain and gladness and dreadful guilt. No friend could ever be as faithful as the man who'd laid down his life for his monarch.

"Aleksandre, please." His mother, his greatest ally, was unstoppable when she'd set her mind to something. Such had been the case when she'd rescued Nico from America. Such was also the case with the reappearance of Nico's birth mother. Though grateful to see her grandson beginning to recover, the topic of Sara turned her into a nag. "What was Sara Presley doing in your room?"

"We were making passionate love."

The queen sucked in a shocked gasp. "Aleksandre!"

He bowed slightly. "I'm sorry, Mother. That was uncalled for and untrue."

And he desperately wished he hadn't put the image in his mind. He was having quite enough trouble with Sara Presley as it was.

Thanks to her, he was exhausted, though not from lovemaking. He might be in a less cranky mood had it been thus. Other than carrying Sara out of Nico's room kicking and screaming, there was little he could do last night but doze in a chair and wait for morning. When he had awakened at sunup from an erotic dream to find Sara still in nightgown and bare feet, it had been all he could do to escape the room with his dignity.

Suddenly, the door to his office burst open without the usual protocol. The prince whirled, on guard and ready for attack.

A harried-looking attendant cried, "Your Majesty, you must come. Nico has taken a turn for the worse."

Late the next evening, Sara's eyes felt like sandpaper and she thought she might fall out of the chair positioned next to Nico's bedside. The little prince had finally rallied after a sudden, unexpected bout of vomiting. The doctors were bewildered but vials of blood were drawn to be certain the new liver was still functioning.

Sara folded her hands in silent prayer. *Please, please, please, let him be all right.*

An hour ago, the haughty Queen Irena had finally departed, though her dark eyes shot daggers at Sara as she swept out of the room.

Aleks himself sat, arms folded, long legs extended, as tired as she, though he would die before he'd admit it.

"You should go to bed, Sara. You're still recovering, too."

"Since when did you start caring?" She bit the words out, tired, achy and a little depressed. The past week had been harder than she'd imagined.

To her surprise, his tired eyes twinkled as he said, "Can't have an American die on foreign soil. You could create an international incident."

Her answer was a droll, "Now you tell me."

He chuckled. The sound lifted her flagging spirits. Was the

ice man finally thawing or was he too exhausted to sustain his fury against her? "The nurse will remain with Nico. Dr. Konstantine thinks the crisis is over and he will sleep the night. You must leave now."

"You're tired, too. I'll go if you'll go."

One aristocratic eyebrow lifted. "Since when did you start caring?"

Was he teasing her? The man must be delirious.

She wanted to tell him the truth—that she'd never stopped caring—but she feared the admission would drive him back into that shell.

"Can't have a ruling prince die on me. It might cause a national uprising."

His mouth curved. He rose and held out a hand. "Come. I'll see you to your suite."

An uneasy truce developed with Aleks, but Sara had no illusions that he trusted her, or even that she was welcome in Carvainia. Most of her visits with Nico were supervised by Queen Irena, a watchful, suspicious woman who had only spoken to Sara once, and that was to ask when she was leaving.

This was a worry that plagued Sara as she recovered from her surgery. After three weeks, she felt completely well, but if she said as much, would she be expected to leave? The thought unhinged her. Now that she was here, she never wanted to return to America. Her heart was in Carvainia.

By the third week post-op, the little prince was up and around, having recoverd from two bouts of mysterious vomiting that the doctors could not attribute to the surgery or to the antirejection drugs. Each day the boy's complexion gained more healthy color and, according to Antonia, the nation buzzed with the good news that their beloved prince would recover.

This particular day, Sara and Nico had ventured onto the balcony to sit in the sunshine and listen to the sea. She'd brought along a deck of cards and was teaching Nico to play Go Fish. Aleks stood at the balcony railing watching the seabirds dip and call along the sandy shore.

"Papa, do come and play. Sara knows the funnest games."

Aleks turned, his expression unreadable as he corrected the grammar. "Most fun games."

The little prince nodded. "Will you play with us?"

"Your grandmother will be here soon. I have a meeting with the parliament in a while."

Though a royal, Prince Aleksandre was not a man of leisure. His duties often kept him away or up late at night, but he spent every extra moment with Nico. Today, he looked particularly tired. His son's illness had taken a tremendous toll on him.

"One game, Papa, just one. Please."

Aleks pulled out a chair from the round patio table and joined them. "Deal me in."

Sara shot him an amused glance as she counted out five cards for each person. "A poker-playing prince?"

"Only when the stakes are high." He didn't offer a smile, and Sara had a feeling he was talking about her, about taking the risk of bringing her to Carvainia.

"Some risks are worth everything." She pointedly slid her gaze to the recovering child.

With a tilt of his head, Aleks lifted his cards. "Indeed."

Oblivious to the byplay between the adults, Nico said, "May I go first, Miss Sara?"

"Yes, you may."

"Do you have any fours? I'm four." He held up four splayed fingers. "My birthday was March tenth. I was sick."

The reminder sent a spear through Sara's heart. She'd missed every birthday but one. "I'm so glad you're better now. The next birthday will be a grand celebration, I'm sure."

She handed over a pair of the requested card and watched like a proud mother as Nico triumphantly counted out a complete set.

"One, two, free, *four*." He put the last card down with emphasis and grinned. "I'm going to win. Papa says a warrior prince must always win. When I'm big I shall be a warrior prince, won't I, Papa?"

Sara shivered at the thought of her son at war. "Let's hope for peace instead." She quickly reverted to the game, asking Aleks, "Do you have any queens?"

"None at the moment," Aleks replied. "Though I am searching. Go Fish."

Nico giggled with glee and high-fived his father, the very small hand colliding against the large, strong one in a resounding smack.

With a short laugh, Sara drew a card from the pile in the center and added it to her hand. "Are the royals ganging up on the poor commoner?"

This time Aleks laughed, too.

"Beware of the guillotine. We royals can be ruthless."

He confused her, this prince of Carvainia. One minute he was as cold as Antarctica and then for a brief, unguarded moment, he'd become the man she'd known and loved in college.

At the end of the game, he glanced at his watch. "I must go, son. Perhaps we can play again tomorrow."

"Sara said tomorrow we could walk along the seashore and gather shells."

"Oh, she did, did she?"

"With your permission, of course," Sara hurried to add. "Little boys get tired of being indoors."

"And what would you know of little boys?" he asked quietly.

Sara blanched at the intentional jab but she stared him down. "Not nearly as much as I'd like to. Thanks to you."

His gaze hardened. "You have only yourself to blame."

Suddenly, Nico clapped his little hands together. "Let's make a picnic and go in the boat."

Aleks stiffened. "I don't think that's a good idea."

"Sara won't capsize the boat this time, will you, Sara?" Big dark eyes beseeched her.

Sara gulped, unsure of how to answer. From Aleks's black expression he was no more enamored of the idea than she. Being with him in the sickroom was one thing, but an afternoon of fun with Aleks could open up a Pandora's box of emotions. In her current state, she wasn't sure she could handle them. Every glimpse of the real Aleks pulled at her like a powerful magnet. Even this new and princely Aleks had moments when she feared that she could love him, too.

And for a plain bookstore owner to love a prince could only bring more heartache.

"Will you, Sara? Say you won't capsize the boat, so Papa will agree. Please."

The child's pleading pulled at her. Poor little man. He thought his father was reluctant because of the long-ago overturned boat. He had no idea that the incident had been one of her best memories, the prelude to a weekend of love she would never forget...or regret.

She treasured her memories of Aleks, but how much longer would she have to make memories with this sweet son of hers?

If Aleks's behavior was any indication, not nearly long enough.

"I would do my best not to cause a problem," she said.

"See, Papa, see? Please say yes. We will have a jolly good time."

Sara could see the war raging inside the prince. He wanted to please his son, but he did not want to be with her. Nor did she want to be with him, though she suspected their reasons for avoidance differed greatly.

Relenting, she said, "I'm not a good sailor, Nico." A lie. "Perhaps you and your father should take the picnic alone."

"No!" The little prince was growing agitated. "I want you."

Those simple words meant more than the child could ever know. He was growing attached to her. She was both glad and afraid. How would he react when Aleks decided her time in Carvainia was over and she had to leave? Worse, what would he think of her someday in the future when he discovered the name of his birth mother, because as sure as his father had the power to adopt him, the son would have the power to ferret out the truth of his birth.

"I want Sara, Papa. And you and me."

Aleksandre's mouth flattened into a tight line. He glared at Sara as he placed a hand on Nico's shoulder. "Do not upset yourself. I'll see what I can arrange."

With that, he spun on his heel and left.

Bright and early the next morning as the first members of the castle staff began to stir, Sara slipped from her bed to shower and dress. While she showered, someone—Antonia, no doubt—had delivered a silver coffee carafe, pastry and fruit. Hair still damp, Sara poured a cup of the fragrant French brew and stepped out on the balcony.

Greeted by the sound of the rushing sea and the pale pinks and grays of dawn, she sipped at her coffee and breathed in the peaceful morning. Last night, she'd talked to Penny by telephone for over an hour. Her friend thought she was crazy to remain in Carvainia in the company of powerful people who clearly despised her. And yet, Penny had also understood. The son she'd mourned for was here.

"What about Aleks?" Penny had asked.

"What about him?"

"Do you still feel—you know—attracted to him?"

"I'd be lying if I said no."

"Oh, girl. I feel so bad that I talked you into this trip."

"I'm glad you did."

"You're going to get hurt."

"Nothing could hurt more than four years of not knowing where my son was."

But this morning, Sara realized the statement hadn't been true. Losing him a second time was going to be worse. Before, she hadn't known him. This time, she did. She knew what made him giggle in that cute little boy way, with his head tilted back and his eyes scrunched shut. She knew how bright he was and his favorite color and the sound of voice and the smell of his hair. She knew too much.

In another ten minutes, the sun would pop over the horizon. Down below, along the water's edge, she spotted a tall, shadowy form. Aleks. Back turned, facing out to sea, he stood with his hands in his pockets, a forlorn figure. He looked as though he carried the weight of the world—and in a way he did. At least the world as Carvainians knew it. He had great power, but with that power came great responsibility. She'd never thought of that before.

Aleks would take responsibility very seriously.

She set her coffee cup aside and watched him for a long time, her heart calling out to him. Though tempted to slip out into the soft morning and stand beside him, she refrained. She could do nothing for the father. But the son was a different matter.

Five minutes later, she reached the medical floor. The dim morning light battled with the pale night lamps illuminating the corridors. No security was posted at Nico's door, a concession to his recovery and the time of day, she supposed, though definitely a change of protocol.

The elevator slid quietly closed behind her. As she started toward Nico's room, a woman appeared from the staircase on the left. Something in her hurried, furtive movements gave Sara pause. She stepped back into the shadows.

Curious, Sara watched the woman glance around before quickly entering Nico's room. In the dim light, Sara could not make out the woman's face, but she was tall and moved with an almost haughty grace. Queen Irena? The nurse, Maria? She was tall, but so were many of the Carvainian women Sara had met. The secretive woman could be anyone.

The question was, why the secretive behavior?

Unease prickled Sara's skin. She hurried down the corridor and pushed open Nico's door.

Except for the sleeping child, the room was empty.

CHAPTER SIX

ALEKS WAS BEWILDERED by his own behavior. He should never have agreed to a boating picnic with Sara Presley along. Yet here he was, rowing lazily around the small, private cove a short distance from the castle proper while Sara listened to Nico's enthusiastic chatter and tried to keep him still inside the boat.

Seeing Nico with this much energy thrilled him. The improved health also assuaged some of his guilt. Had he not taken Nico into the flood-ravaged areas of Carvainia last year, the boy would not have contracted the virus that destroyed his liver. In trying to teach his son compassion for those in need and the duty of a prince to care for his people, he'd nearly cost Nico his life. He wasn't sure he could ever forgive himself for that crucial error in judgment, but he would be eternally grateful that his son had been spared.

His gaze went to Sara. He could thank *her* for that.

She looked up just then and smiled. Something stirred inside him and without thinking, he smiled back.

"I've seen this cove from my balcony," she said, brushing back tiny wisps of dusky red hair from her temples. "It's really beautiful here."

Yes, he'd seen her standing on the railed balcony each morning, usually in that flowing white gown that haunted him. Today, long before dawn, she'd been dressed and drinking coffee. According to Antonia, an able spy when need be, Sara hadn't changed that much since he'd known her. She still preferred coffee to tea and a hamburger to the finest steak.

He wondered if she still mumbled in her sleep.

"I always thought you would like it here." The words appeared on their own, shaking him.

At her quizzical look he gave himself to the oars and pushed his arm muscles as hard as possible, hoping the burn would take control and keep him from saying anything else he might regret. His mother was more correct than she realized. Sara Presley was getting to him.

"Papa, if I stand up, will the boat tip over?"

"Possibly. Stay seated. We'll dock in that small nook just there." He hitched his chin toward a tiny clearing shrouded in brush and trees. The area was invisible from the castle and security would not be pleased with his breach, though they should know by now he could take care of himself.

Sara slipped an arm around Nico's shoulder and snugged him close to her side. "Let's sing a song. Do you know 'Row, Row, Row Your Boat'?"

Nico looked doubtful. "No."

"What?" She flicked a look of mock horror toward Aleks. "You've neglected this boy's education."

Aleks's lips twitched. "Fire the tutor."

"No, Papa! I like Mr. Benois."

Sara laughed, a light, easy sound that he remembered too well. "Your father is teasing, Nico. Come on, now. I will sing a line and you repeat after me."

In a sweet, clear soprano, she began to sing the familiar song, pausing while Nico echoed each phrase in a childish, happy voice.

As he guided the boat onto land, Aleks heard his own baritone join in. Both Nico and Sara looked up in pleased surprise.

In that moment, he saw what he'd never seen before, what he'd never wanted to see.

A mother and son. And the son had Sara's radiant, full-mouthed smile.

His belly sank like the anchor he'd tossed overboard.

"Papa is singing. Papa is singing." Nico clapped his hands. Sara laughed.

And Prince Aleksandre sang a little louder just to watch them smile again.

Sara had stewed all morning about the mysterious woman who had entered Nico's room and disappeared. The incident made no sense, and in the light of day, she questioned whether she'd seen anything at all.

"What did the chef pack for us?" Aleks asked, as he spread a blue blanket on the soft, flower-specked grass. A gold family crest centered the cloth.

"I didn't look in the basket, but I'm sure it's wonderful," she said. "Everything here is."

"Everything?"

"Well, practically."

His answer was a twitched eyebrow and a few crinkles at the corners of his eyes.

He was different today. She couldn't quite put her finger on the change. He hadn't wanted this outing and yet he seemed to be enjoying himself...as was she, though her uncertain future nagged at the back of her brain like an itch she couldn't scratch.

According to the physicians, she should rest and recover under their care for two months. Half of that was nearly gone.

A shudder stole through her. One more month before the doctors released her—and then what? Would Aleks agree to let her remain a part of Nico's life? Or would she be forced back to the lonely life in a bookstore, forever without her son?

The longer she was here, the harder leaving would be. And Nico wasn't the only reason. As confused and hurt and angry as Aleks could make her, her heart remembered a time of love.

Occasionally she caught glimpses of just plain, wonderful, loving Aleks beneath the princely facade, and hope would rise inside her as powerful as a volcano and just as dangerous. She couldn't trust herself with this man who'd left her alone without a word at a crucial time. Even if he'd been to war, even if he'd been wounded, he was still a powerful man. If he had intended to return as he claimed, if he had truly cared for her, couldn't he have sent word?

Sara sighed and opened the lid on the picnic basket. What was the point in rehashing the unchangeable past?

He was a prince. She was no one. Men of his position only played with commoners. They did not marry them.

The truth was as painful as a burn in her chest. Aleks had wanted her body for a while, and that was all. He'd never expected a child to come from their loving.

An insect buzzed her ear. She swatted at it, swatting away the sorrowful thoughts as she kept a watchful eye on Nico. As any small boy would, the little prince wandered around the pretty little meadow, poking at rocks and gathering flowers and weeds into a tight fist. Though he was still far too thin and tired easily, her heart jumped with happiness to see him doing well.

She stretched her arms above her head, feeling only the slight tug of scar tissue at her side, and breathed in the fragrance of sea salt and lush, green meadow. A floral scent she didn't recognize tickled her nose.

"What is that flower I smell?" she asked.

Aleks eased down onto the blanket and stretched his long legs before him. Sara battled a flash of memory. The two of them, a blanket by a lake, the hot summer night pulsing with the beat of two hearts and a hundred whispered promises.

Promises that had been broken.

Aleks sniffed the air. "Delicate and sweet with a hint of fruit?"

"You sound like a perfumer."

He chuckled. "Wine connoisseur. The scent comes from the vineyards. Muscato grapes for spumante."

Another reminder of why she didn't fit in his world. She wouldn't know a spumante from a bottle of beer.

"It smells great," she said, and then felt stupid for the mundane comment.

She bit down on her bottom lip and began to unpack the basket, setting out a stunning array of silver and china and scrumptious foodstuffs. Royalty never skimped. Even something as simple as a picnic was a major production.

The prince said nothing, but he watched her from beneath those enviable black lashes with a pensive expression.

Wondering what went on behind those dark eyes and uncomfortable with the silent stare, Sara threw a napkin at him—a crested cloth napkin in royal blue. "Make yourself useful, Mr. Prince."

The expression disappeared. He shifted closer. "You always were a demanding woman."

His easy reference to their past caught her off guard. "Was I?"

"No." He pulled a bottle of wine from the basket and studied the label. "Quite the contrary. Perhaps if you had been…"

Sara's heart clattered in her chest like a marble in a tin can. What was he saying? That if she'd demanded more, she would have got it?

But that wasn't her way. She believed love was a gift. If he had loved her enough, he would have gone on loving her, regardless of time and distance, the way she had gone on loving him.

The thought brought her up short. Was she still in love with Aleksandre d'Gabriel?

Her gaze flicked to his and then away to stare at an iridescent dragonfly flitting along the shore.

By all that was good, she hoped not. Her greatest fear was to become vulnerable to him again. He'd hurt her before, but this time, with Nico involved, he could destroy her. He was arrogant and curt and loathed her. How could she even consider loving a man such as that?

A little voice whispered inside her heart. She could love him because she'd known the man beneath the prince. And he was wonderful and brave and good. No other man had ever made her feel as precious and loved. He *had* loved her then, perhaps not in the way she'd thought, perhaps far more selfishly, but he had loved her.

And her traitorous heart could not forget.

"Papa, come quick." Nico's excited voice interrupted. "I found something."

Sara's hand went to her chest. "I hope it's not a snake."

With a half laugh, Aleks pushed to his feet. "We have no snakes in Carvainia. They were banished by proclamation."

She looked up the tall length of him. "Is that true?"

Eyes dancing in a way that filled her with foolish, foolish yearning, he reached out a hand. "Come and see for yourself."

She put her hand in his and he pulled her up. She expected him to release his hold, but he tugged her across the sweet-scented grass toward their son.

Her heart skittered in her chest. *Their* son. She couldn't help wondering what life would have been like if Aleks had never left America, if they had married, if the three of them were a family.

But they weren't. And regardless of her silly fantasies, Aleks was no longer the man she recalled any more than she was the same, gullible college girl. By Aleks's own admission, he had played her for a fool even then—a rich, international playboy having his fling with a naive American. He'd no more expected the liaison to result in a child than she had.

He had known what she hadn't. He was a royal, no doubt expected to marry royal. American college girls were only playmates.

An ache much greater than the pain of surgery stole her breath.

She tugged her hand from Aleks's grip. He gave her a puzzled look, but they had reached Nico and his attention went to the little boy. Squatted beside a mound of rocks and weeds, hands on his thighs, Nico peered intently at the ground.

"What have you found, son?" Aleks asked, going to his haunches, too.

"That." Without turning his head, Nico pointed a finger. "Will it bite me?"

Above the two dark heads, Sara bent low enough to see a small turtle. Aleks reached into the grass and picked it up. The animal promptly withdrew into its shell.

Nico gasped and turned huge black eyes on his father. "Papa, what did you do to him?"

From her vantage point, Sara could see the side of Aleks's face. His cheeks creased in an indulgent smile.

"We frightened him." Holding the turtle with a thumb and middle finger, he offered the animal to Nico. "He won't bite unless you put your finger in his mouth."

In total awe, Nico took the two-inch reptile in both his small hands. He lifted the shell to eye level and peeked inside. "Come out. I'm not a mean boy."

Sara's chest squeezed at the sweetness. How many of these moments had she missed? "Is this your first time to find a turtle?"

He nodded, but his focus remained on his father. "May I keep him?"

Aleks shook his head. "No. He would not be happy living in the castle."

Nico seemed taken aback. "But we have the finest castle in the world."

"A turtle is a wild animal. His castle, his home is here in the weeds and rocks."

Nico's face grew long and somber. "But I would be kind to him."

To soften the refusal, Aleks placed a wide hand on the back of his son's neck. With infinite patience he said, "Would you be happy if someone took you away from your home and family? Even if it was a nice place with kind people?"

Sara listened with a terrible intensity. Though afraid she could never gain custody of her child, hadn't she considered attempting exactly that?

The little boy thought it over and then placed the turtle on the ground. "I would be sad to ever, ever leave you, Papa."

And though the mother-wound in her heart bled, that was the moment Sara knew that she could never take Nico away from Carvainia, even if such a thing was possible. He belonged here, with his father and his people.

"My son, you have a strong and kind heart." Aleks tenderly pulled Nico into his arms. "You will make a wise ruler someday."

Like father, like son. The way it should be. And she, though mother by Nico's birth, was an outsider.

The realization nearly brought her to her knees. Just as Aleks had indicated early on, she was nothing but a hired body part.

A short time later, the three of them, along with Nico's turtle as temporary guest, gathered around the picnic basket. Sara bit into an elegant smoked salmon sandwich with cream cheese and nearly moaned from the experience. Though her heart was heavy, her stomach seemed determined to make the most of her dream "vacation."

"Nico," she said, holding out another. "You should try this. It's quite delicious."

He'd hardly eaten anything.

Nico shook his head as he placed one hand to his belly. "My stomach feels strange."

Salmon forgotten in an instant, Sara was up on her knees with a hand to Nico's forehead. She exchanged concerned glances with Aleks. "No fever."

"Are you tired?" Aleks asked, laying aside his own sandwich. "Perhaps we should go back to the castle now."

"I don't want to go yet. I like it here." Nico's bottom lip poked out in an uncharacteristic pout. "I'm not hungry."

Sara longed to take the boy onto her lap and soothe him, but before she could, Aleks said, "Then why don't you play quietly with Mr. Turtle while Sara and I finish our meal. If your stomach bothers you further, you must tell us right away."

Nico looked doubtful. "I don't want Dr. Konstantine to come. I don't like needle sticks."

What could anyone say to that? The child had been through enough to last two lifetimes.

Aleks retrieved his sandwich, though guilt and helplessness pinched his face.

Turtle clutched to his chest, Nico wandered slowly toward the shoreline.

Sara followed him with a worried gaze. "He's not usually fussy like that."

"No. His behavior concerns me."

"I'm concerned, too, Aleks, but for other reasons." She picked at a crust of bread. He needed to hear her suspicions even if he thought she was crazy. "I need to ask you something. Or rather, tell you something."

He sat up straighter, immediately on guard. "About Nico?"

"About these strange bouts of illness that the doctors can't explain."

"They are a puzzle—and a worry."

She popped a tiny piece of bread into her mouth, chewed and swallowed, unsure of how to approach the subject. Would Aleks think she was trying to cause a problem? Would he believe her?

Neither mattered. If there was the remotest possibility that Nico was in danger, she had to tell Aleks.

Swallowing her tension, she asked, "Have you ever considered that someone might want to harm Nico?"

The air around the warrior prince stilled. Eyes narrowed in suspicion, he leaned toward her. "What are you talking about?"

So fierce was his stare that she trembled. Any threat to the royal heir would not be taken lightly and she could almost feel sorry for anyone who crossed the prince of Carvainia.

When she hesitated, his jaw flexed. "Speak, woman!"

Sara's tongue flicked out over lips gone dry as the Sahara. "All right, but you may not like what I have to say. Twice before when Nico's stomach hurt, he had been tended by Maria during the preceding hours. And then this morning I saw someone go into his room. I thought the person might have been her."

Skepticism replaced some of his intensity. "There is nothing sinister in that. Maria is devoted to the little prince just as her son was devoted to me."

"But Nico was sick after her visits. Twice."

"A coincidence. Nothing more. In case you've forgotten, he's been a very sick boy. Maria is devoted to him and has nursed him tirelessly since this nightmare began."

"But what if her devotion is a ploy to do him harm?"

Aleks slammed a fist into his palm. "Enough! You have no idea what you're saying."

Pulse clattering and more than a little nervous at rousing his ire, Sara refused to back down. He might be the all-powerful Oz but he did not rule her. "Then enlighten me. What's so special about this woman?"

"Her son."

"And who might that be?"

His jaw clenched and unclenched, as though he held back great emotion. "Carlo. You remember."

"Carlo? Your friend? Of course, I do." The image of a stocky young man with a wrestler's build formed in her head. "He was very quiet, but a nice guy. A gentle giant."

The prince's voice dropped to a murmur. "The best friend I ever had."

The past tense was not lost on Sara. Dread pulled at her gut. "What happened to him?"

"He died saving my life."

His tortured expression shattered Sara's restraint. She knew how close he and Carlo had been. She also knew Aleks would feel responsible for his friend's death, whether he was or not.

With no thought of the wall that now separated them, Sara moved to his side, circling him with her arms, her need to comfort overriding the fear of rejection.

When Aleks didn't resist, she laid her head on his shoulder and whispered, "I am terribly sorry."

One of his strong, warrior's hands came up to press her back, bringing her closer.

"As am I."

The admission was barely a whisper against her hair, the tension in his body rock hard and thrumming with leashed emotion.

She closed her eyes against the unexpected wash of feelings. No matter the years and sorrows between them, she still loved the scent and texture of his skin, the corded strength of him, the depth of character that had made her love him with every fiber of her being.

She touched his side, remembering the knotty, horrid scars. Aleks flinched but didn't pull away. Instead he buried his face in her hair and sighed, his breath warm against her scalp.

"The grenade that hurt you," she murmured. "Was that when it happened?"

Beneath the smooth cloth of his shirt, the scars were easily felt along the honed ridges of his ribs and belly. With a light touch, her fingers studied the shape and breadth of his terrible wounds, massaging gently as if to erase his pain and memories.

"Yes. Then." She heard him swallow. "Carlo threw himself on the grenade to protect me. I was injured but he was killed. He died in service to his ruler, but more than that, he gave his life for a friend."

He lifted his head and Sara saw the suffering caused by Carlo's sacrifice. She saw something else, too, and her pulse quickened as Aleks's pupils dilated and his gaze flicked to her mouth.

Could he possibly want to kiss her? Did she want him to?

It was her turn to swallow. Her lips parted. Then, as if her acceptance was a turnoff, Aleks gently but firmly pulled away.

The sense of loss stunned her. In that brief moment in Aleks's arms, she'd longed, not only for his kiss, but for his love.

Wouldn't she ever learn? She turned to the side and pressed a fist against her trembling mouth.

After a few seconds of loud silence, Aleks cleared his throat.

"So," he said, as though nothing personal had transpired, as though he'd felt nothing in those sweet moments. Perhaps he hadn't. "You can understand why I trust Maria with my son's life."

She did understand. And yet the strong feeling that something was amiss would not go away.

Reining in her emotions, Sara turned back toward the prince. If he was unaffected, so was she. Nico was the important one here, not them.

"Could there be anyone else who might want to harm Nico?"

"The little prince, as the people call him, is the darling of

Carvainia. You've seen the papers and the television. You've seen the thousands of cards and gifts that have poured in from all over the country."

Sara sighed and pushed at her hair, frustrated. He was right. Who would want to harm an adorable four-year-old boy?

She gave a small, uncertain laugh. "Maybe I've become an overprotective mother, seeing danger around every corner."

Aleks cut a sharp glance toward Nico, who was out of hearing range. "The only person with power to hurt Nico is you. Kindly mind what you say in his presence."

His reaction both hurt and angered. "He didn't hear me."

"And you should be glad he didn't."

The callous remark incensed her. "Exactly what would you do if he *did* hear me? If he found out the truth?"

Fury flushed his dark skin. "Do not challenge me, Sara Presley. This is not a game you can win."

Face burning and tears pushing at the back of her eyelids, Sara dropped her head and began shoving picnic items into the basket. She didn't want him to know how upset she was, not only because he refused to see how much she cared for Nico, but because they were fighting again, their truce broken. She'd thought they were moving toward... friendship, but she'd been wrong. Aleks would always despise her.

"Papa." Nico came toward them, one hand on his abdomen. His skin had turned the color of ashes. He stopped and bent over.

Sara jumped to her feet and hurried to him. "What's wrong? Are you sick? Do you hurt?"

Aleks was beside her in a flash, arriving just as the child pitched forward into Sara's arms and began to retch.

* * *

After an infusion prescribed by Dr. Konstantine and a call to the liver specialist, the mysterious illness disappeared almost as quickly as it had come.

Aleks was beside himself with worry as he stalked back and forth in his office, contemplating the day's events.

Sara Presley's bizarre suspicions had unnerved him. That could be the only explanation for his irrational behavior.

He leaned both hands against his desk and stared down at the gleaming surface. Sara's pale and lovely face seemed to stare back.

He gritted his teeth. What was she doing to him?

In that brief interval in her arms, he'd felt whole again, the raging guilt and anger and sorrow soothed by her touch.

He slammed a hand against the desktop, the sound echoing in the room as he fought back the raw emotions that only Sara Presley had ever stirred in him.

She was a liar, a traitor, a woman who'd abandoned his son. He could not allow himself to be seduced by her sweetness. A principality and a crown were at stake, as well as his heart and his son.

She was wrong about Maria, wrong about everything. She had to be. No one would wish harm upon a four-year-old child.

A terrible voice whispered inside his head. *Unless that child was the son of an old and still-hated enemy.*

"I want a list of everyone who has been in Nico's rooms," he said, barking out the command.

"Your Majesty?" His secretary, Jonas La Blanc, stood at attention beside a computer desk—his work space when the prince was doing correspondence. His bland face showed no reaction to his leader's obvious disturbance.

"I want to know who is in Nico's rooms and when. I want a full report for as far back as you can get it and from this moment forward. And I do not want you to explain this to anyone. Simply do it."

"As you wish, sir." The man bowed and backed away several steps before turning to leave the room.

La Blanc probably thought him mad. Maybe he was. Sara Presley was driving him insane.

Aleks waited until the door soughed shut and then squeezed the bridge of his nose.

She had rattled him, and now his mind jumped from the feel of her in his arms to her dogged insistence that someone might want to harm Nico. Surely no one on his staff, no one in this household would be so diabolical. And yet, Carvainia had enemies. *He* had enemies.

Though they had enjoyed several years of peace, the king of Perseidia had signed their treaty under duress. He was by no means a friend. Had a spy infiltrated the castle?

He shuddered. What if even now an assassin plotted evil against the crown prince.

"No!" He slammed his fist against the stone fireplace. Sara Presley had put paranoid thoughts into his mind. She was the enemy within the walls, seeking to disrupt his household and create dissension.

But she cares for Nico.

The thought hit him like a cannonball. Though he'd fought against believing anything good about her, he could not deny her devotion to the boy—unless that devotion came with an ulterior motive.

He rubbed the tight, tight muscles in his neck.

Were Sara's actions truthful? Were her suspicions spoken because she cared for Nico, or because she sought revenge on the father for perceived wrongs?

At this moment, he didn't know what to believe.

He'd watched Sara at Nico's bedside, still recovering from her own surgery and yet determined to nurse the sick boy. He'd heard her crooning soft words and tender songs when Nico cried with pain. And then today, when Nico had fallen ill, it was Sara who'd held him on her lap while Aleks rowed them back to the castle. It was Sara Nico had reached for.

His gut clenched. Nico wasn't the only one who wanted Sara. He, the leader of a nation, a man in control, could not seem to control his thoughts and emotions when it came to one particular American woman.

But experience didn't lie. She had been false before.

With a groan of frustration, he stormed out of his office and headed toward the security center. He couldn't decide the best course of action with Sara, but he was taking no chances with his son.

CHAPTER SEVEN

SARA HELD NICO'S HAND as they strolled through the vine-yards on their way to the children's garden. In the days since Nico's last bout of illness, his color had improved, his energy increased, and he'd become restless in the sickroom.

A boy needed to be outdoors in the sunshine and fresh air. A boy needed to run and play. She was happy to give him those opportunities.

Nico was not quite as lively as she'd have liked, but he kicked at dirt clods and paused frequently to investigate a bug or a plant or anthill. He was curious about everything, brilliant child that he was.

"What is that bird, Miss Sara?" he asked, head back, shading his eyes with one small hand.

"I'm not sure." She turned to the male nurse who trailed them. "Do you know, Mr. Chang?"

The man, who looked strong enough to hoist a car, glanced upward. "A swift, I believe."

"There you have it, Nico. A swift."

"What about that one?" He pointed to another.

"That one I know. A blue jay."

"And that one?"

She laughed. "I'm afraid I don't know. You must ask your father for a bird book."

"Papa had a meeting with Count Regis."

"Yes. But you'll see him today. He always has time for his favorite son." It was one of the things she admired about Aleks—one of too many. Though the demands on his time were heavy, he popped in to see Nico often throughout the day. He was a good father. All the years of worrying about her baby's welfare had been wasted.

Nico giggled, one sweet hand to his lips in that charming manner of his. "I'm his *only* son, Miss Sara."

She pretended surprise. "Well, my goodness, I guess you are."

She'd been surprised to say the least when Aleks had telephoned her room this morning with the news that his presence was no longer required for her to visit Nico. Did this mean he trusted her? Or that he could no longer stand the sight of her?

Since the picnic, he'd kept his distance, saying little when they were together, but she could practically feel the wheels turning inside his head.

"Look, Miss Sara, the garden." Nico pulled away then and rushed off, short legs churning the grass.

Mr. Chang sprinted quickly after him, remaining watchfully by his side. Sara suspected Chang was more bodyguard than nurse, though she was not privy to such information.

When she caught up with the pair, they were in a colorful garden bordered by thick, green boxwood that twisted and turned into delightful mazes, perfect for a boy to explore.

A small, open area contained a wrought iron bench next to a fanciful wishing well.

"We should have our next picnic here, Miss Sara," Nico

called. He was bent at the waist peering into the well. Sara's heart jumped into her throat.

"Nico, be careful!" Supporting her side, she broke into a run.

"Do not fear," Mr. Chang called, stepping up to balance the boy. "The well is perfectly safe."

"It's only for wishes," Nico said, looking up with a grin.

Sara breathed a sigh of relief. Though the stone and timber exterior appeared as ancient as the castle, the interior had been modernized to a solid surface pool of very shallow, crystal water.

"Papa says when he was a boy his papa brought him here to make wishes. And all his wishes came true."

Sara laughed. "He must have been a very spoiled child."

"Ah, but my wishes were always altruistic." Aleks's amused voice came from behind.

Troublesome heart doing a happy-dance, Sara whirled toward the prince. The usual tension was absent from his expression. His meeting must have gone well.

"Do you mean to say," she asked, smiling, "that you never, ever wished for anything selfish?"

"Never ever." He placed a hand on Nico's head. The boy clung to his father's knees, his face raised in adoration. "Unless you count the pony." Aleks grinned. "And perhaps the sailboat."

Sara laughed, feeling light and giddy in a way she only felt when Aleks was around. "I have no doubt you were the most indulged child in Carvainia."

"Indulged but disciplined. My father thought, and rightly so, that a crown prince could not learn to rule well if he was pampered and self-focused."

"Your father sounds like a wise man."

"A wise and strong monarch, as well as a good father. I hope to emulate him with my own son."

"You are," she said simply and received an intense look for her efforts. Did he think she hadn't noticed? "You must miss your father a lot."

He tilted his head. "I do indeed. Often I wish I could talk to him again, to seek his advice on troubling matters."

Expression pensive, he gazed toward the verdant woods. With a pinch of guilt, Sara wondered if she was one of those troubling matters.

Nico tapped Aleks's thigh. "You told your wish, Papa! Now it won't come true."

Aleks's expression lightened as he exchanged an indulgent look with Sara. "Ah, the rules of wishing. I forgot. Did you make a wish?"

"Yes, but I won't tell." The boy clamped his lips shut and slapped a palm over them.

"Excellent. A wise prince keeps his own counsel."

If Nico had any inkling what his father meant, he didn't show it. Like any little boy, his attention was snagged by a butterfly and he gave chase.

"He seems well today," Aleks said, eyes following his son.

Sara wondered if he was subtly telling her that her suspicions about Maria were nothing but fantasy, but not wanting another argument, she didn't broach the topic. Nico had not suffered any further mysterious bouts of illness, and that's really all she cared about.

"Yes. Much better, I think. No complaints, though his energy doesn't last long."

To prove the point, Nico abandoned his butterfly chase to flop wearily onto the bench.

"Are you tired now, son?" Aleks touched the rounded

shoulders. Nico's breath came in small pants as though the effort of a few seconds had cost him.

He held a forefinger and thumb an inch apart. "Only a bit."

"Perhaps you and Mr. Chang should return home for a rest."

Mr. Chang, who had been standing with arms folded over his chest, moved to take Nico's hand.

By now, Nico's fatigue was as visible as his reluctance to go inside. "But Sara hasn't seen the maze. I promised."

Aleks crouched in front of the boy. "Would it be all right if I kept that promise for you? I can show Sara the maze while you rest."

Sara couldn't have been more shocked. Aleks had never willingly spent a moment alone with her. What was going on with him today?

Nico contemplated for only a moment before nodding. "I want to show her the secret passage."

"Another time perhaps. I'll save it for you."

"Okay."

After a quick hug to both Aleks and Sara, Nico followed Mr. Chang back down the long path toward the castle entrance.

Aleks watched his son depart, expression pensive. "He's taken with you."

Sara didn't know how to respond. Aleks, no doubt, was second-guessing his decision to allow her access to Nico in the first place. He'd wanted only a body part, a donor who would come and go anonymously. He'd never expected this, just as he'd never believed she cared for her baby boy. And now the evidence was mounting. Or at least she hoped it was.

Aleks had never expected, either, that Nico would intuitively respond to the woman who'd given him birth. Part of her was thrilled. Part of her worried. How would the little prince react when she left? Had she been selfish to involve herself in the child's life, knowing she couldn't stay?

She had no answers. Only the ruler of Carvainia had that power. She longed to discuss it with him, but his reaction at the picnic had cut deep. In her precarious situation, she didn't want to risk angering him enough to send her away.

Suddenly, Aleks grabbed her hand. "Come. I promised to show you the maze."

She resisted, uncertain. "You don't have to."

"I always keep my promises."

To his son maybe. Not to her. But she didn't say that either. The prince was in a merry mood and fool that she was, she wanted to enjoy it. Tomorrow he might freeze her out again.

They started through the twisty, turning maze, coming to dead ends and half paths that led nowhere or turned back on themselves.

At one juncture where the path split in two different directions, he said, "Choose a path. Both lead out of the maze."

Sara gazed down the paths and saw nothing but dark, lush green. "I'll take that one."

"Shall we race?" he asked. "I'll take this way. You take that."

Adrenaline kicked in. "What do I get if I win?"

He looked down at her, eyes glittering. "To the victor go the spoils."

Whatever that meant.

Without waiting for a signal, she yelled, "Go!" and hurried off.

Laughing at his yelp of surprise, Sara disappeared into the narrow maze. Blood pumping with excitement, she missed a turn and had to backtrack. After only a minute, her side ached and she slowed. She'd almost forgotten about the recent surgery. But slowing down proved to be the key to noticing the subtle signs of passage. In a short time she found the exit and stepped into the sunlight.

She looked around the clearing, listening for Aleks, but hearing only birdsong and the gentle buzz of honeybees. Seconds passed before he exited the opposite side.

Sara clapped her hands with glee. "I won. I won."

Pretending anger, Aleks stalked toward her with a growl. "I cry foul. You cheated, starting before me."

"Sorry." She giggled, breathless from the run and from his nearness. "Well, not really."

"Off with your head." Like an old-time villain, he pumped both eyebrows. If he'd had a mustache, he probably would have twirled it. "Or better yet, into the dungeon."

This was the Aleks she'd fallen in love with. This was her Aleks, unpredictable, but teasing and fun to be with.

Head back, Sara laughed, the sudden infusion of happiness a stunning, but welcome thing. He was the most complicated, confusing man, but no one else had ever made her blood hum and her skin tingle in quite this way.

She tossed her head, feeling the swirl of hair around her face. "Castles don't have dungeons these days."

"Ah, but some do." Aleks reached to brush away a stray curl and stepped closer. Sara shivered at his feather-touch. "This is an ancient castle, you know."

"Truly?" she said in disbelief, blaming her breathless voice on the race through the maze.

"Truly." He was only inches away, and every cell in her body went on full alert, yearning toward this man who had broken her heart. She was truly a fool.

"Shall I show you?" he asked, eyes twinkling with mischief and a hint of danger. "Do you dare enter the dark and terrible dungeon of Castle-by-the-Sea?"

A tingle of nervous awareness danced down her arms. "Are you trying to scare me?"

His eyes narrowed, but went right on twinkling with mischief. "Are you game? You've explored the maze. Will you also explore the dungeon?"

She patted her heart, nervous but excited, adrenaline revved just to be with Aleks. "Are you going to lock me inside and throw away the key?"

"Are you brave enough to find out?" He laughed and the sound was so like the Aleks she'd loved, she laughed, too.

She yanked at his hand. "Come on, tough guy. I'm not afraid of the big bad wolf. Or his dungeon."

Aleks laughed again, only this time he added a wolfish growl.

A shiver ran down her back, but it was not a shiver of dread.

When they reached the castle, Aleks led the way around to an entrance Sara had never noticed before. He punched a code into an ironically modern security system and a door slowly swung open. They entered an ornately decorated hall-way, similar to those elsewhere in the castle.

"Nothing here looks creepy," she said, torn between disappointment and relief.

Aleks's look was enigmatic as he keyed in yet another security code and part of one stone wall swung inward, creaking just a bit. Musty, much cooler air wafted out.

"Okay, maybe that was creepy." Fresh shivers tingled her spine.

"You might as well get the full experience. After you, madam." The prince bowed slightly and indicated she enter.

"Oh, no, you first. I might faint if that door shut behind me."

"I thought you weren't afraid of the big bad wolf." His grin was lupine.

She thrust out her chin. "The big bad wolf I can handle." She hoped. "But the hidden door and that long dark passageway is another matter."

With a soft chuckle, Aleks stepped around her to enter the passage. Torch holders and candle sconces had been built into the stone walls, but from what she could see there wasn't a light switch anywhere.

"Oops, we'll have to go back." She turned, half pretending to leave. "No lights."

Aleks caught her arm. "We keep a torch here."

"Torch or torture?" she asked.

One eyebrow quirked. "Dare we find out?"

She swatted his hand. "You're trying to scare me."

"Of course. What fun would it be otherwise?" From somewhere in the darkness he produced a flashlight and snapped it on, holding it beneath his chin for macabre effect.

She made a face. "Typical male."

They stepped inside and the heavy door creaked shut. The torch cast a yellow circle of light before them but scarcely illuminated the close stone walls on either side. All Sara could see was empty darkness down a long tunnel. A shiver of fear prickled the hair on the back of her neck, but it was a fun kind of fear, similar to visiting a carnival spook house.

"Five steps down," Aleks said, squeezing the hand he held, his voice hushed now in a way that made her shivers more pronounced. He was playing the part to the hilt. "Beware of loose stone—and the occasional human bone."

She squeaked, to Aleks's obvious delight, and grabbed

onto his powerful upper arm. "Were prisoners really kept down here?"

He turned his head slightly and in a stage whisper asked, "Why are you whispering?"

She giggled nervously. "Good question. Were they?"

"In times past."

"None lately?"

Aleks pumped his eyebrows. "None until today."

She whacked his rock-hard arm and listened to his chuckle as they took the steps down to an enormous barred door.

"This is so cool," she whispered. "Just like in storybooks."

"I doubt the original occupants saw the charm." Aleks shone the flashlight around so she could get a better look. The space was, indeed, an ancient dungeon, dark, damp, cold and lonely. "This same gate has been here since the pits were dug in the sixteen hundreds. Before that, prisoners were housed in the towers of the castle keep."

"Fascinating. It's like walking back in time. Do you have a key to this door?"

"Of course." He reached above the door, scratching around until he came up with a huge skeleton key which he used to unlock the heavy iron door. Its clang echoed eerily off the rocks. Sara shuddered, imagining the fear a captive would have experienced upon hearing that hopeless sound.

Another set of narrow, stone steps took them down deeper into the cold belly of the castle. The darkness increased as did the damp smell.

"The air smells like the old storm cellars in Kansas. Musty and dirty. Do you come down here often?"

He shook his head. "Not since I was a boy and got lost in one of the passageways."

"Lost? You mean there is more than one tunnel?"

"Many. The maze in the gardens is nothing compared to this one. In ancient times, captives went crazy thinking they could escape only to find themselves forever lost in the tunnels. Such was the plan of the builders, an elemental and effective form of torture."

"Eww. Horrid." She stood in the center of a small stone room, rubbing the chill from her crossed arms. "How did you get out?"

"My father and half the royal army searched for hours. After that, Father closed off most of the tunnels, filled in the death pits and placed a small window up there." He aimed the flashlight upward. "Though it gives only a little light, anyone who knows where to look can see down into any open section of the dungeon."

"No more lost boys."

"Hopefully not."

"Will you ever bring Nico down here?"

"Eventually. This is his heritage. He must understand where he came from before he can decide where to lead his people."

Sara didn't say the obvious. Nico had also come from her. Half his heritage was a world away from Carvainia's beautiful shores. Shouldn't he understand that part of himself, as well?

But she didn't voice the question. Aleks had been crystal clear on the topic.

Instead, she slowly twirled around, taking in her surroundings. "Is it safe to explore?"

"As long as you have a guide." He lowered his voice to a spooky whisper. "Though beware. The place is haunted and the cries of the tortured can be heard on moonlit nights."

"Stop it," she said, laughing though a bit nervously.

By now, her eyes had adjusted to the dimness and Sara

began to move around, morbidly fascinated by the dungeon and its beastly history. The chamber was small and narrow with stone ledges built around the walls and divots here and there in the rock. Though she didn't know their purposes, she could imagine men lying on the ledges to avoid the rats and filth. The divots were a puzzle.

Like dark and deathly fingers, passageways led off in several directions from the central room so she could fully comprehend the false hope of escape. She shuddered to think of the real people who had perished in this place.

She was studying yet another wall divot when Aleks touched her arm. She jumped and spun around, bumping into his chest. Without thinking, she latched on like a frightened child, pulling him tight. He wrapped both arms around her.

"A bit edgy, aren't you?" A soft laugh rumbled against her ear.

Embarrassed by her reaction, she started to pull away. He held her for moment longer and then stepped back, his face unreadable in the shadowy light.

Sara turned her face aside, heart thudding for far more reasons than fear of the dungeon.

"It *is* creepy down here." Stirred by the strength and nearness of Aleks she moved away to touch a place in the wall. "What is this?"

A beat of silence passed. She could feel Aleks behind her, but she could not read his thoughts. Did he suspect her emotional turmoil? Did he realize how confused and troubled she felt because of him? Did he know what power he wielded over her? Not only the power to keep her from Nico, but the power to break her heart all over again.

After a bit, he lightly touched her elbow. "Come. I'll

show you." His voice held a strained note that she didn't understand.

Saying little, they journeyed out of the central chamber down a tunnel so low they had to crouch and their bodies pressed close. Sara had never been more aware of Aleks's size and strength than she was in that tunnel.

Once, she bumped her elbow and an involuntary gasp of pain hissed out. Aleks maneuvered her to his front, spooning his body around hers.

She felt strangely, wonderfully protected as he guided her through the tunnel.

Too quickly, the moment was over. They stepped out into a second, larger chamber and separated. Sara felt the loss clear to her cold feet.

Seemingly unaffected, Aleks shone the torch around the walls.

"Here you go," he murmured. "These are still intact. The ones in the anteroom were removed before my time."

Rings of iron hung in pairs at the top and bottom all around the room. Here and there, a piece of heavy chain still dangled from the rings.

"Stocks?" she asked, gruesomely fascinated.

At Aleks's nod, Sara went to one pair and stretched her hands up to grasp the rings. "Like this?"

"If you were a prisoner, would you want to face the hard stone?"

"Probably not." She turned to face him, leaning her back into the wall while grasping the rings above her head. "Would I get a choice?"

"Good point." One hand on his hip, he cocked his head. "I think I like this."

"What? Me in stocks?"

"Hmm. Definitely." He came closer.

Sara dipped her chin, feeling saucy and tingly. "Why? So you can control my every move?"

A slight smile tugged at the corner of his mouth. "Now, that would be a wondrous ability. Nothing more to worry about."

Certain he meant the situation with Nico, Sara was insulted. She started to step away.

Aleks blocked her. "Not so fast. I've been thinking…"

Her heart began to hammer, but most definitely not from fear or insult. Aleks's dark eyes held no animosity, no hostility. What she saw there was powerful male desire.

A responding ache settled low in her belly.

Her tongue flicked out nervously. "Thinking about what? Taking me prisoner in your dungeon?"

"I should have considered it sooner." Eyes teasing, lips curved, he moved closer, trapping her against the stone wall. She couldn't have moved if she'd wanted to. And she certainly did not want to.

A sexy, passionate prince was irresistible. Even in a dungeon.

He slid his hands upward along the length of her bare arms. When he reached her fingers, he twined his with hers. His warrior's body, firm and sleek, pressed into hers. Goose bumps followed in the wake of his touch. She shivered, deliciously.

He noticed. His nostrils flared.

"You are torturing me, Sara Presley," he murmured, his mouth close enough to brush hers in a tantalizing tickle.

With a soft laugh, Sara said, "I think you'd better look again, Prince Charming. I'm the one held captive."

Did that breathless, sexy voice belong to her?

"What shall we do about this?" he murmured. "What shall we do?"

Sara had no answer. They could never return to their carefree youth, nor could they move forward with no trust between them. No matter how attracted she was, her heart remembered the long, lonely years after he'd left. Regardless of his excuses, he *had* left her. And he had not returned.

If Nico hadn't fallen ill, Aleks would never have contacted her. He would have forever kept her son a secret.

How could she forgive him for that?

Yet, she'd been the one to give away their child. His loathing was not without reason.

She sighed. The dilemma had no resolution. She could not change what was.

She studied the strong lines of his aristocratic face and knew she desired him, but more than this, she still loved the man inside the handsome body. What kind of crazy woman continued to love a man who hated her?

Or did he?

The emotion emanating from the prince was not loathing. It was desire.

Was desire enough?

"Aleks," she murmured, every nerve in her body more alive than she'd been in years.

He shook his head slightly, his rapid breath fanning her cheek. "Shh. Shh."

His heart pounded against hers. Two hearts beating. One restrained, the other yearning but afraid to trust again, afraid to hope.

Tension pulsated from Aleks in waves. He wanted her but he didn't want to want her.

Sara experienced a rush of power in that sudden realization. She longed to break through that control of his, to force him to be *her* Aleks again even for a moment.

Though she would willingly remain trapped against the wall for as long as Aleks was here, the hard, irregular stone was cold against her back. Aleks, on the other hand, exuded heat.

"Are you going to kiss me or kill me?" she murmured, so close to his mouth that she could have made the first move if she'd wanted to. But she wouldn't. She might be the captive, but Aleks needed to surrender.

"So impatient," he whispered, but one hand slid down to stroke her cheek. She shivered. He smiled. She turned her head to one side. He brought it back to center and traced her mouth with one finger.

"Arrogant pig," she said.

"Tempting wench."

She nipped at his finger. He laughed softly, dark eyes glittering like onyx, as he finally, finally touched his lips to hers.

He was worth the wait.

A shock of sensation washed through her like a tidal wave. She twisted free from his grip, wanting, needing to touch him. With both arms, she clasped him to her, reveling in his power and maleness.

When Aleks felt her response, he dropped his hold to thread his fingers through her hair, capturing her more completely with his kiss than he ever could with stocks and chains.

She murmured softly, feeling the hum of yearning take control. It was as though her whole being had been in a state of suspension, waiting for her prince to come along and bring her back to life.

She wanted the moment to never end. Reality had problems neither she nor Aleks knew how to resolve. But here, in his dungeon hideaway, she could forget all of that, forget the reasons they could not be together, forget the years of heartbreak.

When the kiss ended, far sooner than she'd have liked,

Aleks didn't move away. He kissed her nose, her eyelids, her forehead before resting his face in her hair. His strident breathing matched her own. She could feel the powerful beat of the pulse in his throat.

For a while, they remained still; both seemed satisfied just to hold the other.

Aware now that she had one arm around his waist and another around his neck, she let her fingers trace the coarse outline of hair at his nape and gloried in his soft murmur of pleasure.

Did the tough warrior prince never experience tenderness?

The thought touched her to the core. Someone as strong as Aleks never wanted to exhibit a perceived weakness. He would deny himself the most basic emotional needs to remain strong and in control.

She stroked the back of his neck and traced the lean shape of his jaw.

His eyes dropped shut. Sara kissed them. A smile lifted the corners of his mouth.

"You smell good," he said, inhaling deeply.

"Like a cold, damp dungeon?"

The smile widened. "Like a soft, warm woman. Like sunshine and flowers. The way I remember."

The answer stunned her. "You remember?"

"Always." The admission seemed to bother him.

"You never told me." Silence and secrets had cost her everything. "Why didn't you tell me?"

"Were compliments that important to you?"

"I'm not talking about compliments and you know it."

His whole body stiffened. She felt his withdrawal long before he pulled back from touching her. And when he did, the chilled air rushed in to fill the space. She crossed her arms, afraid now that she'd spoiled their afternoon.

"You were the one with secrets."

"We both made mistakes—"

He cut her off with a slice of his hand. "Don't talk to me of mistakes. My son is not a mistake."

"I didn't mean—" She reached for him. He backed away.

"Come. Security will be concerned."

The return trip through the tunnels was made in silent regret.

Sara wondered why she couldn't keep her mouth shut.

CHAPTER EIGHT

"YOUR MAJESTY? SIR? Prince Aleksandre?"

A hand touched his arm and Aleks jerked to attention. A dozen curious faces stared at him around the meeting table. Ambassadors from around the globe had gathered to discuss energy concerns, and he hadn't heard a word they'd said.

"A thousand pardons." He dipped his head. "My mind wandered."

Sara had bewitched him. He could think of nothing but her taste and scent and the way she'd melded against him as though she were part of him. Last night, he'd slept little and when he did, a red-haired woman tortured him with kisses and lies.

The ambassador from Great Britain frowned in sympathy from the far end of the table. "How is your son?"

Though ashamed to use Nico as his excuse, Aleks answered, "Much better, thank you. He's encountered some rejection issues but for the most part is recovering well at present."

"Excellent. You have our kind regards."

"Thank you. And again my apologies. Shall we address the next item on the agenda?"

The company returned to the issues at hand, haggling over

a variety of concerns. He reached for his pad of paper. Note-taking should keep him focused. To his dismay, doodles filled one side of the page. Doodles of flowers and handcuffs. His thoughts turned again to Sara, to their afternoon together. What was he going to do about Sara Presley?

When the meeting finally adjourned, Aleks had no idea what had been decided.

An hour later, he stepped into Nico's playroom, fully expecting—and if he was honest, hoping—to face the tormenting woman. She wasn't there. A disturbing tremor of disappointment passed through him.

Nico jumped up from a small chair and ran to him. He enveloped his son in a hug, holding back the question pressing on his tongue. Where was Sara?

The attending nurse, Maria, dipped into a curtsy. Behind her, a small table was set with several open jars and a loaf of bread.

"Your Majesty. What a pleasant surprise." Carlo's mother smiled as though delighted to greet him. As always, seeing her brought memories of the man who'd saved his life.

"And I am delighted to see you." He took her hand, raised it to his lips. "How is the mother of Carvainia's finest soldier?"

Sadness flickered through her eyes. She glanced away. "I am faring quite well, thanks to your generosity."

"It is nothing." He could not bring back her son but he could give her a home and a place of respect within his court. Carlo would be pleased, though Aleks's regret would never be assuaged.

"Where is Mr. Chang?" he asked.

"He was called away."

"His duty is here. I do not want Prince Nico left alone."

Maria's dark eyes registered hurt. "Sir, do you not trust me, the mother of your best friend and most loyal servant, to care for our prince? I have no son of my own now. The young prince has become my life and soul. Surely, you know that."

Guilt punched him in the gut. "Of course. I meant nothing except that Chang must not shirk his responsibility."

She inclined her head in acceptance. "I'm sure he will return shortly. Would you care to join us in our snack?"

"Yes, Papa, please." Nico bracketed his father's face with both hands. Aleks's heart lifted in his chest. "We're having an American original. Peanut butter and jelly. I have never tasted anything so grand."

Aleks chuckled. "And who told you about this delicacy?"

"Miss Sara. Her friend sent it all the way from America just for me. She said all little boys in America love PB and J."

It was the perfect opening. "Where is Miss Sara today?"

Nico's thin shoulders arched. "I don't know. She brought the peanut butter and went away again."

"In her suite with Dr. Konstantine, I believe, sir," Maria answered. As she spoke, she lovingly stroked Nico's hair with her fingers. Nico looked up at her with happy eyes.

The woman adored Nico. Any fool could see that. He was the son she no longer had.

The knowledge eased the worry nagging in the back of his mind. Nico was safe with Maria. Sara was wrong.

"Is Miss Presley unwell?" he asked.

Marie gazed at him with curiosity. Had she noticed the tension in his voice?

"My apologies, Your Majesty. I do not know."

Aleks fidgeted, torn between Nico and Sara. Was she all

right? She'd had surgery, too. Had she overdone yesterday in their race through the maze? Or had he pushed her too hard, holding her captive against the cold wall? Was she injured?

The memory of those moments roared back. She had made him laugh. She had made him feel. For those few hours, he'd forgotten the weight of a nation, the horrors of war, and he'd felt young and free again.

He spun around. "I will return soon."

"But Papa—"

Over one shoulder, he winked and said, "Save me a peanut butter sandwich."

By the time he reached Sara's suite, tension corded his neck, but another emotion plagued him, too. The need to see her was as strong. He knew she was trouble, and yet he could not seem to stay away.

He lifted a knuckle and rapped softly. If Dr. Konstantine was still present, he could apprise Aleks of Sara's condition.

Sara opened the door. His stomach dipped. Red hair flowing around her shoulders, she was barefoot in a long terry cloth robe. And she'd been crying.

An alarm went off in his head. He pushed his way inside the room. "What's wrong? Why are you crying? Are you unwell?"

She stared at him standing inside her room, fists clenched at his side, and said drily, "Come on in, Aleks. You're welcome to burst into my room at any time."

He reached behind her and closed the door. "Answer me. What's wrong?"

"Don't be imperative with me." She sniffed and brushed away a tear glistening on one cheek.

He took her shoulders. "Did I hurt you yesterday?"

She blinked. "What are you so fired up about?"

"Dr. Konstantine was here. I thought—" Beginning to feel like a fool, he shut his mouth and crushed her to his chest.

With a sigh, she settled against his shoulder. He stroked the back of her hair, loving the texture of silk against his skin.

"I'm fine, Aleks," she murmured, her mouth dangerously close to his neck. He felt the softness of her lips as they moved against the stiff collar of his shirt. If he moved his head just a little, she would be kissing him.

"Then why was Dr. Konstantine here?"

"An exam. That's all." But her voice quivered as she spoke.

He pushed her a little away, but was reluctant to turn her loose. She seemed fragile today, not at all her usual feisty self.

"Then why are you trembling?"

She shook her head. "No reason. All is well. Please."

She tried turning away, but he drew her back to him.

"Come. Let's sit down. You are shaky and we need to talk."

"That's a first. You, the king of silence, want to talk."

"Prince," he corrected with a slight smile. "Not king."

Her smile returned, watery and weak, but at least present.

He led the way to a settee in the living space of her suite. She sat down and curled her feet beneath her, pedicured toes peeking out from her long robe.

"That color becomes you," he said, nodding toward her feet.

She lifted her hands to display fingernails in the same pale shade. "Your staff is exceptional. I've never been so pampered in my life." Again, tears sprang to her eyes. She dashed them away with the sleeve of her robe.

"What has upset you, Sara?" Aleks moved closer on the settee, knees turned toward her, aching to touch her again, and not sure what she needed. Why would the mention of a manicure bring tears?

"Is there something else you need that is not being provided?" Heads would roll if anyone had disobeyed his orders.

"Oh, Aleks, don't you know? Don't you get it?" She turned her face away, her delicate profile tragic as tears slid down on her cheeks.

He stopped resisting and touched her, using the tips of his fingers to wipe away her tears. "Was I too rough in the dungeon? Did I ask too much of you in the maze? Are you injured?"

Her look was indulgent as though he was a dim-witted child. "Yesterday was...wonderful."

Her admission forced the words from him. "I thought so, too."

"But you got angry again. You walked away." She grasped his hands, leaning toward him, her face earnest. "Couldn't we just this once have a conversation the way we used to? Could we please forget everything that's come between and just be honest with each other?"

Unease quivered in his belly. Did the woman know the meaning of honesty? Was this merely a skillful maneuver to get her way?

"What would you like to discuss?"

"Anything, everything except the hurt we've caused each other. Talk to me of your work, your vineyards, your boats. Let me know you again. Help me know my son. Tell me about him as a baby. When did he take his first steps? When did he get his first tooth?"

As a leader and strategist, he prided himself on being able to read the intent of others. In Sara's sea-colored eyes, he saw no hidden deceit, only longing. She had missed Nico's infancy. Yes, the fault was her own, but she had suffered for it. There could be no harm in sharing memories of their son.

And so he talked. Occasionally, she interrupted with a question, a laugh, a touch. When the topic of Nico was exhausted, they moved on to memories of each other. The time she sobbed so loudly at a sad movie that he'd grown embarrassed. The time she'd baked him a lopsided birthday cake.

"You ate every bite."

"It was delicious." He had long since relaxed into the sofa, his legs stretched out before him. Sara had always had the ability to take away his worries and make him relax. Even then, he'd had the troubles of a nation on his mind, and though she hadn't known, she'd had a soothing influence on him.

"Really?" she asked, grinning. "Then I'll ask the chef to let me bake another just for you."

With a laugh, he pulled her to him, resting her head on his shoulder. She fit well as though her curves were made for him.

He sighed, a gusty sound. What was he going to do about Sara Presley? She was under his roof and in his mind all the time. And she challenged everything he knew to be true. At least where their son was concerned.

Desire swamped him and he kissed her, reveling in the sweet way her arms snaked around his neck and in the way only Sara could make him feel.

As much as he despised the weakness, he was irresistibly drawn to this woman who'd given him Nico.

Desire. Yes, it must be desire, for that was the only emotion he could allow himself to feel for Sara Presley. He let himself wonder if he dared take her for a mistress. If he did, would he ever be able to let her go?

Sara leaned on the door facing and watched Aleks's lean, straight back disappear into the elevator. Happiness danced in her heart. She raised a hand to well-kissed lips.

They'd spent two hours together without once fighting.

Granted, they had not discussed their hot button topic, but still, they'd communicated. Today gave her hope.

The elevator pinged, taking Aleks away. Sara started back inside the room when a movement from the opposite end of the hall caught her attention. She turned, sure she saw the edge of an arm before it disappeared. Hair stood up on the back of her neck.

"Silly," she said. But a shadow sprawled along the floor, as if someone stood against the wall, just out of sight.

Why would anyone do that? Was it a servant, aware that Aleks had been inside her room and now eager to spread the gossip? Not unlikely.

Curious, she traveled the length of the hall. As she approached the shadow withdrew. Turning the corner, she saw no one.

The short hall opened into a stairwell on one side and into the exercise room on the other. She peeked through the small observation window. A man in shorts and tennis shoes pumped madly on a stationary bicycle. He glanced up, raising an eyebrow.

Sara gave an embarrassed wave. She wasn't the only guest in this wing, though she seldom saw the others.

The man nodded and went back to his sweat and bicycling.

Unable to shake the creepy feeling that someone had been spying on her—or maybe Aleks—Sara considered taking the stairs down. As she placed one hand on the cool knob, she chided herself as being silly.

The shadow must have belonged to a servant. Castle servants, as she'd already discovered, loved to carry gossip. No reason to see intrigue around every corner.

Wrapping her robe tighter, she padded barefoot back to her room. Aleks's expensive, subtle cologne lingered in the air.

She breathed it in, wondering if they could find their way to each other again.

During his visit, they had shared a cup of tea. The dishes remained on her table. She went to it, lifted his cup and kissed the edge where his mouth had been.

Was there any way she could ever repay the mistake she'd made? Was there any hope that he could forgive her? And that she could forgive him? Today she almost believed it could happen.

But time was short.

Tears prickled the back of her eyelids. Aleks had thought she was crying from discomfort. She'd been afraid to tell him the truth. That Dr. Konstantine had pronounced her fit enough to travel soon. Very soon.

Her time with Nico, and with Aleks, was running out.

"Nico."

She hurried to the closet and began to dress. Though she had hope, Aleks could very well send her away with nothing. Every moment with her son was precious.

In ten minutes flat, her sandals made soft click-click sounds on the carpeted corridor of the family wing. She shook her head in wonder that a child of hers would have an entire suite to himself. The playroom, where he now spent much of his time, was a wonderland of toys and equipment. A climbing toy and tube slide occupied one side of the big room. Colorful game rugs, blocks, a train, electronics, books, art supplies and shelves of toys filled the space.

He son had everything…except his mother.

Eager to tell Nico about the flock of feeding cranes she'd seen from her balcony, she sailed inside the playroom without knocking…and came up short.

Nico played at a sand table.

The nurse Maria stood at his side, a glass in hand that she was offering to Nico.

Her little prince took the drink and sipped.

Sara's stomach hurt. Why was Maria here, alone, with her son? But she knew the answer. Aleks had considered her concerns as nothing more than hysteria. Or manipulation.

She must have made a sound because Maria turned, smiling. "Miss Presley, welcome."

"Sara, Sara!" Nico handed the glass to Maria and rushed to Sara.

As she went to her haunches to embrace her son, Sara watched Maria over Nico's shoulder. The woman looked on, a fond expression on her face.

Maria's friendliness made Sara feel ridiculous. Maybe there was no connection between Nico's bouts of vomiting and this particular nurse. After all, Maria was with him every day. If the nurse had an ulterior motive, wouldn't Nico be sick more often?

Perhaps she was imagining things. Perhaps the stress and emotional turmoil of recent weeks had stolen her common sense.

Much later, when Nico had grown tired enough for a rest, Sara made her way back to the guest suite. Dinner would be served soon and she wanted to relax in the spa tub first and consider today's events. Once she returned to Kansas, there would be no more servants, no more spa treatments, no more candle-lined hot tub.

Not that she craved any of those things, but they were nice.

After Antonia filled the private tub, lit the candles and sprinkled fragrant bath salts into the water, she left a tray of fruit and mineral water on the edge of the room and slipped out of the room.

Sara took her cell phone and settled into the steaming water. She made a habit of calling Penny every night. Her friend, though furious at Aleks, remained enamored of the "royal treatment" as she termed Sara's experience in the castle. So, to please her friend, Sara kept her worries to herself and told story after story about the beautiful castle and luxurious treatments.

Using her big toe, she pressed the jet button and slid down into the swirling water as she punched in the long-distance numbers.

She and Penny chatted for a while, laughing above the noise of the tub. Sara told her about the maze and the dungeon, but kept the kisses to herself.

"You sound happier today," Penny said.

"I'm feeling better."

"No, it's more than that. I've known you a long time, girlfriend. You sound different."

"I've found my son."

"Yes, but you found him weeks ago. What's going on? Tell Aunt Penny."

Sara chuckled. "Stop prying. I'll tell you when I come home."

"Are you falling for that prince jerk again?"

Sara couldn't answer without lying.

Penny groaned through the receiver. "Sara, honey, be careful. He hurt you before. He'll do it again."

Wasn't that what she feared?

"Don't worry about me." She tried to sound breezy. "I'm having the time of my life. Servants, massages, pedicures. You should see my toenails."

Penny said no more but Sara knew her friend was worried. So was she.

After the call ended, a thoughtful Sara placed the phone

on the edge of the tub and leaned her head back. She needed to get out soon before she was wrinkled as a raisin.

As she silenced the jetting tub, she heard a noise. She sat up, listening. The walls in this place were too thick to hear through. Was someone in her suite?

"Antonia?"

No answer.

Frowning, she exited the tub, dried quickly and slipped into the thick robe, pulling it close around her. Aleks had toyed with the belt of this robe earlier today. It was the first time since coming here that she'd considered what it would be like to make love with him again.

Dangerous thoughts, to be sure.

She padded out of the bath into the living space and found it empty.

Her imagination was playing tricks on her today.

A knock sounded on her door.

Like a lovesick teenager, her mind immediately thought of Aleks.

She rushed to the door and opened it.

Looking down her aristocratic nose with disapproval was Queen Irena.

CHAPTER NINE

"YOUR HIGHNESS." Not well versed on the proper way to address a Queen Mother, Sara dipped in a half curtsy.

The queen arched one brow. "Miss Presley. May I come in?"

How did she refuse a royal? She didn't. She and the handsome queen had been introduced, but the woman had never before made a point of starting a conversation. On the contrary, Queen Irena had hiked her nose and hurried away every time they met. It didn't take a genius to figure out that she disapproved of her grandson's mother.

Sara opened the door wider and the queen swept inside with the air of one accustomed to being in charge and having her way.

Like mother, like son.

The thought amused Sara, but she didn't smile. She was far too uncomfortable in the queen's presence. What could the woman possibly want?

Eyes so like Aleks's swept around the room before coming to rest on Sara.

"I trust you are well." Rather than a kindness, the words sounded like a command.

"Yes."

"Excellent. Then I expect you shall be leaving us soon. May I enquire as to when that might be?"

Sara blinked, stunned by the obvious effort to get rid of her. "I—I—I'm not sure yet."

The queen looked disappointed but was undaunted. "I'll be happy to have my secretary make the arrangements. How would tomorrow be?"

"Tomorrow?"

"Surely, you see the reason behind leaving as soon as possible? The longer you remain in Prince Domenico's company, the more difficult the parting will be." She offered a smile that never reached her eyes. "Especially for the child. Our prince is too fragile for emotional upheavals, don't you agree?"

"Yes, of course, but—"

"Wonderful. I will send my secretary to you, and let Antonia know to prepare your belongings for travel right away."

"No!"

The queen looked taken aback. "I beg your pardon?"

"I'm not leaving tomorrow."

"But you must."

"I can't." Grasping for a reason to stay, Sara latched onto a thin hope. "Dr. Konstantine has not yet released me medically."

"I see." The queen's nostrils flared, but she kept her composure. "Very well, then. But do keep me informed as to your plans. I want very much to accommodate you in every way possible. We are ever so grateful for all you've done."

Right. That's why she was so eager to have Sara gone. But this was Aleks's mother, Nico's grandmother, and Sara would be civil even when deeply offended by the woman's carefully worded rudeness.

"Helping Nico has been one of the greatest joys of my life."

One side of Queen Irena's mouth twisted. "How kind of you."

The words were polite but her expression was nothing short of hostile.

"Not kind, Your Highness," Sara said. "Love. I'm his mother. I love him."

Queen Irena seemed to weigh a response but in the end, chose to switch strategies. That she disliked Sara was obvious. Apparently, Aleks had poisoned her mind with his anger, and there was nothing Sara could do about it. To all the royal family except Nico, she was the evil American who had abandoned the heir to a throne.

The fact that they were correct didn't help one bit.

"I saw Prince Aleksandre leave your rooms."

Ah, now they were getting somewhere. But Sara was not about to satisfy the woman's curiosity, particularly now, when she and Aleks seemed to be opening up to each other. The relationship was far too fragile to share.

If Queen Irena wanted to know why her son had been in this suite, she would have to ask him.

When Sara kept silent, the queen said, "Did His Majesty mention the grand affair coming up this weekend?"

"No." That she was not privy to such details of his life pained her.

"Of course not. Why would he? It is a royal affair that has nothing to do with you."

Sara tried not to let the words affect her, but her insides trembled. "Why indeed."

"Diplomats from around the region will be dining and dancing in the Grand Ballroom."

"How nice." Sara was not an idiot. She knew very well she

did not fit into this lifestyle, but Queen Irena seemed intent on forcing the issue.

"I wouldn't want to—how shall I put this delicately—offend Prince Aleksandre's fiancée. She doesn't know of your *previous* relationship and we can't have her upset."

Sara felt the blood drain from her face. Her body went numb. "I didn't know Aleks was engaged."

"Well, not officially yet, but very soon. I wouldn't expect you to know anything about that. How could you, not being privy to the inner workings of royalty. Marriages in our class are always among our own kind. Aleksandre has known Duchess Philamena since they both were small children. They've been in love for years. She will make a wonderful queen to my son."

But he'd kissed *her*. He'd fathered a child with *her*. Did his fiancée know that?

Of course she didn't, which was exactly why Queen Irena was here. She wanted Sara out of the way, fearful that a plain bookshop owner from Kansas could shake the royal family tree.

Sara wanted to laugh hysterically. Or maybe she wanted to weep.

She was a nobody from Kansas who didn't even know who her father was. Aleks was a prince with a pedigree as long as history. She was nothing but a fling who had surprised him with a child.

And yet, he'd come to her today. He'd expressed caring and concern. They'd laughed and touched and kissed. He felt passion for her, she was certain.

But did he feel anything more?

According to Queen Irena, he did not. He could not.

Regardless of these last few days of hopefulness, Prince Aleksandre was completely out of her league.

If only she could accept it and let him go.

* * *

Humming softly, Aleks tucked the photograph album under one arm as he stepped off the elevator. Earlier when he and Sara had talked, Sara had eagerly soaked up every scrap of information he shared about Nico. It had occurred to him this afternoon, in the middle of a news conference, that she had never seen any photos of her son as an infant.

He paused, staring down at the crested album. He'd referred to Nico as her son. Odd. When had he switched loyalties? When had he come to think of Sara as Nico's mother?

Concern fluttered under his ribs like a case of indigestion.

He'd never fully listened to her side of the story. Part of him wanted to, but he'd spent so many years despising her, blaming her, he was afraid of her lies.

What if she hadn't lied?

The elevator doors rumbled open.

But she had. He was certain. His mother had told him of Sara's treachery. Mother would know. She'd been there.

He gripped the photo album tighter. He and Sara had shared a pleasant interlude. That was all. Nothing serious. And she *had* given Nico new life when Aleks feared all hope was lost. She deserved this gift in return. It was the least he could do to show his gratitude.

The thought of that million-dollar contract nagged the edges of his mind. Wasn't that gratitude enough?

The conflicting ideas annoyed him. He tried to shake them off. Sara would be gone soon and none of this would matter.

A sick feeling pulled at his gut. Sara would be out of his life again.

Would this time be forever?

He wasn't ready to let her go again.

Desire. That's all it could be. He was a man, accustomed

to having women, though he was rigidly discreet. Since Nico's illness he had been celibate.

Yes, desire was as good an excuse as any for this fixation on Sara Presley.

As Aleks stepped off the elevator, his mind jumping from the reasons he should despise Sara to the reasons he shouldn't, he was surprised to observe Queen Irena coming down the corridor. She wore her usual two-piece suit, probably silk, only this one was blood-red and screamed power. Her hair, always immaculately groomed, appeared freshly coiffed. Her pumps made firm taps on the floor. He knew that walk. She was annoyed.

"Mother?" he said, curious.

Her hand went to the creamy scarf at her throat. "Aleksandre. You startled me."

Indeed. She sounded breathless.

"What are you doing in the guest wing? Has someone arrived already?" With the event planned for this weekend, he would not be surprised to find guests arriving early. Carvainia Castle was noted for its luxury treatment of all guests.

"No, I—" His mother looked extremely nervous for some reason. "I was speaking to Miss Presley."

Knowing how the queen had both ignored and avoided "that American woman," Aleks went on alert. "Sara? Why would you want to talk to Sara?"

"I wished to express my gratitude in person. She has done our country a great service."

Something in his mother's manner didn't ring true. "I see."

"Do you?" She gripped his elbow, eyes narrowed. "Why are *you* here, my son? To express your *gratitude*, as well?"

Aleksandre knew from her tone that the queen suspected

more than gratitude drew him to Sara. At the moment, he couldn't say for certain if she was right or wrong. Regardless of his reasons, he would not share the information with his mother.

All he knew was that he had to see Sara.

"I do not need to explain my activities."

With a sharp gasp of hurt, she dropped her hand. "Gossip is flying, Aleksandre. You were in her rooms earlier. Now you are here again. Have you no sense where this wicked American is concerned? Does she have some sort of power over you?"

He'd wondered the same thing. "Don't be ludicrous."

"Listen to me, my son. I am not without sympathy. You are a man without a wife. You have needs, and yet as prince you bear a responsibility to be especially careful. There are Carvainian women who would welcome your attentions."

"Mother—" he started. Though his thoughts had been along similar lines, his libido was not something he cared to discuss with his mother.

She raised a hand to silence him. "Hear me. Duchess Philamena will be here this weekend as well as other beautiful women of royal blood. It is time for you to choose one of them. Take a queen. Take a mistress. But this attraction for the American is dangerous."

"Do you think I am not man enough to handle Sara Presley?"

She drew up to her full height, head high and eyes of dark fire. "You are a warrior prince, a ruler with ice in your veins and the heart of a lion. You serve your country with honor and dignity every day. Five years ago, you were young and untried. The unworthy woman turned your head and broke your heart. You are too strong, too proud and too wise to allow this to happen again."

As her lips quivered with the passion of her words, Aleks saw her intent. She was not interfering. She was afraid for him.

He touched her shoulder and said gently, "I will think about these things."

Seeing that she could do no more, the queen nodded once and continued her journey, leaving him in the corridor with Nico's photographs in his hand.

Mother was right in many ways.

Sara had fooled him before. He glanced toward the closed door of her suite.

Even now, after his mother's impassioned speech, the thought of being with Sara called to him like a siren's song. As long as she was under his roof, he could not stay away.

Sara awakened at dawn, inexplicably drawn to the balcony. A hill gently sloped from the castle to the seashore. A fading moon cast a silvery reflection across the water and dimly lit a solitary figure walking along the sandy beach below. Head down, hands in his pockets, he looked more than alone. He looked lonely.

What must it be like for a man so young to have such responsibility on his shoulders? Granted, Aleks was a man born and trained to the role and yet, the Aleks she'd known would care deeply, worry too much and try too hard. Failure, for Aleks d'Gabriel, was never an option.

In the last few days she'd seen more and more glimpses of the old Aleks beneath the angry face he'd first presented.

She suffered for him, wishing for a way to ease his burdens—a laughable sentiment.

"Aleks," she whispered, fingers touching the spot over her heart that called to him as eagerly as her lips.

As if he'd heard, he turned toward the castle. The sea breeze caught her hair and tossed it back, then played with the edge of her robe, baring her legs and unshod feet. She lifted a hand in greeting.

She could almost imagine Aleks's smile as he waved in return.

Heart lifting, she waved again before going to the balcony gate. The last few days had been wonderful. Though she'd battled falling in love with Aleks again, yesterday, she'd lost the fight.

Nico's baby photo album had broken down the last barrier. She'd cried, her heart aching for all she'd missed, but she'd also cried with joy that Aleks would intuitively understand how important those pictures were to her. He had held her and kissed away her tears.

Then he'd paged through the album, telling sweet stories behind each photo until she'd almost felt as if she'd been there.

Last night, she had taken dinner with him and Nico, and later, after reading a story to the little prince and tucking him in bed, the two of them had watched a movie in the theater room. Rather, the movie had played. They had not watched.

They had talked. And touched. And used the cover of darkness as an excuse for more kisses. He wanted to make love to her. She could feel it in the passion of his kiss and tremble of his body against hers. She wanted that, too, but she would not because other than renewed desire for one another, nothing had really changed. They had never resolved the terrible rift lying dormant like a volcano waiting to erupt.

Yet their attraction couldn't be denied, an attraction that, to Sara, was far more than physical. She loved him with a love that wanted what was best for him.

But what exactly was best for Aleks? A duchess he had known from birth? Or a commoner from Kansas who'd given him a son?

Beneath the austerity of his position, Aleks was still Aleks. She knew he'd suffered terribly in the war. He'd told her as much. War had changed him, hardened him, shattered his faith in humanity. He was edgier and more cautious, but he could still make her feel like the most incredible woman on earth.

Now, she rushed through the semidarkness, feeling the soft sea spray blowing in from the shore and the fine-grained sand against her feet. Aleks had turned to watch her approach.

He pulled her to him. She tiptoed up for a morning kiss.

"A princess risen from the sea to beguile me," he said, his deep voice hushed against the backdrop of rushing waves.

Smiling, her head tilted up, she asked, "Are you beguiled?"

"Completely."

The reply sent her soul soaring like the first waking seagulls. She, too, was beguiled.

He kissed her nose and then looped an arm around her waist drawing her to his side. They faced the sea and the eastern sky where the first tinges of pinks and grays heralded the coming sun. The moon turned to white and the last visible star clung to the fading night.

They were quiet for a while, absorbing the peaceful morning, content to be together. At least, Sara was content. If only there was a way to make things right so that she never had to leave this place. But the thought was useless. Even if the issues between Aleks and her were resolved, he was still a prince. And royals married royals, as his mother had so carefully pointed out.

A wave crashed against the shore, sending a mist over them. Sara drew back with a laugh, but crossed her arms against the coolness.

"You are cold?"

"No. I'm fine." More than fine. Being here with Aleks in the breaking morning filled her with a sense of completion. Here, there was no one to interfere. There was no painful past, no argument, no feelings of loathing, no prince and pauper. Here in the darkness, they were simply Aleks and Sara.

"You shouldn't get chilled."

"I'm not, Aleks. Truly." The thought came that he might be trying to politely rid himself of her. "Unless you want me to go."

Aleks shook his head. His arm tightened around her. "Stay."

That one word warmed her as no blanket could. "I can see why you come to the beach at dawn. There's a serenity here."

"You feel it, too?"

"Yes, as though I belong to the sea. I feel like the grain of sand here on the shore, a mere speck in the universe, and yet, it takes all of us specks to make the world revolve. We are part of the sea, part of the universe, part of each other."

He smiled down her. "Well said."

He drew in a deep breath that lifted his chest and pressed his side closer to hers. She placed a palm over his heart, feeling the strong thud of a warrior's heartbeat.

"What heavy thing is on your mind today, Prince Aleksandre?"

"Nothing heavy. The usual crises to thwart and decisions to be made."

"You're a good ruler, Aleks. Your countrymen adore you. When Antonia accompanied me into the city, tourists were spending money like crazy, the city is old-world gorgeous, and the Carvainian people seemed happy and thriving."

"True. The city thrives, but not all of Carvainia is this

modern and prosperous. Last year floods wiped out hundreds of farms and villages. I took Nico there." She felt him tense. "I shouldn't have."

"Why do you say that? I'm sure he loved going with you."

"He did, but it was there he took ill. Something he contracted from the floodwaters destroyed his liver."

"Are you sure?"

"It was the only possible explanation."

"And you feel guilty, as though you were to blame."

"I was."

"You want to know something I'm learning about blame, Aleks?"

"What?"

"It has no value. It solves no problems."

He pondered for a bit before saying, "You've changed."

"Older, more wrinkles, fatter?" She tossed her head, hoping to make him smile. "Maybe some cellulite?"

The effort succeeded. Aleks laughed softly. "Older, yes, but also wiser—" his voice became tender as his fingers found the nape of her neck and massaged "—and infinitely more beautiful."

"Why, Mr. Prince, thank you. I'm flattered." Though her insides danced happily, Sara responded with a playful flutter of her eyelashes, refusing to let herself hope that his words were anything more than flattery from a smooth, cosmopolitan prince with a silver tongue.

But Aleks's expression had grown soft. His eyes caressed her face.

All the silliness fled. Sara swallowed, her tongue darting out to moisten dry lips. Aleks followed the action.

With the roar of the surf at his back and the wind whipping at her clothes, he groaned and slowly drew her closer. One hand in her hair, he tugged her head backward and pressed his lips to her throat. Sara shivered with sheer pleasure.

Aleks smiled against her skin. Then he worked his way to her waiting lips and kissed her with such tenderness she wanted to weep. How could a man claim to hate her and still kiss like that?

She wished the moment would never end but, of course, it did. Aleks grasped her hand and said, "Come. Let's walk awhile before the sun is up and the tourist boats come."

Sara cast an anxious glance toward the sea. "Tourists boats pass by here?"

"All day, every day, except in the family's private cove."

Feeling exposed and self-conscious, Sara wondered what a newspaper would give for a photo of their prince kissing a stranger on the seashore. A stranger in her robe.

"We shouldn't be together in plain sight like this. And you certainly shouldn't be kissing me. What if someone snaps a photo?"

He lifted one elegant shoulder. "I long ago stopped worrying about the press. Carvainians are generally protective of their royals."

"Tourists aren't polite Carvainians."

"Are you afraid to be photographed with me?"

"What a silly question. I would think it's the other way around. I'm the outsider. I no more fit here than a pig belongs in a ballet."

He chuckled. "I have something to ask you."

She glanced at the lightening sky and then at the still-empty water. "The sun is coming up. Ask quick."

"The crown is giving a Grand Ball this coming weekend."

"Yes, I know and I'll do my best to stay out of sight. Your mother mentioned it to me."

"She did? I find that interesting."

"Trust me, she wasn't inviting me to attend."

"She doesn't have to. I am."

She spun toward him so fast, her robe flared. "What?"

Aleks reached down, untied and retied the sash. After the bow was made, his hands lingered at her waist.

"*I* am hosting the affair. I would like you to attend as my guest."

Her belly was already going crazy from his touch, but now it leaped into her throat. Was she hearing correctly?

"But Duchess Philamena will be there."

Aleks loosened his hold on the belt to stare down at her, blinking, but he didn't step back. "Philamena? What do you know of the duchess?"

Apparently more than you would like. "Your mother believes Duchess Philamena is perfect for you."

"Perhaps. At least by Carvainian standards."

Her stomach dropped. "Your mother believes the two of you will marry."

He sighed and looked back toward the sky. "Yes, I know."

She waited, hoping he would assure her that no other woman held his heart. He didn't.

"Are you going to?" Please say no. Please say no.

He was silent for a moment, staring down at the white sand. When he answered, his voice was pensive. "I can't say."

It wasn't the answer she wanted to hear.

Sara turned, leaving Aleks alone as she ran up the incline and back into the castle.

CHAPTER TEN

THE APRICOT ORCHIDS ARRIVED at midmorning, approximately an hour after she'd left Nico's playroom. The tender blossoms were accompanied by a vellum note embossed with the royal crest and seal. It said, "You will come to the Grand Ball. A."

Sara kept the orchids but turned the note over and wrote "No, I won't. S." and sent it back with a rather stunned-looking deliveryman.

A dressmaker arrived an hour later with sample gowns and a measuring tape. Sara thanked her kindly and tried to send her away. The woman wept.

"Ma'am, you are cruel. I cannot refuse the prince. Think what this will do to my reputation. I will lose my position as dressmaker to the royal family."

After a round of argument in which both Antonia and the dressmaker, Carlotta, insisted that Sara cooperate, if not for herself for the sake of the seamstress, Sara gave in.

"All right. You can make a dress, but I'm not wearing it."

The woman broke out in sobs again.

Horrified, Sara recanted. "Never mind. Stop crying. I will wear the dress." Under her breath she murmured, "But not to the Grand Ball."

She had no idea why Aleks wanted her to attend the function, but she was certain it was not for the reasons that mattered to her. Maybe he was being kind because of their shared past. Maybe he needed to discourage pursuing females. Whatever the reason, Sara couldn't go. The ball would only emphasize their differences and prove that a bookshop clerk from Kansas didn't belong with the Prince of Carvainia.

Long before Queen Irena had driven the point home, Sara had known she didn't fit in Aleks's world. She once had in America, but not here. Here, he would kiss her in a dark dungeon or under a dark sky where no one in the world could see. In the next breath, he'd admit that a wealthy duchess could one day be his bride. Sara accepted that he wanted her as he had in America.

This time, desire was not enough.

By afternoon when the women finally departed, Sara was anxious to see them go. She wanted to be with her son. Regardless of dresses or balls or kisses on the beach, her time in Carvainia grew short. A lifetime wasn't enough to spend with the child she'd given up at birth.

As she traversed the unusually empty corridor toward his rooms, she heard voices coming from inside an opened doorway.

"I want her released for travel immediately." The queen's precise, imperious command could not be mistaken.

Sara slowed, curious. The old adage that eavesdroppers never hear anything good about themselves came to mind. She started to hurry past, but Dr. Konstantine's words stopped her.

"I am a physician, my queen, not a magician. I cannot make her body heal before its time."

A prickle raised the hair on Sara's arms. They were discussing her!

"She and the prince are becoming close again. She must leave before she finds out the truth."

Sara's pulse began to drum erratically. What truth? What were they talking about?

She glanced down the hallways to be sure no one was watching. Then she edged closer to the door, staying out of sight.

"Perhaps the truth would serve us all better, my queen. The secret weighs heavily on you. Your blood pressure—"

A hiss of disgust from Irena. "Forget about my blood pressure. The crown is at stake. The secret must remain here in the castle and she must go before both of them discover what I did."

"All of your effort does not appear to have destroyed their feelings for one another."

"I did what I had to do for Prince Aleksandre and for all of Carvainia. The woman is a commoner, Doctor. A common American."

"Nonetheless, my queen, Prince Nico is her child."

At the mention of her son, Sara's heart pounded so hard, she feared the pair would hear it.

"The matter of Nico has been taken care of. Now you must do your part, Doctor. Get rid of Sara Presley." The queen's dismissive tone left no doubt that she'd issued an order and expected it to be followed.

At the sharp tap of heels against flooring, Sara jerked away from the door and made a dash for the stairwell. She pounded down the echoing steps to the next floor. A stitch pulled at her side. She stopped, breathless, panting, the ramifications of the overheard conversation swirling in her head.

What were they talking about? What had the queen done that she didn't want Sara and Aleks to find out about? And what did she mean that the matter of Nico had been taken care of? Was the venom in the queen's voice intended for Sara? Or for her son?

But queen Irena adored Nico. Didn't she?

Mind reeling, Sara stood with one hand on the closed stair-well door until she stopped shaking and normal breathing returned. The fear that something was terribly amiss refused to go away.

Aleks was teaching Nico the chess pieces when it happened.

"Papa, I don't want to play this." Nico rubbed the back of his hand over his eyes.

The boy was tired. His energy wasn't what it had been before the fateful trip to southern Carvainia. He was better, but far from his normal self. "Another time, then. The game will keep."

Aleks began gathering up the hand-carved chess pieces, rubbing his fingers over the smooth surface. The set had been in his family for generations. His own father had taught him to play with these very pieces. Just touching them made him feel close to his mentor, his idol, his beloved parent. Someday Nico would also appreciate this small, but meaningful con-nection with the line of monarchs who'd come before him.

"Papa."

"Hmm." Aleks carefully placed the kings into the velvet-lined case.

"Where is Sara?"

Aleks tensed, a bit surprised by the question. This was perhaps one of the few times in the day he hadn't been thinking about her. "I can't say. Why?"

"She didn't come. She always comes. I want her here."

Aleks understood the sentiment. As hard as he fought against feeling anything for her, Sara had burrowed beneath his skin. Perhaps Mother was right. It was time for him to find a wife.

"You haven't seen her today?" On the beach this morning she'd become upset with something he'd said. He still didn't know what he'd done but he suspected his invitation to the Grand Ball had offended her somehow. A mystery, for certain. So he'd sent flowers and a dressmaker. "She can't be here every moment, son."

"Why?"

"Sara is a guest. Soon she will go back to America."

Nico's face crumpled. "Why can't she stay with us? Doesn't she like us? She said I was a good boy."

"I know for a fact that she likes you very much." Aleks tapped the tiny nose.

"She likes you, too, Papa."

He thought she did, but her affections could also be a ploy to gain custody of Nico. He didn't understand why she had changed her mind. She'd given the child away and now she wanted him back.

But he'd watched her with the boy. Her tears over the photo album had been real. It had taken him a long time, but he was starting to believe she truly loved their son.

And if she truly loved the son, what of the father? Could that have also been true?

"Perhaps she likes us both, my son, but Sara has a life in America. She wants to go home." Even as he spoke the words, he wondered if they were true. Sara's talk of her life in Kansas was factual but held little passion.

"I don't want her to go." Nico's bottom lip quivered.

"If we care about her, we can't be selfish. We'll want what's best for her."

His words mocked him. When had he wanted that? When had he ever considered what was best for Sara?

"Papa?"

"Yes?" By now, he'd lifted Nico onto his lap. The boy curled into him, too-thin arms snaking around his neck. The balloon of joy that came only from Nico swelled inside Aleks.

"I love you."

"I love you, too."

"Is it okay if I love Sara a little bit, too?"

Aleks breathed in the sweet fragrance of his son's hair. "Love is magic. The more you give away, the more you have."

"Okay. I'll love her. She loves me. She told me when I was asleep. She kissed me, too." Nico touched his forehead. "Right there."

Aleks was at a loss for words, so he simply stroked Nico's straight, black hair and held him. For the first time, he considered the emotional toll this trip to Carvainia must be taking on Sara. He'd wanted her to suffer for abandoning their son, for abandoning him, too. And his wish had been granted.

He'd expected to feel triumph. He felt like a jerk.

Closing his eyes, he rested his cheek on Nico's head and tried not think so much about Sara Presley.

Nico's breathing grew slow and deep.

They both must have dozed for Aleks was suddenly jarred awake by his son's moans. Head fuzzy with images of Sara dancing through his dreams in a gauzy white gown, he felt the weight and heat of Nico against his chest. He tilted the child back into his arms.

"Nico, what's wrong?"

Nico looked at him with scared, glazed eyes. Then the terrible retching began.

Sara was taking a sundress from the armoire when the door to her suite suddenly banged open.

"Sara, hurry."

She spun around, arms instantly covering her state of un-dress, to find Aleks standing inside the room. He hadn't even knocked.

She started to protest, but one look at his face froze the words in her throat. Beneath the usual swarthy complexion, Aleks was pale as sand, and the stark terror in his eyes shot adrenaline into her veins.

All concern about being seen in her underwear evapo-rated. "What's wrong? It's Nico, isn't it?"

She knew even before his grim nod.

"He's taken ill again. Dr. Konstantine is deeply concerned."

"Oh, no."

Hands shaking, she grabbed the closest dress and dropped it over her head. Aleks crossed the room and raised the zipper while she shoved her feet into sandals.

"He asked for you." His breath brushed her neck.

"He did?" Had she not been so afraid, she would have rejoiced. But under the circumstances, her knees quaked.

"We've come so far. Nothing can go wrong now. He has to be all right."

Aleks extended a hand. It trembled. Stomach knotting, Sara grabbed on and they rushed out, anxious to be with their sick child.

When they reached the medical floor where Nico had been taken, the news was not good.

"My concern is for the health of the new liver," Dr. Konstantine said, his kind face particularly grave. "We've drawn blood to determine enzyme levels."

Sara had heard the terms enough during the last few weeks to understand. Elevated enzymes indicated possible damage to the liver. If Nico's transplanted organ failed, hope was gone. Her baby would die. She swallowed back a sob of agony. Histrionics would do no one any good.

"When will the results be known?" Aleks asked. The tension in his jaw was so tight, his lips barely moved. He was like a leashed tiger, ready to spring.

"I've ordered a rush on them but it will be hours at the least. Dr. Schlessinger is on his way from Switzerland now."

"What can he do that you haven't?"

"I can't say, Your Majesty, but he is the specialist."

"Is Nico awake? Can we go in?" Sara heard the fear and trembling in her voice.

"Of course." The doctor bowed slightly to Aleks. "I've given him a mild sedative to ease the sickness. He will sleep."

But Aleks was already tugging her through the doorway.

As too often had been the case, Prince Nico lay with eyes closed, looking fragile and ill. Thick black eyelashes brushed the crest of his cheeks. He was such a beautiful child.

A soft moan escaped Sara's lips. "I hate this."

Aleks said nothing, but he slid an arm around her waist and pulled her to his side. She was grateful, for she feared her legs would not hold her.

"What can we do?" she whispered.

"I wish I had the answer."

She tilted her head toward the ruler of Carvainia, a man in charge of an entire country, who was every bit as helpless as she.

"This is not your fault," she said. "Stop thinking about it."

She didn't know how she knew, but she did. Aleks would blame himself if the unthinkable occurred.

His gaze flicked down to hers and held. He swallowed, emotion emanating from him, though he kept himself in rigid check. "Thank you for that."

In that moment Sara realized a fascinating truth about

Prince Aleksandre. He was a facade, the outward presentation of the real man she knew. As prince he had a duty to appear strong at all times. But the man inside hurt and struggled and felt just like everyone else. Only this man was alone in his pain.

Her heart reached out to him.

"Sometimes even a prince needs someone to lean on," she whispered, touching his granite-hard jaw. "You can lean on me, Aleks."

His eyes fell shut.

Sara wrapped both arms around his waist and rested her head against his chest. He engulfed her then, the trembling in his body matching hers.

They were like any other parents in the world, terrified for their dangerously ill child, and taking comfort in one another. In this space of time, they could forget their differences and focus on what really mattered—the health of their son.

And if the experience made her love them both even more, there was nothing at all she could do about it.

Three days crawled past in an agony of worry. Aleks canceled the Grand Ball and all but the absolute essential affairs of state. Neither he nor Sara slept much.

His mother was so upset she'd taken to her bed with another migraine. This worried Aleks, as well. The migraines had increased in frequency and intensity since Sara's arrival. Mother had begged him to send "that American" away so that they all might live in peace again. Though he agreed in theory, Aleks could not bring himself to force Sara to leave until Nico was stable.

He seriously wondered if he could send her away at all. But that was a problem he would deal with later. Nico was his focus now.

Doctors came and went. Tests were run and read. The young prince neither worsened nor improved, and the physicians began to suspect something other than host-graft issues. More tests were ordered until Nico whimpered in dread whenever a nurse or doctor entered the room.

Aleks wanted to command them to stop hurting his son. Sara must have felt the same for silent tears flowed down her cheeks as she and Aleks together held and comforted Nico during the blood draws.

She loved their son. Perhaps she hadn't when Nico was born, but she did now. In the endless nights and long days since Nico's latest crisis Sara slept little and ate less. If Nico moved, she was at his side instantly to caress and coo and tell him what a fine, brave boy he was.

At the moment, she slumped exhausted in a chair pulled close to Nico's side, one hand touching her child at all times. Her cinnamon hair lay lank and untended on her shoulders. Her eyes were red-rimmed and glassy. Yet, she refused to leave.

"You should sleep," he told her. "You have healing to do yourself. You can't heal if you don't rest."

"I'm all right." She shook her head. "I promised Nico I'd be here when he wakes so we can finish the gingerbread story. You go. You have a country to run and you're so tired you can barely stand."

She was not far from right. During the two-year war with Perseidia, he had faced fatigue and despair, but nothing like this. This was his son.

He scrubbed both hands down his face. "No. I cannot leave. What if he—?"

Aleks could not voice the terrible fear. What if his son, his only beloved child, died? They'd had such hope in the days following the transplant. And now, this.

Sara reached out and squeezed his hand without comment. She understood, and the bond between them deepened.

The door whispered open and Dr. Schlessinger, a white lab coat covering his gray suit, entered the room. Both adults swiveled toward the specialist.

"Doctor?" The tension in the room was thicker than London fog.

"Miss Presley." The doctor nodded toward Sara and then spoke to Aleksandre. "Sir, may I have a word with you in the hallway?"

Aleks glanced at Sara and saw the hope and worry etched in her face. "You may speak in front of Miss Presley."

The specialist bowed slightly. "As you wish. In our search for answers, I ordered a number of tests to rule out every possible, even improbable, cause. I did not expect to find anything."

"But you did?"

"Unfortunately."

Aleks gut tightened. "Meaning?"

By this time, Sara had risen and moved to Aleks's side. Without giving the action any thought, he reached down and clasped her cold fingers. She held tight, a small but comforting anchor in a great storm.

"One of the tests revealed a disturbing drug in Nico's system."

"He's been given many drugs since his illness began."

"Indeed. But no knowledgeable person would administer acetaminophen to a child with liver disease."

"I'm afraid I don't understand, Doctor. Explain please."

Dr. Schlessinger adjusted his wire-rim glasses. "Acetaminophen is a common and generally safe analgesic, but it is stressful to the liver, especially to a liver already struggling to function. In large doses the drug can cause liver failure, even death."

Aleks blinked, not confused exactly but wary. "Then why was it ordered? Who gave it?"

"That is the most bewildering issue, Your Majesty. There is no order on his charts and no record that Nico has ever taken the medication. But it is undeniably in his system."

Sara's sharp intake of breath sounded loud in the quiet room. "Someone gave it to him secretly? Why? Are you saying someone tried to hurt him?"

"We would hope not, madam. Our thoughts are otherwise. Dr. Konstantine assures me that the child is quite safe here. He is much beloved by all." He gave her a small, bloodless smile. "We conclude, therefore, that someone thought they were helping the little prince. When he complained of discomfort some kindhearted though misguided soul gave him acetaminophen believing it harmless."

"When, in fact," Aleks growled, teeth tight with the implications, "the drug is killing him."

"Exactly."

"But who would give Nico medication without discussing it with Dr. Konstantine?" The very idea infuriated him. "Everyone in the palace knows of his delicate condition."

"You will have to discuss that with your staff."

"You can be assured I will."

Aleks clenched his fists. Anger bubbled up like hot lava. Sara squeezed his arm reassuringly, but he was not to be mollified. Someone within the palace was responsible for Nico's condition. Even if accidental, there was no acceptable excuse.

"Now that we suspect the cause, we have an antidote," the doctor continued. "The nurse is preparing it as we speak."

"Thank God." Sara's body sagged against Aleks. Somehow his arms had circled her waist, and his hand now rode on her hip bone. He gave a gentle squeeze, trying to reassure her. "Will this make him well?"

"Time will tell. Hopefully, we have caught the problem before irreparable damage is done to the new organ." The doctor started to leave, then stopped and turned around, pale blue eyes piercing in their intensity. "But you must inform everyone who comes in contact with the boy that he is never to have acetaminophen again. Ever."

"You need not concern yourself about that, Doctor," Aleks said. "I will deliver the message loud and clear."

"Very good." The doctor dipped his head. "Good night then."

"Good night. And thank you."

After Dr. Schlessinger departed Aleks's shoulders relaxed, though his mind buzzed with the news. Nico would recover but someone had made a deadly mistake. And that someone must be found before the mistake was repeated.

He moved to Nico's bed and gazed down at the beloved boy. "I am relieved to have a solution but also upset that such a serious error could occur. Why would anyone give medication to a seriously ill child without consulting the physician in charge?"

Sara had come to stand next to him. Oddly, he was still holding her hand and until this second, had not realized it.

"I don't know," she said, "but the possibilities scare me."

Aleks recalled her earlier insistence that someone wished Nico intentional harm. He still didn't believe it. He couldn't. Not someone in his own household.

"You don't think the acetaminophen was an accident, do you?" he asked quietly, gazing down at the gleam of red hair over her temple.

"No, I don't. Not for one minute." She cast a pensive look

at the sleeping face of their son before capturing Aleks's gaze
with hers. She reached for his other hand, holding both in her
chilled grip. "And you may hate me all over again when I tell
you what else I think."

CHAPTER ELEVEN

SARA SHOOK FROM THE TOP of her head to the bottom of her feet. The coming confrontation was not something she relished, but for her baby's sake, she would face the devil himself.

Last night, Nico had rallied after the administration of the antidote and subsequent medications to cleanse his new liver. It was clear now that acetaminophen, a common pain reliever, had caused Nico's bouts of illness. What wasn't clear was who gave him the drug.

Sara didn't know, but she had some ideas, and she would never believe the overdose was accidental. Someone wanted to hurt her baby. The questions were who and why?

Long after midnight, she had fallen into an exhausted, dreamless slumber. Antonia had awakened her moments ago to the smell of French roast coffee and waffles swimming in butter and maple syrup.

"His Majesty said these were your favorites."

"He remembered that?" Sara fought back a blush, realizing she'd said too much. Antonia did not know of her and Aleks's former relationship. She might suspect but she'd not been informed.

To cover up, Sara said, "I mentioned it to him the other day, but I never expected him to remember. I mean, he's a prince and all with so much on his mind."

Antonia only smiled and Sara worried that she'd babbled on too long.

Now that breakfast was over and she'd soaked away some of her fatigue and stress in a fragrant jetted tub, Sara could procrastinate no more.

Last night, Aleks had refused to discuss her suspicions. He'd called her overwrought and too tired to think clearly. He'd been right on that account, but this morning after rest and food, she was more determined than ever to find out who might intentionally want to harm her son.

Her first concern was the smiling nurse, Maria, but the woman had never actually done anything suspicious. She'd simply been present before several of Nico's bouts of illness. Even though she gave Sara an odd feeling, that was not enough to accuse her of attempted murder. Maria was the grieving mother of a fallen hero. She'd given her all to the service of the royal family. Aleks thought highly of her.

Sara blew out a discouraged breath. Maybe she had been wrong about Maria.

Then who?

Aleks admitted having enemies, particularly the King of Perseidia. Would the king have sent a spy into Castle-by-the-Sea to murder Prince Aleksandre's son? Why Nico instead of Aleks? Revenge of the most heinous kind?

Or what if the perpetrator was a radical Carvainian? Every country had them, those who wanted a perfect society. What if that person knew Nico was not full-blood Carvainian?

No, that was unlikely. Though rumors had raced like Thoroughbreds since Sara's arrival, very few people in the castle had that information. To the nation at large, Nico was their little crown prince, a Carvainian through and through.

Reluctantly, her thoughts turned to Queen Irena. The queen knew of Nico's parentage, and she loathed the "common American" who had given him life. At the same time, she appeared to adore Nico. She was his grandmother. Surely not the queen.

And yet, who else knew except Dr. Konstantine? Would the gentle doctor do such a thing to a child?

Both of them had been discussing Sara and Nico in a less than friendly manner.

With a sigh, Sara drained the rest of her coffee and plunked the cup onto the saucer. Her head ached with trying to figure it out.

Even if she knew who to blame, she could do nothing until she spoke to Aleks. He *had* to listen to her. She must convince him of the danger before the enemy, whoever it might be, tried something more desperate.

At the thought of discussing her concerns with Aleks, dread weighed her down. The light, tender waffles lay like bricks in her stomach. These were his people. People he trusted. People he loved. How could she ever convince him that one of them was evil? He would think her either mad or a troublemaker.

In the three days of agonizing over Nico, she and Aleks had supported and comforted one another. They'd grown closer, talking in quiet whispers during those endless hours from midnight until dawn. He'd been Aleks as she knew him. Not a warrior. Not a prince. Just a scared father.

Often during the long days and nights they'd sat without talking, hands clasped in silent support. When she'd dozed, she'd awakened to find Aleks covering her with a velvet-soft blanket. When she'd blinked up at him, he'd smiled tiredly, kissed her forehead, and said, "Sleep. I'll wake you if anything happens."

She'd believed him.

If he ever slept during those long nights and days, she hadn't seen it.

She'd even begun to think he might soften his stance on allowing her contact with Nico in the future. Worse still, she'd started to believe he cared for her.

After this morning, he'd hate her all over again.

The red uniformed butler with the stiffest back in the world gestured her into Aleks's office. She'd phoned the prince's private number, expressed her desire to talk, and he'd invited her here. She'd expected him to be resting but he was back at work, as though he'd slept for days.

As soon as he saw her, he tossed aside his pen and rose to embrace her.

She leaned into him, relishing the moment. After this conversation, he might never touch her again. She breathed him in, absorbing all the nuances of Aleks. Subtle, expensive cologne. Powerful, leashed muscles wrapped in a perfectly tailored suit.

Saints above, she loved him.

"I can't believe you're working," she said when she stepped back a little. "You look like death warmed over."

Still holding her upper arms, the corners of his mouth tilted. "Flattery, my darling?"

His darling. An impossible dream.

Sara touched his smooth-shaved jaw. "Will you rest? You have to rest. He's going to be all right now."

His chest heaved. "I could not have borne these last days without you."

"I'm glad I could be here. Thank you for giving me that much."

"No gratitude is required. You are his mother."

Sara's eyes filled with tears. She'd waited a long time to hear those words. "Oh, Aleks. This is so hard."

He kissed her temple. "Hard? What is hard? Being Nico's mother?"

She shook her head. "No. Never that. It's all I ever wanted." Well, not all. She'd wanted to be Aleks's wife, as well, but she couldn't tell him her impossible dream.

He cocked his head, dark, dark eyes searching her face. "Then what? You have a sadness about you this morning."

She broke away and went to the window overlooking the seashore. The day was overcast, an unusual occurrence. Waves crashed against the sand, harbingers of a coming storm.

Sara wondered if the storm outside would be repeated inside this office.

"There's something I have to discuss with you, Aleks. Even if it makes you angry, you must consider what I have to say."

She heard the soft pad of his footsteps across the plush carpeting as he came to her side. "The sea is wild today."

"I was thinking the same thing."

"Were you?"

"Partly." Her head swiveled in his direction. Standing ramrod straight, he looked as powerful and dangerous as the sea, and every bit as magnificent. "Aleks?"

"Speak. I can tell you have something heavy on your mind."

"You aren't going to like it."

"Is this about Prince Nico?"

"Yes."

"I've been giving the situation some thought."

"So you agree that the overdose was not accidental?"

He gave her a strange look. "The overdose?"

"Yes. Wasn't that what you meant?"

"No." But he didn't elaborate, and Sara was left to wonder what "situation" he'd been considering. Instead, he said, "Dr. Konstantine agrees that someone likely gave Nico the medicine in ignorance."

She knew he didn't want to hear it, but she had to say, "What if they didn't, Aleks? What if it was intentional?"

"It was not."

Pigheaded Carvainian. "Are you willing to bet your son's life on it?"

He laced his hands behind his neck and stared up at the ceiling. "You are determined to fight about this."

"I am determined to protect my son."

"And you think I am not?"

"No! You adore Nico. You would do anything to protect him."

"Correct. If it soothes you to know, I have taken every precaution. Security is alerted to your concerns. A camera has been placed inside Nico's room. An extra guard keeps watch."

There was a measure of comfort in knowing that he hadn't completely ignored her. "But what if Nico is in danger from someone the guards trust?"

"Maria again? Will you continue to malign my best friend's mother?"

"I'm sorry. I know you hate that, but we have to consider her and anyone else with easy access to Nico's rooms."

"Certainly, but the question is why? Why would anyone within these walls want to harm the crown prince?"

"Maybe for precisely that reason. Because he *is* the crown prince."

Something in his tight demeanor changed. Sara could see the wheels turning inside his brilliant head. "Elaborate, please."

Taking a deep, shaky breath, Sara started with the idea of a radical Carvainian. Aleks's eyes narrowed and he nodded. "Possible. But who?"

"I don't know. It could be anyone, but I've wondered about Dr. Konstantine as well as Maria. They are often with Nico."

A muscle twitched below his right eye. "Are you determined to make me angry this morning?"

She shook her head. "No. I only want to keep Nico safe." She grasped Aleks's hand and brought it to her cheek. "The last thing I want is to make you angry."

"Then don't." He moved closer, turning his hand to brush the knuckles over her cheek. "Let us celebrate our son's recovery."

"But—" He placed a finger over her lips.

"Shh. Today I have hope. Don't take it from me."

Torn between what she feared and what she yearned for, Sara's heart sank lower and lower. He would hate her once she mentioned the queen.

He drew her close and she went to him, belly fluttering with conflicting desires. Soon she would destroy this sweet emotion brewing between them, so for these precious moments, she would let him hold her. And she would pretend he loved her enough.

His warm, supple mouth found hers, and she was lost in him for a few, wonderful seconds. When he lifted his head to gaze tenderly at her, her pulse rattled wildly against her collarbone. She saw something in his eyes, a look she'd seen before, years ago. A look she'd never expected to see again. Hope and despair mingled like warring sisters.

"Aleks," she whispered.

"You are like a drug in my blood, Sara Presley. The more I have of you, the more I want. And yet—"

It was her turn to place a finger to his lips. "Shh."

She wasn't ready to remember the reasons they could never be. She knew them better than he did. Right now, she wanted to love him and be with him in this sweet moment when Nico was healing and they were at peace. Soon enough, the storm would break and she would be washed away in a sea of his anger.

"Remember," she said, caressing his face, tracing his lips and noble jaw, "the first time I cooked for you?"

"I remember everything about our time together."

"You do?"

The corners of his eyes crinkled. "The casserole was hideous and you cried."

"And you ate it anyway."

His face softened. "Because I loved you."

"Yes. And I loved you, Aleks. Then and now. Nothing has changed my feelings."

He inhaled deeply and drew her against his chest, saying nothing. His heart thudded beneath her ear.

"It's okay, Aleks. I understand." He was a royal and she wasn't. They were from different worlds and different backgrounds. The only things they had in common were love for their son and a passion for each other.

"I don't think you do," he murmured against her hair. "If you loved me, why did you give away our child?"

His voice was weary, as though he'd struggled with the question for a long time. "I've explained what happened. I hate what I did, but I thought you'd abandoned me."

"You see, Sara, this is where the story becomes a problem. I did not abandon you. I sent someone to you."

"Who?"

"My mother, and she returned with the news that you wanted nothing to do with me or with my child."

"That's not true." The knot in Sara's stomach twisted until her belly ached. "I don't care what you were told. That is not true."

Aleks stiffened. All the tenderness they'd been sharing disappeared. "My mother would not lie."

She'd opened this can of worms. As much as she dreaded the end result, she couldn't stop now until everything was said.

"But what if she did? She despises me, Aleks. I'm an American commoner. What if she lied to get me out of your life?"

He jerked away from her. "I will not hear this."

"Yes, you will." She reached for him, imploring. "You're going to hate me anyway, so I have to tell you everything. I overheard your mother and Dr. Konstantine talking. Your mother wants to get rid of me. I heard her say so. I also heard her say, 'the problem of Nico has been resolved.' What does that mean, Aleks? What problem of Nico has she resolved? Is my son a problem because he's half-American and not worthy to take the throne?"

Aleks went as still as death. Disbelief rose from his stiffened body like heat from a tin roof.

When he spoke, his tone was low and threatening. "Are you accusing the queen of trying to murder her own grandson?"

"No." Sara shoved at a lock of hair, frustrated, distraught, and terrified that she was making a huge mistake. But Nico's life was at stake. She had to bring every possibility into the light. "Aleks, I don't know. Maybe I'm wrong—"

"You most decidedly are."

"But what if I'm not? You have to consider the possibility."

"Enough." Face dark and livid, he chopped the air with his hand.

Sara latched onto his forearm with both hands. "No. You will listen to me, you pigheaded prince. Someone lied to you, and it wasn't me. Someone kept me away from my baby—and the man I loved—for five years. And now, someone has poisoned Nico. We don't know why, but you have to consider that there are people who are not pleased at having a future prince who is not purely Carvainian. You have to consider everything."

He shook her off as if she were lint on his suit. "Your accusations are ridiculous."

"What if they aren't? What if I'm right?"

"You are accusing the one person in this world who I trust with my life. She is my mother and she is a good and beloved queen. If not for her, I would never have known my son." He whirled away to storm across the room. Outside the rain cried against the windows.

Sara followed him, intent on making him understand. As she'd feared, her suspicions had destroyed the sweet relationship developing between them. There was no point in stopping now until Aleks agreed to investigate every potential reason for Nico's illness.

She knew for certain that Queen Irena had developed an elaborate plot five years ago. Could she still be plotting?

"If not for the queen, I would never have been forced to give Nico up for adoption in the first place. We could have been together."

"You don't know what you're talking about." Aleks turned, eyes hard, though the emotion behind them was raging. "I was warned that bringing you here would cause trouble, but I was determined to save Nico's life at all costs."

"That's what I care about, too, Aleks. Please believe me. I'm not trying to cause a problem. I just want my son to be safe."

"From his own grandmother? Woman you are insane, a pathetic, ranting lunatic. My mother was right. You are a dangerous woman."

"Listen to me, Aleks, please. I'm only asking you to check into everyone and everything. I'm not trying to accuse her or anyone. I'm just scared and confused and—"

"And finished."

Sara went as still as the tomb. "What?"

He stalked to his desk and yanked open a drawer. "We have a contract. It is completed."

Sara rocked back. "I don't understand."

"Your vacation in Carvainia is over. Your visa is hereby revoked. I will alert the staff to prepare for your departure."

Sara's hand went to her throat. "Aleks, no. Please. I can't leave my son."

"He is not yours."

"I beg you not to do this. Give me a little more time. Please."

He thrust an envelope toward her. "Here is what you came for, the one thing I know that matters to you. Take it and go."

She drew back. "No."

He pried her clenched fingers open and forced the envelope into her grasp. "I do not wish to see your face again. Goodbye, Sara Presley."

And with that, he spun on the heel of his gleaming shoes and stormed out.

Sara couldn't move. She couldn't breathe. In fact, she didn't want to. She wanted her rampaging heart to cease beating so she could die right here in Aleks's office.

The room grew cold and her knees trembled. Outside the storm had broken upon a swirling, surging sea.

The storm had broken inside the castle, as well.

She glanced down at the envelope in her shaking hand. Slowly, she opened it to find the dreaded contract. She'd agreed to give Nico life in exchange for one million dollars. The bank draft was like a snake in her hand. She hated it. Why had she ever agreed to such a travesty?

She tore the draft into small pieces and replaced it in the envelope. With feet of lead, she walked to the desk.

"All I ever wanted was you, Aleks. You and our son." She opened the top drawer and slid the envelope inside.

But not before the paper was wet with tears.

CHAPTER TWELVE

"SADDLE WINDSTAR."

"Sir. Your Majesty, begging your pardon, but you should not go out in this storm."

Aleks speared the groom with a look. "Saddle him."

"As you wish."

In moments, Aleks was astride the sleek black horse and galloping headlong across the castle grounds. The cold rain slashed against his face, but he barely felt it. He needed to ride and to think. If only his father were still alive, they would ride together and laugh at the storm. They would solve the problems of the nation and of the heart.

But his father was gone.

The curse of being a ruling prince was the terrible aloneness. Though surrounded by people much of the time, there was no one to whom he could turn, no one with whom to share his heartache, no one to offer comfort or wisdom.

Without warning, his thoughts went to these last three days and nights at Nico's bedside. Sara had been there for him. She had felt his pain. She'd been his comfort and strength and shared his burden.

But now she accused his mother of lying and perhaps even of attempted murder?

The rage of such a ludicrous accusation had passed and he simply felt bereft. Sara had fooled him again. He'd started to believe that they could set things right somehow.

The queen had been right all along. Sara had her own agenda. She'd done nothing but stir up trouble since she'd entered the castle. Nico would be brokenhearted to know his new friend was abandoning him—again.

Aleksandre should have never allowed the contact with his son to begin with, but Sara had outmaneuvered him.

He dug his heels into Windstar and felt the spurt of power beneath him. Windstar would run until his lungs exploded, though he was not overly fond of storms. When lightning shimmered in the distance and thunder rumbled the horse reared slightly. Aleks held strong, bringing him down. The animal pranced sideways, head shaking. Aleks patted the quivering neck. "Easy, old man."

They were a matched pair, the horse and the prince. The horse instinctively seemed to understand the prince's need to let the wind and the rain and the ride purge his tattered mind. Both horse and man were soaked through, and yet they thundered on. Past the dozens of outbuildings, past the private cove and down to the sea. Waves crashed over the sand and sent sea spray up the beach for more than a hundred yards. Aleks pulled up, he and the horse facing the endless expanse of dark, boiling sea and sky.

He saw her there as they'd been that one morning when she came to him in white robe and bare feet. She'd brought with her something he'd never expected to experience again. She'd brought love. At least, he'd thought as much.

On that twilight morning with the moon white above and air warm and redolent of the seagull's song, she'd broken down his rigidly erected wall. He'd built a fortress against her and she'd walked through it on bare feet.

A man's heart was a traitorous thing.

He'd started to believe her assertions that Nico was in danger. He was not a fool. The possibility was real. But not from Nico's own grandmother.

A vivid flash of lightning danced over the waves. He held tight to Windstar's reins and the big gelding didn't falter this time.

Aleks had no doubt about his mother's negative feelings toward Sara. Sara was bright. She felt the hostility.

Perhaps Sara was trying to cause dissension between him and his mother because the queen was wise to her ways.

Yet, as hard as he tried to envision Sara as the villain, his heart bled with wanting her.

But the die was cast. She must leave before he became more of a fool than he'd already been.

He turned the big steed up the coast, letting the driving rain pound into his face, and rode them both into exhaustion.

"I'm coming home tomorrow." Sara heard the quiver in her voice as she talked to Penny.

"What's wrong? You sound upset."

"Aleks asked me to leave." She lay prostrate on the massive canopy bed, clothes strewn around her. She didn't want to go. Not yet. Not ever.

"Prince Jerk. I don't know what you ever saw in him."

He wasn't always a jerk. Sometimes he was warm and funny and loving. "He adores our son."

"Did he agree to visitation?"

Sara rubbed a hand down her throat. Antonia had lit a

scented candle but the smell set her stomach to churning. She was sick, all right. Sick with grief. "No."

A beat of silence. "What are you going to do?"

"I don't know yet. Right now, I'm coming home. Maybe I can figure out something later. At least I know where my baby is now."

"And you know he's safe. Remember how you used to worry about that?"

Sara's eyes fell shut. She still worried about his safety, but she didn't say as much to Penny. "I need to hang up now, Penny. I want to spend as much time with Nico as I can before tomorrow."

She glanced at the clock. If only she could stop time.

"Okay." And then, "Sara, I'm sorry. I never should have made you go on that fake vacation."

"Don't apologize, Penny. As sad as I am tonight, it was the best thing that has happened to me in years."

That much was true. Though she had no idea how she would get through the days ahead, this time with Nico and Aleks was worth any amount of suffering.

After they ended the call, Sara looked at her meager belongings but didn't pack. Antonia had insisted the job be left for her. Fine. She didn't want to pack anyway. She wanted to run and lock herself in the dungeon where no one could find her, sneaking out at night to see her son.

Shaking her head at the ludicrous fantasy, she went to the closet for a sweater to wear against the cool air brought on by the storm. The ball gown hung there, a vision of aquamarine satin. It was the most beautiful garment Sara had ever owned. She let her fingers drift over the smooth fabric before closing the closet and heading to Nico's room.

A rumble of thunder drew her to the window. The storm had not let up for nearly an hour.

Sweater over her shoulders, she stared out at the sluicing rain. In the distance, a lone figure rode a dark horse with as much wildness as the storm.

Her heart lurched.

"Aleks." She placed the palm of her hand against the cold windowpane as though she could touch him.

He looked as alone as she felt. No, more so. Aleks carried the weight of his family, his people, his nation on his shoulders. And he carried it well. He was an excellent leader. His people loved him.

So did she.

Fool that she was. Her heart still reached out for him.

As the thought came, he rode out of sight, as lost to her as if they'd never been.

Sara spent the late afternoon and evening playing with her son. The attendants, accustomed to her presence, went about their business and for the most part left her and Nico alone. Though she wondered if someone would come along and force her to leave at Aleks's orders, no one did.

Regardless of her false smile, Sara's heart was heavy and a thick knot of dread had settled in her stomach. This evening would fly by. Tomorrow she would be gone from her beloved child and his equally beloved father. Perhaps she'd never see either of them again, a painful possibility she wasn't ready to face.

She puffed gently against the bubble wand. An iridescent soap bubble emerged and hung suspended above Nico's enchanted face.

He clapped his hands. "I see a rainbow."

Sara laughed, storing the memories of every moment. "Now you blow one."

With great concentration, Nico dipped the circular wand into the bubble jar and blew. His eyes widened with amazement as the bubble grew larger and larger before popping. He jerked back. "It splashed me."

Sara laughed again and Nico joined her. She grabbed her cell phone and videotaped the sight and sound of his laughter.

"Let me see." Nico leaned in toward the small screen. The little boy smell of playtime and Play-Doh was a scent Sara would never forget.

"You're a handsome boy."

"You are, too." And then he giggled. "You're not a boy."

She rubbed her nose against his. "No. I'm a...silly rabbit."

His nose wrinkled with glee. "You are not. You're a girl. A real pretty girl. I like your hair, too." His little hands stroked the side of her head. Sara closed her eyes from the pure joy of being caressed by her son.

Would he remember these moments? Would he ever know that the woman who sang silly songs and blew bubbles and finger-painted the sea and the sun was his mother?

Would she ever see him again?

As the evening slipped away, Sara struggled with how to break the news of her departure. She had to tell him, for her sake as well as his.

Finally, when they were in the midst of a jigsaw puzzle, she said, "I have something important to tell you, Nico."

His intelligent face tilted upward with happy expectation. "A surprise?"

"No, not really a surprise." Determined to keep the departure light, she smiled, though the action felt as fake as this "vacation." "I will be going back to America tomorrow. We may not see each other again before my plane leaves. And I want you to know that meeting you has been the best thing in my whole life. You are a wonderful boy."

His face fell. His fingers tightened on a piece of puzzle. "But I don't want you to go, Miss Sara. I want you to stay here and play with me."

"My vacation time is over, Nico. I'm sorry." So sorry that her stomach hurt and her heart was shattering in her chest. "Staying would be lovely, but I'm afraid I cannot."

"Papa said you're lonely for America."

"He did, did he?" So Aleks had already been preparing the boy for her to leave. He must have intended all along to find a reason to rid the country of her, and she'd made the task so easy.

"When will you return? In one week? Papa always promises to return in one week." His handsome face twisted. "Or sometimes two when he goes far, far away. Will you come again in two weeks?"

Sara forced her breathing to appear normal, though tears burned her throat. "No, darling boy, not in two weeks."

"When?"

Staring down at a yellow puzzle piece to hide her tears, she said, "I don't know, sweetheart. I just don't know. America is very far away."

Nico pressed a piece into place before raising puzzled eyes to hers. "But you will come back, won't you?"

Not knowing what else to say, Sara said, "If I can, I will come again."

The answer was enough for the four-year-old. He picked up a green-and-brown puzzle piece, examined it, and snapped it into place. A dinosaur was beginning to emerge.

"Papa says you have a bookstore in America."

So he and Aleks had discussed her. She wondered why.

"Yes, I do, with lots and lots of books exactly right for little boys."

"Books about horses?"

"Lots of books about horses." She thought of Aleks riding like the wind along the seashore. "Perhaps I can send you one."

"I have a pony. When I am well Papa will allow me to ride again."

Sara longed to see that day. She longed for the time when Nico was well enough to run and play like a normal boy. But regardless of his return to health, Nico d'Gabriel would never be a normal boy. Like his father, he was bound by the rules and conventions of his inherited place in Carvainian society. And like his father, he would someday be a fine ruler. Even though she would not be here to watch him grow, she had no doubt Aleks would raise him to become a fine man.

As long as he was kept safe.

Her gut tightened at the thought that would not go away. What if Aleks and the doctors were wrong? What if Nico remained in danger and she was the only one who suspected? How could she leave when he was still vulnerable and when the person who'd overdosed him had still not been discovered?

Aleks was certain palace security could adequately protect their son if needed, but the guards had not stopped someone from poisoning his new liver with acetaminophen. What if the old liver had been intentionally destroyed in the same way? What if Nico had not contracted a viral illness during the flood zone trip as suspected?

The notion shot a spear of terror through her soul.

With all her might, she prayed that the doctors were right and the overdose was nothing more than an unfortunate accident. Maybe she was simply too overwrought and overprotective. Perhaps the stress of these strange weeks had distorted her thinking.

She wished she could believe that.

"May I come to your bookstore sometime, Sara?"

Unwilling and unable to admit that Aleks would never allow such a thing, Sara gathered the thin body into her arms. "I would love for you to visit my bookstore. You can choose any book you want."

"When I am well Papa will bring me." The phrase had become a mantra to Nico. When he was well again he wanted to do so many things.

"Don't be sad if he doesn't. America is a long way to travel."

"Papa has an airplane. He likes you, too. He will come."

The words brought a renewed ache to her heart. She'd begun to believe Aleks cared for her, as well. She'd even dreamed he could love her again, but a dream was all it was or could ever have been. She hadn't known that in America. Now, she did.

But even though Aleks was a ruling prince destined to marry a duchess or a princess, Sara would always be the mother of this child. Not even Irena could change that.

She rested a hand atop her son's head. "If Papa will bring you, you can come to visit me in America anytime. I will be waiting."

For the rest of my life.

The rest of the evening passed far too quickly as they played and talked, sang songs and made up rhymes. Too soon, the nanny reappeared.

"It is time for Prince Nico's bath." The woman held a hand out. Nico's little shoulders drooped in resignation.

"I could give him his bath," Sara offered, almost too eagerly. Every moment grew more precious as the clock ticked cruelly forward.

The nanny seemed taken aback by the suggestion. "But this is my duty. You are a guest."

"Please. I'm leaving tomorrow." She kept the tone light, lest she break down in front of her son. "Tonight is my last night in Carvainia. I'd like to spend as much time with Prince Nico as possible."

The woman studied her with dark Carvainian eyes and Sara wondered if she suspected that there was more to the relationship between Sara and Nico than a donor and recipient. "His Highness will miss you, ma'am. And all of Carvainia will be forever grateful for your sacrifice."

"It was no sacrifice," she said honestly. "Nico has won my heart."

The nanny tweaked Nico's chin with a smile. "He has that effect upon everyone."

Sara hoped that was true, but the warning bell inside her mother's head would not shut off.

"That bath?" she asked.

The nanny's face softened. "Certainly, if Prince Nico agrees."

The boy was already selecting toys to take into the water. "I want Sara to see my boat. It's blue like Papa's. And it goes, *brrr, brrr, brrr* in the water." His little mouth made a motor-boat noise that had the women sharing indulgent smiles.

Keeping her plastic smile in place, Sara went to give her son a bath for the first time…as well as the last.

Long after, when Nico was freshly scrubbed and smelling of bubble-gum-scented soap, Sara dressed him in pajamas and tucked him into his own bed. Now that the acute illness was over, he'd been returned to the normal nursery suite in the family wing.

Knowing that Aleks's room was only steps away gave Sara a strange feeling. She wanted to see him, but she didn't. Sad to say, she feared he'd drive her out of Nico's room. Tonight she would fight to stay.

But the thought of leaving Carvainia without one more glimpse of him and without a final chance to set things right, hurt almost more than she could stand.

"One more story, Sara?" Nico's eyes fluttered shut but he forced them open again. "One more."

She'd read until her throat was sore and the nanny had retired for the night. Still, she was as reluctant as her son to end the evening.

"One more." She selected a board book and began to read the gentle rhyming text about a little train that would not give up. Nico wanted to see the colorful pictures but by book's end, he could stay awake no longer. His eyes fell shut, the thick black lashes fluttering against his cheeks like dark butterflies. Clad in race car pajamas, his thin chest rose and fell in peaceful slumber.

Sara closed the book and held it in her lap, gazing down at her son with all the love bottled up inside. After the longest time, she snapped off the lamp, leaving only the sailboat night-light to cast a glow in the room. She leaned forward and kissed him.

"I love you, Nico," she whispered against his velvet cheek. "Your mommy will always love you."

The night had come too soon. She was not yet ready to be separated from her heart and soul. So she remained on the edge of the mattress, watching her baby sleep. Tomorrow night, she'd have only the memories.

When the night deepened, Sara began to nod, too tired and emotionally spent to remain upright. Unwilling to leave her son's side on this final time in his company, she lay down on a rug between the bed and wall. No one would see her here. No one would ask her to leave. Not even Aleks.

Sara stretched one hand onto the bed to touch Nico and then she dozed.

She didn't know how long she slept, but some time later, Sara awakened with a start. Suddenly alert, she remained still, listening. Had she heard a noise? She listened hard, barely breathing.

Nothing except the rhythmic in and out of her son's breathing.

It occurred to her then that she was no longer touching Nico's foot. With a self-deprecating huff, she pulled her sweater closer against the chill. The noise she'd heard must have been her own hand falling off the bed.

But then the noise came again. An infinitesimal squeak of movement.

Her pulse kicked up. Someone *was* in the room. And that someone moved slowly across the floor and came to a stop on the other side of Nico's bed.

Swallowing a lump of anxiety, Sara eased up to her knees.

What she saw made her blood run cold. A woman, shadowed by darkness, stood over Nico with a syringe in hand.

Sara leaped to her feet and demanded, "What are you doing?"

The woman jerked back, eyes blinking rapidly in confusion. In the night-light a familiar, ghostly face stared across at Sara.

"Maria," she whispered. Her suspicions about the usually smiling nurse pushed to the front.

"It's time for his medication." There was something hard and desperate in the other woman's voice.

A shot of fear-fueled adrenaline surged through Sara. Something was very wrong.

"He's not supposed to have anything else tonight." She stretched across the bed to grasp Maria's upraised wrist. "What are you giving him?"

And why are you doing it under cover of darkness?

Maria yanked. Sara held fast.

A tug of war ensued. Leaning across the wide bed, Sara was in an awkward position, but she was not about to give in.

"He must have it. He must." Maria's eyes widened to a point of wildness. Tension corded the veins in her neck. "You don't understand."

"Then let's call Dr. Konstantine. He can explain."

"No!" she shouted. "Time is running out, you stupid American. All you've done is cause problems. It would have been over if not for you."

Fear grew with every word that tumbled from the nurse's mouth. "What would be over?"

"Recompense. Carlo deserves recompense."

Sara clung hard to Maria's hand. One slip and she could plunge the poison into Nico's vulnerable body.

"It was you, wasn't it? It was you trying to hurt Nico." As she spoke, Sara held tight to the nurse's wrist and crawled across the bed to form a shield between Maria and the child.

With a hiss, Maria yanked hard. Unbalanced, Sara lost her grip and fell headlong onto the floor. She watched in horror as the syringe plunged through the thigh of Nico's pajamas. The child awoke with a scream. His small hands instinctively pushed at the offending needle.

Terrified, heart thundering, Sara grabbed Maria's legs and forced her back from the bed. She grabbed for the syringe, knocking it away from her son.

Please don't let any poison be injected.

By now, Nico sat up on his knees, eyes wide, sobbing uncontrollably. Sara longed to offer comfort but she was locked in a struggle with the wild and furious nurse. Arms around the woman's waist, she tried to pull Maria as far away from Nico as possible.

"He must die," Maria groaned, pounding at Sara's hands, straining toward the little prince. "Your son must die."

Stunned that Maria knew of Nico's parentage, Sara's grip went slack. The nurse whirled and slammed a fist into her still-tender side. A groan of pain *oomphed* from Sara. She doubled over.

With what little breath she had, she yelled, "Run, Nico! Run to Papa. Run!"

Though he had to be terrified, the little prince obeyed, his short legs flying over the floor. Maria lunged for him, screaming like a madwoman.

Though hurting and breathless, Sara grabbed for the woman's knees, pulling her down. They grappled on the floor. Maria quickly gained the upper hand. Somehow she'd retrieved the needle. She jabbed at Sara. Sara dodged to one side but not before the sting grazed her neck.

"Why did you come here? Why did you interfere? It would be over now." Maria slammed another vicious blow into Sara's side. Air whooshed from Sara in a scream of agony. Tears blinded her eyes. She struck out with her fingernails, clawing at Maria's face. Maria's strong fingers closed around her throat. Astraddle Sara's chest, she leaned in close, spittle appearing at the corners of her mouth. "Die in his place. The mighty prince will suffer either way. He will suffer as I have suffered."

The woman was raving mad. And insanely strong. She squeezed Sara's throat and with a gleam of sadistic pleasure in dark, Carvainian eyes watched her adversary struggle for breath.

Spots danced before Sara's eyes. She clawed at the larger woman's hands to no avail. Her head throbbed. She was dying.

But her son was safe. Aleks was safe. Even if she died, Maria's insane vendetta would end here and now.

A deeper darkness than she'd ever known began to close in. Maria's rambling tirade against Aleks went on and on, but Sara could no longer comprehend. Her hands went lax. A quiet humming filled her ears.

Suddenly, light flooded the room and the terrible pressure disappeared. Sara coughed and instinctively rolled to one side, knees drawn up.

Maria's stream of obscene ramblings increased, but she didn't touch Sara again.

Forcing her eyes open, Sara saw Aleks restraining the woman. Maria kicked and thrashed and spat. Face grim and full of sorrow, Aleks simply held her and let her rage.

"Murderer, murderer! You killed my son. You deserve to suffer the way I have. A son for a son. A son for a son."

The thunder of footsteps shook the floor as a host of security guards rushed in to take charge. Maria's cries of "a son for a son" echoed in the corridor as she was dragged away.

Certain now that Nico was safe, Sara let the blessed darkness overtake her.

CHAPTER THIRTEEN

ADRENALINE JACKING from every pore, Aleks fell to his knees beside the red-haired woman. Curled in a fetal position, she was unconscious. Blood oozed from scrapes on her face and neck, and bruises in the shape of fingers already formed around her throat. But she lived. Thank God, she lived.

He shuddered to think what might have happened had he not been sleepless tonight. When he'd heard Nico's cry for help, he'd known something terrible was happening and had not hesitated.

"Sara." Heart in his throat, he scooped her easily into his arms, cradling her against his body as he would a child. "Sara, my love. Sara, my love."

His voice broke. She'd always been his love and out of fear and stupidity, he'd rejected the best thing, other than Nico, that had ever happened in his life. All this time she'd been correct about Maria. Was she correct about other things, as well?

Her eyelashes fluttered. Her mouth barely moved.

"Nico?" she said through a throat hoarse from trauma.

Aleks's insides ached. A nightmare had unfolded but he was wide-awake. Thank God Sara had not given up. "He is safe with his grandmother and a host of bodyguards. No one will get near him. You have my word."

"Check his blood. She stabbed him. The needle. I think I got it in time. Be sure."

Aleks cast a quick look around the floor and saw a filled syringe resting against the leg of the chair. The pounding in his head increased.

"Landish," he said to one of the remaining bodyguards. "Take that syringe to Dr. Konstantine. Tell him Nico may have been injected."

"Done." The man was gone in seconds.

Relief flickered through Sara's sea-blue eyes before she closed them again.

Around him, the remaining pair of bodyguards stood, normally placid faces furious at this affront on their ability to protect the castle. He understood. Sometimes a man failed to protect what mattered most.

"I will take Miss Presley to my apartment. When Dr. Konstantine is available, ask him to come to her. She needs attention."

If the men thought anything unusual about the royal prince taking a woman to his rooms, they didn't show it. One left straightaway while the other trailed Aleks down the corridor to stand guard outside the door. Aleks thought the effort useless at this point. The threat was over, but tonight was not the time to address the security breach. They had erred, but so had he.

Carrying Sara through to his sleeping area, he gently placed her on the bed. She was beautiful beyond words, inside and out. Why had he ever doubted her?

"Ah, my Sara, I am a fool."

Just then, Dr. Konstantine bustled in, hair sprouting in all directions. "By the heavens, Your Majesty, what is going on here tonight?"

"Did you receive the message about the syringe?"

"Still full. But I have ordered blood work to be certain. I cannot believe Maria is responsible. Tell me this is false."

"I wish I could."

Aleks apprised the physician of what he knew. He still could not fathom the kind and smiling mother of his best friend as a murderess. The truth wounded like a poison arrow.

"Security is questioning Maria but she seemed completely deranged." And he had been completely duped by her smiling pretense. Maria's grief had festered into hatred, poisoning her mind and heart. "I doubt they'll determine much tonight. For now, I must go to Nico and the queen and assure them that the threat is over." And to assure himself that his son had, indeed, escaped further harm.

"Go then, I'll take good care of your woman."

Aleks was halfway out the door before he realized what the doctor had said.

Sara awakened in a strange room. Her body ached all over, and she could barely swallow. She touched her throat. Was she coming down with the flu?

As she pushed back the fluffy covers, the events of last night flooded in. Her pulse bumped.

"Nico," she whispered.

She grabbed for the telephone beside the bed and dialed Aleks's private number. When he answered, she blurted through a raspy voice, "Is Nico all right?"

A pause on the other end. "You are awake?"

Obviously. "Nico? Tell me."

"He is well and full of an adventurous tale of a brave

woman who saved him from the bad nurse." Aleks's tone was tired and sad. "He is in the next room having breakfast with his grandmother."

"Thank God."

"Indeed. You can be proud of your son. He sounded the alarm. But if not for you…" His voice trailed off. He cleared it.

Sara gripped the receiver, reliving last night's close call. "We were fortunate Maria decided to make her move before I left Carvainia."

"It was not luck. According to her confession, a rendering that made my blood run cold, she overheard our argument yesterday. She had planned to poison Nico over a period of months and force me to sit by helplessly as he died."

"Why did she change her mind?"

"You."

"Me?"

"She intended to administer the final overdose last night and leave evidence blaming you. You and I were already at odds. You were the obvious outsider. She had somehow learned of your relationship to Nico…and to me. She thought we would believe you had poisoned Nico as payback for revoking your visa."

"I would be blamed, and you would be punished."

He emitted a tired sigh. "Her revenge knew no bounds."

Sara's heart ached for him. "She truly is deranged."

"Yes." His voice was sad. "She even knew of a secret passage in the medical wing."

Sara gasped. "So I did see her go into Nico's room that time?"

"Yes. She laughed, rather maniacally I might add, because you'd seen her and no one believed you. I had no idea she hated me. None. And yet, you saw what I couldn't."

"I saw because I *am* an outsider, Aleks." A fact that pained her no end. "Your loyalty to Carlo's memory blinded you."

"Emotion. How does a leader separate emotion from reason?"

She had no answer for him. And in truth, one of the things she loved about him was his depth of feeling. No matter how hard he tried to hide it, he cared deeply. "What will happen to Maria?"

He drew in a long, quivering breath. "No matter what she's done, she is still the mother of the man who saved my life, a man who was my best friend. For him, I will take care of her."

"I expected no less."

If her sentiment surprised him, he didn't react. "There is an exceptional facility in Switzerland. She is on her way there, under heavy guard and sedation, of course. She will receive excellent care, but she will never be released."

"You must be shattered."

"I have suffered worse. Much worse." But he didn't elaborate. Instead he said, "I will send breakfast and Antonia to you. Rest. Last night was terrible for all of us, but for you most of all."

"But, I'm leaving today."

There was that pause again. "We need to talk. I will be up soon."

Before she could respond, he hung up.

An hour later, after she'd eaten and dressed, Sara paced the apartment, aware that Aleks had brought her to his room last night. But he had not slept here. Why had he done so? And what did he mean when he'd said they needed to talk?

Did she dare hope that he'd let her remain in Carvainia in some capacity? Perhaps as a nanny or a maid? At this point, she'd do anything to be near her son—and the man she loved.

Penny would call her a blind doormat, but she would rather be a servant here with the people she loved than alone in her Kansas bookshop.

A soft knock sounded on the outer door. She hurried to open it, finding both Aleks and his mother outside. She shrank back. Was this a two-pronged attack?

"May we come in?" Aleks asked, his expression giving nothing away.

Regardless of the grave situation, Sara couldn't help herself. "Considering this is your apartment, I suppose so."

She stepped aside and let them enter, trailing along, as tense as a bowstring as they went into the living quarters. The room was tastefully sumptuous, as befitted a prince, but the only thing in it that mattered to Sara was the prince himself.

The two women chose sofas opposite one another. Sara perched on the cushion edge, anxious and uncertain. The queen smoothed the unwrinkled hem of her suit skirt and sat with stiff, boarding school posture. As though purposefully choosing a neutral position, Aleks took a chair at one end between the two women.

The tension in the room was nearly visible.

Queen Irena spoke first. "I don't expect you to welcome me, Miss Presley. But you must hear the truth before you do anything else."

The queen, whose nose was normally raised in distaste, seemed subdued this morning. Her hands twisted in her lap, worrying an elegant, crested handkerchief. Black eyes, filled with loathing only yesterday, now swam with some other emotion.

Sara glanced from the queen to Aleks and back again. "The truth about what?"

"That's what we've come to talk with you about, Sara,"

Aleks said. "My mother and I had a long conversation this morning. She has something to tell you. And so do I."

In fisted hand, Irena's handkerchief went to her lips. A sob broke through, stunning Sara. The stiff-necked queen was crying? In the presence of a peasant?

"I have done you a great disservice," Irena said with a wobbly voice. She glanced at Aleks, eyes full of sorrow. "Both of you. Five years ago, Aleks was at war. He could not stop thinking and worrying about the red-haired American he had left behind. He could not come to you himself, so he sent me as his envoy."

Sara sucked in a stunned gasp. Her gaze flew to Aleks. "You were telling the truth?"

"Yes." His look was grim. "And there is more."

"You must understand, Miss Presley, I had nothing against you personally but you are not Carvainian. You are not of royal lineage. I could not allow my son, the ruler of a great nation, to marry a common American."

Sara's hand went to her throat. The ramifications of the queen's confession ricocheted through her. Aleks had not lied. He *had* loved her. He had tried to contact her.

She began to tremble with a great and terrible sorrow.

But the queen was not finished. "When I discovered the pregnancy, I went to great lengths to obtain the child. A beautiful son would be enough to soothe Aleksandre's pain when he learned of your rejection."

"But I didn't—I never—"

Queen Irena lifted an elegant hand. "No, you did not, but Prince Aleksandre believed you did. I told him this and many other untruths about you, including the payment you exacted for the sale of your child. You must believe me. I thought I was doing the right thing for everyone. For my country, my son and my grandson."

"And for yourself?"

Fresh tears sailed down Irena's proud face. "Can you forgive me?"

On shaky legs, Sara rose and moved away from the queen's pleading gaze. Forgive? How did she forgive such a wrong? How did she put aside the ocean of tears and the months of depression?

"I never fed him a bottle," she murmured, as much to herself as to the present company. "I wasn't there for his first steps. Or his first words."

She'd only dreamed about them, imagining each and every milestone.

"I am sorry, so very sorry."

"All that time Aleks hated me. He believed the worst lie of all. He thought I did not want him or his son." Glaring at the queen, Sara squeezed both hands against her bursting chest. "*Our* son."

With a soft groan, Aleks bolted from the chair and moved to the fireplace where he braced both hands against the stone mantel.

Queen Irena's dark gaze followed her son. "Prince Aleksandre has never hated you, my dear. That has been the problem. He wanted to hate you. I wanted him to. But he could not." She patted her cheeks with the handkerchief. "Please, come and sit. Hear me out. If you judge me harshly, it is no more than I deserve. But you must hear what I have to say—all of it."

Agitated, but relieved that the truth was finally coming to light, Sara did as Irena asked. Her stomach cramped and her back still hurt from fighting Maria, but an odd kind of hope kept sprouting up inside her like a persistent weed that simply would not give up and die.

"I failed my son and my grandson," Irena went on. "Both then and now. During the months since your arrival, I have been so focused on ridding the castle of your presence lest Aleksandre discover my deception, that I did not see the danger to Nico. You saw it." Reaching out, she leaned forward as if to touch Sara's knee. "A mother knows things with her heart that others cannot see."

Sara knew the words were true. Her heart had known something was wrong, even when she'd had no solid evidence. "Yes. I knew. Somehow I knew."

"I am grateful beyond words, Sara Presley. If not for your persistence and determination and yes, your love, Nico may have died." She choked on a sob and took a moment to compose herself.

Tears welled in Sara's eyes, too. "Last night could have been worse. Maria could have succeeded."

"Except for your bravery, she would have." Haughtiness gone, the queen rose, still worrying the now-wrinkled and damp handkerchief. "That is why I am here this morning. I deeply regret my actions as well as my arrogant pride and elitism. I was wrong. A queen is not made by blood. She is made by strength of character and her love of country and of her prince. You will make a far better queen than I."

With a deep, sweeping curtsy that stunned Sara and left Aleks gaping, Queen Irena took her leave.

As the door whispered shut, Sara murmured, "What just happened?"

Aleks pushed away from the fireplace. "I have only seen her this broken once before—when my father died. My mother did us both a terrible disservice, Sara, but she is a fine woman and a good queen."

"She loves her princes very much." It was the only concession Sara was ready to give to a woman who had ruined her life.

"Indeed. She loves us enough to do anything to protect us, even if we do not wish to be protected."

In a way, Sara understood. Didn't she feel this way about Nico? "But all these years, you believed a lie about me."

"A fact I deeply regret. Though this is no excuse, the months after I returned from war were a terrible time. I was wounded and angry. I'd lost my dearest friend and thousands of fine warriors. My father was recently dead. My country was in postwar chaos and I was her young and inexperienced leader. Being betrayed by the only woman I'd ever loved seemed to fit into the general theme of my life. Without our son to live for, that would have been a hopeless time."

"No, Aleks. Even without Nico, you would have served your people well. You would have turned Carvainia into the thriving, beautiful place it is today. You are a born leader." A reminder of her commoner status. Aleks was born to the throne and required a woman of equal quality. She was born a nobody.

He smiled a little. "So, you like my country?"

"I love it." Just as I love you, she thought. But she didn't say as much. Instead she spoke of the one wish he might grant. "I want to stay in Carvainia."

"This is good to know because I have something to discuss with you."

"About?"

"Nico's future."

Sara's chin went up. "I want to be in that future, Aleks. Don't deny me that, not now when you know how much I love him."

"And what do I get in exchange?"

"Whatever it takes. Anything you ask."

"Anything?" His eyes twinkled. "Why, Sara, you have no

idea what a man of my stature might require of such a beautiful, desirable woman."

She shook her head. "It doesn't matter. I'll do anything. I love my son that much."

"And what of the father?" His face became intense. "Do you still love the father as you once did? For you cannot deny that. I know now that you loved me."

Hopeful about the undercurrent flowing between them, Sara could answer with nothing less than the truth. "Yes. I do."

A soft sigh issued from his broad chest. He slid to one knee in front of her, clasping her hands in his. "Sara Presley, my beautiful, courageous, red-haired woman, mother of my child, heart of my heart, I, who was a blind man, will be blind no longer. I love you, too. No lies or raging anger could ever remove the wanting from my soul. I will want you until I die."

Heart lifting with each beautiful word, Sara touched her beloved's cheek. "But I'm not a Carvainian. I'm not royal."

"Those are my mother's requirements, not mine, and certainly not the rules of this nation. Carvainia needs *you* for her queen. Nico needs his mother. And the Prince of Carvainia requires a brave and fearless red-haired wife. Will you be that woman, Sara Presley? Will you grant me my fondest desire and marry me?"

Head reeling, heart thundering like a Kansas tornado, Sara opened her mouth to speak, but before she could say a word, the door slammed backward on its hinges.

Aleks bolted up to his feet, stance protective.

And then he laughed.

The most beautiful little boy in the world rushed inside the elegant room and threw his arms around Prince Aleksandre's legs. Earnest face turned upward, black eyes batting, he said, "Did you ask her, Papa? Did she say yes?"

Voice amused, Aleks stroked his son's hair. "I asked, but she has not given me an answer."

Nico's eyebrows furrowed in bewilderment. "But she must say yes, Papa. It was my fondest wish. I wished in the garden and I never, ever told."

By now, Sara vacillated between laughter and tears. She pressed her fingers against trembling lips.

"Yours, too?" Aleks asked with mock gravity. "Then, come, we must convince her together." The warrior prince returned to one knee and drew Nico down with him. "Now, you on the other side. A proposal must be done properly."

Adorably serious, Nico imitated his father, one knee on the floor and his tiny hand reaching for one of Sara's. The sweetness of the moment wrapped around her, warm and beautiful, a moment in time to capture for eternity. Her son. Her man. What more could she ask of life?

"We're waiting for an answer, Sara." Aleks's deep baritone was warm with love, the cold facade of Prince Aleksandre completely gone. "Will you marry us?"

Nico shot his father an exasperated look. "Wait, Papa. What about the Mama part?"

Sara's pulse stuttered. Did Nico know? Her gaze flew to Aleks. He nodded. "I told him that his mother—*you*—had been separated from us during the terrible war, but that you had finally found him again when he needed you most."

The tears shimmering on Sara's eyelashes broke loose. "I have looked for you for such a long, long time, Nico. For you and your Papa."

"Now that you're home, don't ever leave us again. Okay?"

This was the moment she'd dreamed of but never believed would happen, and all she could manage was, "Okay."

EPILOGUE

Six months later

THE WEDDING OF THE CENTURY took place on a day when the sun was ordered to shine, the sea instructed to remain calm and blue, and every flower in Carvainia was expected to bloom.

Heart thundering in his chest, Aleks stood at the top of the left staircase, looking across the wide expanse of ancient, shining hall to his bride on the opposite side. After all that happened, he'd never expected to see this moment, but there she was. It was his first glimpse at her wedding dress, an American custom he found amusing. He'd seen everything else about her. Why not her wedding dress?

But Sara was worth the wait. Resplendent in creamy satin that nipped her narrow waist and hinted at her luscious curves, Sara was as regal as any royal-born queen. In a gesture that had touched him deeply, she had accepted his mother's offer to wear the simple diamond tiara Irena had worn in her own wedding. The concession gave him hope that the two could become friends.

Beneath the tiara, Sara's cinnamon-red hair was a crown of glory from which flowed gauzy layers of double veil as featherlight and airy as a Carvainian spring. She moved, flowing toward the steps, one hand on the banister, her glowing face turned toward him.

Aleks dipped his chin, unable to keep the smile from blooming. His wedding would not be a stiff and emotionless event, joining two royal houses. His was a wedding of love. He had every right to smile.

Sara smiled, too, and holding each other's gaze, they took the steps in unison. Sara's long train followed, a frothy, elegant entourage befitting his bride.

At the bottom, they turned together and met in the center hall. In this final moment of semiprivacy, with only the uniformed doormen waiting at the huge double doors, Aleks took the tips of her cold fingers and gently drew his bride to him.

"Shall I muss your lipstick?"

Her glossy-peach mouth curved. "Please do."

He did.

"What will the photographers think?" she asked, eyes shining with a love that was all his.

"They will know their prince married for love."

Carvainians had rejoiced at the announced engagement, though some expressed concern that Sara was not of royal lineage and brought nothing with her to the country. Aleks knew better. He'd left his heart in America. She'd brought it back.

"Your people await," she whispered, and he saw her nerves. They'd chosen a very public ceremony on a yacht in the harbor so that as many Carvainians who wished could attend the nuptials. Afterward, they would sail along the coastline for a day to greet thousands of others before heading out to sea for a much-anticipated honeymoon.

"*Our* people await," he corrected. Holding her soft, chilled hand in his, he started forward, eager to claim his bride.

* * *

The massive doors swung wide and the noise rushed in. Sara vacillated between incredible joy and pure terror. She'd have preferred a quiet wedding in the children's garden or the family chapel, but she understood the important symbolism of this public ceremony on Aleks's beloved sea.

In the days since the announced engagement, she had become a public figure, meeting and greeting at dozens of functions around the beautiful little nation. The Carvainian people had welcomed her, accepting Aleks's choice, and she was determined to give them a loving and kind queen.

Besides, what woman didn't dream of a wedding so grand and perfect with a handsome prince at her side? Even cynical Penny had been won over by Aleks's charm.

Scanning the ship's deck, she searched for her friend and spotted the shining blond head, bouncing up and down like a rubber ball. Yes, Penny was here and as excited as a puppy. Aleks had brought everyone that mattered, though the American contingent was small, a handful of friends and a few distant cousins who had kept in contact after her mother had died.

There was nothing left in America to return to, even if she'd wanted to go back. Everything she loved was here.

Penny was now the sole owner of the bookstore, for a sum of one America dollar, though Sara would visit. After all, she'd promised Nico some wonderful books.

Sara squeezed Aleks's fingers and he winked at her. She laughed, partly from nerves but mostly from happiness.

Cheers and applause swelled as the wedding couple exited the castle and began walking the long path down to the sea. Military men and women in crisp white uniforms lined the pathway. The crowd, huge as it was, remained polite behind the low, decorative barriers, though flashbulbs snapped at a constant rate.

A red carpet sprinkled with a rainbow of tiny flowers led the way down to the shore and the moored yacht where the wedding party was already in place.

Sara's magnificent train trailed behind her for yards, held up by eight young ladies, four on each side. Half of the dark-haired girls were commoners, the other half of the royal line, but all had been selected for their good deeds and not for their last names. The announcement had pleased the Carvainian press, who heralded their soon-to-be queen as a friend to all. And that's exactly what she wanted to be.

From a flatboat in the harbor, a military band, their instruments glistening in the sunshine, played the Carvainian national anthem as Sara and Aleks proceeded across the lawn. All around the yacht, a flotilla of flower-bedecked boats bobbed gently on the serene sea.

With sabers drawn and resting at their sides, military attendants, stiff and proper in white uniforms, lined the boardwalk up onto the ship. This was Aleks's honor guard, a group of men with whom he'd served. As the couple passed, the men snapped the sabers to their shoulders, symbolically ready to defend and protect their prince and his bride. Sara felt Aleks's quiver and understood his emotion. He loved these men, as they loved him.

In the months of the betrothal she'd learned much about the man she was about to marry. He was a loving father, a good son, a true and worthy prince who grieved for the loss of his soldiers and provided generously for their families. He ruled his nation with a gentle hand and a wise heart.

She was proud and blessed to join herself to such a man.

As they ascended to the deck and the waiting wedding

party, Aleks held her elbow. She was glad for the support because her knees wobbled. In this surreal moment, the swell of music and people and the smell of ocean and flowers overwhelmed her senses.

"Papa, Mama." Nico's whisper came to her through all the noise. She turned to find his wide, white smile and excited black eyes peering at her from beside Queen Irena.

Irena guided the little prince forward. He was dressed in white tails and crimson cravat exactly like his father's. Together the pair was stunning. Her love for them left her breathless.

She held out a hand, embarrassed to see it tremble. Nico wiggled into place between her and Aleks. The three of them stood beneath an arch of feather flags, white-columned banners of sheer fabric billowing in the sea breeze. The clergyman, decked in long, flowing robes of crimson and cream, began the ceremony.

Even with thousands of spectators crowding the shoreline and spreading up over the hillsides, a reverent hush fell, broken only by the lap of water and an occasional birdcall.

Beautiful, though unfamiliar words were spoken joining Prince Aleksandre Lucian Domenico d'Gabriel with Sara Elizabeth Presley. And though the pomp and ceremony went on for a while, Sara lost track of time as she treasured every word, every Carvainian tradition kept, every glimpse into her beloved's eyes.

And then it was over and Aleks reached for her.

"This is an American tradition I must keep," he said, a half grin on his face as he kissed her.

A shout of approval went up from the shore but was drowned out by a deafening roar overhead. Bemused and happy, Sara held tight to Aleks's hand as they raised their faces to the sky. A precision team of Carvainian Air Force jets swooped past, leaving a wake of red-and-white contrails to honor their prince and his bride. As the planes disappeared from sight, fireworks exploded in a kaleidoscope of color against a backdrop of blue sky and fair sea.

"In my loneliest hours," Aleks said, gazing down at her with a look that melted her bones, "I pictured you here exactly like this."

She laughed softly. "In my wildest dreams I never imagined *anything* like this. You a prince. The two of us married. Here with our son."

"Would you have dreamed it if you'd known?"

"Oh, yes." She cupped his firm, smooth jaw. "My dreams were always of you, no matter who you are or where you live. The man you are inside is the man I love."

Heedless of the crowd, he drew her close again. She placed a hand against his strong, warrior's heart, content to know that it beat for her.

Cameras flashed. But they'd carved out these seconds of privacy and they would have them.

"Your love is a powerful thing, my queen. It has healed me. It has healed our son." He reached inside his jacket and withdrew an envelope. "I have a gift for you."

Curious, with shaky fingers, Sara opened the flap. Inside were the shredded bits of a million-dollar bank draft.

"I don't understand."

"I discovered it in my desk that night before Maria's attack on you and Nico."

"Before the attack? Then you knew—?"

"Yes, I knew you were sincere, that you had not agreed to the transplant for money. I was bewildered and broken and unable to sleep. That's why I was awake when Nico called for help. When I saw these scraps of paper, I knew I could never send you away. Even if my mother had told the truth, I couldn't let you go. Even if I was the worst kind of fool, I could not lose you again. You owned my heart. A warrior dies without his heart."

Tears prickled the back of her eyelids. "Oh Aleks. Of all the gifts you've given me, this one is the most beautiful."

With a smile, he bumped his forehead against hers. "That was exactly what I expected you to say." He arched his eyebrows toward the water. "Shall we?"

She caught his meaning instantly. "Yes, let's do."

Together they went to the railing, trailed by attendants and photographers. Each took a portion of the shredded paper, then joined hands, lifting them high. Nico ran to join them, raising both hands to clasp his parents' sleeves.

"No looking back," Sara said.

"Only to the future," Aleks added. "*Our* future."

And with a whoop of delight they released the offending bits of paper, letting the wind and sea carry them far, far away—along with the pain and sorrow and grief that had kept them apart for so long.

Across the way, the band struck up a rousing song of victory and exuberant joy.

The trio on the yacht, the prince, his queen and the little prince, fell into a satin and tulle embrace, laughing and crying all at once.

The past was over. Let the future begin.

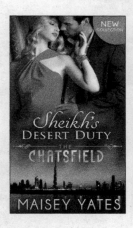

 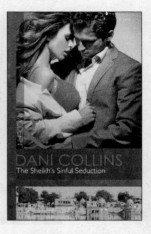